S.O.S.

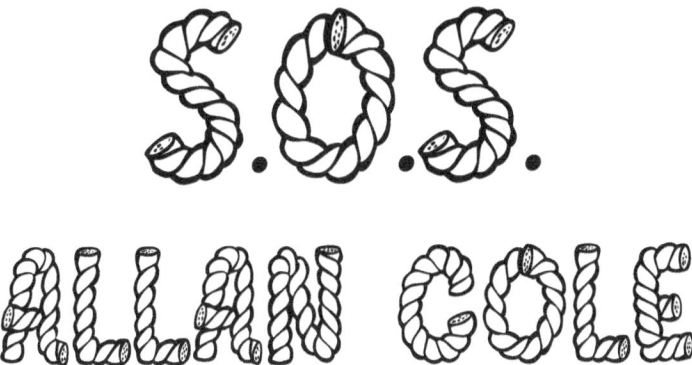

S.O.S.
ALLAN COLE

WILDSIDE PRESS

For the real Verne Sullivan
and
Kathryn, Drew, Vicky and Scott:
I never would have reached this journey's
end without your help and support
and
My grandchildren: Ryan, Layne, Darby, Tristin,
Asher, Colton, Wyatt and Marley.

Published by Wildside Press LLC.
wildsidepress.com

AUTHOR'S NOTE

War Comes to Paradise

Between February and May of 1942, German U-boats operated with impunity off the Florida coast, sinking nearly two dozen freighters from Cape Canaveral to Key West and killing five thousand people. Residents were horrified witnesses of the attacks—the night skies were aflame and in the morning the beaches were covered with oil and tar, ship parts and charred corpses. The Germans even landed teams of saboteurs charged with disrupting war efforts in the factories of the North. This novel is based on those events. For my own purposes, I set the tale in the fictitious town of Juno Beach on the banks of the equally fictitious Seminole River—all in the very real Palm Beach County, a veritable wilderness in those long ago days. Among the witnesses were my grandfather and grandmother, who operated an orchard and ranch in the area.

ONE

Philadelphia

The 30th Street station was a sea of uniforms and tears.

There were soldiers and sailors and U.S. Marines and crying mothers and daughters and women of all kinds, children in tow or on their hips, crowding around the platforms where the big locomotives hissed and smoked and sparked and steamed.

And everywhere Ryan went Pearl Harbor was on everyone's lips and in their minds.

Dec. 7, 1941. Only few months gone now since the Japanese attacked Pearl Harbor on the same day that Ryan Karr entered his 12th year of existence.

Peering down from the overlook on that roiling sea of people and gigantic machines, Ryan thought back on that moment, reliving the shock as the radio announcer's words sank in. Wondering, to his immediate shame, if Aunt Cassie would still bake the cake she'd promised for his birthday.

He was sinking back into that miserable moment when Uncle Tom caught him by the elbow, saying "Come on. There's the Professor."

Then they were pushing through the crowd, Uncle Tom waving his badge, shouting "Police Business! Police Business!"

The crowd parted and Tom used his big Irish shoulders to bull through, carrying Ryan and Aunt Cassie in his wake. The two were suddenly struck with a case of the giggles because it was such a big lie.

There was no police business. Just the three of them running to help Ryan catch the Florida Special where they would all say their goodbyes.

A wrench. Thinking: it could be forever.

Now they were following the line of cars, chains rattling, wheels shrieking, engines chuffing, dodging a woman lifting her little boy to a window to kiss his daddy goodbye, until they came to the car where Uncle Tom's friend waited.

The Professor was a stocky, middle-aged black man in a conductor's uniform, and he was lifting his cap and mopping his bald head with a kerchief when they reached him.

He looked down at Ryan—rimless glasses glinting—and Uncle Tom was saying, "Can't tell you how much we appreciate this, Professor. Cass is worried sick about the boy traveling all that way by himself."

But the Professor was waving the appreciations aside. He was in a hurry to get everyone aboard and he grabbed Ryan's small suitcase, saying, "No thanks needed, Tom. I'll take as good a care of your boy as you have mine."

The professor was referring to his grandson, Josh, a rookie Ryan's uncle had taken under his wing at the department.

A tearful Aunt Cassie fussed over Ryan, patting his hair into place, rearranging his collar, and pulling his jacket aside for the tenth time that morning to make sure the five- dollar bill was still pinned safely on the underside of the lapels. A fortune, especially when you added in the two quarters and five dimes in his pocket.

"I know you'll be good, as good can be, hon," she said in her Philadelphia Irish lilt. "So I don't have to be telling you to mind your grandmother and Verne, because I know you will."

Uncle Tom pulled Ryan aside, gave him a quick hug, whispering last minute uncle-like advice as he handed over the old Navy knapsack he'd been carrying for him.

"Don't take any guff from those rednecks," he said.

"Nossir."

"But don't you go looking for it, either."

"I won't, sir."

Another hug then he swiped at his eyes as he handed the boy over. Ryan paused at the top of the stairs. Resisting the Professor for just a minute to face his aunt and uncle.

"What about—?" he stopped midsentence. Voice trembling, tears threatening.

The train jolted, wheels screeched, cars bumping all along down the line.

"This way, young man," the Professor admonished him. "We have to get going."

"Don't you worry, hon," Cassie called out, her own eyes brimming. "We'll tell your mother you love her, God bless us all."

And then the train lurched and the Professor caught Ryan's elbow to steady him, then led him into the car—empty except for several black servicemen near the back, who were playing cards on a suitcase turned on its side.

The Professor put Ryan in one of the middle seats. Across the aisle there was a well-worn leather satchel, with a sweater on top.

"My regular base of operations," the Professor said, rearranging the stack. "Run the entire train from this spot."

Smiling, he said, "You'll keep an eye on my things for me, won't you?"

"Yessir," Ryan said, sitting straighter.

Now the train was picking up speed, the ride smoothing out.

The Professor turned to go, but paused to say, "I'll be back by and by, so you make yourself at home and if you need anything, just wait until I come around again."

He started to leave, then laughed. "Almost forgot," he said, motioning at Ryan, who gave him a quizzical look. "Your ticket, son. I have to punch it."

"Oh," Ryan said and got out his book of tickets.

The Professor fished through them, found what he wanted, pulled the punch machine from his belt and—ka-chunk! And then another: ke-chunk! And one more: ka-chunk! Paper bullets falling to the floor.

"There you go, Ryan," the Professor said, holstering his little machine. "Good all the way through to Jove Beach, Florida."

Ryan scooched back in his seat. He looked out the window at the slow moving industrial cityscape. There was an acrid factory stink to the air, infused with the train's sweet diesel odor. And there was nothing to see but the backs of factory works and warehouses with broken windows. A few bums moved through the piles of rubble, looking for something worth a pony jug.

But he really wasn't seeing any of it. Instead, his thoughts had turned inward. To his mother at the little picnic they had for her on the hospital grounds the previous Sunday. Beautiful as ever, with her long dark hair, blue eyes and milk white Irish complexion.

"Hi, Mom." Eyes wet. Voice cracking. But her eyes were glazed and Ryan had to repeat himself... "Mom? Mom?"... before she acknowledged him.

Then all she did was pat his cheek and say, "I love you, too, hon." And turn away with a vacant smile.

Finally, there was his father. Vanished in the storms of war somewhere in the North Atlantic. Ryan imagined him in a submarine many fathoms deep, icy seas raging overhead. Enemy destroyers on the hunt.

Suddenly, it became difficult to breathe. Heart trip hammering. He took several deep breaths, then pulled the knapsack onto his lap and unbuckled the straps.

Inside was the small practice Morse Code key set his father had given him. A handsome one with a black stippled metal base and a chromed key and springs. Tucked into a velvet-lined metal case—stippled black like the base.

He put his suitcase on his lap, and used it for a desktop. He started tapping away, trying to compose a message without looking up the letters in his Morse Code book.

Ryan practiced every chance he had, wanting to develop his own style. His own "hand." His father said a skilled telegrapher could tell an operator by his "hand." His style of tapping the key—tapping the short and the long. The dots and the dashes. The "Diddy, dah, diddy." Except with no speaker the only sound was just a faint clacking.

He tried out his key now, wanting to send "I love you, Mom," but he kept losing his way and forgetting the sequence. His heart started racing again. Hooked up to squawk box it would have made a hellacious racket.

In a panic he kept tapping out the same signal string over and over again: ...---... And again: ...---... And again: ...---...

S.O.S. S.O.S. S.O.S.

The international plea for help.

Soon, the sound of the train's wheels racing over steel rails took over from the clacking key. Like many voices chanting: *S.O.S. S.O.S. S.O.S.*

His heartbeat became less erratic. His breathing slowed.

S.O.S. S.O.S. S.O.S.

Then the tapping stopped. His eyes closed.

And he fell asleep.

TWO

The Professor

Something was wrong.

Ryan sensed a hovering presence. A reeking, boozy breath. Someone gripping his hand.

His eyes snapped open and he found a red-eyed soldier standing over him, pulling at his Morse key set. His pale jowls were unshaven, his uniform dirty and in disarray, his breath stinking of stale booze. He had the look of a mean drunk.

"Hey!" Ryan shouted, jerking away.

"Gimme that!" the soldier growled, pulling hard.

Ryan curled his body around the key. The soldier grabbed his arm and yanked harder.

"Let go, kid!" the soldier said. "Or I'll give you such a shot."

A deep voice right out of a gravel pit rasped: "What is going on here?"

And then the soldier was dragged away. Ryan looked up to see the Professor push the man against a seat.

"Mind yer own, ya dirty coon," the soldier rasped, fist coming up.

"I am minding my own, sir," the Professor said. "That young man is in my charge."

The soldier tried to swing, but the Professor caught his wrist, twisting it. There was a yelp of pain.

"Okay, okay," the soldier whined. "Just let me go."

The Professor stepped back, releasing him. At the same time, he plucked the ticket puncher from his belt, wrapping his fist around it.

For a minute, Ryan thought the soldier was going to make something of it, but then he started to retch. He moaned, grabbed at his belly, then turned and raced for the exit. He barely cleared the door before spewing his guts.

Ryan looked up at his savior, heart starting to slow.

"Are you okay?" the Professor asked.

Ryan nodded. "Thanks," he said. It seemed a weak response, but it was all he could manage at the moment.

"I am so very sorry about that," the Professor said. "I was gone longer than I planned."

Ryan just shrugged, but he did it with a smile.

"That Morse Code set is pretty fancy," the Professor said. "Would I be wrong if I supposed your father or an uncle gave it to you?"

"Nossir. I mean, yessir—it was my father's. He bought it when he finished sub school up in Connecticut."

"Ah, your father is an undersea mariner, is he?"

"Yessir."

"Which, I presume, is why you are studying Morse Code so assiduously?"

Ryan didn't know how to reply, so he resorted to his all purpose shrug.

"Must be difficult practicing without sound," the Professor said.

"I'm saving up for a squawk box and earphones for back up so I don't bother people," Ryan said. "Besides, I can hear it in my head."

"Is that so?" the Professor said. "In your head?"

"Yessir."

There was a long silence, and it was only then that Ryan realized the train had stopped and was pulled over to the side.

Puzzled, he asked "Sir? Where are we?"

"Just outside the city," the Professor said.

Ryan frowned, "Why did we stop?"

Before the Professor answered, there was a rumble and a roar and he looked out the window in time to see another train thunder by. Soldiers were staring out. A couple of them caught Ryan's eye. One smiled and managed a thumbs up before he whipped past.

"Troop train," the Professor said. "Two more coming along after this, so we'll be held up for at least an hour. On the Miami run last week we were delayed by trains hauling tanks and half tracks. When you see that you know full well that our country is truly at war."

"I guess," was all Ryan could manage.

Silence followed. Then, curiosity overcame shyness and he asked, "Why do they call you the Professor, sir?"

The Professor chuckled. "You mean, how is it that a man wearing a conductor's uniform, and who is actually working as a conductor, has claim to such a lofty title?"

Ryan reddened. "Nossir," he said. "I didn't mean…" And he trailed off, realizing that's pretty much what he *had* meant.

"I did not receive a formal education," the Professor said. "I never progressed beyond the third grade at the colored school down Miami way. But, I was a bright lad. A curious lad. It seemed that the only way I could make friends was to feign ignorance. Otherwise they thought I was putting on airs."

Ryan smiled. "Feigning ignorance," he said. "I know what you mean."

The Professor grinned. "I expect you do," he said. Then: "So out of pure loneliness I started haunting the library. Then one day the library took possession of a brand new edition of the Encyclopedia Britannica. I heard people say it contained all the knowledge in the world."

Ryan nodded. He'd heard that as well. "It doesn't really," he said. Then, afraid he had been rude, he quickly added, "Does it?"

More chuckling. "Of course not," the Professor said. "However that is what I believed at the time. But I also realized I was never going to be able to avail myself of a formal education. Certainly not a university education. And so I made it my young life's work to read the entire Encyclopedia Britannica, from A to Z."

"And did you?" Ryan asked. "Get all the way to Z, I mean?"

"I did," the Professor said.

Ryan was dumbfounded. He'd never heard of such a feat. "Wow!" was all he could manage.

"Nothing to 'wow' about," the Professor said. "All it did was prove to me just how ignorant I was. How ignorant all of us are. Even so, I went about spouting facts left and right, driving people crazy. Until they started calling me 'The Professor.'

"It was a joke at first. Mockery. But then I started tutoring people's children. Kids who had fallen behind. Or kids who were whip smart, but weren't challenged by school. And that is when the name really stuck."

Ryan could see how it would.

"Now, I have a question for you, young man," the Professor said.

"Yessir."

The Professor said, "I understand that you will be visiting with your grandmother and grandfather."

Ryan's heart skipped a beat. It'd be more than a visit. He'd be living there. For how long, he didn't know.

But all he said, was, "Yessir." A pause, then: "She's my father's mom. My grandmother, I mean."

The Professor nodded.

"And he's... he's not really my grandfather. More like a step grandfather. She was, you know, like married before."

He hesitated. Looking to see disapproval in the Professor's face. Actually, she'd been married twice before. Twice! Which his Aunt Cassie said was scandalous. But the Professor's features remained merely interested.

"Verne Sullivan is a well known and respected figure in Jove Beach," the Professor said. "I have had the pleasure of meeting Mr. Sullivan many times. Coincidentally, my cousin Samuel and his wife work for him. They have nothing but good things to say. 'A wonderful old gentleman,' my cousin attests. Over time that has become my impression as well."

Hearing this, he felt a little better. He'd never met Verne Sullivan.

His grandmother had come alone when she'd visited. She was a chilly woman. Aloof. Quite unlike his mom's mom—the warm and loving little Irishwoman he'd called "Grandmom" since... since... well, forever.

It had been so many years since he'd seen his father's mother before that he barely remembered her. He wondered if he should embrace her. Hesitated, then was saved when she took his hand and shook it.

"Hello, Ryan," was all she said. Then she turned away to talk to Aunt Cassie and Uncle Tom.

His fate had been decided during the visit. Over the weekend they'd gone to the hospital to see his mother. Byberry wasn't a regular hospital. It was for people who'd had suffered what Aunt Cassie called, a "nervous breakdown." The kids at St. Gabriel's called it a loony bin.

That night his aunt told Ryan that it was his father's wish that he live with his grandmother in Florida.

Ryan was horrified. Since his mother's illness—and with his father in the Navy—the boy had been bounced around among friends and relatives for longer than he liked to remember. He had finally found a haven these past months living with his aunt and uncle. He had hoped to stay with them until his mother was well again.

Suddenly, that hope was snatched away.

"But she doesn't even like me," he protested.

"Oh, that's just her way, hon," Aunt Cassie said. "She loves you just as much as the rest of us."

Ryan was not convinced. But there was nothing he could do about it.

Aunt Cassie tried to lighten the burden. "It's just for the time being, Ryan, hon," she said. "Theresa will be better soon. You'll see. And then you'll have a home together again."

With a jerk and a groan the train suddenly came alive, bringing Ryan back to the present.

He heard the Professor say, "I believe you will enjoy your time in Jove Beach. It is a wonderful place to be young. Fishing. Boating. Swimming. Hunting... And—he paused to add an exaggerated Dixie accent—"Yewe know what Ah mean? Awl that thar kuntree stuff."

Ryan couldn't help but laugh. "Kun-tree stuff," he said, trying to mimic the accent and blowing it badly. "Awl that thar kun-tree stuff."

The Professor grinned. "By Jove, I think he's got it," he said, but this time he used an English accent.

Ryan didn't get it, but laughed anyway.

"Also, you'll enjoy meeting Samuel's son, Alex," the Professor said. "He's a bright young lad that I'm tutoring from afar and he'll offer you the intellectual companionship that I'm sure you find lacking in your daily life."

Ryan grimaced. Few of his peers liked to read, or discuss anything but sports and cars, or tell lies about their exploits with the opposite sex.

Before he could reply, there came a loud Crash! and a rumbling shudder traveled the length of the train and back again. Then a metallic shriek and a jolt as the train slowly got underway. After a few parting words, so did the Professor—hurrying out the door to attend to "my train."

When he was gone, Ryan found that his mood had lifted. He looked out the window, but they were going through a boring industrial section. Then he brightened, remembering the books in his knapsack. His little traveling library included a brand new issue of Astounding Science Fiction, featuring a Robert Heinlein story: "Orphans In The Sky."

A few minutes later he settled back in his seat and let the story and his imagination sweep him light years away from his troubles.

THREE

The Train

For most of the passengers it was a wearying, fitful journey south, with the train sidelined by war traffic for what seemed like hours at a time.

But for Ryan it was a grand adventure. Never mind that it was going to take at least thirty five hours to reach their destination, instead of the regularly scheduled twenty five. That meant he'd get to spend two adventurous nights aboard the Florida Special by himself, instead of just one.

He roamed the train, investigating every nook and cranny. He came upon soldiers and sailors playing cards and spinning tales of derring do that would be impossible for most grown men to accomplish, much less these city boys and farm boys off to play war.

He met moneyed men and women, with private cabins and the best tables in the dining cars. And he met young mothers whose husbands were off to war and were spending the last of their savings to move themselves and their children back to their parents' homes where they'd huddle together and wait out the war.

Mostly the other passengers seemed to welcome his presence. They had so many worries and troubles with no one to tell them to. And so they poured them out to the earnest young man with the sad blue eyes who listened so intently to every word they had to say.

The common topic wasn't just about war—but wondering how long this one would last. There was talk of being home for Thanksgiving or even Christmas. Some feared it would last another year or more. When Ryan asked the Professor, he only said that "wars always take longer than people expect."

Ryan was at an age when he was always hungry. He was tall for a 12-year-old, and skinny with what Uncle Tom called "a runner's build" and it took a lot to fill him up.

After he'd gone through all the food Aunt Cassie had packed the Professor brought him leftovers from the kitchen, so he didn't have to cash in the five dollar bill pinned to his jacket.

A black family sat behind him during one part of the journey and when supper time rolled around they broke out a feast of cold fried chicken and fixings that filled the car with tantalizing odors.

It was a big family—five little kids and their parents, Mr. and Mrs. Johnson.

Ryan buried his head in his book, trying desperately to ignore the tempting odors wafting over the seats—his stomach rumbling like crazy.

Perhaps they heard it over the train sounds and took pity, or they were just generous people because after a few minutes a little boy about eight tugged at his sleeve and said his momma wanted to know if he wanted some.

Did he!

Hunger overcame shyness and he was soon stuffing himself with chicken and potato salad and hard boiled eggs and biscuits with homemade strawberry jam and a big piece of sweet potato pie, which he'd never tried before and it was so delicious he had the heretical notion that sweet potato pie might even rival some of Aunt Cassie's baking wonders.

The family was lively and full of talk, filling the car with their chatter and Ryan missed them when they got off in Jacksonville.

Now the ride started getting really interesting, as they swept past great swamps on their right and the Atlantic on the left. It also became noticeably warmer. The Professor said some passenger trains were air conditioned, but it was a slow and costly transition that might take years to complete.

Once he saw a rickety shack perched high above the swamp on stilts. A black kid about Ryan's age was fishing off a narrow porch, a broad-brimmed straw hat shading his head, sitting with such nonchalant ease that Ryan was stricken with envy. He'd never seen anyone who looked so free of the cares and troubles of the world.

Sometimes when the train pulled over to let military traffic pass, Ryan hopped off to investigate the mysteries of cars being coupled and uncoupled, or to watch workmen clamp off leaky lines that hissed and steamed.

Curious animals crowded pasture fences to see the strange goings on. A city boy, it had never occurred to Ryan that cows and horses could be as curious as people and it made him laugh as they quarreled and pushed one another aside to get a closer look.

Ryan also spotted the occasional old bo creeping along looking for opportunity, only to be chased off by the keen-eyed Professor.

Every time they stopped he found himself anxious to get going again. A little fearful that they wouldn't get started and the whole world would have time to catch up to him.

The train itself seemed to match his mood. Strung along the tracks for hundreds of yards, hissing and smoking and jerking, like an animal brought briefly to ground by a trapper—waiting for its chance to break free and run again.

That night all the bad old memories came crawling out of the dark to find him huddled beneath the rough blanket the Professor had given him. The Morse Code set clutched in his lap.

Once Ryan came awake with a start. He was soaked with the cold sweat of night fears. Fingers tapping wildly on the key set's closed box: S.O.S … S.O.S … S.O.S.

He looked about, disoriented. Out of place. Out of time. Then he saw the dark form of the Professor curled up in the opposite seat, the old sweater pulled up under his chin. He gave a long snore. Then a snort! Like a dog rooting for a bone. Followed by the continuation of the snore.

Ryan smiled. Another snort! The smile became a giggle. Loud enough for the Professor to stir. The boy pulled the blanket over his head to suppress another laugh.

His fingers automatically went to the Morse set to resume their tapping. Then he thought of the song his Aunt Cassie started singing after they bought the train tickets. When he was in the dumps, she'd tease him, tickle his ribs and sing:

> *"Pardon me, boy*
> *Is that the Chattanooga choo choo?"*
> *Track twenty nine*
> *Boy, you can give me a shine…*
> *I've got my fare*
> *Just a trifle to spare…"*

A few bars more, then the voices of the Andrews Sisters took over the song:

> *"So Chattanooga choo choo*
> *Won't you choo-choo me home?*
> *Chattanooga choo choo…"*

Now the train's chattering wheels picked up the song. *"Chattanooga… Chattanooga… Chattanooga…"*

Before long he was caught up in the embrace of the Florida Special as it charged along, mile after mile, a marvelous lullaby of rhythm and sound and chattering wheels and soft voices whispering deep into the night.

And he fell into a sleep so peaceful, that later on he thought of it as delicious.

FOUR

Jove Beach

In the early afternoon they broke out of a fierce rainstorm to be greeted by the sunniest skies Ryan had ever seen. They were startling blue with marshmallow clouds and soaring birds circling sparkling seas rimmed with tropical green trees and blazing white beaches.

The storm had buffeted them for hours limiting their view to a few feet and then bursting out into the sun as if emerging from a never-ending tunnel of watery gray broken by startling flashes of objects that seemed to charge out and then were gone so quickly that they made only the slenderest of impressions.

Up ahead, Ryan saw a long bridge curving over the mouth of a river. He unfolded the map he'd kept handy to track his journey. It seemed to him that they were getting close to their destination. He ran a finger down the map, looking for the river.

As if reading his thoughts, the answer came from behind him. "That's the Seminole River, young man," the Professor said. "Named for the tribe that never surrendered to the federal government. Technically, America is still at a state of war with them."

He sighed. "Not that it did them a lot of good," he said. "They're almost all gone now."

The Professor put a hand on his shoulder. "It also means that we're coming up on Jove Beach and you had better collect your belongings. Anything you forget will end up in 'Lost And Found' in Miami."

A friendly shoulder squeeze and then he moved on about his duties.

As they rounded the bend, Ryan saw the big locomotive in action for the first time since they left Philadelphia. It was a magnificent sight. The big diesel-electric streamliner looked like it had charged straight out of a travel poster. Shaped like a gigantic torpedo, the engine was painted a pale purple with a broad white band running along the whole length.

After the locomotive came the purple and white passenger cars, streamlined like the locomotive and drawn up close behind her on mighty tie bars and chains.

And now the locomotive vanished as the train continued across the bridge and then after a long while it was Ryan's turn and he peered down at the gray green water flowing between lush tree-lined banks. He thought he saw a fish jump and then what he thought must be a hawk soared over the water and then the river was gone and he found himself looking at swamp grass and stately magnolias dripping with long, glorious nets of Spanish moss, which quickly gave way to fences and farms and animals and dirt roads.

On his left the windows looked out over the Intracoastal—a narrow waterway that cut through the entire length of the state, and beyond—all the way to Boston.

Strange white birds with stilt-like legs patrolled the banks, stirring sand and soil with long curved bills. An old man with bare skinny legs and bushy white hair and a long beard was reeling in a line—the tip of his pole bending under the weight of his catch so he looked a little like the birds. Several battered fishing boats plied the waters beyond. Ryan spotted an old tug, sitting low in the water, pushing a line of barges up the Intracoastal.

Past the barges was a slash of deep tropical green—the other side of the Intracoastal—and sometimes Ryan caught glimpses of the white breakers of the Atlantic. And once—far away—the outline of a south-bound freighter.

A pang. The freighter looked as lonely as he felt and he wished he were on its deck. On the way to anywhere, or nowhere. It didn't matter. As long as it didn't stop.

The short time on the train had been a respite from his troubles and he dreaded the journey's end when it would all come crashing back, but without the comfort of his Aunt Cassie and Uncle Tom. Instead, there would be that cold-eyed woman who professed to be his grandmother. A woman who shook hands when greeted by her grandson.

Now they were slowing and up ahead he saw a long dock with a fishing boat tied up at the end. Big gulls circled the boat—swooping and diving—as the fishermen gutted their catch and tossed the offal into the water.

The dock led to a long weather-beaten, tin-roofed building with a battered sign announcing that this was JOVE BEACH.

In case anyone doubted that they had reached their destination, the town's number one landmark—a marvelous red lighthouse—towered over the landscape.

The engineer hit the whistle, making him jump. Then came the long suspense of shrieking brakes, rattling chains and bumping cars until the train came to an abrupt jaw-snapping stop.

A moment of silence followed and then there was a cacophony of sound as passengers and crew went into motion.

Only about a dozen other people were disembarking—all but a few in military uniforms. They were whisked away and Ryan found himself alone, standing beside the train blinking in the bright sunlight. His only company seemed to be that big red lighthouse looking down at him from afar.

Then, as if his ears had popped at altitude, the world came rushing back and he heard the birds calling overhead and breathed in the rich odor of fish carried on a salty breeze to mingle with the heavy tropical scent of the lush vegetation surrounding the station.

A small crowd gathered near the station's entrance—a few railroad employees and a dozen or so locals.

He looked the crowd over, searching for, but not seeing his grandmother. A moment of panic. The train was late. Maybe they became tired of waiting and went home. But what would he do? Where would he go?

From behind him came the rumble of the Professor's voice. "Not to worry, young man. I'm sure your grandfather will be along directly."

Ryan almost corrected him and said, "Step grandfather," but it seemed mean-spirited, so he let it go.

The Professor checked his big railroader's watch, then returned it to his vest pocket. "I still have a few minutes," he said. "Let's check with Mr. Donaldson, the station master."

He steered Ryan toward the station's entrance. Chuckling, he said, "Brace yourself," he said. "You are about to meet your first genuine Jove Beach eccentric—'Dadburn Donaldson.'"

Ryan grinned. What joke was this? "Dadburn, what, Professor?"

"You will soon see for yourself," the Professor said.

They paused at the entrance to let two beefy black men heft a long wooden crate into the station. The men set it against a wall plastered with tattered travel posters and a dusty rack containing a few yellowed brochures. Obviously, Jove Beach was not a prime travel destination.

A short, squat middle-aged man with a round, cheery face held forth behind the counter. He wore a shabby blue uniform coat with frayed sleeves and an open collar shirt that was more gray than white.

When he spotted them he called out, "Dadburn it, if it ain't the dadburned Professor!"

"Mr. Donaldson," the Professor said. "Always a pleasure. I am here on an errand of mercy."

Mr. Donaldson nodded. "Been dadburned expectin' you. Got it dadburned here some dadburned place." He fumbled through a heap of papers on the counter. "Gotta dadburned message for you," he said.

Then he spotted Ryan. "Dadburn it. You must be the dadburned Yankee kid the dadburned Sullivans been waitin' on."

Before Ryan could reply, Donaldson turned back to the Professor, motor-mouthing away. "That's what this here dadburned message is about," he said, still flipping through the pile. "Dadburned storm tore up the dadburned bridge. Mrs. Sullivan called me on the dadburned phone. Said to tell the dadburned kid she was gonna be a little dadburned late."

Then, he found it. "Aha!" he said, holding up a crumpled scrap of paper. Ryan reached for it, but the station master pulled the message back, holding the note close to his face and squinting with short-sighted eyes.

He perused it, nodding as he read, lips moving. "Yep, that's what it dadburned says," he reported. "Dadburned storm busted the dadburned bridge piling. Gonna be dadburned late."

He tossed the scrap of paper back on the counter. "You know how it is with that dadburned bridge," he said to the Professor. "Always been pretty dadburned rickety. Gets dadburned pushed about when the dadburned creek's up."

Donaldson looked over at Ryan. "Only dadburned way onto dadburned Sullivan's Island," he told the boy, "'Cept for the dadburned ford down by dadburned Hobe Creek."

Ryan goggled "They have a whole island?" he marveled.

The Professor smiled. "It's nice, but not all that grand, Ryan," he said. "You'll see for yourself. Like most people in these parts, your grandfather does a bit of everything. A little ranching. A little farming. A little fishing."

He started to say more, but the engineer gave a warning toot of his whistle. "I'd best be going," the Professor said. "You will be in good hands with Mr. Donaldson until your grandmother arrives. Poke around and do a little exploring, if it suits you. Just don't wander too far."

"I won't, sir," Ryan said, his heart speeding up. The Professor would be gone soon. It was like his last connection with home.

The Professor offered his hand. "It has been a real pleasure to know you, Ryan."

"And me... uh... the same, sir," Ryan mumbled, suddenly shy. He shook the big hand. "Maybe I'll, you know... see you sometime."

"Of course you will," the Professor said. "I come through here regularly. And, like I told you, my cousin Samuel works for your grandfather. I visit him now and then."

They shook hands. Ryan's small hand in the Professor's firm, smooth grip. It was a powerful moment for the boy. Emotion roiled through him. His eyes became a little bit wet.

And then the Professor was saying a few more words of farewell, and there was another whistle toot and he hurried away. Expert eyes swept the platform for signs of anything amiss and then—just as the train started moving forward—he swung through the door and was gone.

Mr. Donaldson spoke up. "If you want a dadburned Coke, or somethin', kid," he said, "got a dadburned cooler just by the dadburned door. Costs a dadburned nickel, but seein' as how you're dadburned new to town, the first dadburned Coke's on me."

Ryan thanked him and went outside. The cooler was right where Donaldson said it would be. Big enough to hold a couple of cases of soda pop, it was long, about belly high, and so rust-eaten he could barely make out the "Coca Cola" sign. When he opened the lid the smell of cold rusty water rose up. A mixture of Cokes and other varieties of soda bobbed around amid chunks of dirty ice and water.

He fished around, the bottles bumping and clanking against one another, enjoying the chilly air. Ryan had just become aware enough to realize how hot it was. Sweat poured off him, but when he looked around the few other people he spotted were bundled in jackets and sweaters as if they were cold. A thermometer/barometer display hanging in the station window said it was 75 degrees. When he left Philadelphia it hadn't been that long before the last of the snow had melted.

Ryan stuck the top of his Coke into the recess for the opener, popped the cap off, then took a long, frosty swallow. Suddenly overtaken by thirst, he drained the bottle. The cola burned all the way down. Burped. Fished out a nickel and bought seconds.

Another long drink. Oh, that was so much better. Feeling more confident, even a little cocky. After all, he had just traveled twelve hundred miles on a train all by himself. Never mind the Professor. Mostly he had done it on his own.

He looked about and saw a fishing boat tying up to the dock. Two pelicans followed the boat into its berth. Ryan considered wandering over to watch the fishermen work, but then he heard a familiar, rhythmic tapping. The dah-dah-diddy of Morse Code.

Ryan followed the sound until he came to a boxcar that had been lifted off the rails and set up next to the station house. The overly large sliding doors were sealed shut and a normal door had been cut into them. Over the open door was a sign announcing that this was the station's Western Union office.

Sipping his Coke, he strolled over and peeked inside. To his surprise, he saw a woman seated before the operating station, tapping away on the key. It was just one more sign that they were at war, with women taking on jobs normally reserved for men.

She paused in her operation, swiveled to the typewriter stand and started taking down the reply. A moment later she was done, snatched the typed sheet from the roller and stuck it on one of several spikes set up on her desk. Then, as if sensing Ryan's presence, she turned and spotted him in the doorway.

"How can I help you, young man?" she inquired in a soft southern drawl. She was a plump woman in her middle thirties, with a kind, motherly face.

A little embarrassed, Ryan said, "I'm fine, thank you, ma'am. I was just watching. I didn't mean to bother you."

She smiled, waving his apologies away. "No bother," she said. Then, "Are you interested in telegraphy?"

"Yes, ma'am," Ryan said. "My father is in the submarine service. And on his boat he's, you know, 'Sparks.'" This was the nickname all the Naval telegraph operators went by.

"Oh, now I know who you are," she said with a broad smile. "Verne Sullivan was in the other day talkin' about you."

Ryan didn't know what to say, so he just gave his universal shrug and replied, "Yes, ma'am."

The woman offered her hand. "I'm Etta Wilkinson," she said. "Normally, my husband runs the telegraph office, but he's doing that job for Navy now and I've taken his place."

There was a clatter of an incoming message and Mrs. Wilkinson excused herself and turned back to her board.

He watched as she worked, admiring her smooth, unhurried way with the key. Women telegraph operators weren't unheard of. But usually they were very young and just out of operator school, working until they got married and started a family.

But the war had turned everyone's world upside down. Ryan spotted a family picture on her desk showing a man, a woman he took to be Etta and two girls in their late teens.

Outside, he heard Mr. Donaldson shout to someone: "I think he's over to the dadburned telegraph office."

Ryan's heart gave a bump. His grandmother must have finally shown up.

With great trepidation he turned and stepped outside, momentarily blinded by the dazzling sunlight.

FIVE

Verne Sullivan

When his vision cleared, Ryan found himself gawking at the most magnificent animal he had ever laid eyes upon.

It was a horse rivaling in looks and size any sculpted heroic scene portrayed in a museum, or city park. Powerful muscles. Fiery eyes. Magnificent head. Broad back. Rippling flanks. And it towered over Ryan as if he were a midget, instead of a boy who at 5'6" was tall for his age. And under the blazing Florida sun the animal's color was a beautiful shimmering red.

His eyes traveled upward and he found a man sitting astride that fabulous animal who was ever bit its equal. He was easily the biggest human being Ryan had ever seen. He was so tall that if he shook his feet free of the stirrups they would have practically scraped the ground.

And he was huge. Grizzly bear huge. Ryan couldn't imagine how many yards of material it took to make the faded blue dungarees the man wore, or how many cows had given up the ghost to create the tooled leather boots the dungarees were stuffed into. A white cotton shirt was stretched over an immense torso with axe handle shoulders and bulging biceps.

Topping all this off was a broad, white Panama hat, shading an immense head. The man's hair was silver and he had a wide smile set in a jolly Irishman's face.

Ryan was startled to see only one bright blue eye looking down at him. The missing left eye was concealed by a black, piratical patch.

"You must be Ryan," the man said, in a flat Midwestern accent. "I'm Verne Sullivan." Then, a little shyly, he added, "I'm your grandmother's husband."

Ryan finally came unstuck. "Yessir, Mr. Sullivan," he said. "I'm Ryan. Ryan Karr."

The big man chuckled—a sound like a rumble in a deep cave. "Let's get this started on the right foot, Ryan," he said. "Rule Number One: no more 'misters.'"

Ryan blushed. "Yessir." He hesitated, then, "Uh… But what should I call you?"

Another rumble of amusement. "Call me what my mother called me," he said. "Verne." A grin. "But unless you can run real fast don't you dare call me what my father called me."

Ryan laughed and suddenly he felt light and relaxed. He didn't even mind the tropical heat. He said, "Yessir. Verne is fine."

The marvelous animal Verne was sitting on snorted and stomped an impatient hoof. Verne laughed and said, "Here, now, I'm being rude. I haven't introduced you to my friend."

He stroked the animal's neck. "Ryan, I want you to meet Big Red. Red, this young man standing before you is none other than Ryan Karr."

Then he reached down with a long arm and tapped Big Red's left leg. The horse snorted, then dipped down, making a graceful bow. At the same time, Verne swept off the Panama hat, revealing a shock of dazzling white hair.

"Welcome to Jove Beach," Verne said as animal and master came erect.

Delighted, Ryan laughed. Totally charmed, he reached out a hesitant hand.

Looking up at Verne he said, "Is it okay?"

"Go ahead," Verne encouraged him. "He won't bite."

As if on cue, Big Red tossed his head then leaned toward Ryan, offering his nose. Ryan complied. The horse snuffled his palm with a velvety nose. It tickled and Ryan suppressed a giggle.

"Here, give him this," Verne said, fishing some sugar cubes from his pocket, and handing them over.

"Put 'em on the flat of your hand," Verne directed.

Ryan did so, hand tingling in anticipation. Snuffle. Snuffle. A soft, wet muzzle investigating. Then Big Red sucked up the sugar cubes and crunched them.

"You've just made a friend for life," Verne said. He glanced around. "Where's your luggage?"

Ryan indicated the small suitcase and knapsack at his feet. "That's all I've got, sir."

"You travel light," Verne said, approvingly.

"Yessir. We move around a lot. My dad being in the Navy and all."

Verne offered a hand. "Give me your stuff, then climb aboard."

Ryan was thrilled. The only horses he'd ever ridden were the ones little kids sat on for birthday pictures. He handed up the suitcase and shouldered the backpack. Then grabbed Verne's offer of a hand the size of catcher's mitt. Verne effortlessly lifted him off the ground and swung him around onto Big Red's back.

"Hang onto my belt," Verne said, making a clicking sound that put Big Red in motion.

Ryan grabbed the thick black belt that encircled Verne's huge waist, assisting a set of sturdy red suspenders.

A cluck of the tongue and the horse started moving faster. Big Red's gait was so smooth that Ryan was barely jostled by the motion.

Behind him, he heard Mr. Donaldson call out, "Say, Verne! We got that dadburned delivery you was waitin' for!"

Verne waved a big hand and raised his voice to reply, "Thanks! Sammy will come fetch it tomorrow."

Another cluck and a snap of the reins and they speeded up, but the horse's motion was so smooth he barely noticed.

Ryan would vividly remember that ride for the rest of his life. Years later he'd be able to recall every detail, from the deliciously rich odor of Big Red's healthy sweat to the fantastic sensation of sitting so high off the ground that he had the view of a giant. Verne smelled of tobacco and Old Spice and there was a rough red raw spot by his Adam's Apple where he had scraped himself with his straight razor.

Soon they were cantering out on a narrow blacktop and then turning toward the lighthouse. A flock of a dozen or more elegant white birds with long curved beaks crossed the road and they parted before Big Red's approach, moving in unhurried unison around and through his long legs.

Verne's big thumb indicated the lighthouse. He turned his head slightly to say, "Only a blind man can get lost in Jove Beach. Wherever you go, just keep that lighthouse in sight, and you'll have a pretty good idea which direction to take."

"Yessir," Ryan said. "I read up about it at the library in a book about American lighthouses. It's pretty famous, too. They gave it a whole page."

Verne whistled. "That much!" He patted the horse's neck. "You hear that, Red? A whole page." The horse snorted, as if in reply.

With the sun overhead and the sea breeze rustling his hair and tickling his nose, Ryan sat easily on Red's broad back, big muscles moving effortless, the rhythmic clop, clop of his hooves soothing to his ears. And he thought, maybe this won't be so bad after all.

Then they were coming to a long wooden bridge, crossing over from one side of the river to the other. A high-masted Coast Guard boat had just gone through and the bridge was still split in the middle. Ryan saw the small figure of a woman operating the machinery inside the bridge house. On the other side of the bridge a line of military vehicles waited.

Red eyed the vehicles suspiciously. Verne patted him, whispered a few soothing words, then fished out the makings of a cigarette. He rolled it one-handed and lit up with a wooden match.

Slowly, but surely, the two bridge halves swung down and joined up with a loud thunk! An elderly black man with a game leg limped out of the bridge house, double-checked the connection, then waved the traffic through.

"That's Mrs. Turner and old Noah," Verne said, breathing out a cloud of rich-smelling tobacco. "Her husband joined up the day after Pearl Harbor, so she and old Noah have to tend that bridge pretty much by themselves around the clock."

Indicating the approaching military trucks, Ryan asked, "Where are they going? I thought the only base down here was the Coast Guard's."

Verne chuckled. "Well, that's the official picture," he said. "Actually they're building a new naval facility up the road a piece. Supposed to be a secret." He snorted. "Some secret. Jove Beach is a Small Town with a capital "S" and a capital "T." Everybody knows everybody's business. Even the U.S. government's."

Red did a little nervous dance as the heavy trucks neared, the boards under their wheels popping and crackling. Verne leaned forward, patting Big Red and whispering in his ear. The horse grew easier, tossing his head and glaring at the vehicles as they moved past.

When he was calm again, Verne field-stripped the remains of his cigarette, and pocketed them for later disposal. Then he made another cluck of his tongue and they moved across the bridge, hooves drumming the wooden planks in a perfectly measured beat.

Mrs. Turner leaned out her window to wave. Verne waved back, shouting, "I'll stop by next time we're goin' to town in the car, Ruth. Keep your list handy." The woman waved back and shouted her thanks.

To Ryan, he said, "With her husband gone and old Noah getting—well, older—some of us have been pitching in to fetch groceries and run errands."

"Maybe I can help out sometimes after school," Ryan said.

"She'll appreciate it," Verne said. Then: "About school. Tomorrow's Friday, so you'll have a long weekend to get settled and we'll take you in on Monday and sign you up. The principal—Hank Jordan—is a pal of mine.

"We hit town about the same time—fifteen years ago—which makes us newcomers to the locals. And since we both had the bad grace to be born in the North, we're also Yankees. Which makes us figures of fun on some days, and on others we're—"

Verne paused, then switched to a mock Southern drawl... "Nothin' but dirty Yankee devils, lowern' yeller dogs."

Ryan laughed. "By Jove, I think he's got it," he said in a fake British accent.

Verne slapped his leg and guffawed. "You've been talking to the Professor," he said.

"Guilty," Ryan said.

"He's quite a man," Verne said. "A pure American original."

As they crossed the bridge, Ryan craned to see the waterway and got a jolt when he spotted his first alligator sunning itself on the banks.

At first he thought it was nothing more than a large log, but as he watched the log opened its mouth, displaying a frightening array of teeth. The beast was easily twelve or thirteen feet long and probably weighed hundreds of pounds. Fascinated, he watched it move slowly forward, then slip gracefully into the water without a sound or even a splash.

Verne pulled Big Red up. "You'll want to see this," he said.

At first Ryan didn't know what he meant, but then he saw the gator, which was almost completely submerged, moving silently toward a flock of ducks leisurely paddling around hunting for food.

Just before reaching the flock of ducks the gator vanished. Fascinated, Ryan waited for it a to reappear. Suddenly, a huge tail emerged just ahead of the ducks and came crashing down so hard that it sounded like an explosion. A huge wave of water engulfed the ducks, stunning them.

Then Ryan saw the gator shoot to the surface, great jaws spreading wide to engulf a duck. Then, snap! snap! and two more ducks went down the enormous gullet.

A moment later it was all over. The rest of the flock recovered and took flight, and the gator turned and headed back to take its ease in the sun while it digested its meal in peace.

For a moment, Ryan was speechless. Then all he could say was, "Wow!"

Verne clucked and Big Red moved on.

Nervously, Ryan asked, "Do you have those on Sullivan Island?"

"Gators are everywhere in Florida," Verne said. "But they're nothing to be frightened of, unless you're a child or small dog. They don't often attack full grown adults and then it's a matter of stupid people showing off, or becoming careless."

He turned his head slightly to say, "Don't let fear of gators keep you from enjoying swimming and fishing. Just stay alert and if you see gator signs, steer clear of the area."

"Yessir!" Ryan said, with feeling.

Now they were nearing the lighthouse, which towered over a rocky beach where the Seminole River spilled out into the Atlantic. It was an impressive sight and Ryan's imagination ran wild with visions of ships caught in storm-tossed seas, and the captain spotting the welcoming beam of light warning him away from sharp coral shoals.

The Coast Guard base was just beyond the lighthouse and Ryan saw a score or more white clapboard cottages and metal Quonset huts. The cottages had Victory Gardens in their small yards and Ryan spotted a few women with young children tending the gardens and hanging wash. A two-story, white colonial building perched on grass-covered dunes on the side nearest the road.

"That's the Coast Guard base you mentioned," Verne said. "It's starting to grow like crazy. New families have been moving into the cottages every day since the war started. That big house has rooms upstairs for visiting big shots."

Ryan nodded. Then, realizing Verne couldn't see him nod, he said, "Yessir. I've lived on bases like that before. But bigger. Lots bigger."

Ryan grew up on a dozen or so naval bases across the country and knew first-hand what that sort of itinerant life was like for the families. You had to be ready to adjust to new, not always friendly, people and circumstances.

Ryan had moved around with his parents so much that he thought he'd seen just about everything. But he'd never been south of the Mason Dixon line before and his journey from Philadelphia to the tropics of South Florida had opened his eyes to so many bewildering changes that he felt disoriented and more than a little confused.

Ever since he left Philadelphia he'd felt like a character in one of his science fiction time travel stories, moving from the modern industrial cities of the North to the Grecian style courthouses and the disturbing "Whites Only" signs of the South.

The further south they went the more outdated and primitive the farms became. Going from state of the art tractors to animals and men straining against plows. And there seemed to be so many poor people. Not just the colored fieldhands he saw through the train windows, but equally ragged white people his city relatives would have dismissed as rednecks, crackers and white trash.

And now, here on the banks of the Seminole River, it was like he'd traveled back two hundred million years or more to the Jurassic era. He felt like he was in that King Kong movie. It wouldn't have surprised him if a brontosaurus or the deliciously scary T-Rex had emerged out of the tropical wilderness the rutted dirt road meandered through.

But sitting behind Verne, moving slowly through the countryside on Big Red, he felt at peace and safe for the first time since he left his aunt and uncle at the 30th Street Station.

And now he was soaking up new sights and sounds and experiences, amazed at the beauty of wilderness in the raw.

There were reedy swamps spreading out from the riverbank on one side and on the other dense forests of immense trees draped with thick blankets of lacy Spanish moss and knuckled roots the size of a large man rising above the water.

Once they passed a rotten log half in and half out of the water and it startled him when he realized the fat mottled green and brown lumps that speckled the log were turtles—dozens of them, all lined up to bask in the sun.

Big Red snorted as he went by and the startled turtles scurried over one another to plop into the water. They looked so comical, Ryan laughed aloud.

Verne smacked his lips. "Snapping turtle soup," he murmured. "Delicious!"

There were birds everywhere of every imaginable color, shape or variety, swooping overhead, or running alongside the road. Or even—and this was as funny as the fleeing turtles—water birds that looked like chickens, but ran across lily pads on oversized webbed feet like circus clowns.

Clouds of insects filled the air, desperately squeezing in a few days, or even hours, of life while escaping the constant threat of being eaten by the birds, or the fish that moved through the water in schools so thick Ryan imagined he could walk across their backs from one side of the river to the other.

"Do you like to fish?" he heard Verne ask.

"Yessir!" he said with alacrity.

He loved to fish. Before he became ill with the cancer that would carry him painfully away, his grandfather in Philadelphia took him fishing on the Schuylkill River. But there were never as many fish as this.

"Good," Verne said. "We'll try to get some fishing in before you start school on Monday."

As they passed by, wildlife of all kinds peered out from the tropical underbrush. A momma raccoon hustled her young into the brush as they approached. An incredibly ugly possum snuffled in the dirt. A gray heron almost as tall as a man hunted the shallows. When they passed it took off in an explosion of air—its wings spreading so wide they didn't seem real.

Finally, they came upon a fork in the narrow dirt road. On the left, there was a weather-beaten hand lettered sign that read, "Sullivan's Island." On the right there was a barely legible official Palm Beach County marker. Squinting, Ryan could make out the words: "Hobe Creek."

Big Red automatically turned toward the left but Verne pulled him up. Patted his neck and said, "Not today, Red. No bridge, remember?" He clucked his tongue and guided the horse to the right.

Just then, gunfire erupted up ahead. One, two, then a whole flurry of shots and Verne was fighting to control Red who reared back.

Ryan started to slide off, but Verne reached around and grabbed him with one hand, while he muscled Red back to earth with the other.

No sooner had the shooting stopped, when they heard a loud crash, followed by the ear-splitting blare of a car horn that went on without stop.

A minute later, there was the clatter of small hooves and then a half dozen pigs burst into view. These were not the big fat, spoiled porkers Ryan had seen on farms in the north, but smaller, leaner beasts covered with splotches of wiry hair.

"Razorbacks, by God!" Verne exclaimed. "Keep your feet in!"

Heart hammering, Ryan clutched Big Red's belly with his heels. Meanwhile, Verne had his hands full, keeping control of Big Red, while dodging the pigs.

Ryan clung to his belt for dear life, pulling his feet up higher as the pigs charged through, missing Red's legs by mere inches. Up close they had mean little eyes and sharp tusks bared against any and all comers.

A moment later the pigs disappeared into the brush, but no sooner were they gone then there was the roar of a truck engine and the screech of tires.

Then a bizarre vehicle came charging into view. It was a 1941 Ford pickup, painted a bright red, with yellow flames shooting back from the grill to the doors.

Shouting, cheering boys were crammed into the truck's bed, waving bottles and .22 rifles. Four more boys were crammed into the cabin.

Ryan caught a look at the driver's face—it was round and pudgy and boozy red, framed by greasy blond hair under a black Stetson. To Ryan's surprise the person behind the wheel was barely of drivable age, if that. The boy sneered as they went by, flipping the finger, while his friends shouted obscene insults.

"No surprise there," Verne murmured. "It's Jim Collins's kid."

Then they were gone, the shouting and jeering fading away. Somewhere up ahead, the car horn persisted.

Verne nudged Red and the horse moved onward, clearly agitated and rolling his eyes.

They rounded the bend and came upon a pitiful sight. An old, black Chevy roadster was stranded half on and half off the road. A dark haired girl about Ryan's age was tugging futilely at the hood, trying to get at the horn. Leaning against the truck was a woman who looked enough like the girl that Ryan took her to be the mother.

Verne snorted. "It's Mrs. Peters," he said. "I swear, every time I see that woman she's in some sort of trouble."

Then he sighed. "Guess we'd better help," he said.

He clucked at Red, who picked up his pace and a moment later, they were coming up on the roadster.

The woman turned as they approached. She put a hand on her hip and bleared up at them. "Well, well," she said, "if it ain't Verne Sullivan again. Come to rescue a couple'a dam-shels in dish—I mean, dis-tress."

She straightened, staggering a little—which was when Ryan realized she was quite drunk.

SIX

Hattie and Gig Light Sally

Mrs. Peters kept talking a blue streak, but between her slurring and the blaring horn Ryan couldn't understand a word she was saying. As for the girl, she was clearly mortified and trying her best to make herself small enough to vanish from sight.

Finally, Verne had enough. "Jesus Christ," he said. He slid off Big Red, handing the reins to Ryan, who took them, scared as hell he'd do something wrong and Red would bolt. But the animal stood perfectly still, except for swishing his tail and stomping his hooves to chase off the flies.

Verne popped the Chevy's hood, reached into the guts, gave something a twist and the horn stopped so abruptly that Ryan nearly overbalanced and fell off the horse.

Turning to Mrs. Peters, Verne demanded, "What's going on here, Bridget? How'd you get into this fix?"

The woman looked up at Verne, eyes red and weepy. "I don't know, Verne," she said, voice all a tremble, "We were just... well, you know... just, um... And then those boys, umm... "

"Wasn't Momma's fault," the girl broke in, embarrassment boiling off in a flash of anger. "It was that Joe Collins and his gang," she said. "Shooting at those pigs from their truck like nobody was around."

The girl pointed at the left front tire, which was flat. "And then one of their bullets got Momma's tire and we went off the road."

As she spoke, she grew angrier. She stomped her foot. "Joe could have killed us for all he cared. But he just kept driving when we went off the road. Like nothing happened. Shouting... you know... things. Nasty things."

"That's all right, Hattie," Verne said, his voice turning gentle. "We get the picture. That Collins kid's a piece of work. Everybody knows that. Now, let's see what we can do to put things right."

Verne got the spare tire, which was mounted just behind the engine compartment. Bounced it a few times, handling the tire as if it were no bigger than a basketball. "Pumped up nice and tight," he said, trying to sound encouraging.

After investigating the untidy jumble in the back seat, he nodded in satisfaction, adding, "We've got ourselves all the tools we need right here."

More fishing about, then a smile. "And look at this," he said, "we've even got some rope. Just what the doctor ordered."

With that he dumped out a thick coil of rope that was all knotted and twisted together.

"Why don't you kids make yourself useful," he said, "and uncoil that rope."

He turned to Mrs. Peters, his smile gentle. "You'd be a big help behind the wheel, Bridget," he said. "Turn the key when I give the signal."

Ryan didn't know what he meant by that. Turning the engine on and off had nothing to do with changing tires. But then he noted the sparkle of humor in Verne's single, bright blue eye and realized what Verne was up to as he helped Mrs. Peters into the roadster, then gently shut the door.

"Just take a little rest, Bridget," he said, surreptitiously removing the keys and pocketing them. "I'll give you a shout when you're needed."

He'd taken no more than three or four steps back to the spare tire when Bridget's head slumped forward and she passed out.

Ryan thought he heard Hattie mutter, "Thank God for small favors," but when he looked she turned away.

Bridget was in her thirties, attractive, but definitely a rose whose beauty was fading. And she was pale, as if she didn't get much sun. Hattie—who was tanned from head to sandaled feet—had her mother's looks, without the fading part. She wore dungaree cut-offs, displaying long foal-like legs, and a sleeveless blue blouse tucked around a slender waist.

Encouraged by Verne's example, Ryan did his best to put her at ease, listening to her pour out the story of their ordeal while Verne changed the tire. With her dark brown curly hair and flashing black eyes, she was easy to listen to. Her accent was southern, but not heavily so. And when she was excited—like she was now—it became a little thicker and more colloquial.

Hattie was a little hazy on what they were doing so far from town and when Ryan asked, she nervously said, "Oh, Momma just wanted to go for a drive and see what there was to see. We're new here—my daddy's just down from Georgia."

Her daddy turned out to be a chief petty officer—an important man at the Jove Beach Coast Guard station, which Hattie said had been getting bigger every day.

But a thrill ran through him when Hattie added, "I guess it's no secret that they're hunting U-Boats. Daddy says the Germans are getting pretty bold along the coast. They're after the British freighters."

"My dad's in submarines," Ryan said, forming an instant military brat bond with Hattie. It was a small, insulated world that only the inhabitants understood. "Last we heard," Ryan added, "he was hunting U-boats in the North Atlantic, just like your dad."

Ryan felt the tension go out of Hattie. She flashed a shy smile and patted his hand, as if to say: *Then you know what it's like.*

He glanced over at her mother, who was snoring peacefully behind the wheel. When you lived on a base everybody knew your business. Unless you wanted the whole world to know you were a drinker, you never purchased all your booze in one place.

In a low voice, he said, "Was she... uh... looking for a... you know... store, or something."

Hattie nodded. "Or something," she confirmed. Then, "With all the U-boat stuff, dad's been pretty much working around the clock. He's hardly ever home and things get... well, you know."

He did, indeed, know how things got.

Verne spoke up. "You kids got that rope untangled yet?"

They looked over and saw Verne on his feet, wiping his hands with a rag. The tire change was complete.

"Now we have to get the car off the river bank," he announced.

Verne stood back and examined the situation. The roadster was hanging off the side, dangling about six feet above the river. Ryan couldn't see how the job was going to be accomplished. One false move and the car would slide off into the river. Verne must have been thinking the same thing, because he sighed and shook his head.

But just then they heard someone shout, "Halloo the car!"

Ryan looked up to see a strange sight coming along the river. An incredibly skinny woman of indeterminate age, with long tangled hair streaked with gray, hove into view.

She was standing upright in a flat bottom boat, pushing it with a long pole. She had hawk-like features, with a sharp, hooked nose. From many years in the sun she was tanned the color of old leather. She wore raggedy sailor's bell bottoms, a faded navy blue shirt, stitching scars where rank badges had once been, and a battered captain's hat with crossed anchors.

When they saw her, Hattie and Verne both brightened. "Hi, ya, Sally," Hattie called out. While Verne said, "Little late in the day for frog gigging, isn't it, Sally?"

The woman chortled. "I ain't catchin', now, Verne, I'm sellin'," she said, as she poled her way to the bank.

She tossed a line to Hattie who tied it to a nearby tree. Sally studied the scene, then—in unconscious parody of Verne—sighed, and shook her head.

"Quite a fix you and your momma got yourselves in, Hattie," she said, with sympathy. "It was that Collins gang, weren't it?"

"Yes'um," Hattie said. "They were chasing pigs and shooting up the riverside. Hit one of our tires and ran Momma right off the road."

"Figured," Sally said. "I seen them hoorawing that colored hooch joint back aways. Then somebody shouted 'Pigs! Pigs!' And they took off, shootin' and shoutin' and raisin' all kinds of hell."

She looked over at Hattie's mom, who was snoring peacefully behind the wheel of the car. "Saw you and your mom in the neighborhood just afore that, and I was worried there might be trouble so I come along this way, case you needed help."

Ryan was starting to put two and two together. The hooch joint was obviously a place that sold illegal booze. Which, Hattie had hinted, was the purpose of Mrs. Peters' journey off the beaten track.

Verne said, "Sally, with your help I think I can see a way out of this."

"Sure, Verne," Sally said. "What'cha got in mind?"

He held up the rope. "If you can reach up from where you are and tie this end around the right wheel, I'll hook up Big Red and swing the car around."

"Good plan," Sally said. "Toss us the rope, big man."

Verne grinned and tossed her the rope. Oddly elegant for such a gawky-looking figure, Sally balanced in her boat, which rocked dangerously back and forth, and tied the rope to the wheel.

Verne took up the slack and looped it around Big Red's saddle horn. "Okay," he said. "Here we go."

Everybody scrambled out of the way, while Verne gently coaxed Big Red forward. Slowly, with a lot of grinding and ripping of dirt and rock and brush, the car swung around, uprooting plants and showering debris into the river.

Then, just as success seemed assured, a wheel got hung up on the embankment. Big Red strained, but the car barely budged. There was a grating sound and Ryan worried that the oil pan might be yanked off, then there'd be Hades to pay. Plus, the saddle horn was being pulled so hard Ryan thought the stitching might burst apart.

"Hold on, Red," Verne said, patting the horse. "Don't want to wreck your saddle."

He motioned Ryan over, saying, "You keep him steady."

Ryan's eyes widened. He'd never done anything like that before.

Verne patted him on the shoulder, a little like he'd patted Red, Ryan thought. "You'll do fine," he said. "Big Red likes you. Never saw him take to somebody so fast." He fished out more sugar cubes. "Just to make sure here's a little more friendship bait," he said, chuckling.

Ryan offered the cubes, which were snuffed up and crunched with relish. Then he held Red steady while Verne moved over to the car's back wheel.

He reached down, got a grip with one hand, then heaved a mighty heave. At first the car didn't budge. Verne's big forearm swelled to half again its size, muscles rippling and straining. Despite Verne's size, Ryan couldn't believe his eyes when the car slowly began to give way. After much ripping and tearing of foliage the vehicle was forced to come all the way around until it was resting safely on all four wheels.

Ryan looked over at Mrs. Peters and saw that she was still snoring peacefully away, blissfully unaware of everything going on around her.

Verne straightened as if nothing unusual had happened and brushed himself off.

He turned to Hattie. "Now, Hattie," he said, "I don't want to be rude but your momma's in no shape to drive. So if you'll just be patient, me and Big Red will take Ryan to Sullivan's Island, before Myrtle has conniptions wondering where we're at. And I'll send Sammy back to drive you two home."

"Thank you, Mr. Sullivan," Hattie said in a small voice, mortified at her mother's state.

But Sally broke in. "No need to go to all that bother, Verne," she said. "I was on my way to town to sell my catch. I can drive Hattie and Mrs. Peters to the base and get somebody to fetch me back for my skiff."

She looked over at Hattie. "That okay with you, hon?" she asked in a gentle voice.

"Yes ma'am," Hattie said. Even with her tan, she was scarlet with embarrassment. "We'd be ever so grateful for your help."

"Well, don't you worry about a blessed thing, honey," Sally said. "Life can sink a body lower'n old gator hole. Sometimes it can drive even a strong woman to hooch." Shook her head. "Old Sally's been there herself, hon. I know how she feels."

Hattie flashed a look at Ryan, then looked down at the ground to mumble her thanks.

Sally threw two gunnysacks up on the bank. They smelled of fish and another richer odor that Ryan would later learn were frogs.

"Thank you, Sally," Verne said. "As always, it's been a pleasure."

He mounted Big Red, hauled up Ryan and his luggage and clucked his tongue. Red started off down the trail. Ryan turned back to give Hattie a wave goodbye. She just ducked her head in a little nod and then she and Sally were gently moving Mrs. Peters aside so Sally could take the wheel.

Before she climbed into the car, Sally called out, "That boy Myrtle's grandkid, Verne?"

"Sure is," Verne called back. "Sorry I didn't introduce you. His name's Ryan. You'll be seeing a lot of him from here on out."

"Glad to meet you, Ryan," Sally shouted. "Mind you stay clear of that Collins gang. Nothin' but trouble."

And then Big Red went around a bend and they were out of sight.

Verne chuckled. "Pretty big day for you, Ryan," he said. "Got to meet another of Jove Beach's many characters. First, Dadburn Donaldson. And now the one and only Gig Light Sally."

"What about Joe Collins?" Ryan asked. "Does he count as a character?"

"Only in his own mind," Verne said. "His father owns the Ford Dealership in these parts."

He said the last as if it somehow explained everything.

Later, Ryan would learn that it pretty much did.

SEVEN

Sullivan Island

A barking dog announced their arrival at Hobe Creek. They were immersed in tropical foliage so thick that Ryan could barely see the narrow track they had been following.

They emerged where the track ended at a slow-moving stream. On the opposite bank, Ryan saw the source of the barking: A big Dalmatian was jumping up and down and yapping joyfully at their arrival.

"That's Rex," Verne said. "Told him to stay, and by God he *stayed*." Shook his big head. "That was a couple of hours ago. I expected he'd get bored and go home to chew on the new bone I gave him this morning."

"That's a *good* dog," Ryan said, impressed.

"That he is," Verne said. A cluck of the tongue, a motion with the reins and Big Red stepped into the creek.

Then Ryan heard a high-pitched whistling and he looked up to see an enormous bird swoop down from on high. It skimmed along the creek at about their height, turning slightly toward them as it went by.

Ryan caught a quick snatch of fierce eyes and a hooked beak, then the bird was soaring away, up and up, on nine-foot wings.

"You've just been dive bombed by Orville," Verne said. "Our resident Bald Eagle."

Ryan was too dumfounded to reply.

On the other side, Verne reined in and Rex rose up on his hind legs to get a pat and a rub behind the ears. He dropped to all fours, sat back on his haunches and stared up at Ryan, interest in his dark eyes.

Ryan reached down with a tentative hand. The dog hesitated, made some sort of judgment, and then a warm tongue flicked out to lick his fingers. Boldly, Ryan stretched down as far as he could and rubbed Rex vigorously behind the ears. The dog woofed in pleasure.

"Down," Verne said. Rex obediently dropped to all fours. Verne clucked for Big Red to continue on and Rex padded along beside them.

Then, casually, Verne asked, "You ever have a dog, Ryan."

"Nossir," Ryan said. "We moved around too much. But I always wanted one."

Verne chuckled. "I think you've just been adopted."

Ryan could smell the sharp, sweet scent of citrus even before they encountered the first orange grove. And then they broke out of the foliage shielding the creek onto a broad, well-tended dirt lane. It ran toward its destination straight as an arrow. The trees drawn up on either side as orderly as a regiment greeting its commanding general.

The trees were covered with oranges in various stages of ripeness and clumps of snowy white blossoms graced the branches, promising more fruit to come.

Off to their left—and beyond the orchard—Ryan heard a heavy engine at work. It seemed out of place here. All else was quiet on the island. Nothing but bird song and insect buzzing, with the occasional splash in the creek of leaping fish. Then he caught a whiff of diesel fumes on the breeze and wrinkled his nose. Like the engine noise, it seemed almost a desecration of the peaceful scene.

"That's Sammy and his crew fixing the bridge," Verne said, anticipating what was on Ryan's mind.

Gesturing, Verne said, "The main house is up ahead, where the river cuts back in. Got a dock there and a couple of boats. Truck garden on past there. After that there's the barns, a stable for the horses and a corral. Then there's Sammy's house and…well… you'll see for yourself. There's a lot to explore."

Just as barking had announced Hobe Creek and the scent of citrus, the orange grove, the rich smells of something good cooking announced the presence of the Sullivan home.

Verne sniffed the air and grinned. "Chicken and dumplings," he announced. "That's my darling, Myrtle!"

His big belly rumbled, sounding like the Florida Special charging through a tunnel. Verne laughed. "In case you can't guess, I've got a Big Red-size hunger coming on."

Ryan's belly rumbled in sympathy and he realized he hadn't eaten since his scrambled eggs and country sausage breakfast on the train.

Another laugh from Verne. He patted Red. "I think we got some competition, big fella," he said.

They came out of the orchard to find a Spanish style house, with a white stucco exterior and a red tile roof. Deep verandas embraced the house in dark, cooling shade. Bougainvilleas climbed the walls and clay pots of tropical flowers and plants were tastefully arranged. A broad lane of crushed white seashells led up to the house, with ancient oaks, dripping with Spanish moss shading the avenue.

Then Ryan saw that one side of the house was blackened, as if from a fire. Charred beams came into view, confirming his guess. Fresh cut lumber was stacked neatly on the ground—obviously, repairs were under way.

Parked nearby, Ryan saw a long, silver Airstream trailer. A gleaming, freshly varnished deck with a blue canvas awning ran along the side to the door near the front the trailer.

As they approached, the door came open and a middle-aged woman stepped out. Slender. Elegant. Her artfully arranged hair was dark and dusted with silver. She wore a light summer dress, protected by a crisp white apron. And, despite the heat, high heels and stockings. A touch of lipstick and a little expertly applied makeup to smooth out the age lines completed the picture.

It was his grandmother.

Verne grinned, swept off his Panama and bowed in the saddle. "Madam," he said, speaking as if he were a picture show hero home from some grand adventure, "you take my breath away."

Ryan was so relaxed after their journey that he nearly laughed, but he cut it short when he saw that his grandmother hadn't cracked a smile.

"Mind your manners, Verne Sullivan," she said, "What will the boy think?" She sniffed. "Calling me madam."

To Ryan's surprise, instead of being admonished, Verne only gave another belly laugh.

"I'm too hungry for manners, Myrtle," he said. "And as for the young gentleman, here, I suspect he's thinking that he's hungry too and would the old folks quit jawing and get him something to eat."

He elbowed Ryan. "Isn't that so, Ryan?" Avoiding taking sides, the boy only mumbled. "See, Myrtle?" Verne said. "He agrees. Two to one. I win." More laughter. "I'm gonna to like this arrangement," he said. "A new majority on Sullivan's Island."

Ryan nearly protested that he hadn't said a thing, but Verne reached around to get a grip, then swung him off the horse and deposited him on his feet. Then handed over the small suitcase.

He said, "Now, why don't you go in with your grandmother and catch up over a nice, tall glass of lemonade. Myrtle always keeps two jugs going in the fridge. One for her and one with lots of honey for me."

He turned Red away. "I'll join you after I give Red a good rubdown and some grub." A cluck of the tongue and they trotted off.

Ryan stood there, the suitcase on the ground, the knapsack digging into shoulders, his hands dangling foolishly at his side. Feeling a little like a waif out of Oliver Twist.

As he stood there, his grandmother looked him up and down. He couldn't tell what she was thinking and so after the silence became uncomfortable, he assumed disapproval.

Not knowing what to do, he shoved his hands in pockets.

Finally, she sniffed and said, "Well, you might as well come in out of the sun." Opening the screen door, she said, "Be sure to wipe your feet." As she stepped inside, she added, "And take your hands out of your pockets."

Mortified, Ryan yanked his hands out. Then, after a moment's hesitation, he followed her.

The interior of the Airstream was dark and unaccountably cool, considering that his grandmother had the oven going and had pots and pans bubbling on the stove.

He sat at the built-in table, sipping lemonade from a frosty glass, while his grandmother read the letter his Aunt Cassie had sent along.

When Myrtle was done, she rattled the pages, sniffed, then said, "Where are you school records? I specifically asked Cassandra to send along the transcripts."

It took a minute for Ryan to realize that "Cassandra" was his Aunt Cassie. Then he said, "Oh. Um… The secretary said they weren't done yet because the transcripts from my other schools hadn't shown up."

"Well, I never," Myrtle said. "I expected more competence from a Philadelphia school." Another sniff of disapproval. "Of course, it is a parochial school, isn't it? And a Catholic school at that."

Ryan made no comment. His mother had never been particularly religious, although he was raised Catholic. Mostly he'd gone to public schools, transferring from one to the other as they followed his father from one Navy base to another. From his experience—which was rather wide from attending so many schools—Catholic schools were academically far ahead of their public school cousins. For this reason he was pretty confident he'd have an easy time with any school work thrown at him here in Jove Beach.

Weary from a long day, his mind drifted and he was wondering about the humming noise in the background, when he realized that his grandmother was speaking to him.

"Did you hear what I said, Ryan?"

Covering quickly, he said, "Yes ma'am. It was about the transcripts. And how they hadn't shown up yet."

Mollified, his grandmother nodded. "Yes. And I plan to write and complain. I can't abide incompetence. Especially with public employees. We pay their salaries, after all."

Of course, Catholic schools weren't public and didn't get tax money, but Ryan wasn't so brave—or foolish—to point this out to his grandmother.

It was about then that he realized why the trailer was so cool. It was because of that humming noise he heard in the background.

"You have air conditioning!" he blurted.

"Well, of course, we do," his grandmother said. "The Airstream is brand new and quite expensive." A sigh. "Pity we don't have air conditioning in the house. It's far too costly."

Until now, the only time Ryan had experienced air conditioning was in the movie houses in Philadelphia. And he'd heard that places like fancy department stores were installing them.

"But we have nice thick walls, high ceilings and fly fans in all the main rooms, so that's a blessing," his grandmother said.

Ryan made bold to say, "I noticed you had a fire. Hope nobody was hurt."

Myrtle sniffed. "No, it was just a kitchen fire that got out of hand," she said. "Verne *will* try to cook himself sometimes, despite all evidence that he is incapable. I hope the fire cured him of the habit."

"Yes ma'am," was all Ryan said.

"Now, about sleeping arrangements," his grandmother said.

"Yes ma'am?"

"The fire smell is gone from the house, thank goodness, so that won't be a bother. However, your bed hasn't arrived yet and we don't have any extras. So you'll have to make do with a mattress on the floor until it's delivered."

Another sniff. "The bed was quite expensive, you know," she said in a wounded tone. "I swear, the government ought to look into the prices merchants are charging. In my opinion, they are taking advantage of the war. One might even say, criminal advantage."

She sighed. "Prices are going up all over," she said. "On top of that, there's talk of rationing." She frowned. "Serious talk, mind you. And now that you have arrived we'll have another mouth to feed on top everything else."

Ryan didn't say anything, although there was a momentary flush of anger. Shoot, if she wanted she could send him on back to Philadelphia. He was tempted to make a big pig of himself. Eat her out of house and home and bankrupt her and make her send him back.

He cut off his mental tirade, hoping his anger didn't show. He covered by taking a long drink of his lemonade. Before he knew it he had drained the glass and ice was rattling against his teeth. He set the glass down. Wanted to ask for more, but after the "another mouth to feed" remark he was afraid to bring it up.

Then he remembered something. He fumbled in his jacket. "Aunt Cassie gave me this before I left," he said, unpinning and offering the five dollar bill. "You can have it to help for—you know—expenses and stuff."

Myrtle was taken aback. She straightened in her seat and fussed with her hair. Then she shoved the bill back at him.

"I won't take money from a child," she said.

At the door, Ryan heard a loud scraping of feet and then a big voice boomed: "Money? Did I hear someone talking about filthy lucre?"

Ryan turned as Verne entered—the Airstream settling under his weight. "And before dinner, too," he added.

"Oh, it was nothing, Verne," his grandmother said, composing herself. "Ryan was just showing me his pin money. A very generous gift from his Aunt Cassandra, especially with a husband earning a policeman's salary."

"Uncle Tom didn't mind," Ryan hastily added.

A sniff. "Yes, I'm sure," said his grandmother.

"Enough money talk," Verne said. "Let's eat!"

A few minutes later, looking over a mountain of cornbread dripping with butter and the heaping platters of chicken and dumplings and steaming side dishes spread out on the table, Ryan saw a side of his grandmother he wouldn't have guessed existed.

And the way her husband dug in with such undisguised gusto he understood a little of the attraction Verne had for such a seemingly cold and distant woman.

Myrtle Sullivan was one heck of a cook.

EIGHT

Night Sweats

It was a difficult night. A spooky orchestra of tropical wildlife serenaded him without end, booting aside any notion that country life had ever been quiet.

Besides the usual chorus of animal and bird calls, there were strange, ominous clicking sounds, the scurrying of little feet across the roof, accompanied by something scratching at the exterior walls.

He'd read that panthers and bears inhabited this part of Florida and his imagination went wild when a breeze picked up and the shadowy foliage outside swayed and whipped back and forth in a macabre dance.

Ryan had just seen a revival of the film, "King Kong," complete with klieg lights and a stage show as if it were first run, instead of ten years old. And the shadowy foliage aroused scary memories of the gigantic beasts that stalked Kong Island, making sleep even more difficult.

During one period, something out by the river croaked mournfully. It didn't make Ryan feel better the next day when he was told that the noise was probably a bull alligator looking for a girlfriend.

Occasionally, he heard dogs barking in the distance, but he was pretty sure none of them were Rex. On one hand, this was comforting. A silent Rex most likely meant nothing bad was happening. On the other, what if Rex was a lazy no good mutt, so spoiled he couldn't be bothered?

"Just stop it!" he admonished himself. "There's nothing wrong. Go to sleep."

One thing he couldn't complain about was his room. Spacious, with gleaming hardwood floors like the rest of the house, its white stucco walls glowed when the light was on. A dark oak armoire served as a closet and bureau for his few belongings. And there was a nice old desk, also of dark oak, with many little drawers and cubbyholes that begged to be investigated.

The first thing Ryan did after he'd unpacked was to install his Morse key set on the desk and practice diddy-dahs while sitting comfortably in a cane basket chair with soft blue pillows.

His temporary bed was an elderly mattress whose years of use had flattened everything except for irritating lumps that gathered wherever they'd cause the maximum discomfort.

Thank God he only have to put up with it for one night. Tomorrow, Verne had promised, Sammy would pick up the bed whose cost had so horrified his grandmother.

When sleep finally did overtake him, he was so tired and disoriented from his journey that it was dreamless, which was a definite blessing. For months, worries about his mother and father had spawned nightmares far more tortuous than any of the bug eyed monsters that inhabited his favorite science fiction stories.

Even so, the only way he could finally get any rest was to curl up with his Morse set, clutching it like a little kid's teddy bear and tapping S.O.S. over and over again until sleep overtook him.

Eventually bright morning sun and the scent of bacon and coffee coaxed him awake. He sat up slowly—every muscle groaning and complaining—and craned his sore neck to see the clock on the bedstead next to the mattress.

Six thirty!

He groaned and flopped back onto the mattress. But even with the covers pulled over his head there was no escaping the smell of the bacon and coffee.

There was a knock at the door. Someone called out in a disgustingly cheery voice, "Better get up, Ryan. They're coming to take the bathroom away."

At that very moment bladder pressure made itself known and he sat up in a panic.

"What? Where? Who? What's happening?"

Booming laughter announced that it was all a cruel joke. Rex barked gleefully on the other side of the door, adding to his torment. Groaning and moaning the boy climbed to his feet and got dressed.

After washing and taking care of necessities—thankfully, the bathroom was still intact—he followed his nose to the Airstream trailer where Verne presided over a kingdom of scrambled eggs, bacon and sausage, country fried potatoes, buttered toast, with a big bowl heaped with baked beans as a centerpiece.

Verne gestured to the seat opposite him. "Better get busy," he advised. "We've got a long day ahead."

Ryan looked around, wondering where his grandmother was.

"Myrtle's in the sewing room," Verne said, as if reading his mind. "Listening to the radio, while making socks for the boys."

Ryan nodded. Making socks and scarves for America's fighting men was all the patriotic rage these days. His eyes went to the corner, where a very nice Philco in a gleaming wooden case sat upon the countertop.

Verne saw where he was looking and grimaced. "Heard enough war news to do me an hour or so ago when I got up," he said.

Ryan almost spit out a mouthful of egg. "You got up before six thirty?" he said, incredulous.

Verne chuckled, his single blue eye glittering with amusement. "Force of habit," he said. "I'm pretty near retired now, so I've cut way back. And I've got some nice reliable people like Sammy to do the hard stuff, like getting up early to do most of the chores."

Verne polished his plate with a piece of toast, then pulled over a platter with a large slice of watermelon on it.

"Got time now for important stuff like this," he said, holding up a mason jar for Ryan to see. The contents shimmered in the light. "Always wanted to make my own honey." he said with reverence. "Pure gold. Best thing is that bees pretty much do all the work for you. I'll take you out later to see the hives."

To Ryan's astonishment, he tipped the jar and poured honey all over the melon. Surely, the watermelon was sweet enough.

"I like honey on everything," Verne said. "Perks me up faster than coffee." He offered the jar to Ryan. "Want some?"

Ryan shook his head helplessly. "Nossir," he said, patting his belly. "I'm stuffed."

Verne shrugged and dug into his melon. "If it weren't for the war," he said, "I'd retire all together. But if we're gonna whip those sons of bitches—pardon my French—the country needs everything we farmers and ranchers can squeeze out of the land.

"Army's buying up all my oranges—and then some—to make concentrated juice for the soldiers. And any cattle and crops I can bring to market will help feed people. I even got my fishing boat out of the dry dock and hired a captain and a couple of old boys to go fishing for their country."

Verne settled back, the bench seat creaking, and wiped his face with a napkin. He sighed.

"We all have to do our part," he said. "You know that as well as any of us, don't you, Ryan? With your father in the thick of it all."

"Yessir," Ryan said, voice trembling with feeling.

He thought about his father, off fighting America's enemies, forced to leave his sick wife in a hospital and his son in the care of his mother and the stranger she married.

Outside, Ryan heard Rex bark, then the sound of a vehicle crunching over the seashell driveway, followed by the toot of a horn.

"That'll be Sammy," Verne said, polishing off a final bite of melon and honey and rising from his seat.

The Airstream groaned under his weight as he went to the door, Ryan close behind him. He stepped outside to be greeted by a beautifully re-stored Model T pickup. In the back was a familiar-looked wooden crate.

Ryan stepped off the deck and saw that it was the same crate the two men had lugged into the station office.

"Your bed," Verne announced, moving to the rear of the truck.

Rex came running around, wagging his tail and begging for scraps. Verne fished something out of his pocket. After gobbling it up Rex charged over to Ryan, who kicked himself for not thinking of grabbing a piece of bacon, or something, for the dog. But Rex seemed satisfied with a rub and scratch behind the ears and trotted after him as he followed Verne.

A short, wiry black man had the tailgate down and was fussing with the ropes that held the crate in place. He turned as they approached, flash-ing a wide grin.

"You're back early," Verne said. "Let me guess—old Dadburn was sleeping one off and his wife had you in and out in record time."

"Bullseye, boss," the man said with laugh. Then, in a pitch perfect imitation of Dadburn Donaldson, he said, "Mr. Donaldson got hit by a dadburned hooch truck last dadburn night and dadburn it, if'n it didn't dadburn knock him dadburn flat."

Verne laughed, then reached over and gave Ryan's shoulder a gentle squeeze. "Sammy," he said, "in case you haven't guessed, this young man is Ryan Karr. Myrtle's grandson. He's the reason me and Big Red dared the ford at Hobe Creek. Ryan, meet Sammy—Samuel Davy to be exact—my number one man on Sullivan's Island."

In his early forties, Sammy was a little taller than Ryan—with nar-row features, a sharp chin and close-cropped hair. He wore faded canvas trousers, a long-sleeved red shirt that had been washed so many times it was more pink than red, and his bare feet were stuffed into sturdy farmer's boots.

"Good to meet you," Ryan said, offering his hand.

Then there was a clumsy shuffle as Sammy replied in kind, but shifted to offer his left hand instead of his right.

As Ryan shook it, he glanced down and saw that Sammy had no right hand—only a thick leather-wrapped ball attached to the wrist. Embar-rassed, he quickly shifted his gaze upward, but Sammy caught the look and chuckled.

"Fought a round with a fertilizer spreader when I was too young and dumb to know better," he said. "Me and the hand lost by a knockout."

Put at ease, Ryan grinned. "I heard a lot of nice things about you from the Professor," he said."

"If the Professor said it," Verne broke in, "then you know that every blessed word is true."

A little embarrassed, Sammy said, "He's been a big help to my boy, Alex. Tryin' to get him a scholarship, and all."

Verne slapped the side of the truck. "Okay, let's get goin'," he said. "We're burning good daylight."

They scrabbled around, freeing the rest of the rope, then slid the heavy crate part way off. Ryan flexed his arms, hoping he was strong enough to handle his end, then moved over to one side ready to start lifting.

Verne raised a hand and said, "No need, son. But thanks anyway. Gotta be careful, here. Don't want to scratch Sammy's pride and joy. How many hours did you put into this, Sammy?"

"More than Ada will ever let me forget," Sammy said. He patted a gleaming black fender. "But it was worth every minute of it."

Ryan would never forget what he saw next. In one smooth motion, Verne tipped the big crate upright and slid it onto his right shoulder, curling his arm around the crate and clamping a steely hand against the thick wood.

"Let's go," he called to Ryan, as he lifted the crate off the bed of the Model T, wheeled around and marched effortlessly away, heading for the front door of the house—Ryan and Sammy trotting behind him.

Sammy grinned at Ryan and shrugged, as if to say, that's how the boss likes to do things.

But as they reached the front door, it came open and his grandmother emerged. She looked like she had just stepped out of a modern housewife's magazine. Freshly made up, wearing a light floral dress, protected by a crisp white apron that had a ball of yarn with knitting needles poking out of one pocket.

"Now you mind the walls, Vernon," she said. "Let Sammy and Ryan help you."

"If you'll hold the door for me, darling," Verne said, "That'll be all the help I need."

And he pushed on through, Myrtle backing off to the side. Ryan rushed to help her. There was a screen door, plus a heavy oak main door with a sunburst glass panel.

Verne breezed on through, moving his big bulk as easily as a dancing master, dodging furniture, a standup radio/record player entertainment center, and an upright piano.

When he came to the hallway leading to Ryan's room, he shifted the crate so he was holding it straight out in front of him and progressed down the hallway, leaving the walls on either side untouched.

Ryan followed, marveling at the sheer strength on display.

In the room, they quickly got the bed out of the crate and set up, Ryan and Sammy trotting in and out of the house, carrying away the empty crate, packing material and the old mattress.

When it was done they stood back to admire their handiwork. Verne posed over it, hands clasped over his head like a high diver.

"Should I give her a try?" he asked.

"Don't you dare, Vernon Sullivan," Myrtle squeaked. "You'll break it."

"Then you go, Ryan," Verne said.

Laughing, Ryan jumped on the bed, bouncing up and down on the firm metal springs. "Fantastic," he laughed.

By chance he looked up and saw a strange look on his grandmother's face. For a minute he thought he saw tears well in her eyes.

Verne saw it too and gently folded her in his arms. "What is it, darling?" he asked.

Fighting back sobs, she whispered something. Whatever it she said made Verne draw her closer. She was so small next to him that at any other time it would have looked ludicrous. A lady midget clasped in the arms of a one-eyed giant.

"All we can do is pray for the boy, darling," Verne said in a low voice. "At least we've got this one safe."

And in that moment the far away war crept into the room and Ryan realized the "boy" they were talking about was his father.

In the silence that followed, Ryan eased off the bed. Sammy caught his eye and nodded. Quietly, they crept out of the room.

NINE

Alex

A Jeep pulled up in front of the house just as Ryan and Sammy came through the screen door. Rex burst past them and set about barking, letting potential enemies know they had a resident canine to deal with if mischief was their intent.

Sammy hesitated when he saw the Palm Beach County Sheriff's insignia on the door and the uniformed man behind the wheel. His head jerked back in shock and he cursed under his breath when he spotted the colored kid in the back seat.

Then he pulled on a blank-faced mask as he approached the Jeep.

"Down boy," he admonished Rex. "Don't want the nice deputy to think he ain't welcome."

Obediently, the dog sat back on his heels and Ryan instinctively went to the dog and busied himself scratching behind his ears while Sammy dealt with the deputy, who was climbing out of the Jeep, his wary eyes fixed on Rex.

"He don't mean no harm, Deputy Tindall," Sammy said, pasting a practiced smile on his face. "Like the boss says, old Rex is all bark and no bite."

Tindall was a beefy, baby-faced man in his 40's. Except for a fringe around his ears, he was entirely bald. This, coupled with his broad, pink features, tiny nose and the beadiest eyes Ryan had ever seen, made his head look like it was nothing but face. Ryan bit back a giggle when the blasphemous thought bubbled up that Tindall looked like one of those egg-headed aliens on an Astounding Magazine cover.

The deputy mopped his bald head with a kerchief, then covered it with a peaked khaki forage cap.

Looking past Sammy to Ryan, he said, "You the kid we been hearin' about? Mrs. Sullivan's grandson?"

"Yessir," Ryan said.

"Well, keep that dog close," Tindall said. "I been bit by dogs folks swore were gentle as lambs more times'n I care to recollect."

"Yessir," Ryan said again, putting an arm around Rex, who was perfectly calm and at ease. Tail thumping. Ears at attention. Eyes alert and curious.

Ryan snuck a peek into the back of the Jeep. The boy looked about fourteen and he wore Coke-bottle glasses so thick they overwhelmed his narrow face.

Tindall turned to Sammy. Jerked a meaty thumb in the boy's direction. "Looks like we got ourselves a little problem, Sammy," he said.

Sammy grimaced. "Yessir, I 'spect we do." Ryan noticed that Sammy was copying the deputy's manner of speech. What the Professor called, "Dumbing it down."

Tindall said, "Your son, Alex, there, got hisself into a tangle with Mr. Collins's kid. And little Joe came out on the wrong end of the deal."

Ryan could see the anger building in Sammy. Jaw clenched. Neck veins swelling. But whether he was mad at the boy, the deputy, the Collins family, or a combination of all three, he couldn't say.

"Don't you worry, none, Deputy Tindall," Sammy said through gritted teeth. "I'll give that boy such a whuppin' he won't be able to sit his sorry butt down for a week."

Tindall sighed. "That might not be good enough, Sammy," he said. "No, that might not be good enough at all."

Sammy frowned. Glanced over at his son, then back at Tindall. "How bad was young Mr. Collins hurt, Deputy Tindall?" he asked with some trepidation.

Tindall chuckled. "Oh, it weren't all that bad," he said. "Got a tooth knocked out. Least it weren't a front one. But when he fell he hit his head on somethin' and there was a lot of blood. His momma had conniptions."

"Well, I am sorry as sorry can be about that, Deputy Tindall," Sammy said. "I'll do whatever you say is necessary to make amends."

The deputy shook his head. "Well, like I said, that might not be good enough. His daddy's all for pressin' charges. Puttin' your boy in jail."

Sammy's eyes widened. Ryan could tell he was really scared. "But, sir," he said, "it was just two boys fightin', weren't it? If they was to put all the boys in jail who got into fights, we wouldn't have no kids left."

Tindall straightened, his eyes narrowing. "Now, Sammy," he said, "you know and I know that what we got here is an entirely different situation than an ordinary kid fight. We gots Mr. Collins. An important man." He shook his head. "Kinda man my boss depends on when election time rolls around."

Sammy could see which way the wind was blowing. His shoulders slumped. "Yessir."

"And we got your boy—Alex. Hot tempered kid, from what the principal told me over the colored school."

Tindall pulled a notebook from his back pocket. Flipped pages. Then: "And we got witnesses who said the attack was…" He paused here, frowning at the page. Then he nodded, smiling to himself. "Yeah. Right here. It says the attack was un-pro-voked."

The way he said Ryan knew the word was not his own, but had been dictated to him.

Sammy looked close to tears. "Please, deputy," he said, "just tell me what to do. Anythin' at all. Alex is a good boy. Top of his class in school. Even in line for one of them scholarships. And, yeah, sure, he's got a temper. Ain't nothin' me and his momma can't fix with a fresh cut hickory stick."

"But he's colored, Sammy," Tindall said. "Can't fix that with no hickory stick."

Sammy's head dropped. "Yessir," he said, voice so low Ryan could barely hear him.

Ryan heard the screen door close behind him and he turned to find Verne coming down the steps of the verandah.

When Tindall looked up to see who it was, his entire demeanor changed. He was all smiles as he swept off his hat.

"Mr. Sullivan," he said. "Sorry to be a bother on such a fine day." He waved a hand, indicating Alex in the back of the Jeep. "But I gots my duty to tend to, sir."

"No question about it, Bob," Verne said. "And rest assured the folks in Jove Beach all sleep easier nights knowing that you are on the job—doing your duty."

Tanned as he was from years under hot Florida suns, a blush of pleasure crawled up from under Tindall's uniform collar.

"Thank you, sir," Tindall said. Big as the deputy was, Verne still towered over him, forcing him to crane his neck to look up. "That's mighty white of you to say so, sir."

Ryan saw Verne blink at that, but he recovered quickly, saying, "As for your duty—Well, I was in the living room reading the newspaper and had the window open to catch the breeze, so I couldn't help but overhear your conversation with Sammy."

Ryan knew darned well that Verne hadn't been reading any newspaper. He'd been inside, eavesdropping.

"But, Bob, what I didn't hear," Verne said, "was Alex's side of the story. You say he's got a notorious temper, although I've never known that to be the case. But if notoriety is evidence, then we should take into account young Joe Collins' reputation as the Number One town rowdy."

"I do admit we've had some complaints about Joe in the past," Tindall said. "But it's just kid mischief. High spirits. Tipped over outhouses and stuff. Nothin' the law need worry about."

"That might have been true in the past, Bob," Verne said. "But as it happens, just before you arrived I was thinking hard about paying you a visit today to file a complaint against Mr. and Mrs. Collins's pride and joy."

Tindall stepped back. This was unexpected. "A complaint, sir? What sort of a complaint."

"Yesterday, that *high-spirited* young man almost killed a couple of people," Verne said.

"Whoa!" Tindall blurted. "That's a serious charge."

"And it's a charge I can make stick," Verne said. "Young Joe was racing all over the countryside in a pickup with a half-a-dozen of his buddies shooting at everything in sight with their .22s. Me and Ryan, here, were on Big Red and the horse almost went over, taking us with him."

Tindall grimaced. He did not like what he was hearing.

"And, Bob, you know what the kid did when he went by and saw the mischief he had caused?" Tindall shook his head. "He didn't ask if we were hurt. Or even if Big Red was okay. I mean, Red could have broken a leg and have to be put down. No. he did none of those things. Instead, he flipped us the finger and drove on by."

The deputy looked at Ryan, then Verne. "Why that little—" He broke off in a weak attempt to maintain some sort of impartiality.

"And that's not all," Verne said. "One of the Coast Guard ladies was out for a drive with her daughter. And one of young Joe's stray bullets blew out her tire and she almost went into the river."

Verne gave a sad shake of his head. "Things were lookin' pretty bad for them when Ryan and I showed up. And if wasn't for us and Gig Light Sally—who happened along just in time—you might be dealing with a manslaughter case just about now instead of a fistfight between two quarrelsome boys."

Angrily, Tindall flipped his notebook closed and shoved it into his back pocket. He motioned to Alex. "Come on out, son," he said.

Cautiously, Alex opened the door and climbed out—bare feet first. He was skinny, wore an oversized T-shirt and old Khaki shorts. With his rail thin arms and legs, Ryan couldn't see how he'd be much of a threat to the Collins kid.

Tindall said, "Son, I don't know what really went on back there in Jove Beach. Joe said one thing. And you said another and—"

"I never said nothin'," Alex said, breaking in. He was hot as a pistol and getting hotter by the minute. "You didn't ask. I never had a chance to tell my side. You just—"

"Shut up, Alex!" Sammy snapped. "And stay shut up until further notice. Understand?"

Alex mumbled something. Sammy glared at him "I said, do you understand?"

"Yessir...I understand."

Sammy turned back to Tindall. "Thanks, Deputy Tindall," he said. "Me and Alex's momma will never forget how you went out of your way to keep our boy out of trouble."

Ryan could see that although Sammy's words brought a smile of appreciation to Tindall's lips, his son was so mad his eyes practically burned through those Coke-bottle lenses.

"Well, I'll just leave it for you to handle, Sammy," he said. "And I'll talk to old man Collins about his kid."

To Verne, he said, "About them charges you was consider'n filin'...?" he let the rest trail off, shuffling his feet in the seashells and looking hopeful.

"In the end, no permanent harm was done," Verne said. "And I'll talk to the lady and her daughter. I'm sure they'll want to drop the matter as well."

"Thank you, sir, thank you," Tindall said. Then, after a moment's hesitation, he added, "Maybe this hasn't been a complete waste of everybody's time. I was thinkin' about comin' out to see you one of these days to ask for your help."

Verne's single eye brightened with interest. "You know I'm always ready to pitch in when my community calls on me, Bob," he said.

"Yessir," Tindall said. "Like when the river was threaten' to jump its banks a couple of years back. Everybody on Sullivan's Island showed up on the front line. Fillin' and stackin' sandbags from sun up to sundown. And then some."

Verne shrugged. "Just doin' our part, Bob," he said.

"Yessir," Tindall said. "And it was much appreciated. But what we have now is whole different kettle of fish. Yes, indeed. A whole different kettle. What we got now is them U-boats."

Verne was startled. "U-boats? What about them?"

"Well, you probably heard on the news that there's been a lot of U-boat activity offshore lately. Chasin' freighters goin' up and down the coast and sinkin' anythin' they can catch."

"Yes, I've heard that on the news," Verne said. "What about it?"

"Well, folks are worried some Germans might try and sneak ashore one night and cause mischief," Tindall said. "The sheriff has asked me to put together a posse to patrol the beaches on horseback."

He paused, waiting for Verne's reaction. When none he came he hastened to add, "Well, sir, I was... I mean, me and the sheriff was hopin' that maybe we could persuade you to be in charge of the posse."

Verne thought a minute, then said, "Who would be in charge of organizing the whole program, Bob?" he asked. "I'm pretty busy as it is and I never was a man for detail."

Tindall rushed in to reassure Verne. "No sir. We wouldn't want to bother a man like you with that kind of foolishness. Gloria, over at office, just finished secretarial school and she's full time now. She can draw up schedules for the different patrols. Notify everybody when it's their turn in the saddle. Consultin' with you every step of the way, of course."

The deputy was feeling more confident now, and hurried to close the deal. "Nossir, you wouldn't have to do a blamed thing except put your name at the top of the paper. Soon as folks see that we'll have volunteers comin' out the whazoo, pardon my French."

Ryan didn't know what a "whazoo" was, but he was fairly certain it wasn't French.

Verne said, "I can see the sheriff's problem. What with the war and all, posse material must be pretty scarce. Only civilian males left in town are either in diapers, going to school, or getting fitted for false teeth and wheelchairs."

Tindall started to laugh, then cut it off, nervous that Verne might not be joking.

"Yessir," he said. "That's the situation exactly... Uh, more or less."

"Okay, Bob," Verne said. "Let me think about it. And talk to Myrtle, of course. I'll get back to you in a day or so."

Tindall looked hopeful. "Can I tell the sheriff which way you're leanin', sir?" he said, in a pleading tone. "Will it be more likely a yes, or, or no?"

Verne let him wriggle on the hook of his own making a bit, then grinned. "Most likely a 'yes,' Bob."

Tindall smiled a smile of huge delight. Bobbing his bald head up and down. "Yessir, I'll tell him that! And I thank you from the bottom of my heart."

There was flurry of action as Tindall shook Verne's hand, then Ryan's, almost reached for Sammy's stump, but swapped the shake for a nod and then he was in his Jeep and tearing away, before Verne changed his mind.

When he was gone, Sammy turned to confront his son. "Okay, Alex," he said. "Now let's hear what you have to say for yourself."

Verne stepped in. "Hang on, Sammy," he said. "The boy looks done in. Why don't we go sit up on the porch, have some sweet tea and maybe some of Myrtle's cookies, and hear Alex's story?"

With much visible effort, Sammy calmed down. A minute ago he was facing the prospect of seeing his son go to jail. Now the future held sweet tea and a plate of cookies.

A deep sigh, then he said, "Sure, boss. Sure."

And the four of them mounted the stairs to the cool shade of the verandah.

TEN

Sweet Tea and Fisticuffs

Verne said, "So you knocked Joe Collins's teeth out, did you?"

Alex nodded. "Yessir." Then, he shyly held up one finger. "But it was just the one, sir."

Remembering the sneer on the Joe's face as he gave them the finger, Ryan couldn't help grinning. It'd be a gap-toothed sneer now.

"Funny," Ryan said. "I only met the kid once and knocking his teeth down his throat was the first thing that came to mind."

Verne shot him a warning look, but Alex appeared eminently grateful.

"Hope you had a better reason that that," Sammy said. "You can't just go around knockin' other kids teeth out because you feel like it."

"Nossir," Alex said. Hanging his head he added, "It was even stupider than that. It was all because of this big old ugly ball of oysters Gig Light Sally had."

When Ryan heard Sally's name he leaned forward with even greater interest.

"Oyster ball?" Sammy said. "Never heard of such a thing."

Alex sat up straight, magnified eyes lighting up with excitement.

"Yeah, see, in one of the biology books the Professor gave me I read that oysters like to attach themselves to each other. Then you can get fifty-sixty pound oyster balls. I told Sally about it last summer. And we worked up this little oyster farm experiment—"

Sammy broke in. "So you knocked Joe's tooth out and almost brained him over an experiment, is that what you're sayin', son?"

"Well, yeah," Alex said. "But it's not that simple, dad."

"Then simplify it for me, son," Sammy said.

"Please, dad," Alex said. "Give me a chance, okay? I know I caused a lot of trouble. But it wasn't my fault."

Sammy snorted, and sat back in his chair. Verne took the opportunity to pour glasses of sweet ice tea all around. Everyone drank thirstily and seemed to settle down.

"It was like this, dad," Alex said. "I was on my way to school with Ester and Phebe, when we came on Gig Light Sally."

"She was unloadin' her skiff into that little cart she has. You know, the little two-wheel collapsible dealie she uses?"

Verne and Sammy nodded. They knew about the cart in question.

"Anyhow, she had this big lumpy thing," Alex continued, hands demonstrating the size and shape of the object. "It was round like a basketball, but bigger. And it was made of all these oysters growing together. Must'a been a hundred of them. Maybe more. All clumped together. Weighed maybe twenty pounds. "

"Where'd she get it?" Verne asked.

"It was that experiment I mentioned," Alex said. "We were jawin' last summer about how things can get scarce, depending on all kinds of factors.

"And she said, 'Yeah, like oysters. Season's all messed up this year. Wish I could get them more regular like. Grow them like farmers grow corn, except they'd be shellfish. All the restaurants in town would be beggin' me for fresh oysters.'

"So I told her let me put my thinkin' cap on and I came up with this idea of startin' an oyster farm. I figured out if you got some old fish traps and sank them in an oyster bed you could encourage the oysters to grow together around the trap into one big ball. And they'd be safe there against seasons that go wonky, because they'd be protectin' one another from what the books call the 'elements.' Scatter them around, and pretty soon you'd have your own oyster farm."

Ryan nodded. Made sense to him.

Alex continued, saying, "Well, the idea knocked Sally out and she agreed to try it. So I drew up some plans and she said she'd let me know how the experiment turned out."

Even Sammy was looking on with interest now. "It must have worked then," he said.

"Sure did," Alex said. "And there was proof positive in the cart." Alex took a long drink of tea, then added, "So I asked if I could meet her later after school and take some notes for a science project.

"And that would have been the end of that conversation and we'd have set off to school and Sally would have headed out to make her rounds of the restaurants. But then a blamed wheel fell off her cart. And here she was stuck with all that fresh fish and stuff and the cooks at the restaurants waitin' on her."

"And you volunteered to help her," Sammy said.

"Yessir," Alex said. "I sent the girls on and I was helpin' her unload the cart so we could get at the wheel when Joe Collins and his pals came along in that fancy pickup his daddy gave him."

Ryan could imagine the scene. The Collins kid—his buddies egging him on—sneering down from a rich kid's height, with that look on his face you just wanted to wipe off.

"So Joe starts hoorawin' her, callin' Sally all kinds of names—filthy names, some of them. But she just turned her back on him, ignorin' him."

He looked at his father, almost pleading. "And I tried to do the same, Pop," he said. "Honest I did."

Sammy nodded. "Go on."

Alex took a deep breath, then continued. "So we just kept unloadin' the cart, doin' our best to pay him no mind. But then that big oyster ball fell out and rolled across the dock and Joe says, 'What's this?' and jumps out of his truck. But Sally snatched it up real quick before he could get his hands on it."

Alex shook his head at the memory. "Whoa, did that make him mad. He grabbed for it, but Sally pulled away and said the oysters were promised to somebody else.

"So then he tried to buy it. Shoved a dollar at Sally, but she said that's not near enough, and even if it wasn't, the oysters was promised elsewhere. And Gig Light Sally, she said, never goes back on a promise. I mean, the cook had it on his menu and everything."

"But young Joe wasn't taking 'no' for an answer?" Verne surmised.

"Nossir, he wasn't," Alex said. "He grabbed hold of that ball and tried to pull it away, but old Sally is stronger than she looks and she wasn't gonna let go. So he pushed her and she fell on her back, but she still had hold of those oysters.

"And Joe and the guys were all standing over her, jeerin' and cussin' her and then Joe rears back and is about to kick her."

Ryan felt his own right arm tense, as if for a punch. In his world, the boyhood world of fair fighting and no hitting below the belt, or kicking people when they're down, and above all—never, ever, hitting an old lady—that punch should have been delivered without hesitation and full force.

Alex looked up at his father, magnified eyes pleading. "I couldn't help it, Pop," he said. "No way was I gonna let him kick that nice old lady. So I stepped in and let him have it."

He tapped the point of his chin. "I hit him fair and square, Pop," he said. "Right here. And, boom! he goes down. And he hits his stupid head and there was blood everywhere. I was so scared, Pop. Thought maybe I'd killed him."

He sighed. Took another drink of tea and settled back in his seat. "That's when Deputy Tindall came along. After he made sure Joe was okay—and boy, was I glad to see he wasn't dead—he interviewed Joe's pals. And they all swore I jumped Joe for no reason. Sally tried to take my part, but the deputy paid her no mind.

"And he wouldn't let me talk either. Just stuck me in his Jeep like a criminal and started drivin' around. First to my school. And I don't know why the principal said those bad things about me, 'cause they're not true."

Sammy snorted. "You've been in more fights than any other kid in school," he said. "Me and your mom have been called down to the office more times than either of us like to recollect."

Alex's defiant look returned. "Kids pick on me," he said. "I'm small. I look like a weirdo with these glasses. And I'm smart. They hate that most of all. Maybe I'm too small to lick 'em, but they know they've been in a fight and so they leave me alone."

Ryan reflexively nodded. Being smarter than most of his classmates had caused him trouble in the past. Thankfully, his size gave most of his would-be tormentors pause.

Alex caught Ryan's reaction and smiled. And with that smile the first bond of friendship was formed.

"I'm guessing the deputy took you to meet Joe's folks after that," Verne said, breaking in before an uncomfortable silence infected the atmosphere again.

"Yessir," Alex replied. "But Joe was home by then and had told his lies." He shrugged. "Guess the doctor had seen to him already, so it couldn't have been that bad. But Mr. Collins was yellin' bloody murder and sayin' 'Justice must be done!' And Mrs. Collins was cryin' about her poor baby."

Sammy said, "I'm surprised Tindall brought you home instead of straight to jail."

"Me too," Alex said. "I thought for sure that's where we were headed. You can't believe how happy I was when he took the Sullivan Island turnoff instead."

Verne said, "It's a good thing you got the bridge fixed, Sammy. Otherwise, Deputy Tindall—who does not strike me as the hard-working sort—might've turned around and deposited Alex at the county lockup."

"Thank God," Sammy said. He turned to Alex. "Son," he said, "You did a foolish thing. In a lot of places—even in Jove Beach—a colored kid could get himself killed for hittin' a white boy."

Ryan saw anger flare in Alex, but he quickly got the anger under control. "Yessir," he said, his voice low.

"Even so," Sammy said, "you did the right thing, son. The honorable thing. And I'm proud of you—no matter what trouble it might've caused."

A flush of embarrassed pleasure deepened Alex's dark skin. And a wide grin split his face.

"Thanks, dad," he said.

Verne cleared his throat. Ryan looked up and saw him adjust the patch over his missing eye and he noticed that the good eye was moist.

To Alex, he said, "Your father and I have to go over the orange harvest reports. Why don't you show Ryan around the place? I'll bet he'd like the company of somebody his own age about now."

"Yessir, I would," Ryan said. Then to Alex, he said, "You mind?"

Alex grinned. "Nope," he said. "Don't mind one bit."

He polished off his tea, shoved a handful of cookies in his pocket and got up. Ryan did the same thing, including the cookie stashing business.

"See you at lunch," Verne said, getting up and going inside, Sammy close behind.

When the screen door banged shut, Alex asked, "You like fishin'?"

"Love it," Ryan said.

"Great. Let's go, then," Alex said. "I've got a couple of poles stashed down by the dock."

And off they went, a joyful Rex bounding along ahead of them.

ELEVEN

River Magic

On the way to the dock they went past the stables where Ryan saw a middle-aged black man currying a magnificent black mare. After Big Red she was the largest horse Ryan had ever seen.

"Wow!" Ryan said. "Are all Verne's horses that big?"

"Yep," Alex said. "That's Sheba, sired by Big Red. Mr. Sullivan raises Tennessee Walkers. They're not just big, but they're trained to have a special gait. Sort of a runnin' walk. A four—beat gait, he calls it. Real smooth. When you're ridin' them you don't bounce up and down like on a regular horse. It's almost like they have springs. And they never stumble, or fall."

"No kidding," Ryan said. "I was on Big Red yesterday when that Collins creep almost ran us down. Didn't faze Red one bit."

He told Alex about the razor backs and Hattie and her mom and how Gig Light Sally came along and helped save the day.

Beyond the stables they came upon a broad pasture where Big Red and several other Tennessee Walkers grazed. Red spotted them and strolled over to the fence. As they approached, he pushed his nose through the rails.

Ryan patted him. Although Big Red seemed to appreciate the pat, he nudged Ryan's hand aside and nuzzled his pockets.

Alex laughed. "Smells the cookies," he said.

"Might of figured I didn't become his best pal overnight," Ryan said, reaching into his pocket.

Big Red practically inhaled the cookie, then went after the pocket again. At the same time, Rex jumped up, front paws on the rail, and started snuffling at Ryan's pocket.

Suddenly, Ryan found himself besieged by cookie loving animals, pushing and prodding and slobbering all over him.

"Hey! Hey! Stop that, you guys!" Ryan protested.

The cookies crumbled in his pocket and he found himself fishing out crumbs and trying to share them with his new best friends for life.

Alex burst out laughing.

"You're no help," Ryan said. "Here I am, surrounded by Indians after my scalp and heap big oatmeal cookies and you just stand there laughing."

"Okay, okay," Alex said. "Lemme get in on this deal. Any enemy of Joe Collins is a pal of mine."

And he turned out his pockets to sacrifice his cookie stash to the cause.

Finally, the crumbs were gone and the boys made an elaborate show of displaying empty hands. Big Red snuffed, then strolled away to find a patch of sweet alfalfa. Rex abandoned his post and trotted off, sniffing at fence posts and bushes for signs of intruders. Pausing to soak the spots they'd dared to claim as their own.

A few minutes later, Ryan heard whooping and hollering and they came upon a field fenced with barbed wire, where two swarthy men on horseback were herding a dozen or more of the strangest looking cows Ryan had ever seen. They were huge, with humps behind their short-horned heads.

"What in the world are those?" Ryan said.

"Mr. Sullivan's got a special breed of cattle too," Alex said. "Mix of Texas longhorns and Brahma bulls from India. Better take extra care around them, though. They can get pretty mean. Meaner even than regular longhorns."

As they grew closer, Ryan got a better look at the men. They were dressed in full cowboy regalia: dungarees stuffed into boots and brightly colored long-sleeved shirts, with battered Stetsons pulled over kerchiefs tied behind their heads.

One was whirling a lariat over his head. The other had a whip that he snapped with loud cracks to cut a calf away from its mother. Ryan noticed that the whip ends never touched the mother. Just that loud Crack! to hurry her along. Close up, he could see that both men had narrow faces and high cheekbones.

"Indians," Alex said, guessing what was on Ryan's mind. "In these parts most of the cowboys are Seminoles."

Ryan's eyes widened. Remembering what the Professor had told him, he said, "They're the ones that never surrendered, right?"

Alex nodded. With grim satisfaction, he said: "Yep. They told old Mister White Eyes to stick it where the sun don't shine. Never gave up. Never signed a peace treaty."

Ryan said, "On the train, the Professor told me that technically we're still at war with the Seminoles."

Alex stopped in his tracks. "You met the Professor?" he said.

"Sure, I did," Ryan said. "He's friends with my Uncle Tom. The Professor's grandson is a rookie in the Philadelphia police department. My uncle's a sergeant, and he's taken the nephew under his wing. Helping him get better assignment and promotions, and stuff. They call it being a rabbi, in the force."

Alex frowned. "Rabbi? That's like a Jewish priest. What's that got to do with cops?"

Ryan shrugged. "Beats me," he said. "That's just what they call it. Anyway, that's how I got to meet the Professor. He even told me about you guys."

He gave Alex a playful poke. "He said you were some kind of genius."

Clearly pleased, Alex ducked his head, and kicked at the dirt, trying to look unimpressed. But Ryan could see the edges of a smile creasing his face.

Laughing, he gave Alex another poke. "Come on," he said. "Let's get those fish."

As they continued on, Alex said, "What'd you think about that deal old Bob Tindall was talking about? The posse thing." He waved a hand. "U-boats and saboteurs and what all. Like one of those "Suspense" radio shows."

"First thing I thought about," Ryan said, "was how I could maybe talk Verne into letting me go along."

"Wow! That'd be amazing," Alex enthused. He mocked riding a horse and firing a pistol. "Pow! Pow! Take that you dirty Germans!"

Ryan joined in, hands coming to waist level as he mock fired a submachine gun. "BupBupBupBup—Bup!" he went. "Die Nazi dogs! Die!"

Alex laughed. "Better'n Cowboys and Indians," he chortled.

Ryan joined in the laughter. Then he said, "Wait! Wait!" He gestured at the men in field. "Except with those guys you can't play Cowboys and Indians anymore."

"How come?" Alex asked.

"Well, technically wouldn't it be Indians and Indians?"

Alex groaned, and threw a light punch. Ryan dodged it and threw one of his own. And they danced around for a bit, shadow boxing, until the sweat was streaming down their faces.

"I give," Ryan said. "Maybe let's go see about those fish. I'd love to just crawl into the river with them and cool off."

"That can be arranged," Alex said with a mischievous grin.

The two friends set off again, following the road of hard-packed seashells, Rex running ahead of them. When they came to the river Rex kept going, sailing off the bank and splashing into the water.

Alex led the way to the dock, where several flat bottom skiffs were tied up. Alex hopped down on the smallest one.

"This one's mine," he said.

He rummaged around, then came up with two bamboo fishing poles. "Here we go," he said. "And I got a bucket around here someplace to put our catch in."

Alex found it, then motioned for Ryan to join him, but before he did, he said, "Better shed your shoes and anythin' else that don't like water."

Ryan kicked off his shoes, then his socks. He took off his shirt and laid it carefully over his shoes.

At that moment, Rex came bounding out of the water and ran up to him. Stopping over his little pile of clothing before he gave himself a good shake—water flying everywhere, soaking Ryan and everything else on the dock.

Alex burst out laughing. He fell on his back and kicked his bare feet in the air, the skiff rocking dangerously under him.

"If you could see your face," he chortled. "Look like you swallowed a big fat juicy June bug."

"Actually, that felt pretty good," Ryan said. "Maybe I'll go for a swim first."

With that, he stripped to his underwear and jumped in feet first. The water was cool and delicious and he sank down and down and down, feeling like he was in a wonderful gravity-defying dream.

And then was he coming to the surface. Easy. Not hurrying. It was like he was born of the sea, not the air. Like one of those science fiction transformation stories, where men learn to live in watery worlds by changing their form.

Then his head broke the surface and he drew in a long breath of sweet air, filled with the tropical scents of Sullivan's Island.

Treading water, he looked over at Alex, who was squatting on his heels, unspooling the line from one of the poles. He saw Ryan and grinned.

"This is great," Ryan said.

"If I were you," Alex said I'd start paddlin' my butt over here. But go easy, hear? And mind the moccasins."

"Moccasins?" Ryan said, puzzled. I'm not wearing—" He broke off in sudden realization, heart double-timing. Alex wasn't talking about foot wear. "You mean, like, uh, water moccasins? Snakes not shoes?" he said.

"That's the kind," Alex said. "But don't worry. You scared stink outta them when you hit the water. But they'll be comin' back soon enough to see what was causin' all the fuss."

Quickly, Ryan struck out for the skiff. He reached the side, grabbed hold, and started to pull himself up.

"Wait!" Alex shouted. "You're gonna pull us over!"

Ryan fought panic. Then, with Alex's help, he got a leg over. Then the rest of him. He looked around, searching the water for signs of snaky activity.

"Where are they?" he asked.

"Where are what?" Alex asked, frowning.

"The water moccasins, darn it! Where are they."

Alex looked calmly around. Then shrugged. "Don't see any," he said. "But they don't favor this part of the river. Too many gators."

Finally, Ryan realized he had been the object of an Alex Davy prank. The first of many to come.

"You just wait," Ryan said. "One of these days—when you least expect it. Wham!"

Alex clutched his chest. "He got me, Sarge. Tell Mom I died game."

Ryan snorted, grabbed the other pole and started untangling the line. While he did that, Alex swooshed a small net back and forth through the water. After a few passes the net came up full of little fresh water shrimp, limbs wriggling frantically. Alex dumped them into a waiting pail of water.

"Great bait!" Ryan enthused, threading his hook through a juicy shrimp.

He flicked his wrist, sending the line out over the river. It plopped down in the water. But no sooner had the first ripple cleared when he had a strike and he found himself fighting something huge.

"Wow!" he said. "That was fast!" Expertly, he reeled in a little line, then let the fish run for a beat or two, then started reeling it in.

"Got yourself a snook," Alex said, reaching with the net.

He scooped up the fish and dumped it into the bottom of the boat. It was easily four pounds or more. The fish flopped around and snapped its jaws alarmingly. Alex gave it a couple of whacks with a length of pipe, and it quit flopping.

Ryan looked around for something to put it in, but Alex said, "I'll take care of it. It's your first day, so you just keep goin'. It's your party!"

And so Ryan kept going, threading more shrimp, tossing the line in, and once again, no sooner had the hook hit the water then he had a strike. Into the bottom of the boat it went, where Alex waited like an assassin to club it over the head.

For the next half hour Ryan fished like he had never fished before, hauling in one catch after another. Tossing anything that looked less than two pounds back into the water.

Finally, he was exhausted. He sat back on his heels, a smile as wide as a quarter moon splitting his face.

"For a Yankee fella," Alex said, "you sure know how to fish."

"Thanks," Ryan said. "My grandpop in Philadelphia taught me. Went fishing with him almost every weekend last summer." Ryan sighed. "But then he caught some kind of cold or something, back in the fall. He only had one lung, you know. Lost the other in a German gas attack back in World War One. Anyway, it got worse until they had put him in the hospital." A long pause, then he said, "He never did come back."

"Sorry to hear that," Alex said. "I know what it's like. My grand daddy died a couple years ago." He dabbed at an eye. "Folks said I was just like him when he was young. Bad eyes. Bad temper. Liked books better'n people. The whole Alex Davy thing."

In the silence that followed, Ryan looked around to see what Alex had done with all the fish. Then he noticed a large washtub sitting on the dock next to them.

He stood up, craning to see inside. It was crammed with more fish than Ryan had ever caught in his young life.

"We'll never eat all that," he said, alarmed at the potential waste. Never catch more than you can eat, was his motto. His grandpop had drummed that rule into him.

Alex laughed. "Don't worry," he said. "When it comes to eatin' on Sullivan Island there's always plenty of folks ready to help. We are a hungry bunch. Just look at our boss, Mr. Sullivan."

Ryan laughed. "Can't argue with that," he said.

Alex glanced up at the sky to check the position of the sun.

"We've got some time before they holler for lunch," he said. "Want to poke around the river a bit?"

"Sure, let's go!" Ryan said, putting the fishing gear away.

"Just sit up there," Alex said, pointing to the bow, "and I'll get us going"

Ryan slid into the bench seat, while Alex untied the skiff and pushed it away from the dock. Then he got out a long pole, like the one Ryan saw Gig Light Sally using. And like Sally, he stood in the stern and pushed the skiff along.

His motions were smooth and easy. Pole sliding into the water, finding the bottom. Alex leaning forward, using only his weight to drive the skiff on. Then coming erect to repeat the motion—all without effort. His motions as measured and easy as Big Red's gait.

And soon Ryan found himself floating dreamily along on a magic river.

TWELVE

A Business Offer

A gentle breeze cooled them and Ryan leaned back, enjoying all the marvelous sights and sounds and exotic odors. Birds and insects of every variety flitted about. Fish moved lazily along, digesting their breakfasts. A turtle splashed off a log and swam away, head poking just above the water.

From the river banks, little animal faces peered out at them as they passed. Took their measure, and judged them non-threatening. At least for now.

In a low voice, Alex said, "Look over yonder."

Ryan craned to see and for a moment thought it was just another log. Then with a thrill he saw the twin bumps at the front of the log and realized that he was looking at an alligator. Only the second one he'd seen.

"That's a momma gator," Alex whispered. "This is her territory. She won't bother you none, but later on, when she lays her eggs, you'd best take care not get between her and her nest."

"No worries there," Ryan said. "I'm not getting near her, much less her nest."

Then, curious, he asked, "How'd you know the gator was a she?"

Alex shrugged. "Gig Light Sally told me," he said. "She knows these parts like the back of her hand. Probably saw her nest, or something."

Ryan laughed. "Safer than flipping them over and checking them out for lady parts," he said.

"You wouldn't get away with that more than once," Alex said.

Ryan mused for a minute, then asked, "How did Sally come by her name? You know, the gig light thing?"

"Old Sally does most of her fishin' at night," Alex said. "She's game for anythin', but she favors frogs most of all. Anyhoo, she fixes a lantern on a pole hanging off the bow of her skiff. The fish and frogs all come to investigate—like moths come after a candle. And old Sally is waitin' there with her gig—which is sort of like those trident things in the gladiator movies."

Ryan nodded. "And they've got the net, too," he said. "To go along with the trident."

"Yeah, like that," Alex said. "So when the fish and frogs come swimmin' up to her skiff to check out the light, she stabs 'em with her gig, scoops them up with her net and tosses them into the bottom. There's so many of them, sometimes, she just keeps stabbin' and tossin' half the night. I've seen her come in some mornings with her skiff so full the water was sloppin' over the sides."

"I'd love to try that sometime," Ryan said.

"No problem," Alex said. "We'll check with the folks and I'll take you out one of these nights. Just need to slap on a bunch of Bee Insect Powder to keep the skeeters off."

Ryan smiled, imagining the adventure. "If I got one of these boats, would you mind showing me how to get around on them."

"Sure," Alex said. "And you're right about needin' a boat of some kind. And a bicycle. With those two things you can go just about anywhere. Even places cars can't go. Shoot, no kid can hold up his head in Jove Beach without the two B's. A boat and a bicycle."

Ryan sighed. "Have to save up some money first," he said.

"Oh, there's all kinds of odd jobs you can get around town," Alex said. "Especially with all the men gettin' drafted or joinin' up."

Alex maneuvered around a log—which, to Ryan's enormous relief, really was a log—then said, "I need to make some money myself. Real money. Not piddlin' little nickels and dimes."

Grimacing, he touched the Coke bottle monstrosities perched on his nose. "These things are ridiculous. Used to belong to my grandfather. They work okay, although I get real bad headaches sometimes when I'm readin'."

He looked at Ryan. "But that's just between you and me, right?"

Ryan crossed his heart, then made a locking motion at his lips and threw an imaginary key away. "They'll never find out from me," he said.

"Good," Alex said. "'Cause if you let somethin' slip my folks would go crazy tryin' to come up with the money. Takin' on extra jobs, and stuff. But they work hard enough, you know? Besides, it's my problem and I'd rather fix it myself."

Ryan nodded. He completely empathized with Alex for wanting to stand on his own two feet and take care of himself.

"Okay, so you're saving your nickels," he said. Then he frowned, and added, "But aren't glasses pretty expensive? And you'll need like an eye doctor's examination, and what not."

"Yeah, it's real expensive," Alex said. He glanced about, as if someone might be listening, then added, "But I've got a foolproof plan to make a pot of money."

"What kind of a plan?" Ryan pressed, thinking about the squawk box he wanted to buy. But he'd need a bike first. That was of the utmost importance. "You think maybe there's a spot in it for me?"

"Well, as it happens, I got an idea that's a two-man job," Alex said. "Maybe you'd like to get in on the deal."

"Maybe," Ryan said. "What's the deal you had in mind?"

Alex said, "The word's goin' around about a big order from some of the labs up in Yankee land." He paused in his poling and leaned closer and in a low, conspiratorial voice, he said, "I hear tell they're payin' a dollar a foot for all the rattlesnakes a body can catch. But you've gotta get 'em alive, so they can milk them for the venom."

Alex pointed to a woodsy area off to their right. "I know where there's tons of them," he said. "There' a field over by the Coast Guard base I've been keepin' an eye on. They've got snakes there that're six footers or more."

Ryan laughed. "Knock it off, Alex," he said. "I grew out of being a snipe hunt sucker a long time ago."

But Alex looked serious. "I'm not funnin' you," he said. "It's the real deal."

"Well, they can keep their real deal," Ryan said. "No way am I going to mess with a rattlesnake."

Alex shrugged. "Folks are scared of rattlers," he said. "That's why we can clean up. No competition. But if truth be told, it ain't dangerous if you know what's what."

Ryan gave him a skeptical look. "So, exactly what is 'what's what'?"

Alex said, "When it gets cold a snake can hardly move. A body'd have to stick his finger in its mouth to get bit."

Ryan nodded. "Yeah, snake are reptiles and reptiles are cold blooded. Everybody knows that."

"Sure, but what most folks don't know," Alex said, "is what they do to protect themselves. See, all they have to do is find themselves a nice gopher hole to hide in until it gets warm again."

"Okay," Ryan said. "So it gets cold. And they crawl into a hole. Then what?"

"I get out my snake catchin' kit, is what," Alex said. "All I need is a gunnysack, a long piece of hose, some gasoline and a nice long snake-catchin' pole."

"If it's so easy," Ryan said, still suspicious, "how come you haven't done it already?"

Alex shrugged. "Like I said, it's a two-man job and all I've got is two scaredy cat little sisters."

Ryan was on the verge of being won over. "How many snakes do you think we could get?" he asked.

"Oh, we'd clean up," Alex said. "We'd have to move fast, though. It's still cold snap season right now. But they don't last long down in these parts. One day it's smoke pots to save the oranges from freezin' and the next it's sunburn city.

"Even so, I think we could maybe catch ten or twelve a day. Maybe even before lunch. All of 'em five or six feet or even more."

"Let's see," Ryan said, really getting interested now. "Let's say we got twelve snakes at six feet each. If I remember my twelve times correctly, that'd be—"

"Seventy two bucks," Alex said. "Minimum!"

"That's fantastic," Ryan said, visions of squawk boxes, bicycles and skiffs dancing in his head. "When do we start?"

"Have to wait for a cold snap," Alex said. "Like I said, this time of year, we get them pretty regular. So, you just sit tight and when we get a snap some morning I'll come on by and roust you out."

Ryan held up a cautioning hand. "I don't expect my grandmother will approve of rattlesnake hunting," he said. "And Verne will go along with whatever she says."

"No problem," Alex said. "I'll just sneak around the back and tap on your bedroom window."

He stuck out a hand, eyes glittering behind thick lenses. "Deal?" he asked.

Ryan took the hand. "Deal," he said.

And they shook.

Then they heard a clanging sound coming from the direction of the Sullivan house.

"They're callin' you to lunch," he said.

Another, clanging sound began, but louder and closer. "And that's lunch for me and the hands," he said and started poling back to the dock.

Once there, they tied up the skiff. Got dressed, then checked on the fish in the washtub. A couple of snook had recovered slightly and were moving around.

Alex grabbed the two handles and heaved. The tub came up, but it was heavy. Water sloshed over the sides.

Ryan said, "Here, let me."

He grabbed one of the handles and the two of them started back along the road. Behind them, they heard barking and scrambling in the bushes. A minute later a frightened rabbit charged by, Rex on its heels. It disappeared down a hole beneath a banyan tree and Rex got busy trying to dig it out.

"Hope there's no rattlers down there," Ryan said.

"Oh, don't worry none about that," Alex said. "One thing Rex knows for sure, and that's one end of a snake from the other."

They moseyed along for awhile, until they came to a much-used pathway that cut to the right.

"This way," Alex said. "We can drop off the fish and you can meet my family."

Soon they came upon a grove of coconut and palm trees that shaded a meandering Florida bungalow with a tin roof. A deep verandah cooled the front.

Smoke rose behind the house and Ryan could hear people laughing and talking.

"Sounds like a party," Ryan said.

Alex laughed. "Sounds quiet to me," he said. "My sisters are still at school, otherwise you couldn't hear yourself chew. They never shut up. What makes it worse, is that they're twins and they're comin' at you from two sides at once."

Alex steered them around the house and a little girl shouted, "There's Alex!"

"Oh, man," Alex groaned, "I should'a kept my big mouth shut."

The girl, whom Ryan assumed was one of the dreaded twin sisters, jumped up from a long picnic table and raced across the yard.

"Wait for me!" shouted another girl—the exact duplicate of the other, down to the yellow ribbons tied around their pigtails.

In a flash she was running side by side with her twin, bursting through a flock of chickens pecking away at the dirt, scattering them everywhere, adding flying feathers and scolding hens to the sudden confusion.

"Whatca' got there, Alex, huh, huh?" said the first girl, grabbing the rim of the washtub to peer inside. She looked to be about ten.

"Get out of here, Phebe," Alex said, pushing her away with one hand, and trying to keep hold of the tub with other. "We're gonna have fish all over the place."

"I'm not Phebe," the child protested. "I'm Esther." Then pointing at her twin, adding, "She's Phebe."

"Who's that with you, Alex?" asked the second girl—presumably Esther. "He your new friend?"

The girls crowded in so close that Ryan and Alex almost tripped over them, tub of fish and all.

"Get out of the way, Esther!" Alex said. "Let me get this through."

"We got sent home 'cause you was in trouble, Ryan," Esther said. "Whaja'all do? Huh? Huh?"

Alex pushed past them and he and Ryan staggered the last few feet, dodging the girls, angry chickens and several brown-skinned tots with rattles and toys.

"Put that thing down over here, Alex," a harried looking black woman said.

She was bending over an outdoor grill where sausages and slabs of fish smoked and sputtered over a wood fire. She was sprinkling on herbs, then squeezing a lemon over the fish. Men and women were crowded around a long table that was full of covered dishes of steaming side dishes.

"You'll need to get washed up," she said, still not looking around. "So hurry it up. We're all waitin' on you."

"Mom," Alex said, "we got company."

The woman turned around. She was in her mid thirties, pleasingly plump, and so dark she was almost ebony in color. She wore her hair tied up in an efficient bun.

Her eyes widened when she spotted Ryan. "Oh, my goodness," she said. "You must be Ryan, Mrs. Sullivan's grandson."

"Yes ma'am," Ryan said, standing there awkwardly. "That'd be me." His side of the washtub was dragging him down.

Thankfully, Alex bent so they could rest the tub on the ground, because the woman was offering her hand to Ryan. Awkwardly, he got rid of the tub, then shook.

"I'm Ada," the woman said. "Ada Davy. And I am so pleased to meet you. Mrs. Sullivan has been all excited about your comin'"

Ryan barely concealed a grimace. He couldn't imagine his grandmother being excited about anything—especially him.

But all he said was, "Yes ma'am. And I'm pleased to meet you, ma'am. Back on the train, the Professor told me all about you and Sammy and Alex and... " he waved a hand, taking in the rest—"... the family. He said to tell you he'd be stopping by next time through."

Ada grinned. "Oh, you met the Professor? And isn't he a fine gentleman?"

"Yes ma'am," Ryan said. "He sure is. Took care of me on the trip down."

Ada caught his elbow and drew him over to the table. Two of the Indian cowboys he had seen earlier were there. Ada said they were Charlie Silver Moon and Sawgrass Hank. Then there was Josh, the man he saw currying the mare, and then Ephraim, who was slightly older. More names followed—there were several young women, some black, some with high-cheek-boned Indian features and a bunch of kids, but Ryan soon lost track and just nodded helplessly, repeating the names, hoping they might stick.

He wouldn't have the same trouble with Esther and Phebe who tugged his shirt and pestered him with questions about Philadelphia and the train trip and so many things that they all ran together.

Thankfully, just about then Sammy drove up in his Model T.

"Figured you'd be here," he called through the window. "Boss sent me to fetch you home for lunch."

Ryan turned to Ada. "I'm sorry ma'am," he said. "I have to go. But I was so pleased to meet you."

Alex followed him to the truck. When they couldn't be seen by the others he whispered, "What about the deal? We still on?"

"Heck, yeah," Ryan said. "I need the money."

"Me too," Alex said.

Then he gestured at the tub. "We'll clean the catch and send it on up to the house later."

"We can't eat all that," Ryan said.

Alex laughed. "You don't know Verne Sullivan very well, yet, do ya?"

That got Ryan laughing too. "Probably pour honey all over them," he said.

Chortling, he climbed into the truck next to Sammy. As they drove away, Alex shouted out, "Hey, Pop! Can Ryan go to the movies with us tomorrow night?"

Sammy looked over at Ryan, a surprised smile on his face. "You want to?" he asked.

"Please, sir," Ryan said.

Sammy leaned his head out to shout, "Sure he can. Long as the boss says it's okay."

Ryan had no worries on that score. He settled back in his seat, tired but happy. It had been a long time since he'd felt this good.

Then, for no reason he could fathom, his mother's pale face and vacant eyes suddenly rose up from the depths and his stomach clenched.

With a finger and a thumb, he started tapping away on his knee—
S.O.S. S.O.S. S.O.S.

"You okay, Ryan?" Sammy asked.

"Yessir," he said. "I'm fine."

THIRTEEN
Old Wars

His grandmother served up another delicious meal: thick hamburgers sizzling from the grill, country-fried potatoes, baked beans, and bowls of fragrant soup made from tomatoes and basil fresh from her garden.

By the time Ryan had come to the end of his burger, Verne had inhaled an entire platter, two big bowls of soup and was pouring honey over a thick slice of blood-red watermelon.

Only then did his grandmother sit down to her own meal—a small hamburger patty and a cup of soup.

Verne teased her about "eating like a bird."

She only smiled and said something about needing to watch her figure.

The atmosphere seemed right to broach the subject of the movies.

"I don't see why not," Verne said. "Nothing happening around here, except whatever's on the radio."

Ryan was about to thank him, when his grandmother weighed in. "I don't know if that's such a good idea," she said.

"Why ever not, Myrtle?" Verne asked, frowning.

"That boy—Alex," she said. "Isn't he in trouble with the law?"

"Oh, pshaw!" Verne said. "First off, Alex is something special. Probably one of the smartest kids in these parts. Otherwise the Professor wouldn't have taken him under his wing. He's determined the boy's gonna go all the way to college."

"Well, he won't go very far if he keeps gets into fights," Myrtle said.

"Oh, that was nothing, sweetheart," Verne said. "Just a couple of boys getting into it. Boys will always get into it until the Good Lord stops the world and orders us off."

"It's more than that, and you know it," Myrtle said. "The Collins are an important family in these parts."

Verne frowned. "And Alex is colored, is that what you're saying?"

Myrtle fixed him with a glare. "Don't put words into my mouth, Verne Sullivan," she said. "You know I don't feel that way."

Verne scoffed. "I don't care if the boy is green with polka dots, Myrtle," he said, "Jim Collins is nothing more than a trumped up car salesman."

"He's got the only Ford dealership for miles around," Myrtle said. "He not only supplies cars and trucks, but tractors and harvesters and things. There's even talk of him running for mayor, and maybe even for Congress after that."

"I don't depend on him for my needs," Verne said. "In case you didn't notice, sweetheart, I stick to Chevys and General Motors products. Never could stand that Henry Ford. A damned war profiteer in my book. Rather go back to plowing with mules, than buy Fords.

"And I don't care one whit for Collins' political ambitions. Don't need him, or anybody else for that matter. I've always lived by my wits and done quite well at it."

"Still," Myrtle said. "We live in the South and people down here have their own ways and opinions. And we have to respect that."

Verne snorted. "Myrtle," he said, "we have had this discussion before. And you know my views. Some of these folks don't seem realize they lost the blamed war and I have made it my mission in life to remind the worst of them who won and who lost every chance I get."

Ryan looked over at his grandmother, who was staring off in the corner, her face a mask of disapproval.

He wasn't surprised at her attitude. In his experience white people in the North were as anti-colored as they were in the South. They were just more polite about it. Especially the Irish. His father told him that the Irish had been the low man on the totem pole so long when it came to jobs and homes to live in, that they'd come to take their frustrations out on colored people.

Just before he'd left their posting in Connecticut for Philadelphia the colored sailors on the base had rioted. His father said it was because the Navy and the other services put colored men into menial jobs where there was little hope for advancement. Plus, even with a war on, the military was reluctant to admit them into the services.

He didn't know how the riot had turned out—his father said the newspapers would never print anything like that because of "morale." That mysterious word was used to excuse the most appalling things in the military. Also his father had shipped out a few days later, so there was no one to tell him what happened.

As a committed Navy brat cynic, he strongly doubted any progress had been made.

Then, to his surprise, he heard his grandmother sigh. "Verne's right," she told him. "Compared to the Davy family, the Collins are lowlifes."

"So I can go then?" Ryan asked.

"Yes, you may," his grandmother said.

Hearing that, Verne reached into his pocket and pulled out a wad of bills so thick it'd choke Big Red. Peeled off a fiver and slapped it down on the table in front of Ryan.

"Son," he said, "tomorrow night you be sure to tell everybody that the ice cream is on me."

"Yessir," Ryan said, quick like a bunny grabbing the bill and stuffing it into his pocket. "And thank you."

"Nothing to thank," Verne said and dug into his melon.

Ryan glanced over at his grandmother. He couldn't read the expression on her face.

FOURTEEN

Of Carnivals and Steam Engines

Just before nightfall, Ryan was sprawled on his bed reading Astounding Magazine when Verne came tapping on his door.

"I'm heading out for a ride, son," Verne said. "Want to tag along?"

Delighted, the boy scrambled to his feet. "Yessir," he said. "Are we going to take Big Red again?"

Verne chuckled. "Oh, I think we can manage to find you a mount of your own."

Josh, the stableman, was waiting outside with Big Red and Sheba—the black mare Ryan had seen earlier. But when he approached she was so huge he felt intimidated. She looked at him out of the corner of an eye, snorted and tossed her head. Ryan took a hasty step back.

"Don't mind Sheba, son," Josh said. "She's on'y testin' you."

He fished some hard candy out of his pocket and gave a handful to Ryan. "Feed her some'a these and she'll love you forever," he said. Then, with a laugh, he added, "Or, at least until the next fella comes along with a pocketful of candy."

Hesitantly, Ryan held out a couple of candies in the flat of his palm like Verne had shown him earlier.

"That's how you do it," Josh said, approvingly. "Nice and easy like."

Sheba's soft nose dipped into his palm and she snuffled up the candy. There was a loud crunching sound as she crushed them in her teeth. Ryan grimaced, imagining what those teeth would do to his fingers.

"Okay, all aboard now," Josh said and he made a stirrup of two hands.

Ryan started to put his right foot in and Josh laughed. "Nah, nah, the other foot, son. Or you'll end up sittin' backwards. And won't old Sheba be surprised?"

Laughing and blushing—he knew better than that—Ryan offered his proper foot and Josh hoisted him up and then suddenly he was sitting in the saddle looking out at the world from the height of a giant.

Verne snorted amusement. "You've got a smile on your mug as wide as the quarter moon," he said.

"Now I know what it's like to be you," Ryan said, his grin growing broader still. "It's fantastic!"

Verne laughed and said, "Young man, you wouldn't say that if you had my arthritis."

He clucked his tongue and Big Red started out. Ryan tried to do the same thing, but his tongue had barely touched the roof of his mouth when Sheba fell in behind Red without being asked.

Ryan felt a little clumsy at first, thinking he must've forgotten something, when Josh called out, "The reins, son! The reins."

"Oh, yeah," Ryan said, embarrassed and picked up the reins just before they slid off the saddle horn.

They ambled quietly along while Ryan got used to the saddle. He studied Verne's posture and the easy way he held the reins in one hand. Big as he was his back was straight as a pressed pine board.

Gradually, Ryan relaxed and started to enjoy the ride. They started out on the same path he'd taken with Alex earlier, but then veered off onto a narrow trail that led through a grove of enormous oaks.

Ghostly fingers of Spanish moss brushed his cheeks and the night air was rich with a cacophony competing scents. Tangy oak pollen. The musty smell of moss. Citrus from the groves. The heady odor of tropical blossoms. The earthen smell of the corals and the cow pasture. Wood smoke from a cooking fire. And running through it all, like a melody, the overweening smell of the river and the creeks that surrounded and cut through Sullivan's Island. And then, very faint, the salty mist of the sea.

The first fireflies appeared, flitting about in the gathering dark, little lights blinking in and out in a rhythm that Ryan thought was not unlike wireless messages sent by some great Master Hand Of The Universal Code.

Then Verne's voice came drifting back in a soft rumble, "Just up ahead." And they rode out of a dark avenue of oaks into the slowly dying light of the sun, which dappled the surface of a broad lake.

Verne led them across soft meadow grass to a small covered dock, where a little rowboat was tied up.

He dismounted, but as Ryan started to follow he held up a hand and said, "Hold on. That's a long way down."

Ryan offered a hand so Verne could help him, but the old man just lifted him off as if he were nothing more than a feather pillow. Then he looped Sheba's reins around the pommel and did the same for Big Red. The two animals immediately started grazing contentedly on the sweet meadow grass.

"Won't they run away?" Ryan asked.

Verne chuckled. "What for?" he said. "They're already home and there's plenty to eat right here."

He led Ryan out onto the dock where a enormous wooden chair had been set up, obviously built for Verne. Next to it was a much smaller chair, most likely his grandmother's.

Verne sank slowly down into the big chair—his hands braced on the arms—and gave a long deeply felt sigh. It was as if a mountain had come to rest. Ryan perched on the little chair. He was about to speak—to ask some little question just to fill the silence—but then thought better of it. He sensed that Verne had something to say, so he just sat back and waited.

The silence lasted a long time and soon Ryan found himself watching the dying sun settling behind a distant forest, light filtering through the branches to caress the surface of lake. Then, in one glorious moment, the sun turned the lake a fiery red and vanished behind the trees.

A three-quarter moon took its place, and the surface of the lake turned silvery. Clouds of insects swept across the water and immediately there were shrill cries of birds and swarms of bats who appeared as if from nowhere to feast on the insects. Then the surface of the lake came alive as fish broke the surface to compete with the birds and bats for their dinner.

Spellbound, Ryan wasn't sure how long they sat there in silence and when Verne finally spoke he almost jumped at the suddenness of it. At first he was so befuddled—what his Irish grandmother in Philly called "pixilated"—he couldn't make out what Verne was saying. All he could tell was that he was being asked to do something.

"I'm sorry, sir," he said. "I wasn't paying attention."

"Don't blame you," Verne said. "This is my favorite spot and my favorite time of day."

"It's just become mine too," Ryan said. "Thank you for letting me tag along."

Verne smiled, then repeated his request. He pointed at the rowboat. "If you don't mind," he said, "hop down in that boat and lift of the back seat and bring me what's there."

"I don't mind at all, sir," Ryan said.

He crossed to the edge of the dock and gingerly stepped down into the boat. It rocked back and forth, but not dangerously so. He lifted the seat to find a big clay jug with cork in it.

Guessing what was in the jug, he grinned as he held it up for inspection. "This what you're looking for, sir?"

Verne laughed. "Indeed it is, young man," he said. "My little jug of kindness."

Ryan jumped back up on the dock and carried the jug to the chair. After pulling the cork with his teeth, Verne held the jug up in mock ceremony.

"Just to let the Good Lord know we're serious," he said.

He tilted the jug back, took a long swallow, then cradled it in his lap.

Slapping the jug, he declared, "Rheumatism medicine. A local remedy that I swear does more good for me than anything any sawbones has ever prescribed."

Ryan smiled. "Is that the moonshine stuff we Yankees hear about up North?"

"One and the same," Verne said. "Get it at that roadhouse Sally was talkin' about. They've got illegal stills set up in the woods."

He took another swallow from the jug. "They're pretty touchy about those stills," he said. "The Federals are always looking to find them and bust them up. So, when you're out wandering if you should ever run across a still don't you hang around. Get the hell out of there fast or you're likely to be introduced to the business end of a shotgun."

"I'll have no trouble remembering that, sir," Ryan said, with much sincerity. "It's sort of like gators and their nests that Alex warned me about."

Verne patted the jug like it was a lapdog. "Do me a favor and keep this between us. Me and Myrtle have some different ideas about doctoring."

"Not a word," Ryan said.

Verne took another sip, then fell silent again, staring out at the lake. Ryan didn't mind. It was so peaceful and the play of moonlight on the water was hypnotic.

Then Verne said, "First time I came down to these parts was maybe forty years ago. I was workin' the boiler room in a steamer and me and the captain didn't see eye to eye about certain things. Like good grub and back pay. Since he was the captain and I was nothing but a boiler tender, I lost the argument and we parted company. But not before I loomed on him some and convinced him to part with some of my back pay.

"So I found myself found myself ashore in what was practically a wilderness with almost no money, a growling belly, and no prospects whatsoever."

Ryan glanced at his eye patch, wondering. Verne caught the look and absently touched the leather thong holding it in place.

"I still only had the one eye then," Verne said. "How I lost it is another story that I might tell you about one of these days. Depending on my mood and... " he lifted the jug... "how much rheumatism medicine I have on hand."

"Yessir," Ryan said and left it at that. In his experience adults were apt to talk more if he talked less.

"As luck would have," Verne said, "I came across a wildcat timber crew. Actually, my good luck was another fellow's misfortune. He was cutting boards for them with a little steam-powered donkey engine and he made the mistake of mixing this stuff... " Verne indicated the jug "... with work and wound up confusing his hand with a board."

Ryan gulped, imagining the bloody scene. "Did he, uh… die, or something?"

Verne grimaced. "No. But he wasn't much use to anybody after that." He consoled himself with another swig, then continued. "Thing is, the donkey engine gave out just about then and I was probably the only fellow with steam engine experience this side of Miami."

He raised a finger. "But there was only one problem," he said. "It was an all Negro crew. And the white owner of the operation, who ran crews up and down the coast, didn't believe I'd take orders from his Negro foreman."

Verne took a nip from his jug, then said, "I argued with him. Said I had no bad feelings about colored people. When I was a kid I worked the traveling carnival circuit up on the Canadian border and half the performers and most of the roustabouts were Negroes."

Ryan gawked. "Carnivals?" he said. "You were a carny?" He couldn't think of a job that was more romantic than that, except maybe the circus, which he admonished himself, was practically the same thing.

"I grew up in it," Verne said. "My grandparents were carnies and they took me in when my folks died in a train wreck." He smiled. "If you're thinking that carny life was fun, well it was. It was also damned hard work and you couldn't always count on regular meals."

He patted his belly. "I wasn't always fat," he said, "but I was always big and big requires a lot of feeding. So, I got into other things. But we'll save that for another day."

Like the missing eye, Ryan thought. But he just nodded, encouraging Verne to continue.

"Like I said, the bossman didn't believe I'd get along as the only white man on the crew so it looked like I was back where I started from. Even worse, along about then my old captain was nursing a grudge for me looming on him and on his way back through he set the crew on me.

"I was drowning my sorrows at a rum joint when they came upon me and big as I was I didn't stand a chance against a sap alongside the head. And then they set to giving me one of the worst beatings of my life and then dumped me in the swamp to leave out for gator food."

Verne sighed, shaking his head at the memory, then added, "And that would have been the end of my sorry tale if weren't for a fellow named Christian Little."

He tried to continue, but his voice got rough and he took a swig off the jug to smooth the edges.

After a minute, and another application of rheumatism medicine, he said, "Mr. Little was the Negro foreman the timber company boss said I'd never get along with. As it happened, Mr. Little and his crew were clear cutting the area I'd been dumped in. They found me all bloody and beat to hell and covered with skeeter bites. Don't think I'd have been long for this world if they hadn't come along.

"Anyway, they took pity on my sorry behind, and hauled me to their camp where Mr. Little's wife doctored me with remedies so old they go all the way back to Africa. Then, just as I was gettin' better, that old donkey engine gave out again. And this time it looked like it had given it up forever.

"Well, I opened it and then rebuilt the whole thing with parts I made myself out of tin cans, pins I carved out of bone and gaskets made of snake hide."

Verne chuckled. "If you're ever in the same kind of fix," he said, "tanned moccasin skin makes tolerable gasket material."

Ryan laughed. "That's a good thing to know," he said. Privately, he wondered if moccasins fetched a dollar a foot like their rattler cousins.

Verne said, "I spent a better part of two months with Mr. Little and the others before the bossman found out. But when he did—and saw how well everything was going—he not only kept me on, but paid me for the time I'd already worked.

"So I spent another five or six months with the crew and before long the sun had burnt me almost as black as they were and if wasn't for my good blue eye, you'd have thought I was one of them."

He paused to oil his throat, then said, "Truth tell, I felt like one of them. And I heard all their stories and learned a little of what it was like to live in their skin. Although I couldn't ever really know what it was like. My folks had been brought over in Irish famine ships, not slave ships, and there is a powerful difference. Mrs. Little's grandmother had been a slave on a Georgia plantation—"workin' in the big house"—is how she put it."

Verne leaned forward, his single blue eye burning with purpose. He said, "That time I spent with the crew did more to form me than almost anything else I experienced in my life.

"And, Ryan, if you get anything at all from living here on Sullivan Island with me, I hope it will be that you come to share my feelings of kinship to folks whose only difference is the color of their skin."

Ryan started to reply, but his emotions had been set to hard boil by Verne's story, so he just nodded.

"I wanted to tell you about that," Verne said, "to sort of explain why I went against your grandmother in the matter of Alex and the movies."

"I understand, sir," Ryan said, although he didn't.

"It was wrong of me to contradict her in your presence," Verne said. "She's your grandmother and is legally and morally responsible for you until you come of age. I only spoke up because of my strong beliefs."

Verne leaned closer to underscore his point. "So please don't make the mistake of thinking it's you and me against her. Ninety nine and nine tenths of the time I will back her all the way. She's the boss lady and her word is law."

"Yessir," Ryan said. Then he grinned and pointed at the jug. "As long as I remember that's part of the leftover tenth, right?"

Verne frowned, not getting it at first. Then gave a huge belly laugh. Reached out and clapped Ryan on the shoulder with a blow that nearly knocked him off the chair.

"Oh, we are going to get along, you and me, young Ryan Karr," he said. "Like biscuits and gravy."

Then, out of the corner of his eye, Ryan caught a glimmer of light. He looked up to see the shadowy apparition of an open boat moving across the lake.

A bright light extended several feet from the bow. And in the back someone was standing up working a stern paddle, slowly driving the boat through the water.

"That's Gig Light Sally," Verne said in a low voice. "Making her nightly rounds."

It was a marvelous, deeply moving sight. Almost like a painting. Except better, because it was real.

Ryan felt wetness on his cheeks. He'd never seen anything so beautiful.

FIFTEEN
Bedsprings Mystery

That night Ryan heard music in his bedsprings for the first time.

Well, maybe it wasn't actual music. But there seemed to be some kind of rhythm and a beat to the faint sounds.

He pressed his ear closer to the mattress. Were those actual voices he was hearing? Singing voices? Country music, maybe?

Ryan sat up and the sound went away. Of course, it was nearly impossible to hear anything properly over the din of nocturnal birds and animals and insects.

Even so, the night sounds weren't as bothersome as before. He had a good idea what everything looked like beyond his bedroom walls. To his chagrin, he discovered that the huge spooky figures he'd imagined creeping around the verandah were just the leaves of an elephant plant blowing in the wind.

Besides, if something nasty came along Rex would raise the alarm, which would be backed up by the shotgun Verne kept handy in a rack above the front door.

Calling himself all kinds of a scaredy cat fool, he plumped his pillow and sank back into the mattress again.

There. Nothing, right?

Yeah, but the pillow was in the way.

He moved the pillow aside and experimented: First his left ear—nothing; then his right—still nothing.

See, you jerk. It's all in your imagination.

Ryan sank back onto the bed then tried to compose himself for sleep. There was a little trick he'd invented to overcome restless nights. He imagined that the bed was an anti-gravity machine like the one H.G. Wells used to fly to the moon. Except, Ryan turned it into a soft platform that he sprawled across with his arms and legs stretched as far as they would go.

Then he imagined that the mattress was lifting slowly away from the bed frame. Rocking back and forth ever so gently. Then he was lifting away, mattress and all. He gripped the mattress edges, imagining that he was controlling this remarkable machine.

In a minute they'd fly right through the walls and out onto the grounds of the island itself. And he'd soar above everyone, peering down through the night, and he'd be freed from all the cares of the world.

And he'd fall into a deep, peaceful—

Wait!

There it was again!

That sound.

But this time it wasn't music. At least he didn't think it was music. It was more like the diddy-dah-diddy of Morse Code.

But faint. So very faint and far away.

First the three dashes and a dot that formed an *"O."* Then the dash-dot-dash that made a *"K."* Meaning OK. An actual word. Big deal. Random letters plucked out of the ethers of the imagination could easily produce words like OK.

He snorted. Disgusted with himself. This was foolishness. He was just tired. The journey had been long. The worries about his mother and father constant. He'd barely slept the night before. And the day that would be gone in an hour or so had been so full of events that when supper time came around he had barely been able keep his eyes open at the dinner table. Or, ruder still, stop yawning.

His grandmother had said something biting. Remarking about how she'd been saddled with such a lazy boy.

"Your father wasn't lazy," she informed him. "And if something needed doing, he'd do it without being asked."

"Yes ma'am," Ryan said, getting up from his chair and starting to collect empty dishes.

"What are you doing?" his grandmother demanded.

"Clearing the table, ma'am," he said. "That's what I always do at home."

"You're just being fresh," his grandmother said, eyes flashing.

Ryan was genuinely puzzled. She complained about him being lazy, but when he tried to do something, she got mad.

"Besides, that's Ada's job," his grandmother went on. "She'll be over directly to fetch the dishes to the kitchen for washing up in the house."

"Well, that's okay, then," Ryan said. "I can help Ada clean up. I don't mind. And it'll save her the long trip from the trailer to the house."

His grandmother started to object, but Verne intervened with a gentle, "Now, darling, don't go getting yourself all upset. You know what the doctor said."

Ryan was taken aback. Doctor? Was his grandmother sick? Then—so fast he was almost ashamed himself—if she was sick why couldn't he go back to Philadelphia?

"That quack!" his grandmother said. "I don't know why I should listen to him. He's just a cracker doctor."

"But a cracker doctor who makes sense, darling," Verne said. "You have high blood pressure. Headaches. All kinds of other nervous symptoms. He gave you a tonic, which I think seems to be helping."

He fixed her with a challenging look. "Doesn't it?"

"Well, yes," his grandmother admitted.

"And he said to avoid unpleasantness as much as we can. That's why we ration the war news to a few times a day. Most people never turn their radios off. He doesn't want you worrying about things nobody can do anything about except maybe a four-star general or the president of the United States." He patted his wife's hand. "Unless I'm mistaken," he said, "you don't resemble Franklin Delano Roosevelt one darned bit. And you certainly don't look like Eisenhower."

Ryan bit back laughter. His grandmother started to speak, but then blushed furiously and lapsed into silence. At least it didn't seem to be an angry silence.

Verne turned to Ryan. "You go on, son," he said. "I'll clear the rest by and by. You look kind of sleepy."

"That I am sir," Ryan said, suppressing another yawn.

"Go on, then," Verne urged.

Ryan got.

Now he was sitting up in bed too tired to fall asleep. His imagination running wild with foolishness. Like listening to a radio through mattress springs. And Morse Code?

Come on, Ryan! That was Ridiculous—with a capital dot-dash-dot *"R!"*

SIXTEEN

Movie Night

"You comin' to the movin' pitcher show with us, Ryan? Is ya? Huh? Huh?"

Since Ryan was already crammed in the back of Sammy's Model T, along with the rest of the Davy clan, the answer to the child's question should have been self-evident. But she and her twin, Esther, had latched onto him the moment he'd hopped aboard.

Esther was on one side, Phebe the other. With great seriousness, they had explained to him that they were wearing different colored pigtail ribbons just for him so he could tell them apart. Phebe wore blue, Esther yellow.

But the way they kept at him, laughing and teasing and asking a steady stream of questions, he soon lost track of which was which.

"You got any brothers and sisters, Ryan? Do ya? Huh? Huh?"

"No, I don't."

"What're their names? Huh? Huh? Their names?"

"I already told you, Phebe, I don't have any brothers and sisters."

The girl giggled. "You didn't tell me, silly. You told Esther. We changed ribbons to fool you."

"Well, can't you hear?" Ryan teased. "You got wax in your ears?"

And he pretended to grab Phebe's head to look into her ear. She squealed with pleasure and pulled away.

"Wow! You've got enough wax in there to grow potatoes."

The twins kicked their heels and squealed with laughter.

"Hear that, Alex?" Esther chortled. "Phebe's got taters in her ears."

"I do not!"

"You do. You do."

"Momma! Tell Esther to quit sayin' I got taters in my ears."

Since Ada was safely ensconced with her husband in the truck's cab she was blissfully unaware of her daughter's demands. Besides, Esther was already on to her next round of questions.

"You have movin' picture shows in Philadelphia? Do ya? Huh? Huh?"

"Thousands."

An outraged little face, yellow pigtails bobbing indignantly. "Thousands! Naw! You're fibbin' me. Momma, tell Ryan to quit fibbin' me."

Just about then they bounced off the hard-packed dirt road onto the asphalt of Dixie Highway. In the distance, Ryan could see the red lighthouse towering over what Alex had informed him was the Jove Beach Inlet.

The ride was smoother now, especially since they all sat on old mattresses and fat pillows made of canvas stuffed with Spanish moss.

Two young colored women—Tamar and Eve—joined Ryan, Alex and the twins in the back of the pickup. They wore light cotton dresses and were barefoot—just like the others. Ryan felt definitely out of place in his pleated pants, and striped sports shirt. Normal relaxed wear for a Philadelphia neighborhood movie night. But, hot, sticky and confining in a little town in the tropics a thousand miles away whose only claim to fame was a big red lighthouse.

"Truth tell, Ryan," Eve said. "You was joshin' Esther. How many pitcher shows do they really got in Philadelphia?" Eve had long hair, tied back with a red ribbon and was more gregarious than her friend and co-worker, Tamar.

"Well, maybe not thousands, but close to it," Ryan said. "Chestnut Street—just up a little ways from my aunt and uncle's house—must have twenty or thirty, easy. And that's just one street."

"Naw! That can't be!" That was Tamar finally speaking up.

"Honest," Ryan said. "Why, me and my cousins used to walk up one side of Chestnut and down the other picking the shows we wanted to see. One theater might have nothing but jungle movies. Another Westerns. And cops and robbers. Jimmy Cagney and Edward G. Robinson."

"Do they have any, you know, colored movies?"

Eve's shy question caught him by surprise. He thought minute, then recalled bus rides through some of the colored neighborhoods.

"Sure," he said. "Lots." But his hesitation gave the true answer away and her face fell. Not so many.

Just then, up ahead, he saw a familiar figure walking along the highway. A white girl in blue shorts, a tan blouse and sandals.

"That's Hattie Peters, Alex," he said, nudging him with an elbow. "Can we give her a ride? Maybe she's going to the movies too."

But it wasn't necessary. Sammy was already pulling over to the side of the road. Ryan would learn later that in Jove Beach everybody who had cars stopped for people who didn't.

Hattie turned as Sammy leaned out to ask, "Need a ride, Hattie? We're headin' into town."

The girl hesitated, then spotted Ryan in the back. He waved to her.

"We're going to the movies, Hattie," he yelled over the engine noise. "Want to come?"

The hesitation turned into a wide grin. "Thanks, Sammy," she said and came up to the truck, where Alex and Ryan were waiting to help her climb aboard.

Moments later they were off again and to Ryan's relief the twins shifted their attention to Hattie.

"Whatch'all doin, Hattie? Huh? Huh? You got a boyfriend? Huh? Huh? Is he cute? Huh? Huh?"

And on and on with such nonstop fervor that Hattie collapsed into helpless laughter, shouting "I give up! I give up!"

But then things quieted down as they entered the town proper and the twins, along with everybody else, rubbernecked the village, seeing who was there and studying the shop signs and windows.

Ryan spotted his first gas station since leaving Philadelphia. This one had two pumps with a glass bowl filled with gasoline on top of each pump. He'd heard that the government might start rationing gasoline soon, along with tires.

It was Saturday evening, so the town was busy, although it took Ryan a moment or two to realize that the only people he saw on the street were women, children and old men. The only young men were in uniform, and there were few of those.

When they went by the Western Auto Association Store Ryan heard a war news broadcast playing over outside speakers. A dozen people stood around listening intently.

Alex tapped him on the shoulder, then pointed at the store.

"Look at that!" he said, his eyes huge behind the bottleneck glasses as he pointed to the store window.

Ryan caught it right away. And the sight was glorious! A sparkling new Schwinn bicycle with a green and black frame and centerpiece, a beautifully shaped matching cuff guard, a molded front light, a rear rack, and black leather- wrapped handlebars.

"I think I just died and went to heaven," Ryan said.

"Come on, cold snap!" Alex said, immediately setting the twins off.

"Cold snap? Whatch'all mean, cold snap, Alex? Huh? Huh? Whatch'all mean?"

Ryan started tickling one of them and the questioning died in a torrent of giggles.

Hattie nudged Ryan. Grinning, she said, "Yeah, Ryan? Whatch'all mean?"

"Never you mind, Hattie Peters," Ryan said with a laugh. And then they were moving past the store and the magnificent bicycle.

A few minutes later they drove by Seminole Drive, and Hattie pointed out the two-story building that housed the school Ryan would attend Monday. She said little kids were on the first floor, older students like Hattie and Ryan—all the way up to 12th grade—were on the second floor.

"We go to the colored school," Phebe informed him.

"That's 'cause we're colored," Esther said with great solemnity. "Ain't we, Alex? Huh? Huh?"

Alex looked at Ryan and just shrugged. Ryan wasn't shocked that there were two separate schools—one for white and the other for colored people—in Jove Beach. But for some reason he suddenly felt out of place—and guilty. But then he thought, at least with Alex he finally had a colored friend. A definite first.

Then they were passing by an open air drugstore, with chairs and little tables sitting under an awning. The store advertised a soda fountain, which was where Ryan presumed he could buy the ice cream Verne had given him the money for.

Sammy spun the wheel and they pulled into a broad parking area behind Martha's Sundries. The lot was paved with crushed seashells. A dozen or more vehicles had already parked there and the audience—mostly women, little kids and teenagers—were gathered in groups. Sammy found a spot near the front, reversed the truck so the back end was facing the broad whitewashed wall of the store, and parked.

As they climbed out, Ryan looked around. "Where's the theater?" he asked.

Alex laughed. "Right over there," he said, pointing at the store.

"Oh, you mean it's inside the store?" This was puzzling. The sundries store didn't look big enough to house a theater.

"No, right there," he insisted, jabbing his finger at the store's white washed rear wall. Just then Ryan noticed that a teenage boy was hosing the wall off. "That's the screen. Mr. Carney will be here in a little bit with the movies and he'll project the pictures on the wall."

"We have to wait for dark, though, don't we Alex?" the twin Ryan thought must be Phebe said. She looked up at Ryan and explained, "Can't see the pitchers so good when it's daytime out."

"Also, when it rains," Esther joined it. "It's not good for the electricity. Rain makes electricity go all sparky."

"I guess it would," Hattie said with a laugh. Then to Ryan she said, "Closest real movie theater is down by West Palm Beach."

"Yeah, but they ain't half so comfortable in West Palm as we are here," Sammy said as he moved to the rear of the truck.

He motioned to Alex. "Come on, son, help me with this."

And he started tugging at the mattresses, using his one good hand and his leather wrapped left wrist to muscle the awkward objects about. Alex ran to help. Ryan soon caught on what they were trying to do and joined in.

In no time the truck's bed was as comfortable as the padded floor of an Arab sheik's harem. Or, at least, what Ryan imagined such a harem might be from reading "Yankee Pasha." He'd read that book several times now, imagining himself as Jason Starbuck, the buckskin-clad hero of Edison Marshall's tale.

Meanwhile, Ada and the two young women were unpacking food and drink from boxes stacked in the cab.

Hattie looked shyly about, then started away. "Well, guess I'll see you later," she said.

"Nonsense, girl," Ada said. "Stay here with us. We got plenty, don't we Sammy?"

"Sure we do, hon," Sammy said. Then he glanced around the lot, where people had arranged themselves in white and black groups. "Unless... well... Hattie has someplace she'd rather be."

"No, no," Hattie said. "I've got no place to be." Then, to Ryan, "You know how it is." She started to go on, but then shrugged, repeating, "You know..."

Ryan nodded. He certainly did. He'd been a new kid in school his whole life. It was hard to make friends when you were a military brat.

"I'd like to stay, then," Hattie told Ada. "If it's okay?"

"It sure is, honey," Ada said. "Now you just find a place and make yourself comfortable."

"Thank you, ma'am," Hattie said. Then, after a moment's hesitation, she said, "But first I have to buy some things for my momma." She held up a little purse. "Gotta get some aspirin and stuff."

Ryan remembered the soda fountain sign outside the drugstore and said, "Wait a minute everybody. Verne gave me some money to treat us all to ice cream. Who wants some? And what kind?"

The twins shouted, "Me, me... I want chocolate... I want chocolate too... You know that's my favorite. No, you love vanilla. I do not. You do too. Momma make her quit sayin' I love vanilla."

And then the others were weighing in until it got so confusing that Ryan begged everybody to hold on.

"Maybe I'd better write this down," he said, automatically patting his pockets for pencil and paper.

"Here, I've got some," Hattie said, digging into her purse.

"Hold on, Ryan," Sammy said. "Ephraim and the other hands will be here soon. So, why don't you just get a gallon or so of each kind? Chocolate, strawberry, vanilla and maybe even some Spumoni."

"That makes everything easy," Hattie said, putting the paper and pencil away. "Come on, Ryan, I'll help you carry."

On the way, Hattie said, "We're supposed to get a theater at the base soon." She gave Ryan a shy look. "I'm pretty sure I can invite guests."

"That'd be great," Ryan said. A moment's hesitation, then, "Think Alex would be able to come?"

"Sure," Hattie said. "It's the Coast Guard, isn't it? Everybody's supposed to be equal." She grimaced. "Least that's what they always say."

Ryan nodded. He knew how it was.

They went by a group of teenage girls who looked up as they passed.

"Hi, Marla," Hattie called to one of the girls. "And Jean. You too, Patty."

The girls made perfunctory, barely heard greetings, then turned away, rolling their eyes. One of the girls made a tipping motion, putting her thumb and an outstretched pinky to her lips.

They laughed and started whispering furiously together. Ryan thought he heard the one called Marla say something like, "Her momma's a dipso." Ryan glanced over at Hattie and saw tears welling up.

She gave a quick swipe with her hand and pasted on a smile. "Some of the kids are friendlier than others," she said.

"But not them," Ryan said.

A bitter laugh. "No. Not them."

Casting about desperately to say something to make her feel better, he said, "My mom's been pretty sick. She's in the hospital and all. That's why I'm down here."

Hattie touched his arm. "Oh, I'm so sorry," she said. "What ailing her? Hope it's not cancer, or somethin' awful like that."

"No, it's not cancer," Ryan said. He started to say more, but snapped his jaws shut with a hard, almost audible click.

Hattie squeezed his arm. "So we both have sick mommas," she said. Then, embarrassed, she snatched her hand away.

Loud engine noises split the night and a familiar, flame-painted Ford pickup screeched to halt beside them.

It was Joe Collins and his cronies. As wild and jeering as ever.

"Hey, Hattie, Hattie, Hattie," one of the boys shouted in a mock falsetto. "Momma know you're out tonight?"

Joe grinned at them from the driver's seat, displaying a gap-toothed smile.

"You come see me in a couple a years, girl," he said. "I'll take you out for some shine."

"Better yet," said one of his friends. "Let's go fetch her momma right now. She's old enough."

"What about it, Hattie?" Joe said. "I hear she'll do most anythin' for a jug."

Instinctively, Ryan stepped in front of Hattie. "Get lost," he said. "Or somebody might knock out your other teeth."

Joe looked him up and down and laughed at what he saw.

"Ooh! I'm scared." He turned to his friends. "I'm pissin' my pants I'm so scared."

He opened the door and stepped part way out. Tall as he was, Ryan was still just a skinny 12-year-old facing a muscular boy of fourteen.

Even so, he took a step forward, raising his hands. Remembering what his grandfather had taught him. "Don't wait. Hit first and put him down."

Just then a crackly voice called out, "Here, what're you up to, ya little peckerwood?"

It was none other than Gig Light Sally, pulling a little cart along. It was empty, except for a pile of burlap sacks and a big red can of kerosene.

Joe's face went white when he heard the voice, then turned red as he saw Sally standing there, a skinny old rag of a woman looking like a nautical scarecrow in her captain's hat and ragged swabbie pants and shirt.

"You old bitch!" he snarled. Then, "By God, I would have done you good if that jungle bunny hadn't sucker punched me."

Sally's eyes lit with fire and with her hooked nose she looked like a raptor about to skewer its prey. She placed a bony hand on an outthrust skeletal hip. She was defiance roused from the grave.

She said, "Sonny boy, you ain't nothin' more'n a busted carbuncle on your daddy's fat rich ass. Your momma must love ugly, 'cause a tree toad's warts are purty next to the two of ya."

Joe took a step forward, rubbing a fist into an open palm.

Sally held up a warning finger, her face turning so fierce that it stopped the boy in his tracks.

She said, "And another thing folks have been wantin' to tell the whole Collins clan for years now, but have just been too skeered to. You're a bunch of greedy pigs feedin' on gator slops. Your old man and his Tallahassee pals have been cheatin' folks in Jove Beach for too long now.

"Man needs a tractor, your old man makes him pay twice what it's worth 'cause he can't pay cash. Man gets drafted into the war, and he's out lookin' to grab that tractor back, before the profiteerin' laws catch up to him.

"And no woman who works at his lot dares be alone with him. And if he corners her and she yells, he fires her and blackballs her so she'll never get a job of work again. And you—you're no better. Runnin' around with your kiddie army beatin' up boys to get at their girls.

"Yeah, I know all about you sonny boy. And I'll tell you this—I see you fussin' with these two kids again, I will tell Deputy Tindall that I've changed my mind and want to file official type go-to-jail charges against you and your pals for attackin' poor defenseless ole me the other day when I was goin' about my lawful business."

Joe barked laughter. "Fat good that'll do ya. Who's gonna listen to an old bag who hunts frogs for a livin'?"

Now it was Sally's turn to laugh. It came out like a storybook witch's cackle. "Oh, won't you be surprised, sonny boy," she said. "He came to me this very afternoon when I was sellin' my catch and he said that if I should ever have trouble with you again all I have to do is grab his ear. He's wise to yer peckerhead ways, sonny boy. And he's talked to the sheriff, so he knows about ya too."

Joe snorted. "Shoot! The sheriff's bought and paid for by old man."

Sally wagged a bony finger at him. "Oh, no, no, no. That's not how it is at, at all. Not any more, it ain't." She indicated Ryan. "Old man Sullivan—this boy's grandpappy—is friends of the sheriff too. And if the sheriff's spine needs stiffenin'—and I think it do—Verne's the man to do it."

Joe was wavering. His friends were silent. They'd watched the old woman bring him down and were having their doubts.

Suddenly, he whirled. Jumped into the truck. Slammed the door. And sped away, burning rubber all the way down the street.

Sally turned to Ryan and Hattie who stared at her with unbelieving eyes. And she said, "How are you young folks doin' this fine evenin'?' Come to see the movie, have ya?"

Then she trundled off, one cart wheel squeaking as she slowly made her way.

Ryan and Hattie looked at each other.

"Wow!" Ryan said.

Laughing, Hattie said, "Wow is the only word for it."

"Let's get some ice cream," Ryan said.

And they marched into the store.

SEVENTEEN

A New Business Partner

Ryan and Hattie were greeted by a lively scene when they returned to the makeshift outdoor theater. A hot Glen Miller number was playing on loudspeakers and little children were dashing through the growing crowd. Half-a-dozen young women were dancing together, while older folks looked on with amusement.

The music was coming from speakers mounted on an old Model A truck where an enormous fat man was fussing with equipment set up in the back.

Alex spotted them and hustled over to help with the ice cream. "That's Mr. McNash," he said as they neared the truck.

McNash seemed to have solved whatever problem he had been working on and was mounting a reel of film on an ancient projector. Several boxes with neatly stacked film cans were set up within easy reach.

Two teenage boys were lifting down an oversized chair. From the deeply concaved seat, and stuffing poking through stress tears in the upholstery, Ryan presumed it was where Mr. McNash rested his extra large self during the shows.

"What're we going see tonight?" Ryan asked.

Alex shrugged. "Never can tell," he said. He indicated the oversized cowboy hat sitting next to the projector. "He always dresses the part, so I guess we're still into Westerns."

Mr. McNash looked up from his work and spotted Alex. A big grin lit his huge face. He wiped a river of sweat from his face with a sopping hankie and said, "Alex, my boy. How are you this lovely evening?"

He spoke with a deep theatrical voice with just the trace of a British accent. He wore black trousers, a white shirt beneath a black broadcloth coat, and a black string tie.

"I'm just fine, Mr. McNash," Alex said. "Momma said to tell you that I'll be bringing by a couple of her pecan pies in a little bit."

"Well, you tell that fine woman that Amos McNash will treat her culinary treasures with the deep, unwavering respect that they deserve."

He patted his belly. "My gastronomic friend here and I always look forward to our visits to this little community and your sainted mother is the unchallengeable number one reason for my partiality to the little town of Jove Beach. Small as it is, Jove Beach will always be on my motion picture circuit."

"I'll be sure to tell her that, Mr. McNash," Alex said.

The man peered into the box Alex had taken from Hattie and spotted the ice cream. He licked his lips.

Alex grinned. "Would you like some ice cream to go with that pie, Mr. McNash?" he asked.

"Indeed, I would, young man," Mr. McNash said. "And you, sir, are a gentleman and a scholar."

The three of them went on their way, managing to stifle a fit of giggles until he turned back to his task.

"I think I just met another of Jove Beach's characters," Ryan said.

"You ain't seen nothin' yet," Alex said.

Then the twins came rushing over and it was all they could do to escort the ice cream safely to where the rest of the clan had gathered.

Ephraim and Josh and the Sullivan Island hands had also shown up, and they were sprawled around an old flatbed farm truck, munching on plates of goodies Ada and the other women were passing around.

Alex directed Ryan and Hattie to a washtub full of ice and jars of lemonade and sweet tea, where they deposited the ice cream.

"Mr. McNash says he'd like some ice cream with his pie," Alex informed his mother.

She smiled. "He's a greedy old rascal," she said, "But I don't mind. Fair enough trade, considering how many of us there are. They don't take pies for the price of admission over in West Palm."

Ryan saw other people gathering around Mr. McNash, with little baskets and bundles of food. Some elected to give him pennies and nickels, which they dropped into the big white cowboy hat.

In a few minutes the music changed to a swelling orchestra number and in the gathering darkness Mr. McNash switched on the projector and a night of flickering magic began.

First they saw a carton—a *Silly Symphony* about the hilarious misadventures of a cat. Then, to Ryan's supreme delight, this was followed by a full-length Laurel and Hardy movie—*Way Out West*. Another cartoon filled space while Mr. McNash lined up the reels for the main feature: *Ghost Patrol*, with America's favorite cowboy, Tim McCoy.

The excitement proved too much for the twins. By the time *Ghost Patrol* was half over they were sound asleep. Later, they barely stirred when the truck was repacked and they were laid gently on a mattress and covered with blankets.

Despite her polite protests, Sammy insisted that they give Hattie a ride home, and as they turned toward the lighthouse—which revolved majestically in the night—Alex tipped Ryan the wink.

"Hattie," he said, "by any chance are you lookin' to earn some extra money?"

"I sure am," Hattie said. "I don't get an allowance. Momma always says just take what I need from the kitty she keeps in the kitchen with the household money. But a dime doesn't last in that jar longer than a tadpole out of water. There's lots of little jobs a body can get, like weeding ferns at the Pennock Plantation, or picking berries, or hunting clams and oysters. But none of them pay much."

"Well, how would you like to make some serious money?"

Hattie's eyes narrowed. "How serious?"

Alex said. "How does seventy dollars a day sound?"

"Seventy dollars?" she exclaimed. She looked at Ryan. "He's fooling with me, right?"

"No, he isn't fooling," Ryan said. "Of course, we'd be splitting the money three ways."

"Even so," Hattie said. "That's a lot!" She leaned closer, voice dropping. "What do I have to do?"

"What do you know about rattlesnakes?" Alex asked.

She gave Alex a hard look. Weighing. The she turned to Ryan. "Is he serious?" she asked.

"He is," Ryan said.

Ales proved to be a consummate salesman and by the time they dropped Hattie off the deal was signed, sealed and delivered.

But as they were driving away Alex suddenly came up to his knees and looked out into the darkness. "What's that?" he said, pointing.

Ryan looked and far out to sea he spotted a bright yellow light.

"A ship, maybe?" Ryan speculated. "Running lights?"

But he was enough of a Navy brat to know better than that. Then a cloudbank swallowed the light.

Later, Ryan heard the faint sounds coming from his mattress. A little music. Then the Morse Code-like sounds. He tried to listen—to make some sense of the strange phenomenon. As the minutes went by he became more certain that he was hearing Morse Code. And the diddy-dahs were coming at a furious rate.

He tried to concentrate. But he was so tired it was difficult to focus and then he became less sure that it wasn't just a product of an overactive imagination.

Just before he fell asleep he thought that next time he was in town he'd stop by the telegraph office and ask Mrs. Wilkinson's advice.

EIGHTEEN

The War Hits Home

The following morning, after a sumptuous Sunday breakfast, Verne said, "Sorry I didn't ask before, Ryan, but are you a church going man?"

Ryan looked cautiously over at his grandmother, who was putting on another pot of coffee. "Not normally," he said. "In Philadelphia I was going to a Catholic school and church attendance was pretty much mandatory. But, ordinarily, my mom and dad never went."

His grandmother sniffed. And to his surprise, she said, "It's just superstition," she said. "I never believed that Jesus Christ was the son of God, born of a virgin woman and it's just foolishness to think otherwise."

"Yes, ma'am," Ryan said.

Verne chuckled. "Then you won't mind spending the day with me," he said, "helping with the chores and things."

"Nossir," Ryan said, with feeling. "And about chores, sir. I've been meaning to tell you that I'm ready to help out around here anyway I can. If you make me up a list of chores I'll get to them every day. I used to wash Uncle Tom's car every weekend and I always did the windows for Aunt Cassie. And before I left she started a little Victory Garden and I helped her weed that."

"Well, don't you go near my garden," his grandmother warned. "I have some special vegetables I've been growing that I brought down from Ohio. And I don't want some clumsy boy with a hoe whacking away at them."

"No, ma'am," Ryan said. "I'd never do that. But if you just tell me what to do, I'll be ever so careful."

Another sniff from his grandmother. But she did seem mollified. "Very well, but just as long as we understand one another. And you ask my permission first."

"Yes, ma'am," Ryan said.

Verne rose from his seat. "Let's get started," he said. "Sunday might be a day of rest for some, but on a farm or a ranch there's always something that must be done."

On the way out, he gave Ryan a mischievous grin and added, "But, first I want you to meet a friend of mine."

He set off for a distant Banyan tree that grew along the banks of an irrigation ditch. Rex tried to follow, but Verne raised a thick finger.

"Stay!" he said in that deep, commanding voice. Rex stayed.

They passed a melon patch on the way. Verne leaned over and scooped up a monstrous fruit that easily weighed twenty five pounds or more. As they walked, he juggled it like a ball, tossing it from one hand to other with no visible effort.

When they got closer, Ryan heard grunting noises coming from a large pen that had been built in the shade of the tree.

Verne called out, "It's daddy, Bertha! Come to get his morning kiss."

While Ryan wondered who in blazes Bertha was, and why she should expect a kiss, an enormous pig rose out of the pen, snuffled the air and made oinking noises.

"That's Bertha?" Ryan gasped.

"None other," Verne said. He handed Ryan the watermelon. "Here, hold this, son," he said. Ryan nearly buckled from the unexpected weight.

At the pen Verne said, "Give Daddy a kiss, Bertha."

The pig offered up its big snout, going, "Oink, Oink," and by gosh and by golly it made kissing noises and Verne gave it a lip smack.

Ryan never dreamed a pig could get this big. It was easily five hundred pounds and four feet high at the shoulders. With its front legs braced against the pen, the animal towered over Ryan.

Verne said, "Lie down for Daddy, Bertha. Show Ryan here what you can do."

Making little squealing noises, Bertha flopped on the muddy ground.

"Roll over, Bertha," Verne commanded. "Go on, now. Roll over."

He made kissing noises, and then, to Ryan's amazement Bertha rolled over like a five hundred pound dog. Lying on her back, she waved her four feet in the air, looking so silly that Ryan nearly burst into laughter.

"Don't laugh," Verne warned him under his breath. "She's a sensitive pig and you'll hurt her poor feelings."

With difficulty, Ryan stifled laughter.

Verne grabbed a rake that was propped up against the pen.

"Does Bertha baby want her belly scratched?" he asked.

The stream of oinking noises coming from Bertha made Ryan guess that would be a "Yes."

Making kissing noises all the while, Verne scraped her enormous tummy with the rake and Bertha squealed and wriggled with undisguised pleasure.

When he thought she'd had enough, Verne put the rake away and took the watermelon back from Ryan.

"Thanks," he said, then, holding the melon between two hands, he gave it a whack on the fence, splitting it neatly in half.

Bertha scrambled to her feet.

"Oh, baby knows what's coming next, doesn't she, girl?" Verne said and he tossed first one half, then the other into the pen.

Bertha got busy munching them down.

"Come on," Verne said. "Let her eat in peace."

As they walked away, he said, "If you can imagine, she was only this big when I found her." He spread his hands about a foot apart. "About the size of a pup."

"You found her?" Ryan asked. It never occurred to him that you could find a pig. He figured farmers bought them from breeders, or bred their own.

"Florida is full of wild pigs," Verne said. "Razorbacks left by the Spanish years and years ago. They can be a nuisance, getting at our crops and stuff, so we usually hunt them down and kill them for meat and sport.

"And, just like you noticed the other day, they can be dangerous as all get out. Grow big old tusks, six, eight inches long. First thing I did was clip hers, so she wouldn't grow any.

"I think old Bertha's momma was movin' her litter from one place to another and little Bertha got stuck in the barbed wire fence. I rescued her and she was such a cute little thing I didn't have the heart to put her down. I thought I'd let her be and maybe raise her for some gourmet-style bacon and hams."

He smacked his lips. "No kitchen scraps for Bertha," he said. "I feed her nothing but the best. Melon and apples and oranges and whatever nuts and berries that are in season. Vegetables from the truck garden."

Verne shook his head in wonderment. "Can you imagine what her bacon's gonna taste like with a diet like that? And shoot, what could be better than apple-fed ham smoked over apple chip coals?"

"You mean, you really are going to eat her?" Ryan asked.

"Of course I am," Verne said. "Why else would I go to all that trouble? God made pigs so we could eat bacon and ham and deep fried crackling."

"I suppose so," Ryan said, trying not to laugh.

Verne gave him a stern look. "You doubting me son?" he asked.

"Nossir," Ryan said. "I'd never do that."

On the way back to the house Sammy and Ada came driving up. They were dressed in their Sunday best, as were the twins who sat between them, uncomfortable in flowery dresses and little black Mary Janes with white lacy topped socks. Alex was perched in the back, wearing long pants a crisp white shirt and polished shoes.

"Off to church, Sammy?" Verne asked.

"Sure am boss," Sammy said. "Sunday morning chores are done and everybody's either visitin' family, or at church. It's Charlie Silver Moon's turn to mind the stock. Hank'll pick it up next Sunday."

Verne nodded. "Well, you'd best get goin' then," he said. "Deacon Jones'll give you what for if you're late."

Sammy laughed. "Don't worry, boss," he said. "Got a couple of Ada's pies to smooth the way."

Then, after a pause, Sammy said, "You hear the war news yet, boss?"

Ryan's heart gave a bump. Could the news have something to do with his father? He kicked himself. That was ridiculous. He was too far away for news to filter down this far.

Still.

He crossed his fingers behind his back and waited.

Verne said, "Haven't had a chance yet. I try to catch a listen when Myrtle isn't around. Doctor's orders, you know."

Sammy nodded. "Yessir," he said. "Good thing, too. This was awful close to home."

Verne's eyebrows rose.

"German U-boat hit a freighter off our coast last night," Sammy said. He shook his head. "Word is, there ain't no survivors. Radio said the sub surfaced and machine gunned 'em all."

Verne's face went pale and he suddenly looked twenty years older. With the way his own stomach took a multi-story tumble, Ryan guessed he didn't look much better.

"That's terrible," Verne said, deep voice atremble. "They were just unarmed merchantmen. Civilians. No threat to anybody."

Sammy sighed. Reflexively, he touched the place where his left hand used to be. "If they'd take me," he said, "I'd join up tomorrow. Shoot the hell out of them Germans."

Ada leaned over the twins, so her head was closer to the driver's side window.

"I suspect we'll all be speakin' to the Lord about those poor boys this mornin', boss," she said. "And they'll most likely be takin' up a collection for the families."

Verne reached into his pocket and pulled out a roll. He peeled off a thick sheaf of bills and handed them to Ada.

"Put this in for me and Myrtle, would you Ada?" He looked at Ryan, then back at Ada. "And for Ryan, too." He looked at the remaining money in his fist, then shrugged. "What the hey," he said. "Make it from everybody on Sullivan Island." And he handed it all over to Ada.

Ada gave a sad smile. "I'll be proud to boss."

She shifted back to her place and Sammy slowly drove away. In the back, Alex gave a shy wave. Ryan waved back.

When they were gone, Verne said, "When we go to town tomorrow to get you into school, I'll swing by and talk to Captain Frank."

Ryan gave him a quizzical. Verne said, "He's the fellow I hired to operate that fishing boat I told you about earlier," he said.

The boy nodded, remembering. "I'll get him to prep the boat for rescue operations," Verne said. "First aid stuff. Food. Blankets. That sort of thing. Then, next time one of those merchant ships are hit maybe we can help."

"You think it's going to happen again?" Ryan asked.

"Unfortunately, I do," Verne said. "And anybody who thinks otherwise has their heads stuck way up their behinds."

It suddenly occurred to Ryan that the flash of fiery light that Alex had pointed out last night was very likely the merchant ship sinking in burning seas.

In his mind's eye he saw the U-Boat surfacing. The German gunnery crew pulling the tarps back from the heavy machinegun with fast well-practiced ease.

And he imagined them opening up. Aiming for the bodies thrashing around in burning seas.

"You alright, boy?" he heard Verne ask. His voice seemed to come from a distant place.

Ryan sighed. "Nossir," he said. "I am not."

NINETEEN

Car Magic

All Ryan could see in the bathroom mirror was an idiot wearing clothes that shouted "I'm A Yankee." He was clad in heavy cords, a dress white shirt and black, spit-shined leather shoes.

And no matter how many time he pushed down on it, the Our Gang Comedies cowlick sticking up on the back of his head insisted on staying as erect as a steel bar.

Making matters worse, it was only seven thirty in the morning and he was already dripping sweat in the south Florida tropical heat.

In short, Ryan was desperately trying to shake off the Monday morning first-day-of-school blues. And right now—staring in the mirror—it not only looked hopeless. It was hopeless.

His suitcase was packed tight with equally unsuitable clothes and so from now until some distant point in the unforeseeable future he'd be condemned to look like a rube.

He'd be the target of every Florida Cracker's sneer from here to Key West, where the sun mystically fell off the ends of the earth in a green flash. Ryan had read that in a column in one of his science fiction magazines, and had an itch ever since to see the phenomenon.

Ryan would have to ask Alex about the green flash. He perked up. For a change he had somebody intelligent to talk to. Actually, that was *two* somebodys. Alex and Hattie. He'd rarely found one—much less two—friends like that in all the schools he'd attended. They were gone now in the mist of other schools, other half-semester friends, and if not for Hattie and Alex the days that came might be the same as all those in the past. He was suddenly aware that he might have just found a treasure.

Outside, Verne beeped the horn.

Okay, Ryan Karr. Time for the pep talk. New school. New teachers. New kids. Keep your head low. Mouth shut and do not draw attention to yourself. That is Rule Number One: Do Not Draw Attention To Yourself.

In dismay, he looked down at the clothes he was wearing. He hoped to blazes they'd get a cold snap soon so he could buy new duds—never mind the bicycle and the boat. First things first.

Outside, a particularly humongous car horn blast almost made him jump out of his skin. And he heard Verne bellow: "Time's a wastin', Ryan!"

Ryan snorted amusement. What in the world was Verne up to? He gave the cowlick one more futile push and hurried off to investigate.

A moment later he stepped through the screen door to be greeted by a magnificent sight: a car whose like he'd never seen before except in a few men's magazines in barbershops. Which practically every schoolboy visited once a month—twice if you were a Navy brat, or a kid in Catholic school.

Also, like any red-blooded American boy of his time, Ryan could spout the pedigree and specifics of any automobile on the road. And the 1941 Cadillac Convertible sitting before him was at the top of any list of a young man's favorites.

Streamlined like the Florida Special that had carried him to Jove Beach, it was long and low and gleaming black, with the spare tire mounted on the side. The chromed grille and window frames sparkled in the morning sun. With the top thrown back showing off the rose-colored leather upholstery, the vehicle looked like it was right out of a travel poster depicting beautiful people standing around admiring the car and each other.

Ryan was so transfixed it took a moment before his eyes fell on Verne sitting behind the wheel, sporting a grin as wide as the Seminole River. He gave the horn another shot.

He clapped the big Panama on his head and grinned the widest grin Ryan had ever seen, his single blue eye sparkling with fun.

"Those aren't school bells you hear ringing, young man," Verne said, playing a little drama of his own making. "Let's get goin', Pard, 'fore they send the truant officer out to lasso us and haul us away to the hoosegow... or school... whichever is worse."

"Please, Verne," his grandmother said. "You're going to give me a splitting headache."

With a start, he realized she was sitting in the back seat, dressed for town in a gray suit, gloves to match and a string of pearls around her slender throat. Her makeup was light.

"My God, the man can make an event out of the smallest endeavor," she complained.

Verne patted the passenger's side. "Get on in, Ryan," he said. "You'll be riding shotgun today."

Delighted, Ryan hopped in, sinking luxuriously into the soft leather.

In the back, his grandmother was going on about the things she needed to pick up in town after they got done with Mr. Jordan, the school principal. Thankfully, she was talking to Verne because Ryan was so knocked out by the car he only made out every third word or so.

He watched, fascinated, as Verne pressed the starter button with his thumb and the big V8 engine rumbled into life. Then he smoothly shifted the lever of what Ryan realized was the new 4-speed hydromatic transmission all the guys were talking about back in Philly. Verne applied gas and the car moved forward, seashells crunching under its wheels.

Magic!

Then he heard Verne say, "Myrtle, we have to do something about the boy's clothes. It's just morning and he's already sweating like Bertha on a hot August day."

That got Ryan's attention. He glanced up at the rear view mirror and saw his grandmother's lips tighten.

"Another expense," she said. "I told Cassie what kind of clothes to send down with him. I swear, that family is so scatter brained that—"

Verne broke in. "Myrtle, darling," he said. "Seems to me the folks up in Philadelphia have pretty much got their hands full. And with the war and, uh…" he glanced over at Ryan… "Well with the war and all, I suspect they're pretty distracted.

"Besides, I don't mind us taking a little of the burden off them if we can. They're family after all. Sure I married into it, but that's how I feel darling, and you know it.

"We can certainly afford it. The feds bought our entire crop of oranges at top dollar to make concentrate for our boys in uniform."

Ryan could see his grandmother's eyes narrowing. She was not mollified.

"We can talk about this later," she said.

"That we can, darling," Verne said. "That we can."

He nudged Ryan with his elbow. "What do you think of my pride and joy, son?" he asked, patting the steering wheel. "I think she's a work of art. Or pretty near to one. How about you?"

"She's fantastic!" Ryan enthused. His excitement carrying his mind away from his grandmother's pettiness.

"Wait'll we get out on Dixie Highway," Verne said. "I'll open her up and show you what she can do."

"Oh, boy!" Ryan said.

"Now, Verne," his grandmother said. "Don't be going too fast. You know how I get."

"Not to worry, darling," Verne said, giving Ryan another elbow nudge. "Not to worry at all."

Ryan could hardly wait for Dixie Highway.

Magic!

TWENTY

Philadelphia Blues

"Class, may I have your attention, please? We have a new student joining us today."

Ryan stood straight as a board as twelve pairs of eyes took his measure. Even though he'd done this many times before, he was nervous. He'd never felt so out of place, standing there in his sweat-soaked Yankee clothes.

Beside him, Mrs. Carlin—a pinch-faced woman with graying hair—held forth with practiced ease.

"This is Ryan Karr, class," she said in her soft southern accent. Turning to Ryan, she offered him a piece of chalk. "Ryan, would you write your name on the board for us, please?"

"Yes ma'am," Ryan said, voice cracking a little, eliciting giggles—immediately cut off by Mrs. Carlin's fierce glares.

Ryan wrote his name on the blackboard, the chalk screeching, then breaking in half from nervous pressure.

More giggles.

Mrs. Carlin snapped—"Class! This young man is not here for your amusement. Kindly give him your full attention, please."

"Yes, Mrs. Carlin," came the practiced chorus of agreement.

"Now, Ryan," Mrs. Carlin said, "where are you joining us from?"

"Philadelphia, ma'am," Ryan said.

"Philadelphia," Mrs. Carlin said, nodding as if this was of great significance.

Titters broke out and she rapped a pointer on her desk to silence them.

"Marla Gentry," she said, indicating one of the girls Ryan had seen on movie night, "please come up here and show the class where Philadelphia is on the map."

Blushing, Marla came shuffling up to the front and took over the pointer from the teacher. She went to a large map of the United States and started searching for the city, the rubber-tipped point trailing across the map.

"Where are you going, Marla?" Mrs. Carlin said. "I can assure you that Philadelphia is not in Texas."

This time the entire class laughed. And this time, Mrs. Carlin let them. A quick look at her face and the pleasure shown in her eyes told Ryan what he needed to know about the woman. If kids were flies she'd enjoy plucking off their wings.

"Thomas!" she snapped. "Come up here and show Marla and the rest of us where Philadelphia is."

A chubby, pimple-faced boy reluctantly rose from his seat and approached the board. Marla gave him the pointer.

"You may sit down, Marla," Mrs. Carlin said. The girl did so, scurrying away, head ducked low in embarrassment. If she hadn't cut Hattie dead Saturday night, Ryan would have felt sorry for her.

Speaking of which, Ryan spotted Hattie in the back, sitting alone in a row of empty desks. He smiled when he saw her, but she gave a little negative shake of her head. Ryan quickly got the message—Eyes front!

Meanwhile, poor Thomas was having no better luck.

Mrs. Carlin gave a dramatic sigh of frustration. "That is Illinois, Thomas. You'll find Chicago in Illinois. Springfield. And even Rockford. But you will not find Philadelphia in the great state of Illinois."

"Yes, ma'am," replied a glum Thomas.

"Ryan," Mrs. Carlin said. Ryan snapped to. Shoulders back like a regimental soldier.

"Yes, ma'am?"

"Kindly show the class where Philadelphia is."

"Yes, ma'am," Ryan said, taking the pointer from Thomas. Then he turned and touched the proper spot on the map.

"And what state would that be in, Ryan?" Mrs. Carlin asked.

"Pennsylvania, ma'am," Ryan said.

"Very good, Ryan," Mrs. Carlin said. Then turning to the class, she said: "Tonight, I want everyone to write a two-page essay on Philadelphia."

Everyone groaned. Two pages!

"Yes, two pages," Mrs. Carlin said. "Along with all your other homework. You'll find the information you require in your geography books."

"But we didn't get there, yet," somebody complained.

"We're only up to Georgia," said another.

"Thank you for reminding me, class," Mrs. Carlin. "To reward you for your diligence, let us make that assignment three pages."

She held up three fingers. Someone else groaned. "Shall I make it four?" she said, another finger coming partly up.

Silence.

"Very good, then," she said. "Three it is and three it shall stay." A dramatic pause, then: "For the time being."

She turned to Ryan. "Take your seat, Ryan," she said.

Just then the bell rang. Ryan's eyes jumped to the clock on the wall. Thank God, it was three on the dot. For Ryan the school day was over before it had barely begun.

After his grandmother and Verne had left the principal's office where they'd signed various papers and Mr. Jordan and Verne had exchanged pleasantries, he was given a sheaf of papers to fill out and several folders containing state-mandated tests.

Fortunately, he'd done this many times before and the tests were so easy it was laughable. The room was steamy hot and coated with a thin layer of dust that kept him sneezing until he took it upon himself to crack a window.

A sea breeze swept into the room, giving him a fright when it set the blinds to rattling. Quickly, he tied them back and hopped into his seat before someone came to investigate. No one did, so he pulled out a Reader's Digest condensed book he'd found at home. He placed it close to his knapsack, left open so he could quickly hide the evidence.

He made use of it a little later when Mrs. Keys, a cheery little woman who served as Mr. Jordan's secretary, brought him a lunch tray from the cafeteria. He dawdled over this, just as he dawdled over the tests. Sneakreading another story in the book. He was not eager to start the day with his new classmates.

Ryan gazed longingly through the window at the sparkling blue Florida skies. In Philadelphia they would be gray and overcast. When all the city's backyard incinerators were going palm-size "snowflakes" of ashes would be floating down, coating clothes and skin.

Jove Beach's big red lighthouse beckoned in the distance, instead of the towering Dupont Chemical factory towers in Philly. The sea breezes blowing in from the Jove Beach inlet were fresh and invigorating, instead of the awful stench from the Dupont factories lined up along the banks of the Schuylkill River.

Now, the sea breezes and bright skies elicited daydreams of exotic lands and faraway places. Then reality jumped him like a cat on a mouse. At this moment the Allies were locked in a desperate struggle with Rommel in Africa, while in the east the Marines were battling the Japanese in Bataan. And those were just miniscule examples of the rivers of blood being shed all over the globe, from Australia to Zanzibar.

And Saturday night, while he had watched a movie and enjoyed Ada's pecan pie topped with fresh churned ice cream, the blood of innocent merchantmen had flowed into the seas that lapped the shores of Jove Beach.

He shivered. It was time to face the music. He gathered up his forms and test papers and went to the door to tell Mrs. Keys he was done.

Now, fifteen minutes after he joined the class, he found himself moving hastily aside as the other students hurried out of the room to freedom.

When the way was clear he went to Mrs. Carlin's desk where a stack of textbooks and workbooks awaited him.

She looked up as he approached. "Here is your class schedule, Ryan," she said, handing him a blurred mimeo. "You have PE first thing in the morning. Two periods with me in this classroom. Then there's math and general science with Mr. Jackson down the hall, and then back here with me for your remaining classes."

"Yes ma'am," he said.

"And here are your books," she said.

"Thank you, ma'am," he said.

He stuffed them into his knapsack, noting how battered and out of date they looked. The good news was that he would likely be far ahead of the other kids. His previous school had all the latest textbooks. The bad news: the next time he transferred he might be far behind. No problem. He'd write to Aunt Cassie and see if she'd send him his cousin Sandy's books from last year. Sandy was a grade ahead of him.

Next, Mrs. Carlin handed him a worksheet, with hand scribbled notes.

"And here is the homework you'll be expected to hand in tomorrow," she said.

"Yes ma'am."

She gathered up her own things and rose from her desk. "See you tomorrow, Ryan," she said.

"Yes ma'am," he said. "And thank you."

"No thanks required," she said. "It's my job."

As he was leaving she called out, "Oh, Ryan?"

He turned back. "Ma'am?"

"I won't be expecting a paper about Philadelphia from you," she said. "Obviously, you know where it is."

"Yes ma'am," he said.

And he left just as fast as could without appearing in too much of a hurry.

A grinning Hattie was waiting for him in the stairwell. "Stretched the tests as long as you could, did ya?" she said.

Ryan smiled. "That what you do?"

"Every darned time," she said. She patted her stomach. "Helps settle first day butterflies," she added. Then: "What did think of Mrs. Carlin?"

Ryan sighed. "She couldn't have done a better job getting the other kids to hate me if she tried. Now everybody has extra homework all because of me."

"Too true," Hattie said. "Never mind that it wasn't your fault."

"At least with only twelve kids in the class," Ryan said, "and most of them girls, I won't have too many guys wanting to fight."

Hattie snickered. "You don't know the girls," she said.

They exited the school into bright sunlight, scattering little curly-tailed lizards that escaped under the building, which rose two or three feet off the white sandy ground. Other than the lizards and a flock of egrets pecking at the base of several palm trees and coconut trees, the school grounds were mostly empty.

A newly familiar car horn honked. They looked up to see Verne waiting in the Cadillac. He waved to them.

"Wow!" Hattie said. "That your grandfather's car?"

By now, Ryan had given up explaining the relationship. Instead he just grinned.

"Something, isn't it?"

"Something is right!" Hattie said.

She pointed to a bike rack, where only one lonely bicycle waited. "That's my ride."

It was blue, with gold trim and Ryan noted with approval that she kept it sparkling clean and the chain was freshly oiled.

"That's nice," he said.

Hattie shrugged. "Gets me here and there," she said. Then, waving, she said, "See you tomorrow. Oh, and if you need any help on the homework, just call. Mrs. Richards, the local operator, will put you through."

"Thanks," Ryan said. "See you."

Approaching the Cadillac he glanced in the back and was pleased to see that his grandmother wasn't there.

But wait. What was that? He looked closer and saw a long object stretched across the back seat. It was green and black and it was-

"Holy cow!" he cried out.

Verne grinned at him, his single eye alight with pleasure. Ryan was so overcome he could hardly speak. Finally, he got it out:

"It's the Schwinn!" he cried.

"None other," said Verne.

TWENTY-ONE
Bikes, Boats and Bedsprings

"I'll pay you back Verne, honest I will," Ryan said. "Even if it takes a thousand years."

Verne adjusted his eyepatch. "A thousand years?" he said. "Hmm. I wasn't thinking of terms that strict. Maybe two hundred. Or even a hundred. With compounded interest that ought to make me pretty rich."

"You know what I mean," Ryan broke in. "And even after I pay you back, I'll never be able to thank you enough. Alex and I saw that bike in the Western Auto window the other night."

"So he said," Verne replied, a twinkle in his single eye.

"Why that—" Ryan slapped the seat. "He's... he's..."

"... a pretty good friend?" Verne filled in for him.

"He sure is," Ryan said. He almost leaked tears. He'd never had a friend like that before.

"Besides," Verne said, "you need a way to get to school that doesn't involve me or Sammy driving you every morning. And the school bus doesn't come anywhere near Sullivan Island.

"Also, the Feds'll be hitting us with gasoline rationing pretty soon, although as a farmer and a rancher it'll be easier on us than others."

"But, it's so much money," Ryan continued to protest. "We could've gotten a used bike."

"Look at this way," Verne said. "Your father will be sending us money for your keep every month. He has the Navy automatically deduct it from his pay. So, it's really your father buying the bike. Not me."

"Still," Ryan said. "Still."

He looked around, noting for the first time that they weren't heading home.

"Where are we going?"

"Down to the port to see Captain Frank," Verne said. "Remember what I said about stocking the boat for trouble?"

"Yessir," Ryan said, sitting up straight. He was eager to see Verne's boat.

Even so, on the drive over he kept glancing in the back, checking to see if the Schwinn was still there.

Soon they were driving into the lot where Ryan had disembarked from the Florida Special a few days before. They had to pause while a gaggle of ducks waddled unhurriedly across the road, then pulled past the train station and telegraph office to the docks, where pelicans and seagulls squabbled over fish offal being dumped off the boats.

The Myrtle turned out to be one of the fishing boats Ryan had seen when he disembarked from the train. Its hull was a dazzling white and its flying bridge and cabin areas were mahogany polished to a high gloss, with gleaming brass rails and fittings.

Captain Frank, a grizzled mariner with a silver beard and dark piercing eyes set deep in a face weathered to the same mahogany as the craft he commanded, ran down the specs for Ryan's rapt edification. The *Myrtle* was 38 feet long, had dual Chrysler engines with a combined 75 horsepower and did 16 knots—"18 miles an hour for you landlubbers"—and had a livewell for fish.

The captain was all for Verne's plan to equip and provision the *Myrtle* for rescue operations.

"I was overhauling one of the engines last time," he said, "otherwise I'd have called you for permission to go out to help."

"Next time no need to call," Verne said. "Just go!" Then, after a minute's reflection, he said, "Well, call anyway. If I can get there in time, I'd like to go along."

"Sure thing, Skip," Frank said.

Then, after showing Ryan around, he and Verne got together in the galley to draw up a list of necessaries and discuss the engine overhaul.

"If it's okay," Ryan said when Verne asked him to be patient for a bit, "I'm going to visit with Mrs. Wilkinson over at the telegraph office."

"Tell her I said hello," Verne said.

Mrs. Wilkinson was munching on a sandwich and flipping through a magazine when he came in. She pushed them both aside when she saw him.

"Sorry," she said. "I've been swamped all day, what with all these new military folks in town. And it just quieted down enough for me to grab lunch."

"I didn't mean to interrupt," Ryan said. "I just stopped by to ask a technical question."

Mrs. Wilkinson gave him the sweetest smile. "Well, you go right on and ask, hon," she said. "I'd enjoy the company."

Ryan blushed, suddenly embarrassed. "It's probably silly," he said. "In fact, the more I think on it the sillier it seems."

"Can't learn unless you ask, sweetie pie," Mrs. Wilkinson said. "That's what my instructor at telegraph school always said. And that answer has served me well over the years."

Ryan gathered his thoughts, then plunged ahead. "Well, it's like this," he said. And then he explained the whole thing. The new bed. The faint sounds of what he thought might be music. And then the sound of what seemed to be somebody sending messages in Morse Code.

Mrs. Wilkinson thought, then said, "I suppose it's possible, hon. Unlikely, but possible. The bed springs could be acting like an antennae. I mean, an antennae is just wire stretched into various configurations to catch a signal."

"Like the bedsprings?" Ryan asked.

"Yes, like the bedsprings," she replied. "It could be that the music is from the local radio station. It's signal isn't that powerful, but it is close. And if the cloud cover was just right and the bed was in the perfect position, I suppose you might pick up a kind of ghost signal."

"What about the Morse Code?" Ryan asked.

Mrs. Wilkinson smiled. "No, hon," she said. "I don't see how that could happen. I mean, the atmosphere can cause some strange phenomenon and we don't know near as much as we think we do about radio and telegraphic transmissions. But hearing telegraphy in bedsprings? I just don't think so, hon. Sorry."

"You think it's my imagination?" Ryan asked.

Mrs. Wilkinson chuckled. "You're a smart young man," she said. "After practicing on your key for hours on end doesn't it make more sense that you're imagining the Morse Code sounds just before falling sleep? Or that it's really happening and your bed has been turned into a humongous speaker system?"

Ryan laughed. "When you put it that way," he said, "imagination makes way more sense. And I have been practicing my hand pretty hard lately. But now that I'm starting school again I won't have near as much time to get my imagination all worked up."

Mrs. Wilkinson nodded. "You have Mrs. Carlin at school, right?"

"Yes ma'am."

"Well, she's a monster when it comes to homework," she said. "Drove both my girls crazy before they graduated."

"That's okay," Ryan said. "I'm pretty good with essays."

Mrs. Wilkinson reacted with mock horror. "Essays? On, no, no, no. That would be way too much work for Mary Moore Carlin," she said. "She likes her evenings free for bridge and visitin' friends. No, she relies on the textbooks questions they ask at the end of every chapter. That way she can correct them in a few minutes."

"She assigned everybody a three page essay today," Ryan said, "because they couldn't find Philadelphia on the map."

"That was punishment," Mrs. Wilkinson said, "for embarrassing her in front of a new student. She'll never read them. Just count the pages to make sure there are a total of three."

"But, how hard can it be?" Ryan asked. "There's only twelve kids in the class."

In Philly, the class size had been over forty, although you'd never know it, that's how strict the nuns and brothers were.

"I shouldn't be speakin' ill of your teacher," Mrs. Wilkinson said. "Shame on me." But she didn't look ashamed. If anything, her smile just got broader.

Then lights started to flash and the telegraphy sounds started up and Mrs. Wilkinson made an apologetic smile and got back to work.

Verne was just getting into his Caddy when Ryan emerged from the telegraph office. "Come on, son," he said. "We've got one more errand to run."

"What's that?" Ryan asked, climbing into the car.

"We're gonna fix you up with some sure enough Florida duds," he said in a mock Southern drawl.

Ryan stated to protest. This was too much. Too generous by far. And his grandmother would have conniptions over the expense.

But then he felt sweat trickling down his sides and soaking his shirt and all he said was, "Thanks, Verne."

TWENTY-TWO

The Jove Beach Musketeers

In the days and weeks that followed, Ryan slowly fit into his new life. Spring in the tropics was swiftly becoming his new normal. Or, as Hattie said, "Whatever normal is to military brats like us."

Ryan and Hattie and Alex spent so much time together and had so many adventures they started calling themselves the "Jove Beach Musketeers."

Verne was also a constant presence—but never an annoyingly adult one. It seemed to Ryan that Verne appeared just when he was at his gloomiest, worrying about his mother and father.

Helping smooth things out was the absence of any more mysterious Morse Code signals, if they had existed at all. The more he thought on it, the more it appeared that Mrs. Wilkinson had been right when she said it was most likely his imagination. Although, sometimes he could swear he heard radio music, except the sound seemed so distant—so ghostly—that it was probably imaginary as well.

School was no challenge at all. Mrs. Cardiff's teaching methods consisted of assigning them chapters to read in the various subjects, then—just as Mrs. Wilkinson had said—she used the questions and answers at the end of each chapter to test their knowledge. During class she read a few pages of the chapters aloud in a dry, dusty voice that reminded Ryan of a bluebottle fly trapped on the wrong side of a window.

Mr. Jackson, their math and general science teacher, spent almost all of his time concentrating on war news, instead of the subjects he was supposed to teach. He had maps of the world pinned to the walls and used little stick pins to mark the war's progress.

Ryan and the others were riveted the whole hour, glorying in Allied victories and despairing when setbacks and losses were reported.

Even so, Ryan's worries about falling behind in "the real world" persisted, so wrote to his Aunt Cassie, asking if she'd send down his cousin Sandy's books. They arrived a little later in a box filled not just with textbooks, but with Philadelphia goodies, like several varieties of Tastykakes, as well as enormous pretzels, Goldenberg's peanut chews and Asher's Dark Chocolate Sea Salt Caramels.

If he'd only had a nice cold cream soda to wash all that down he could have closed his eyes and transported himself to 28th and Tasker.

He and Alex and Hattie polished the treats off over several lazy afternoons and Alex allowed—through a mouthful of Tastykake—that maybe city life wasn't so bad after all.

Alex scrounged up some cast off pole boats and he, Ryan and Hattie spent several afternoons repairing them and making them water tight. Sammy helped them build lightweight pullcarts to attach to the backs of their bikes and from then on they were free to roam the Seminole's tributaries and dusty byroads in search of adventure.

Rex was their constant companion, running beside their bikes, or bounding along the river banks when they were water-borne. He even learned to ride the boats—straddling the front while Ryan, or one of the others, poled them smoothly along.

Once a big gator nosed up to Ryan's boat to investigate and got an unpleasant surprise when he raised his head to find a snarling Rex daring him to move one inch closer.

With a flick of its tail the gator slipped beneath the water and ghosted away.

One hot afternoon, Alex took them to see Jove Beach's famous blowing rocks. At first, Ryan didn't know what the heck he was talking about. Blowing rocks? It made no sense whatsoever. Was dynamite involved? Gunpowder?

It turned out to be a marvelous display of Mother Nature's prowess. Up from the inlet was a wild, rocky cove that few people frequented. It was here that Nature displayed one of her many quirks, in the form of a jumble of boulders that hung over the sea.

On certain days—if the tide was just right and the wind was blowing just so—waves would come rolling in, strike the rocks and shoot up through holes carved over thousands of years, creating marvelous geysers thirty or forty feet high.

Ryan stood there transfixed, watching the waves roll in, lifting higher and higher, then crashing—KABOOM!—against the rocks. Then another, louder, KABOOM! as the water shot through the holes as if fired by a cannon, then gravity took hold and the water cascaded down on the rocks with a thunderous roar. Then the hiss of the spent wave as it returned to its oceanic home.

Ryan swore to himself that soon as he had enough money he was going to buy a little Brownie camera so he could send pictures to Aunt Cassie to show his mom. But that thought made him gulp. Would his mom even know what the pictures were about? Or that her son had taken them? Gut wrench: would she even know who or where her son was?

The Jove Beach Musketeers did odd jobs to earn money, such as picking Plumosa Ferns over on Pennock Point—where the ferns were wrapped in wet newspapers and crated for the long journey by train to northern flower shops.

Ryan was amazed to learn that the lacy ferns that decorated the arrangements Uncle Tom gave his Aunt Cassie on special occasions had come all the way from the tropical swamps of Florida. Berry picking at Pennock was another job always in need of willing hands. They got a nickel a pail, although the berries were so delicious it took willpower to leave enough in the pail to turn a profit.

Gig Light Sally generously showed them some of her favorite places where the oysters and mussels grew thick and the crabs gathered in sufficient numbers to fill their buckets. They sold them at crab shacks and oyster bars and even to the Seacrest Hotel, home of one of finest restaurants in Palm Beach County.

Down the road, Alex and Sally had high hopes for their oyster farm experiment, but not enough oyster balls had grown yet for idea to make commercial sense.

Fishing was always on. They kept their gear stashed on their little pullcarts. Poles lashed to the side. Extra line, hooks, and other things were stashed in a bucket that Alex made it his business to carry—he didn't trust Ryan, or even Hattie, who was more experienced in the ways of the Seminole River than Ryan, not to lose them.

Once, when they were racing one another, Alex ran his pole boat into a sandbar. He lost his glasses and sat on the edge of the riverbank half blind and wringing his hands in despair while Ryan and Hattie dived for them.

Finally, just as it was getting dark and the tide was coming in—threatening to sweep the glasses away forever—Hattie made one last dive. Of the three, she was the best diver and could stay underwater the longest.

This time she was under longer than any time before. Every once in awhile her feet would emerge, then she'd muscle her way down again. Then she came up with a loud whoop of victory holding the glasses aloft.

"I got 'em, Alex, I got 'em," she shouted.

And then she waded ashore to be congratulated by her friends. Ryan tied the glasses to Alex's head with fishline as a temporary measure. Later, he bought a strip of leather in town and presented it to Alex for a more stylish safety device.

Sammy taught them how to make spear guns out of tough palmetto leaves. They'd whittle the leaves down to eighteen inch spears with needle sharp points. The gun part was made from slicing up old inner tubes into bands, which were fitted into a y-shaped stock, a little like a slingshot. Fish line was tied to the palmetto spear. The devices were more powerful than they looked. Ryan got so he could sink a palmetto spear half an inch into solid wood.

If they came across a school of mullet, which liked to gather at the surface when insects were thick, they merely had to remember to take into account water refraction when aiming. Then all they had to do was haul in the mullet close enough to net them.

On the hottest days they'd bike over to the Hobe Ice Plant, which provided ice to the bars and restaurants and fishing boats to pack their catches in. There they'd wolf down thick ice cream sandwiches, washed down with frosty bottles of Coke.

There was also a milk bar on the road outside the Pennock Plantation, which boasted the largest dairy in the county. There they'd drink thick root beer malts so cold they made their teeth ache.

Ryan and Hattie had little contact with their classmates. Hattie, because she was a Coast Guard outsider, just down from Georgia. Ryan, because he was a Navy brat plus a Yankee outsider down from the beating heart of Yankeedom—Philadelphia USA.

When Ryan mentioned this to Verne, he laughed and said he and Myrtle had been in Jove Beach for years and were still considered Yankee outsiders down from Ohio.

He counseled patience, saying that by and large the people of Jove Beach had their hearts in the right place and that they'd gradually come around when they saw how well they behaved.

Hattie snorted when he repeated Verne's admonition. "They'll never get over my momma," she said.

When Ryan pressed her on the subject, she just shook her head and he could see tears well up, so he left it alone. From the gossip overheard from Ada and his grandmother, he realized that their first meeting told the tale in full. Her mother was a hopeless alcoholic and not only did the whole town know it, but everybody on the base knew it as well.

Later, she confessed that her mother's weakness was endangering her father's career. After one incident, the base's CO had come to the house and Hattie overheard him warn her dad about her mother's behavior.

Her dad had tried to get professional help. Apparently there was a special hospital—an asylum—she could go to for "the cure." But her mother refused. Hattie was terrified that any day now her father would announce that he wanted a divorce. Which would leave Hattie in the sole care of a woman who could barely take care of herself.

Ryan told her about his own mother and the asylum she was in for crazy people. Like Hattie's mother she had never fit into the life of being a

Naval spouse and over the years it had gradually eaten away at her. No one ever really told Ryan what was going on, but he was pretty sure that pills were his mother's problem, rather than alcohol.

Alex also had little connection with classmates at the colored school. His thick glasses and bookishness made him an outcast and object of derision. He only hinted at this on particularly bad days, but usually kept his problems to himself.

He and Hattie were among the smartest people his age Ryan had ever met. Both were voracious readers. Alex said that decent books were hard to come by in the school library.

"But I have the power of the Professor," he said with a grin. "Every few weeks or so he sends word ahead and I meet him at the train station to get another supply. He has whole courses mapped out for me. Literature, history, math, science."

"Any chance I could borrow a few?" Ryan asked. "I'm worried about getting behind. My Aunt Cassie sent me some of my cousin's books, but it's not near enough."

"Why don't we get together one night a week and study?" Hattie suggested.

That plan was not only adopted, but expanded. Alex's poor eyesight sometimes made reading difficult. And so they got into the habit of reading aloud to him, soaking up the Professor's lesson plans by proxy.

Hattie's father, an engineer by training, was a science fiction buff. He generously allowed them access to his collection of science fiction magazines that went back for years.

Some weekends they'd pack lunches and pedal over to their favorite hangout—Hobe Hill. Alex said that at eighty six feet, it was the highest promontory in Florida.

"One of the books at the library said that most of the height comes from Indians dumping seashells all in one place," he said. "But that never made sense to me." He grinned, eyes alight with humor. "Makes you wonder about the guy who wrote the book, don't it? Why'd didn't he just dig down a bit and see for himself?"

On Hobe Hill, Ryan and Hattie would take turns reading the stories aloud, saving Alex's eyes. Then they'd have long discussions about space travel and life on other planets.

Alex was certain that man would set foot on the moon in their lifetime. Ryan doubted it. For Hattie, the jury was still out.

"Do you think there's life on other planets?" Alex asked his friends.

"Of course there is," Hattie said. "My dad's a trained navigator and he's always going about the billions of stars out there. And with all those stars there's gotta be billions more planets. It'd be stupid not to see that some of those planets would harbor life. Probably life a lot smarter than we are, too."

"Think they ever visited here?" Ryan asked. "And if they did, do you think some of them are still around? Hiding out?"

"I don't know why any intelligent critter would ever want to visit Earth," Alex said. "Look at us. Always at war. Right from the start. Guys come out of the caves and kill other guys. On and on, from throwing rocks to droppin' bombs. Now the whole blamed world is fightin'! And it's not like it's first time. We had a world war before." He snorted. "A war to end all wars, they called it. And look what that got us."

"It got us this war," Hattie said. "The one we're fighting now."

Ryan grinned. "What if it's the fault of the aliens?" he said. "Maybe they visited here. Thought the planet was pretty. And now they're just trying to get us to empty it out for them. Kill each other off so they don't have to."

Hattie and Alex just stared at him minute. Then:

"Wow!" Alex said. "You are really out there."

"It's the Yankee in him," Hattie said. "With Yankees it's always everybody else's fault."

They got together most days and every weekend not just to read, but to explore the wonders of the Seminole River. They suffered many a cut and scrape and a bruise in their various adventures but never complained. They last thing they needed, they agreed, was for some well-meaning adult to step in and set down safety rules.

However, once when Alex and Ryan were picking berries alone—Hattie was off on some errand for her mom—they came across some large paw prints that were bigger than any dog Ryan had ever seen. Rex sniffed at it, gave a bark, and charged ahead, disappearing into the berry bushes.

Alex said the footprints were likely those of a bear, making Ryan's heart jump into overtime.

"You stay back here," Alex said. "Let me scout ahead a bit and see which way it went. It'll be okay. Rex is up there. He's not scared of any old bear."

Well, Ryan wasn't Rex and he was definitely scared and not afraid to admit it. He was all for getting the heck out of there and heading over to the milkbar to meet Hattie and calm his nerves with a nice root beer float. But Alex shushed him, then crept ahead, holding his flimsy little palmetto speargun at the ready as if it were a deadly weapon.

After a minute or two, Ryan made bold and took a few steps forward. He put his own foot next to the bear's print to compare and swallowed hard. This was one big bear!

He bent closer to look, thinking to measure one of the prints with his hand.

And then all of a sudden he heard a sound and a big damned wet nose shoved its way up his butt with a loud SNUFF!

Ryan shrieked and jumped sky high. He whirled around, only to find Rex standing there. Head uplifted, eyes with a big, "what in the blazes is wrong with you," look.

Alex came rushing back to find his friend pale as a ghost and frozen in place.

"What happened?" he asked.

Ryan just pointed at Rex. He could barely speak. "He…he… he… Oh, God. I thought he was the bear."

Rex just thumped the ground with his tail, with a "who me" look on his doggy face.

Alex fell on the ground laughing and kicking his heels. Finally, Ryan recovered. He scooped up his palmetto spear and spun on his heels.

"Where you goin'," Alex asked.

"Out of here," Ryan said.

"But the bear's gone," Alex protested.

"Good for the bear," Ryan said.

And he stalked off, Alex bringing up the rear, occasionally breaking into peals of laughter.

* * * *

There were more worrisome things than bears. Word filtered down that Joe Collins was laying for Ryan and the others, just waiting to catch them alone.

He'd already avenged himself on Sally. Her pullcart had gone missing from its place at the docks where she normally kept it. After searching for several days she'd finally found the smashed up remains dumped in a canal.

She'd complained to Deputy Tindall, but there wasn't any proof that Collins was responsible. Of course, everybody knew it was Joe because he openly bragged about "gettin' even" with a certain "old frog eatin' bitch."

After that, they kept an eagle eye out for Joe and his cronies, taking care not to get caught out on an empty road. They spotted the truck several times and hastily got off the road and hid in the bushes.

Rex redeemed himself a few days after the bear incident. At Myrtle's insistence, workmen putting the finishing touches on the new kitchen set up an outside wash area so they could avoid leaving greasy handprints all over the house. It was also decreed that Ryan and Verne make use of it, instead of dirtying up the bathroom whenever they returned home.

One day, as he leaned over the basin ready to scoop up water and splash his face, Ryan found himself staring at what he at first thought was a discarded flower.

He pulled back a few inches and the object moved with him, rising up from the sink. It was a small snake with red and yellow bands running up and down its body. Fangs exposed. Tongue flickering in and out, no doubt tasting his sudden fear.

Later, he would say he felt like a character out of Kipling's story about the mongoose, Rikki Tikki Tavi. He was unable to move, hypnotized by those beady little eyes. It moved closer to him, rearing back as if getting ready to strike.

Suddenly, he heard a roar and Rex came charging in, knocking him aside. Ryan fell back, cutting his hands on the shell-strewn ground.

He looked up in time to see Rex growling, and shaking the snake back and forth like a whip, breaking its neck. Then he gave a toss of his head and the snake's body flew away, fifteen feet or more.

Rex rushed up to it, barking his head off, but making sure—Ryan noticed—of staying well away from the snake, which was still wriggling and snapping its jaws.

Suddenly Verne appeared, a shovel upraised. He slashed down with it, chopping the snake's head off.

He turned to Ryan, single eye bright with anger. "Didn't you see it, boy?"

"Nossir," Ryan said. "I was just washing up, like I always do."

"Well from now on, look before you wash up," Verne said. "In fact, wherever you go in Florida, mind what's about you."

He pointed at the beheaded reptile. "That's a coral snake," he said. "Deadliest snake in North America. It's like a cobra. Poison works on the nervous system. One bite and you will be lucky to find yourself alive ten minute later."

Ryan's blood ran cold. "Oh," he said in a small voice.

Verne scooped the snake up with the shovel and motioned for Ryan to follow. He buried it deep on the edge of the garden.

When he was done, he said, "I think it's best that we don't mention this little incident to your grandmother. Otherwise, she'll be on you every single day like white on rice."

"Yessir," Ryan said. "And sir... Thank you."

Verne's good humor returned. He chuckled and gave Rex a pat. "Don't thank me," he said. "Thank Rex. In case you didn't notice, he saved your life."

Then all the fear and adrenaline drained out of Ryan and he fell to his knees, shaking all over. Rex licked his face and Ryan threw his arms around him.

"Thank you, Rex," he said, voice trembling "Thank you."

A voice came from behind them. "What are you thanking the dog for?"

He whirled around. It was his grandmother. He forced a smile.

"Nothing, ma'am," Ryan said. "He's just been a really good dog all day and I was telling him so."

His grandmother sniffed. "That's all very well," she said. "But now you have dog hair all over you. Be sure to wash up before you come to dinner." And she turned to go back inside.

"Yes, ma'am," Ryan said, burying laughter when Verne gave him a wink.

Later, when he told Alex and Hattie about the incident, they fussed over Rex, patting him and calling him a good dog. From then on they made sure they took Rex with them in all their adventures.

Rex was a big help sniffing out things of value. When roaming the beaches he led them to many an interesting object that put money in their pockets.

Tourists bought odd looking driftwood and shells. And there were always drives on to collect metal for the war effort. Once Rex found a piece of a ship's boiler buried in the sand. It was probably off one of the merchant ships the German u-boats were stalking just off the coast.

After much digging—with Rex's help—they got it loose, but it was too big for them to move by themselves, so they convinced Sammy to drive out on the beach—letting air out of his tires for better purchase—and haul it to shore. They got a whole twelve dollars for that effort. They each saved a portion to put toward their goals and there was still enough left over for a trip to West Palm Beach to see a movie in a real theater, with real popcorn and soda and blessed air conditioning.

It was a long bus ride to West Palm, and the driver had to pull over several times to let military convoys pass.

The whole venture was nearly spoiled at the start. Apparently two white kids in the company of a colored kid was too much for the good people of West Palm. They drew stares wherever they went. And in the stores, employees followed them around to make sure they didn't steal anything.

They almost didn't get into the theater. The box office clerk served other people in line and ignored them. Ryan wanted to make a fuss, but Alex and Hattie knew it would only cause trouble. Someone would call the cops and who knew what would happen after that.

Finally, Ryan drew on his big city experience. He sent Hattie in first, then he followed. Once inside, while the newsreel was playing, Ryan slipped down the dark aisle to let Alex in the back door. He knew just how to finesse it. Popping the door open a crack and dragging Alex inside before anyone noticed the light streaming in.

Then, at Alex's suggestion, they sat together in the colored section and—except for the other Negro members of the audience—went unnoticed. The ushers never bothered to check that section.

The movie—the 49th Parallel—was a nail-biting thriller starring Leslie Howard and Lawrence Olivier. It was about German saboteurs stranded in Canada trying to make their way to the still neutral United States.

They were quiet on way home, worn out from their big city adventure and the thrilling movie. But then Alex started telling them about his great uncle, who had died only a few years ago.

"Everybody called him Old Daddy," Alex said. "And he was maybe the most famous colored person in Jove Beach. Shoot, if truth be told, he was maybe even more famous than a lot of the whites. One time he came on a whole passel of footballs on the beach."

"Footballs?" Ryan asked. "You mean like the kind you kick and throw?"

"No, no, back in Prohibition times footballs are what they used to call the bottles of liquor that got washed on shore," Alex said. "See, if the Coast Guard spotted a smuggling boat and gave chase, the smugglers would throw these big nets full of booze off the boat. Then, if the wind and tide were right they'd float ashore.

"Well, Old Daddy found one of those nets and he hid the bottles in an old shack over on Sullivan Island. And whenever there was a cookout, or beach party, he'd show up pullin' this little wagon full of booze. And he'd set it up so everybody could get a taste. Then he'd sit back and enjoy all the food folks were cookin' and pretty soon they'd get all friendly and make sure Old Daddy got the best of everything.

"And he'd sit around eatin' and drinkin' and folks would start beggin' him to tell his stories about life on the plantation where he had been a slave. They were stories from old Africa, mixed up with stories from America. The stories had lions in 'em and monkeys and foxes and elephants and big old snakes that could eat a body whole. Like I said, they were all mixed up from both sides of the ocean.

"Then, when he got nice and tipsy they'd coax him into singin' the old slave songs. He played this mouth harp, and beat on his knees to keep time. And he'd sing songs like *Old Mister Coon*, *Graveyard Rabbit*, and *Possum Up the Gum Stump*."

"You remember any of the songs?" Hattie asked.

Alex sighed and shook his head. "Wish I had written them down," he said. "But I was just a kid and I guess I figured Old Daddy would always be around for the next crab boil."

He fiddled with the leather tie on his glasses, then said, "He didn't know how old he was. When we asked he said it was probably more than a hundred."

Alex chuckled. "Funny thing is, when he did go it wasn't from old age. He fished and hunted right up to the end. And then one day he turned up missing, and Pop went lookin' and found him tangled up with some vines along the river bank. Guess his canoe got stuck and he tried to kick it free and the vines pulled him under and he drowned."

"That's terrible," Ryan said.

"Not when you think on it," Alex said. "Old Daddy said he always figured the reason he lived so long is 'cause God forgot about him and thought maybe he was still back in Africa. It made him sad because he said everybody he knew when he was young was gone. And if this kept up he'd never find his way home. So, I always liked to think that God finally found him and took him home to Africa."

A long thoughtful silence followed them all the way back to Jove Beach.

TWENTY-THREE
Morse Code Disaster

"So, you're sayin' that you got a secret way that me and you and Hattie can talk without usin' the telephone?"

"Well, it's not a secret, really," Ryan said. "Anybody can do it."

It was a hot, lazy afternoon and the Musketeers were minus Hattie, who was stuck at home taking care of her mother. The pair were in Ryan's room, where he was showing off his latest telegraphy experiment.

In this instance, he was convinced he'd found a way for the three friends to communicate without using the phone—which was hardly private. One careless word would be immediately picked up by Mrs. Robinson and gabbed about all over town before the day ended. For example, they knew Hattie's mom was suffering from effects of a moonshine bender, but the kids had to use their own special Code to get it across, and even that was suspect.

Alex looked skeptical. He said, "I don't know. Sounds kind of over the top to me."

"No, really," Ryan said. "I finally have it figured it out."

Alex frowned. "Are you sure you're not talkin' about one those fake little kid walkie- talkie dealies with a cord tied between two oatmeal boxes?"

"Come on," Ryan said, outraged. "You know me better than that. This is the real deal. Almost professional."

"Okay, let me get this straight," Alex persisted. "That's me at my house, Hattie at hers and you here, right?" Alex persisted. "No wires, right?"

"Right," Ryan said. "No wires that go further than from here…" he patted his Morse Code key set… "and here…," he laid hands on the small rectangular object, with wires leading off it, that was his latest pride and joy. "A genuine transmitter, good enough to take on Western Union. Well, maybe not that good, but close."

"This I have to see," Alex said.

Ryan popped open the box, exposing a thick copper coil it had taken him hours to wrap and a few other electronic parts. "I made this from a Model-T spark arrester I got off your dad. He said he had plenty of spares."

Alex nodded. "He's got boxes of parts he's scrounged for ages," Alex said. "He loves that truck. Swears he'll keep it to the day he dies."

"Your dad's smart," Ryan said, attaching wires with alligator clips. "Model-T's go forever. And you can do anything with them. Drive them, or run a little saw mill. I even heard of some little newspapers that use Model-T engines to run their presses."

Finishing, he rubbed his hands together. "Okay, here we go," he said, tapping on his key set.

Alex jumped as the little speaker on Ryan's desk made a short, very loud, static bark.

"What was that?" he said.

"That was a dot in Morse Code talk," Ryan said. "Now, here's a dash."

He tapped the key, but held it a little longer. Again, there was a bark of static from the speaker, but it was a longer, stretched out sound.

"What's goin' on?" Alex said. "How're you doin' that?"

Ryan indicated the two wires in the box. They were about an inch apart.

"Watch," he said, tapping the key.

A small spark jumped between the wires, and at the same time there was a static blast on the speaker.

"It's a spark transmitter," Ryan said. "They've been around for ages. A lot of radio amateurs swear by them. They work even when there's a lot of interference, like from a storm. And they're easy to make. I got the instructions from an encyclopedia at the library in Philly, but never had time to make one. Then I read that guys were adapting Model-T coils to do the job. Add more copper wire and you get more power. And you can also skip out mounting parts and soldering things."

"I get it," Alex said. "We put one in my house, one Hattie's and then all we have to do is learn Morse Code, which looks pretty darned easy from watchin' you."

"That's my plan," Ryan said, pleased with himself.

"Let me try," Alex said, eagerly nudging him out of his chair and sliding into it.

"Go ahead," Ryan said. "Let's start with something easy. Like S.O.S."

"Yeah, like we've got a big old emergency fire or something," Alex said, enthused.

"It goes like this," Ryan said, reaching around his friend to tap the key. "Three dots."

He demonstrated, tapping the key three times, quickly, producing three short, sharp blasts on the speaker.

"Now the dashes."

Another demonstration, holding the key just a little longer and getting three drawn out barks of static.

"Then three dots to make the final 'S'," Ryan said, giving the key three quick taps.

"You try it," Ryan said.

Alex tapped the key three times. Got the static dots. Then three more times, copying Ryan's movements and getting three static dashes.

"S.O.S." Alex chortled. "This is fun!"

He kept at it, **S.O.S. S.O.S. S.O.S.** Over and over again.

"Great," Ryan said. "Pretty soon you'll be diddy-dahing with the best of them."

He fished some paper and a pencil from the drawer. "Let's try something new," he said and started composing a short message of dots and dashes.

Alex looked over his shoulder. "What's it say?" he asked.

"In Morse Code talk it says, Joe Collins is an idiot," Ryan said.

Alex laughed. "Go ahead, send it," he chortled.

Ryan did and static dots and dashes rattled the little speaker.

"My turn," Alex said, pushing in to get at the key.

And then he started joyfully tapping away, sing-songing along with the static dots and dashes: "Joe Collins is an idiot. Joe Collins is an idiot. Joe Collins is an idiot."

After a few minutes he said, "How about if we add stupid? Like, 'Joe Collins is a stupid idiot.'"

"Love it," Ryan laughed, making a new Coded message and shoving it over to Alex.

They played like that with different silly messages for twenty minutes or so—sending boyish nonsense out into the ethers. Then there came a knock at Ryan's door.

"Ryan?" Verne called out. "Hattie's on the phone. She says its urgent."

Ryan hurried out to the phone and picked it up.

"Hattie! What's going on?"

She got right to the point: "Ryan, have you been messing with that transmitter do-hicky you were talking about?"

"Yeah, I got it set up and Alex and I were just trying it out and it works great. Why, is something wrong?"

Hattie snorted. "I'll say something's wrong. Apparently you're blowing out local radio reception, plus Mrs. Wilkinson called the base to complain that she's getting blasted out. They've both been blaming it on the Coast Guard."

Ryan stomach's fell from a great height and bounced on the floor. "Oh, boy! That's awful," he said. "I'll unplug it right now!"

"Too late," Hattie said. "My dad and some security guy are on their way over with one of those signal detection trucks."

Ryan was scared. He could imagine his grandmother's reaction to the disaster.

"You mean they tracked it that fast?"

"Well, soon as my dad saw it was coming from your neighborhood he called me asked about your telegraphy experiments. You've mentioned them to him before. And so I had to tell him about your experiment. I didn't have any choice, Ryan."

"No, no," Ryan said. "It's my own stupid fault. I should have realized…"

Outside he heard a heavy vehicle crunching across the seashells and he suddenly found it difficult to breathe.

"I think they're here, Hattie," he said, throat thickening. "I'd better go."

He hung up and went to the door.

Through the screen he saw the tall, ungainly signal detection truck, with a large revolving antennae mounted on the roof.

Verne and Myrtle were already on the porch, saying hello to Mr. Peters. A young man in a Coast Guard uniform remained in the truck.

Ryan went out to join them. He jumped in before a word could be spoken, figuring he'd better spill it fast.

"I'm so sorry, Mr. Peters," he said. "I just got off the phone with Hattie and she told me all the trouble I was causing."

Verne and his grandmother looked at him, puzzled and more than a little concerned.

Ryan turned to them. "Verne. Grandmother. I did something really stupid," he said. "You know that little experiment I was doing with my Morse Code set?"

They both nodded. "Is that what all that static sound was about?" Verne asked.

"Yessir. And I guess it's blasting out all over Jove Beach."

"More like all over the county," Mr. Peters said.

He looked stern, but to Ryan's relief, not really mad. "Ryan," he said, "I guess Hattie told you we got complaints from Western Union and the local radio station."

"Yessir, she did," Ryan said. "I had no idea that was going to happen. I thought stations were shielded and stuff."

"Not against something so out of the ordinary as a hopped up spark transmitter," Mr. Peters said. "That's like putting a gigantic megaphone on a signal that blasts across all the channels on the airways."

"I hope it didn't affect Coast Guard communications," Verne said.

Mr. Peters shook his head. "No, or Ryan would be in a lot more trouble than he is right now. We have special shielding. You'd need a coil the size of an ice box to overpower us."

Ryan hung his head. "I'll disconnect it right this minute," he said, "and I'll never try that stupid stunt again."

"Is there going to be some sort of fine, Steven?" Verne asked.

"No, but if it were malicious, or Ryan did it again, there would not only be a fine, but a possible jail sentence," Mr. Peters said.

Ryan gulped. "Jail?"

"Not this time, Ryan," Mr. Peters said. "But you'd best give us your solemn promise not to do something like that again."

Ryan crossed his heart. "I swear," he said.

Finally, Mr. Peters smiled and patted his shoulder. "You're a nice young man, Ryan," he said. "Bridget and I are pleased that Hattie has found such a good friend in you. But next time you want to experiment, come and ask me."

He indicated the young man in the truck. "Adams, there, is an electronics whiz kid. I know he'd be glad to share his knowledge. And maybe even some spare parts. But ask first, okay?"

"Yessir," Ryan said.

His grandmother broke in. "Would you and the young man care for a cup of coffee and a little piece of pie that I just got out of the oven?"

Mr. Peters sniffed the air, appreciatively. "Mm. Smells like apple. My favorite." Then he shook his head. "Sadly, we have to get back to work and I have to call around and tell everybody the problem has been resolved."

Ryan's gut gave another wrench. "Mrs. Wilkinson is going to hate me," he said. "And she's always been so nice and helpful."

"Don't worry about Mrs. Wilkinson," Mr. Peters said. "I'll let you tell her, okay? I'm sure she'll forgive you if you personally apologize."

Ryan nodded vigorously. "I'll call first thing," he said.

Mr. Peters said goodbye, hopped in the truck and drove away.

Ryan turned to Verne and his grandmother. "I'm sorry," he said. "I didn't mean to make so much trouble."

"We know you didn't," Verne said. He looked at Myrtle.

To Ryan's surprise she just nodded agreement. He even thought he caught the hint of a smile.

Verne said, "Let's put the incident aside and forget about it."

Ryan gave sigh of relief. His grandmother opened the screen door.

"Why don't you call Alex," she said, "and I'll cut you both two nice big fat pieces of apple pie."

"Fantastic," Ryan said.

He went inside and started for his room, then veered over to the phone.

"But I'd better call Mrs. Wilkinson first," he said.

TWENTY-FOUR
The Celestial Queen

It was one of those unseasonable Florida storms that struck without warning. Ryan, Hattie and Alex were exploring the Seminole on their paddle boats when it hit.

The first sign of trouble—although they didn't recognize it right off—was a sudden silence that descended on the river. A little later, for no apparent reason, turtles basking on a log took sudden panic and plunged off a log into the water.

A small gator that had been following them, hoping for fish scraps, gave a flick of its tail and vanished into the depths. Flocks of birds took to the air, swirling and screeching and complaining about the Lord knows what, then charged off in a long stream and disappeared into the tropical foliage.

Peering into the river's depths, Ryan spotted an army of crabs marching hurriedly along—frantically waving their claws as if something was chasing them.

Ryan had a bad feeling and wished he had Rex along to sniff out danger. Rex had a badly infected tick bite and had to stay home to be treated by Sammy.

Dark clouds boiled in, obscuring the sun and turning day into a spooky twilight and then a brisk wind picked up, coming at them face first and making progress difficult.

Lightning strikes came next, blistering the surrounding countryside. One bolt hit just ahead of them, striking an immense dying magnolia that looked like it had been struck several times before.

Flames erupted from the tree, only to be extinguished when the skies opened up and rain torrented down. The rain was so heavy it was hard to see. Rolling thunder battered their eardrums and Ryan had the sensation of being completely isolated, all his senses overwhelmed by the storm.

The wind and surging water drove them onward, and it was all they could do to stay on their feet, poling when they could reach bottom, or futilely paddling with the stripped bamboo sticks that were their only means of locomotion.

Alex shouted, "We have to get off the river!"

Ryan peered through the rain and saw him poling frantically toward an opening in the dense foliage. Hattie was only a few feet behind him.

"Hurry!" Alex cried.

And Ryan did his best to hurry. Pushing against the muddy bottom as hard as he could. His pole boat almost swept past the opening, but Hattie grabbed the prow and hung on. Moments later, Alex joined in and they helped Ryan muscle the little boat into the shelter of tall swamp grass.

They huddled together for what seemed like eternity, lying flat on their boards, their poles jammed into the mud so they wouldn't be driven back into the current by wind and surging water.

And then—as suddenly as it began—the storm passed. The clouds vanished. The sun shone brightly overhead in sparkling blue skies and the wildlife started to appear, beginning with the birds, then the turtles, then the fish. All hungrily chasing the insects and worms that had been churned up by the storm.

Deep in the reeds, Ryan heard critters scurrying about on the hunt. Mother ducks emerged, paddling about with their fuzzy little chicks lined up behind them, frantically trying to keep up.

An eagle soared overhead, then dived into the water to come up with a flopping fish, declaring the storm officially over.

Ryan looked at his companions. He had rarely seen such a sorry sight. Sitting up on their boats, feet dangling on either side, clothes bedraggled, hair stuck with briars and swamp grass and steam rising off them in clouds.

Hattie plucked at briar in her hair. "I feel like a drowned cat," she said.

Alex grinned. "Pretty much how you look, too," he said.

Hattie snorted. "Thanks for being so encouraging," she said.

"My pleasure, ma'am," Alex said, then ducked as Hattie lashed out at him with her gill net.

"I give, I give," Alex laughed.

And then all three of them were laughing, more in relief than anything else.

"We'd best get goin'," Alex said, standing up on his boat.

The other two followed and they pushed out of the reeds. But they hadn't gone more than a few feet when Alex stopped. He turned slowly around on his boat, peering up and down the river. He looked worried.

"What's wrong?" Ryan asked.

"I don't know where we are," he said.

"That's ridiculous," Hattie said. "Your brain is water soaked. Here. Let me take the lead."

She pushed on ahead of him, moving smoothly across the water. But she'd only gone a few a few feet when she stopped. Now it was Hattie's turn to look bewildered, as she futilely searched for familiar landmarks.

"I can't believe this," Hattie said. "I've never been lost in my life. My daddy's gonna kill me."

"That's okay," Ryan said with a grin. He found the whole situation amusing. "Then it's problem solved because he'll have to find you first."

Hattie glowered at him. "This isn't funny, Ryan Karr," she said.

Ryan gulped, suddenly realizing the seriousness of their plight. Ryan had never been lost before and it suddenly occurred to him that getting lost in the Seminole River wilderness could be fatal. When people finally did get the idea something was wrong, how would they find them? No one even knew which direction they'd taken. It had been a day of unplanned exploration, with no particular goal in mind and the storm had struck.

Suddenly he blurted, "Charlie Silver Moon!"

Alex stared at him. "What about Charlie Silver Moon?"

"He'll find us," Ryan said. "He's an Indian, isn't he?"

Alex and Hattie just glared at him. Ryan felt a blush coming on.

"That was stupid, wasn't it?" he mumbled.

"I expect so," Hattie said dryly.

Just then they heard a familiar voice. "You younguns're alright, ain't ya?"

It was Gig Light Sally.

Relief washed over them as she came poling into view.

"Boy, are we glad to see you, Sally," Ryan said. "We got ourselves lost."

Sally chuckled. "Thought ya might be," she said.

She gave her pole two long, slow pushes and she shot up to them, coming to a full stop with little effort.

"You ain't that far from home," she said. "At least Hattie, ain't." She pointed to the right. "Coast Guard base is yonder. About a quarter mile, there's a spot you can pull up your paddle boats and walk to the base."

"Great," Alex said, rising up and getting ready to set. "We can circle around from there and find our bikes and stuff."

"I wouldn't advise it," Sally said.

"Why not?" Alex said.

"Rattlesnakes," Sally said. "There's a whole passel of 'em thereabouts."

"The gopher holes!" Alex said, excited. Then to his friends: "The place I was tellin' ya'll about."

Sally chuckled. "You heard about that dollar a foot deal, did ya?"

Alex suddenly looked guarded. He took off his glasses and wiped them on tail end of his shirt. "Why? Were you thinkin' about given it a try on?"

"No thankee," Sally said. "And my best advice to y'all is to find some other way to make money. Rattlers can get downright cranky."

"We have a system," Alex insisted.

"Just the same," Sally said. "Old Mr. Rattler is best left alone."

Hattie broke in. "Can you show us a nice safe way to get home, Sally?"

"Sure thing, honey," Sally said. "And while I'm at I can show you a little secret." She started poling smoothly away. "You just get in line behind old Sally like little ducklings and come on along."

They followed her through a maze of sawgrass, slipping from one watery aisle to the next until they came to a long, narrow stretch, with enormous banyans growing on either bank that were so tall they blocked out most of the sunlight.

This was an area of the river unlike any Ryan had seen before. The sawgrass gave way to tall, delicate ferns with broad fragrant leaves. And it was almost completely silent. The only sound was that of their poling, water dripping from Spanish Moss, and the occasional splash of a turtle popping off a log when they came too near. Not for the first time since he came to Florida, Ryan had the sudden expectation of a dinosaur rising up from the shallows, its tiny head perched on a neck twenty feet long.

When they came to one sharp bend, Sally stopped and turned to them.

"I'm gonna let you in on a little secret," she said. "But you gotta promise ya won't tell nobody."

The three promised. Sally looked each in the eye, then, after a long moment, she decided to trust them.

"Come on, then," she said. And pushed off with her pole.

Around the bend they went and when they came to the other side they gasped in astonishment.

Up ahead was the wreck of an enormous paddle wheeler. A veritable ghost ship from another century, the wreck looked like a giant had taken a bite out of its side. The gaping hole exposed the rusted out ship's boiler and the brickwork that had once held it in place.

A hand painted sign on the side read:

CELESTIAL QUEEN

"There she be, kids," Sally said, waving an impresario's hand: *"The Celestial Queen!"*

To Ryan the ship looked like some fantastic ghostly wreck straight from the pages of Amazing Stories.

"Wow!" he said.

"Everybody dig in," Sally said. "The river gets kind of rough here after a storm."

And so they dug in, maneuvering their boats through the swift current until they reached the ship. Sally caught a dangling rope, pulled in close, then threaded a line from her boat to a protruding bolt, pulling them up snug. The three friends followed suit.

"Be it ever so humble," Sally said, "there ain't nowhere's like home and all that sentimental beeswax."

"You mean you live here?" Ryan asked.

"Sure do," Sally said. "I've fixed up some parts of the ship over the years so they're fairly tolerable. Got a nice kitchen and eatin' place. Turned the captain's cabin into my bedroom so I'm squattin' in tall cotton."

With practiced ease, she tossed a gunnysack up and over a busted out railing. Gathered up her pole and a bucket of fish and swarmed up the side with an agility of someone half her age.

"Come have a looksee," she said. "I'll rustle up some tea and cookies and y'all can clean yourselves up so you don't give your folks conniptions."

"That wouldn't be all they had," Hattie said. And she shinnied up the side, Alex and Ryan close behind her.

They were greeted by the yowls of half-a-dozen cats who descended on Sally the moment she stepped aboard.

She shooed them off. "Hold onto yer furry britches," she admonished them. "Old Sally didn't forget her little darlin's."

With that, she yanked a big catfish out of the gunnysack, placed it on a chopping block mounted on the side, yanked up an old cleaver stuck in the block and gave the fish several expert whacks.

Before she continued, she pointed to a big hand-lettered sign, that read:

DANGER!
NO TRESPASSING!

"Don't y'all go wanderin' off without me," she said. "I got little surprises stashed all over to warn off boarders. Some'r right hurtful, too. Fella could lose a finger, or a toe, or mebbe even a hand, if he warn't careful."

Then she started butchering out the fish, pushing the cats out of the way as she wielded the cleaver, hacking off hunks of flesh.

Sally made smooching noises as she dumped the catfish offal over the side where an enormous gator was waiting like it was its regular dining spot.

"Kids, meet my pal, Geraldine," she said. "Geraldine, meet the kids. And don't you go chompin' on them if'n they fall off, or you'll have ole Gig Light Sally to contend with, ya hear?"

Nervous laughter from the three.

"Hope she minds you," Alex said.

"Wouldn't count on it," Sally said with a grin. "Ole Geraldine can get mighty hungry."

"Maybe sneak a clock into those fish guts next time," Alex said. "Then she'd go 'Tick Tock' like the crocodile in Peter Pan."

Everybody laughed, except for Sally. "I got that book in my cabin," she said wistfully. "Used to read it to my kids."

The three looked at each other. They'd never thought of Sally in terms of someone with a family, much less kids who enjoyed having stories read to them.

Meanwhile, Sally was divvying up the rest of the fish among tin pie pans lined up on the side.

The yowling cats went at their meal ferociously, Sally calling them each by name and gingerly patting them—always ready to snatch back a hand if a cat suddenly struck out with needle sharp claws.

When she was done, she washed her hands in a tub sitting next to the chopping block, along with a bar of soap.

"You go on ahead and wash up," she told Ryan and the others. "I'll fetch y'all some towels."

Hattie was delighted to see a little mirror mounted above the washtub, using her fingers to comb out her hair after giving her face and arms and bare legs a good scrub. Ryan and Alex followed suit.

But as Alex leaned down to splash his face, the wreck trembled slightly and he grabbed the basin for support.

"Never mind that," Sally said. "The *Queen* can get cranky after a storm. Shifts in the channel, then by and by she settles down."

She shook her head. "One of these days, though…" she let it trail off. Then, brightening—"Never you mind that. Old Sally has it all under control. Come on and I'll show y'all around."

They followed her down a rickety staircase to a lower deck where the rumble of the river rushing by was much louder. Something heavy thudded against her, and once again the old ship shuddered.

A little frightened, the three friends stood perfectly still until Sally got them moving again.

"Happens all the time," she said. "But the river'll be down in a hour or so and she'll be steady as a rock."

Continuing the tour, they came upon more warning signs where Sally would pause and fiddle with a booby trap before they could go on.

At one passageway, she warned them to back off then deliberately triggered a mechanism. There was a loud Crash! and a heavy beam with a sharp blade attached dropped down and slammed into the floor.

"See what I mean?" Sally said, as she tugged the blade loose from the deck.

She showed them how she'd used a machete blade to made the contraption.

"Works like one of them guillotine-thing-a-ma-bobs the Froggies use," she said.

"Viva la Froggies," Ryan said to nervous laughter.

"That's the last of the booby traps," Sally said. "It's all clear from here on out. Didn't want to wake up in the middle of the night to take a whiz and get my tits chopped off."

She glanced down at her flat chest. "Not that I got much to chop," she added.

Hattie giggled—as much from the boys' embarrassed reaction as anything else.

"But, mind you," Sally said, "I always leave that one set in case somebody tries to sneak up on me while I'm asleep."

"Who'd want to do that, Sally?" Ryan asked. "It's not like you're rich, or anything."

"There's a lot of crazy folks wanderin' around the Seminole River," Sally said. Then, laughing, she added, "Y'all are lookin' at one, right?"

"Oh, Sally," Hattie said, smiling, and patting her. "You're not crazy. Just… well…interesting."

"In Yankee talk, she's only eccentric," Ryan said.

"And you should know, right?" Alex said. "You're the Yankiest talkin' son of a gun I ever met."

More laughter. Then Sally said, "Come on and I'll give y'all the cook's tour."

Sally took them around the areas she'd fixed up and the more they saw the more impressed they became. Over the years, she'd hauled in driftwood to rebuild the kitchen and various cabins, including the captain's stateroom, where she'd even gone to the trouble of varnishing the bulkheads and deck.

Library shelves lined one wall, which she'd filled with castoff books, periodicals, and rolled up navigational charts. Maps of the Seminole River and torn out magazine pictures of local flora and fauna decorated the stateroom.

A wood-framed bed was bolted to one bulkhead. The bed was neatly made up with a sleeping bag covering a mattress Sally said was stuffed with Spanish moss.

A silver St. Christopher's medal dangled from a peg just above the bed. Sally was clearly proud of the necklace and she lifted it off and passed it around for them to admire. The medallion was finely wrought, showing the saint carrying the Christ child.

"I ain't superstitious," Sally said. "But that there's my lucky piece. Had it with since… well… forever. Someone special give it to me."

"If it's so all fired lucky," Alex asked, "how come you're not wearin' it?"

Sally laughed. "'Cause it almost kilt me," she said. "Got hung up in the bushes once and it near strangled me to death."

She took the necklace back. Lifted it up reverently, gave it a kiss, then returned it to the peg. She turned her head a moment, swiping away a drop of moisture that had gathered at the tip of her beak-like nose. Then turned back.

"We made a deal, me and old St. Chris," she said. "I just wear him at night when I'm in bed. Then in the morning I hang him up in the place of honor and ask his blessin' for the day ahead."

She shrugged. "'Pears to've worked so far," she said.

Ryan looked around the marvelously restored stateroom. "I'm surprised nobody hauled all this away for salvage years ago," he said.

"Guess they would, if they knew she was here," Sally said. "This channel used to be a reg'lar route for paddle wheelers haulin' folks down to places like Jove Beach. Whole families'd come, along with their belongin's and livestock.

"But then, the story goes, old man Flagler was buildin' his Celestial Railroad and he thought the paddle wheelers were too much competition. So, he bought out the competition and scuttled a couple of 'em to close off the channel. 'Fore ya knew it, Momma Nature steps in and turns ever'thin' back to jungle again."

Sally shrugged. "That's what I hear tell, anyways. Don't know if it's true. Don't care, neither. Makes a nice home for Sally in her old age and I don't owe nothin' to nobody to keep a roof over my head."

She had an impressive galley, with pots and pans hanging from the walls, a marble countertop she said she'd cut to fit with a hacksaw, and an oven and a range fueled by propane.

They snacked on a fragrant tea, which she served with honey and thick slabs of hot buttered cornbread.

After they'd eaten their fill, Sally got out her corncob pipe, tamped in some tobacco and fired it up, making thick smoke rings.

When she looked good and relaxed, Ryan got up the nerve to pry. "How long have you lived here, Sally?" he asked.

She puffed on the pipe, reflecting, then said, "I'm not all that sure. Twenty years. Maybe more." She waved the pipe at him. "I was a right mess when I come down to these parts.'

Glancing at Hattie, she added, "Ain't ashamed to admit old Sally had a wicked problem with the hooch back then."

More puffing, then: "Life didn't seem worth livin' in those bad old days. Never guess it lookin' at me now, but I had me an actual family onc't upon a time. Had me a good man. Some kids. Beautiful, they was. And then one of them went and had a kid of her own, so I had me a grandchile too.

"Had us a nice little bait shop up by Crescent Beach. Couple'a boats to rent out. Caught fish, and frogs and stuff to sell to the local restaurants and markets. We weren't rich, but we weren't poor neither. Sure, we had our problems. But we was right happy, ya know?" She nodded firmly. "Right happy."

A long silence followed as Sally reflected on those long ago memories. Finally, Hattie got up nerve enough to ask, "What happened, Sally."

Sally's face darkened. "Spanish flu." She practically spit out the words. Then, softer: "Took little Billy first. My grandchile. He was only four months old. Still on his momma's tit, he was."

She looked up at them, her face full of pain. "Preacher fellas say the Lord moves in mysterious ways. Well, I'd sure like to know what he was plannin' when he snatched out the life of a chile only four months old. Then he took the rest. Kids first. Little Honor and Justin. Then my daughter, Rita Mae. Then my boy, Jimmy. Smart as a whip, my Jimmy was. And he could sing. Lordy, he could sing. Voice so sweet make the angels weep."

Sally's pipe went out. She fell silent, fussing with it. Sniffling and swiping at her eyes. Although Ryan never saw her leak a tear.

She started to speak again, but her voice was thick and hoarse. She coughed, clearing it.

"Then, it uh... took my darlin' Richard," she said. "A handsome man, he was. Big and strong. That's prob'ly why it took so long for Ole Momma Flu to drag him down. And after she catched him, he just got weaker and weaker... 'til one day he weren't here no more."

"I'm so sorry, Sally," Ryan rasped. He was close to tears. He looked at the others. Hattie was openly weeping, while Alex concentrated on cleaning his glasses.

"Well, I felt so danged sorry for myself it nearly kilt me," Sally said. "I took to the hooch somethin' fierce. Did some shameful things. Lost my home. My little business. Took to the rails, hoppin' trains, lettin' 'em take me wherever they pleased.

"Then one mornin' I woke up in a boxcar and I looked out the open doors and I spied the Seminole River. Sun was shinin'. Fish was jumpin'. Birds was singin'. Everythin' was all cheerful like."

She puffed on her pipe. A little smile on her face as she reflected.

And she said, "I swear I hadn't seen nuthin' so purty since they ran me out of Crescent Beach."

Ryan nodded, remembering his first view of the Seminole River through the windows of his comfortable berth aboard the Florida Special.

"Well sir, the train came to a bend and had to slow down so quicker'n frog after a skeeter, I grabbed my truck and jumped. Found a little clearin' to sleep that night where the skeeters weren't too bad. Caught some dinner and set up camp.

"Next day I gave the place the looksee and liked it so much I stayed on and made a new life for myself."

She grinned. "May not look like it to some," she said, "but it's a right nice life for Old Sally. And I'm happy as I'll ever be in my own skin."

And with that, she took a big pull on her pipe and blew a series of fabulous smoke rings that drifted about the galley like victory signs.

A little later, after they insisted on helping her clean up, she showed them the way home.

They climbed the embankment, then turned and watched for a long while as she poled out of sight.

"What an amazing woman," Ryan said after she vanished like a raggedy wraith as she poled into a mist.

"Can you imagine losing your whole family like that?" Hattie asked. "It'd drive me crazy too."

"I read about the Spanish flu in one of the Professor's books," Alex said. "Killed hundreds of thousands of folks here in America. Twenty, thirty million all over the world. Book said it spread out of the wars in China, or maybe even here in America at training camps for soldiers who were going to fight in Europe. And then spread all over the planet because of World War One."

"You always think people just die from guns and bombs and stuff during wartime," Hattie said.

"Not when the whole world is fightin'," Alex said.

"Just like now," Hattie said.

"Yeah," Ryan said. "Just like now."

TWENTY-FIVE

The Wrestler

Ryan didn't know if the bug that swept through Jove Beach the following week was related to the Spanish Flu, or if it had anything to do with a world at war. Whatever the affliction, it put Hattie and Alex out of action with the heaves and the runs, leaving Ryan by his lonesome the remainder of the week.

Friday after school, where attendance was so sparse the classrooms echoed, he was poking around the island feeling sorry for himself when Verne hunted him down.

"What do you have planned for tonight, Ryan?" he asked.

Ryan shrugged. "Nothing much," he mumbled.

Verne peered at him, amused. "Nothin' much?" he said, "Or, nothin' at all?"

Before he mumbled a less than spirited reply he caught the look of mischief on Verne's face.

Perking up, he grinned. "Nothing at all—Sir!" he said.

"I've got posse duty tonight," Verne said. "Since you don't have school tomorrow, I was wondering if you'd like to tag along."

"Would I?" Ryan said, almost shouting.

"Would that be a yes?"

"Yessir, that's a yes!" Ryan said.

Later, just before dusk, Josh led out Big Red and Sheba. They were saddled and ready to go.

Sheba's Tennessee breeding made her almost as tall as Big Red and Ryan was glad that Josh gave him a leg up, saving him the embarrassment of climbing a rail to get high enough to climb on.

Ryan was thrilled when he saw Josh pass up the shotgun, which Verne laid across his saddle. Then he handed him a .45 automatic, which Verne shoved into the wide belt that encompassed his ample waist. He was wearing dungarees stuffed into gator hide boots and his favorite Panama hat.

Verne caught Ryan big-eyeing the guns and smiled. "Remind me in a couple of weeks or so to give you shootin' lessons," he said. "It's about time you learned."

"Yessir," Ryan said, with undisguised enthusiasm.

"You won't forget, will you?" Verne teased.

"Nossir," Ryan said, dead serious. "I won't forget."

In his world, learning to shoot was a major step in a boy's advancement to manhood. Next up, a driver's license, then 18, then the sky's the limit.

Verne chuckled. Adjusted his eyepatch, settled his hat. He clucked his tongue and Big Red set off in that smooth, steady pace his breed was known for, with Ryan and Sheba close behind.

A gentle sea breeze was rustling the palm trees when Verne and Ryan rode out on the beach to join the other members of the posse. A cloud passed overhead as they emerged and at first all Ryan could see was the shadowy figures of the men and their mounts and the glow of their cigarettes.

"You gentlemen ready?" Verne asked.

"Dadburn right, we're ready," said a familiar voice. "Ain't hardly had the dadburn time to eat my dadburn supper."

The cloud scudded onward, revealing Jove Beach's station master, George Donaldson. He was riding a bay mare whose best days were long past. He carried an old, but well cared for service revolver jammed into a well-oiled holster.

Verne smiled and patted his saddlebags. "No worries there, George," he said. "Myrtle and Ada whipped up enough grub to feed an army."

Another man came forward, riding a nervous, elegant animal that even Ryan, who had no experience with horseflesh, could see was a thoroughbred.

He wore an ostentatiously expensive riding outfit, with a little peaked-brim hat that looked like a helmet. He sported a gleaming pearl-handled pistol in a tooled leather shoulder holster, that he kept fingering as if it were a good luck charm.

The man gave Mr. Donaldson's bay a scornful look. "Jesus Christ, George, when are you goin' to get a decent mount?" he said. "Never keep up with the rest of us.

"Dadburn it! Watch what yer sayin' about my Mary Belle. She might be gettin' on in dadburn years, but she can hold her dadburn own."

"Yeah, well if she can't," the man said, "I intend to complain to the sheriff that you're holdin' up the rest of us."

"George never slowed us down before, Jim," Verne said. "Don't expect he'll start in tonight."

The man snorted. "Whatever you say, Verne," the man said. "The sheriff put you in charge. I guess he had his reasons."

From his attitude, Ryan could see that the man deeply resented Verne's role as leader of the patrol and was having a hard time not showing his disdain. He also kept flashing envious looks at Big Red and Sheba.

He gave the man a closer look and his heart gave a bump when he recognized the sneering look. It matched that of his nemesis, Joe Collins. He had no doubt that the man he was looking at was none other than Joe's father, Jim Collins. Sole owner and operator of Jove Beach's Ford Dealership.

"So, can we get goin' then?" Mr. Collins pressed. "We've got twenty miles to cover tonight and I have to be at the lot early tomorrow. Got a shipment of new cars comin' in. Might be the last until the war's over."

"Since you're riding that magnificent animal, Jim," Verne said, "why don't you take the lead. Show the rest of us how it's done."

Mr. Collins snorted and gave his horse a hard kick with spurred heels. The poor animal was startled and reared back.

"Goddamn it!" Mr. Collins shouted, sawing on his reins. "Behave your fool self!"

Another spur and the horse set off in an awkward trot that sent its rider bouncing in the saddle like a jack in the box.

Mr. Donaldson snickered and from the way Mr. Collins hunched his shoulders Ryan could see that he'd heard.

"Ain't he a dadburn piece of dadburned work," he said, drawing laughter from the other men.

Obviously, the Jove Beach station master was the social equal of the local Ford dealer. Mr. Donaldson made smooching noises and said, "Let's get goin' Mary Belle. Dadburn time's a dadburn wastin'!"

And off they went. Verne waved the others on, then he and Ryan fell in behind them.

Ryan could tell that the men were serious about their duties and kept their eyes peeled for anything out of the ordinary.

It was a moonless night. The only light on shore came from the Jove Beach lighthouse, and that had been dimmed to its lowest level by order of the Coast Guard. There were fears that at full beam it would pick out passing freighters, making them easy targets for prowling U-boats. The few seaside homes and buildings on this part of the wild Florida coast were blacked out for similar reasons.

The first few miles of the patrol were hectic. Collins kept running his horse up and down the column bossing everyone. Saying, "Close it up, there." And, "Keep a sharp eye out, men."

Then he'd charge off, whipping up sand so it got in everyone's face, and driving his mount crazy with constantly changing demands.

He'd kick it up to full speed and tear along the beach, then pull up so hard that Ryan winced, thinking of the poor animal's tender mouth.

Everything roused his suspicion. He'd see an object in the distance and hold up a hand as if to halt a cavalry column. Then he'd pull out his pistol and race along the water's edge waving his gun until he came upon whatever had caught his attention. It was usually driftwood. Once it was a dead tarpon, a fish with a dorsal fin so like a shark's that it had scared Ryan half to death—to Alex's vast amusement—the first time he'd encountered one surf fishing..

Verne and the other men took it all in good humor for a time, laughing as Dadburn Donaldson cussed up a blue streak, "dadburning" this and "dadburning" that.

Then Collins spotted what turned out to be a gigantic sea turtle making its way to back to the ocean after digging a nest in the sand and laying its eggs.

Shouting, "Saboteurs!" he tore along the surf line, waving his pistol. He raced up to turtle—still not realizing what it was— shouting and pointing his gun at the beast as if to fire.

The turtle reacted in surprise, lifting its huge head and opening its jaws—scaring the bejesus out of the Collins's horse.

Whinnying in fear, the animal reared up and the pistol went off, scaring the horse of the next man in line when the bullet struck the sand a few feet away.

Ryan heard Verne mutter, "That's it. I've had enough."

He gave Big Red his head and trotted along the beach until he reached Collins's side.

To Ryan's surprise, his own mount, Sheba, was there seconds later. He'd been so excited, and her gait was so smooth, that he hadn't noticed how fast she was going.

"Hand it over, Collins," he said, stabbing a thick finger the pistol.

Collins glared at him. "What are you talkin' about?" he said.

"You know damned well what I'm talking about," Verne said. "Give it here before you shoot one of us. You obviously have no respect for weapons. Now I know who your boy got his bad manners from, shooting up the countryside like he owned it."

He snapped his fingers. "Now, give it here."

Collins pulled the weapon back, like a caught-out kid, a spoiled look on his face that reminded Ryan mightily of his son, Joe.

"This here gun is mine," he said. "Cost more than most of these crackers make in a month."

Without another word, Verne reached out with one long arm and snatched the gun from his hand.

Collins gawped. "You can't do that," he protested.

"Well, I think I just did," Verne said. "And the others are probably thinking it's none too soon. You're acting like a crazy man with that thing."

"Dadburn right!" Ryan heard Mr. Donaldson say. The other men muttered agreement.

"What am I supposed to do if the Germans come?" Collins whined. "I ain't got no weapon."

"What you can do, is get," Verne said. "Go on home and brag to your poor wife and that juvenile delinquent kid of yours what a big man you are. And what a bunch of crackers we all are."

Collins got a stubborn look on his face, but Verne just edged Big Red in closer until he towered over the man.

"Now, get!" he said.

"But my gun," Collins said.

"You can pick it up tomorrow at the sheriff's office," Verne said. "Now get! I won't say it again."

And Collins got. Charging off on his horse, hurling back a blue streak of curses when he thought he was far enough away to be safe from Verne's wrath.

Verne turned to the others, a big grin lighting his face.

"Gentlemen," he said. "Shall we proceed?"

"Your dadburn right," Mr. Donaldson said. "And we're all dadburneds grateful to you for gettin' rid of that dadburned party boy. Good fer dadburn nothin' but fancy dadburned cocktails and sellin' overpriced dadburned cars."

There were mutters of agreement and laughter and soon the patrol continued on in high spirits, with Verne and Ryan in the lead.

They met the posse coming from West Palm about ten o'clock. Munched on sandwiches, washed down with thermoses of coffee, while sharing gossip—including the incident with Collins and the sea turtle. Repeated with a record number of dadburns from Mr. Donaldson and much laughter at Collins's expense. Ryan could see that the Ford dealer was known and loathed up and down the coast.

The moon made an appearance an hour or so later, lighting the sea and beach for long stretches and making the patrolling job more pleasant for everyone.

Ryan moved Sheba closer to Big Red. He had questions that he wanted ask, but hadn't had nerve until now. He cleared his throat, catching Verne's attention.

"What do you have on your mind, son?" Verne asked.

"Well, sir," Ryan said, "when you told Mr. Collins to hand over his gun, weren't you worried he might get mad and shoot you?"

Verne chuckled. "With that dinky little thing?" he scoffed. "If he had, it would've been the last time he shot somebody."

Ryan grinned. He could hardly wait to tell the story to Alex and Hattie. And wouldn't Sally get a big laugh too?

"I guess you've been shot at before," Ryan said. "Back in the first war against the Germans."

"I've been shot at, yes," Verne said. "But not in any war." He touched his eyepatch. "They wouldn't take me on account of this."

"Oh," was all Ryan could manage. "Then... uh... how..." He gave up. "Sorry, sir. It's none of my business."

"No, it's not," Verne said. "But we're family now and I think we know each well enough now that I can confide in you."

"Yessir, I guess we do," Ryan said, pleased at the compliment.

Verne got out the makings and started building a cigarette. "Back in my carny days," he began, "I took up fairground wrestling. I was no more than nineteen or twenty and full of piss and vinegar, as they say. Those were tough times. Hungry times. And when you are as big as I am, it takes a lot of feeding."

Verne lit the cigarette and tucked the spent match into a vest pocket, then continued:

"Anyway, I struck out on my own, taking on all comers. I put up a hundred dollars against ten. And I'd wrestle five or six guys a day. In one town I took on ten. Although I won all the matches, I was so battered and bruised I couldn't fight again for two weeks, so from then on I limited myself.

Verne shook his head in wonderment at his youthful foolishness. "Those were the days of no holds barred wrestling," he said, "and it was illegal as all get out. Had to dodge the sheriff wherever I went. Or, more often than not, pay them off. Once in a rare while I let one of their deputies take me on with no entry fee."

Verne was silent for a moment, remembering. His cigarette tip glowed as he drew in, then exhaled smoke.

Sighing, he said, "Anyway, last match in my short career was in a logging camp on the other side of the Canadian border. Up past Niagara. They called it, 'Devil's Hole' and the way things turned out, it was well named."

"Because it was in Devil's Hole that I finally met my match. He was a big old boy. Bigger even than me. And he was a scary sight. Had a knife scar running from the top of his head all down his cheek to his neck. I didn't notice until later, but he'd let his thumbnails grow to outlandish lengths. They stuck out almost half an inch and I soon learned they were filed, razor sharp."

Ryan shivered, imagining the scene.

"Well, we must have fought for half an hour," Verne continued. "Men were whooping and hollering for my blood. Finally, he had me flat on my back in a hold I just couldn't break. And he hit me such a shot in my balls that I thought I'd die. I slapped the ground, saying, 'Give!' But he kept on going. And I'm shouting, 'Give! Give!'

"But he just laughed and kept going. Then he reached up and stuck his thumb in my eye."

Ryan gulped. "He what?"

"Stuck his thumb in my eye," Verne said. "Dug in with that long, sharp nail. It was like a red hot poker."

Verne stopped for a moment. Painful memories twisting his features. He pinched out the cigarette, not noticing how it burned and when he spoke next he unconsciously touched the patch covering the empty eye socket. And his voice was so low, Ryan almost stopped breathing in his effort to hear.

"Shoved his thumb right in. So easy, you could tell he'd done that sort of thing before. And then he... well... twisted... and my eye popped right out. I could hear it go. And now I'm not just shouting, but begging him to stop.

"And then... and then..." Verne took a deep breath. "And then he went for my other eye."

Ryan gasped. "What did you do?"

Verne squared his big shoulders. "I don't know how I managed it. But somehow I reached inside myself to a place I didn't know existed. And I found the strength to fight back.

"Big as he was... strong as he was... I broke his hold and came up off the ground. And I grabbed him and flipped him over. Put his back right across my knee and then... well...

"I broke it."

Ryan gaped like a fish. "You what?"

"Broke his back," Verne said. "Killed him dead."

"Oh, my God," Ryan said.

"God had nothing to do with it," Verne said. "To this day I think it was old Scratch himself. Hiding out in Devil's Hole."

A long silence followed. A thousand thoughts and images bounced around Ryan's head.

Finally, Verne said, "I didn't tell you that story to shock you, Ryan. Or to brag about what a big brave man I was."

"Nossir," Ryan said—low.

"I never forgave myself for what I did," Verne said. "For outright murdering a man."

"But it was self defense," Ryan protested.

Verne raised his massive shoulder and lowered them again. "I made that excuse to myself. Although the local law didn't see it that way. I took off on the run, bouncing around the country for years. Even went to sea, like I told you.

"But I was guilt-bit big time and no matter how much time passed, it continued to haunt me. Even after I'd gone on to become a big success buying and selling farm property and breeding horses and all.

"Then I met your grandmother. I'd never met such a fine woman. Didn't think I deserved someone like her. But she got me to see myself a lot clearer than before. And although I never have forgiven myself, she's taught me how to live with it. Put it in the proper perspective."

He chuckled. "She's a pistol, old Myrtle is," he said. "All upright and proper. Sure, she's got some strange ideas about folks. But she has a way of making a man see things in himself he never saw before."

Verne looked over at Ryan. "You haven't met that particular Myrtle yet, son," he said. "But you will, by and by. Just give her a chance."

"Yessir," Ryan said. But deep inside, the jury was still out.

As they neared the lighthouse, and the end of their patrol, a brisk wind picked up. It had a chill to it that Ryan hadn't experienced since he arrived in Jove Beach.

Mr. Donaldson came trotting up on Mary Belle, who, despite her age, looked as fresh as when she started out.

"Looks like we're in for a dadburned cold snap," he said.

TWENTY-SIX

Snake Hunt

Alex came tapping on Ryan's window at daybreak.

On the way to meet Hattie, Ryan teased Alex about the miraculous recovery he and Hattie had made—just in time for the weekend.

"I was sick of bein' sick," Alex said. "Besides, it might be the last cold snap of the season and then we'd be out of luck when it came to snake catchin'."

Trailing their pole boats, they biked to the Coast Guard base, Rex joyfully bounding along behind them. Hattie met them at the gate.

She wore dungarees and a thick sweater against the chill and had a watch cap pulled over her ears. Her feet were shod in rubber fisherman's boots.

"It's c-c-cold," she said. "Last thing I wanted to do is get outta of my n-n-nice warm bed."

"You won't be feelin' like that when we start cuttin' up the money," Alex said. He wore trousers instead of shorts and an oversized flannel shirt against the cold.

Ryan pointed at his friend's feet and laughed. "First time I've seen you wear shoes since we went to the show in West Palm," he said.

Alex shorted. "Oh, yeah. Well you look like Mr. Philadelphia Yankee in the flesh."

Laughing, Hattie said, "He's got a point."

Ryan grimaced. For a change, he felt comfortable in his Philadelphia wear—dungarees, a jacket with a fur-lined collar, heavy shoes and a leather cap, with the ear muffs snapped back. Although, if pressed, he might admit that despite the cold snap he was feeling a trifle warm. He was finally becoming acclimatized to South Florida.

"I don't know why everybody keeps saying that," Ryan said. "I might have been born in Philadelphia, but I've never spent more than a few months at a time there."

"Where were you before that?" Hattie said, with a mischievous smile.

Another shrug. "Oh, you know, Connecticut. New England. Boston. Places like that."

Alex removed his glasses. Polished them with his shirt tail. "And everyone of them in Yankeeland," he said. "I rest my case," he said.

"Got everything?" Hattie asked. "Don't want to be standing there empty-handed when the rattlers come charging out of their holes."

"They won't be doin' no chargin'," Alex said. "It's too blamed cold. They'll be all slow like and sleepy."

"You hope," Hattie said. She pulled a little from her back pocket. "Let's go over the list before we start out."

She examined her list. "Gasoline?" she said.

"Check," Ryan said, lifting up a red two-gallon can.

"Hose?"

"Check," Alex said, indicating the eight-foot length he had in his basket.

"Burlap bags?"

"Check, check, and check," Ryan said, holding up several large gunnysacks.

"Hope they don't have any holes in them," Hattie said.

"They did," Ryan said. "But I fixed them."

"Okay, how about the snake pole?"

"I've got that," Alex said, pointing to the bamboo rod tied to his bike. It had a noose with a slipknot fixed to the end.

"What about Rex?" Hattie asked. "Aren't you worried he might get bit?"

Ryan dropped to one knee and pulled Rex close. "Not a chance," he said. "If you saw him with that coral snake, you'd never doubt him. If anything, he's our weapon of last resort."

"Okay, we all agree he's a wonder dog," Alex said. "Now, let's go make us some money."

Keeping the big red lighthouse over her shoulder, Hattie led them to the back end of the base, where one of the Seminole's many tributaries flowed out of a grove of magnolias.

"I'm pretty sure we were over yonder when Sally brought us in," she said, indicating a familiar spot by the creek.

"Looks good to me," Alex said and started unloading his pole boat and snake hunting paraphernalia.

When they were done, they stashed their bikes and pullcarts out of sight and climbed onto their boats with practiced ease.

"Come on, Rex," Ryan said, slapping his knee and Rex obediently jumped aboard.

Hattie took the lead, poling smoothly away. Of the three, she was by far the most graceful and athletic. They moved in congenial silence for a half hour or more, taking in the beauty of the river and the wildlife.

The deeper they went, the more Ryan thought it felt like a cathedral, with magnificent trees forming the vaulted ceilings and sun filtering in through leaves in a rainbow of colors, like the fabulous array of stained glass windows in the Cathedral Basilica in Philadelphia.

At one point, Hattie came to a stop. She held a finger to her lips to shush them and pointed ahead.

There, perfectly poised on the edge of the far bank, was a blue heron—nearly as tall as a man. It was a shimmering blue gray in color, with long, elegant legs and a fabulously curved neck that carried an elegant head with a long beak. Ryan thought he'd never seen anything so beautiful.

Then Rex spotted the heron and barked. The startled bird took off in an explosion of wings. They were nearly seven feet long from tip to tip. The wings beat once, twice, then the bird soared away leaving behind an empty space in their hearts.

The three friends looked at each other, too overcome to speak. Then Hattie dug in her pole and they moved onward.

Finally they reached the place Sally had indicated. There they beached their boats, gathered their supplies and set off on a deer trail so narrow it was barely visible.

Eventually, it opened on an area teeming with rabbits and other small animals. Rex flushed several of them out to give chase, but Ryan called him back.

"We're gettin' close," Alex said.

They moved onward a few minutes more then broke out of the trees into a dewy meadow glistening under the morning sun.

Rex bounded around the meadow, stopping here and there to bark at unseen presences.

"Gopher holes," Alex announced, getting out the length of hose.

He found a likely snake den, shooed Rex away, then inserted the hose into the hole—standing well back as he fed the hose into the hole—then moving closer until the hose could go no further. He wiggled it around a few times. Nothing.

Then he did it more forcefully, ramming the hose back and forth.

"Appears nobody's home," he said.

"Try this one over here," Hattie said, indicating a spot where it looked like there had been some activity in the surrounding area.

He started to pull the hose out, but then they heard the chilling sound of a dry, angry rattle.

Alex dropped the hose as if he'd been bitten and they all took big steps back.

"Shoot! There's one in there!" Alex said.

"Well, let's get him," Hattie said.

Alex approached the hose. Very gingerly he lifted it up.

Another dry rattle.

Another scramble to perceived safety.

"Here, I'll do it," Hattie said, grabbing the hose before Alex could pick it up again. "Somebody get the gasoline and stuff."

She rammed it into the hole several times, producing more angry rattling sounds. Ryan approached with the can of gas and the funnel. He inserted the funnel into the opening of the hose.

"You pour," he told Alex.

Alex's already huge eyes grew to moon size as he gingerly tilted the can.

Nothing happened.

"It works better if you remove the cap," Hattie said.

"Oh," Alex said, hastily removing the cap.

Ryan couldn't help but laugh. Of the three, Hattie was the only one who managed to stay cool.

Alex poured, sloshing gasoline all the place. He almost dropped the can when the buzzing sound was joined by another, louder one.

"There's two of 'em," he said.

"What'll we do?" Ryan said.

"I don't know," Alex said. "Nobody ever said anythin' about two of 'em."

"Quick! Get the snake pole," Hattie cried, "I think one 'em's crawling out!"

Ryan grabbed the snake pole and freed the noose so a wide loop dangled from the end.

Alex came alive. "I've got a gunnysack," he said, voice full of excitement.

And now Hattie was slowly backing away, pulling out the hose. A moment later a large reptilian head appeared. Nasty fangs exposed. Tongue tasting the air for signs of the enemy. Beady eyes looking for likely targets.

"I got him!" Ryan shouted, pushing the noose over the head, then pulling the cord to close it.

But the noose failed to respond. It was hung up. And the snake was still coming, rattles going like crazy. Rex barking furiously. Ryan trying to push him away with one foot, while he kept jerking on the cord.

Finally, it closed. Caught in the noose, the snake lashed back and forth. Ryan staggered under the onslaught.

"For God's sake, don't let go!" Hattie shouted.

Then Ryan found himself running backwards as the snake came crawling out at full speed.

He fell over something and landed on his back, both hands frozen to the pole. The snake coming with it. Heavy coils falling across his legs.

"The sack! The sack!" he shouted, trying to scoot away on his butt. "Somebody get him in the sack!"

Ryan wasn't sure what happened next, or who did it, all he knew was monumental relief as the gunnysack closed over the snake and somebody drew the neck closed.

"Eureka, we're rich!" Alex cried, lifting the heavy bag up. "He's gotta be seven feet or maybe even more."

He did a little dance, swinging the sack around. "Seven dollars on our first go around."

"Oh, shoot!" Hattie cried. "Here comes the other one!"

Now Rex was really going crazy, bounding around, barking, jumping forward, then back. Ryan tried to call him off, but he kept it up. Leaping to the other side of the hole and barking down into it.

Ryan got the nerve to come closer to pull him away, but then he realized Rex was the only thing keeping the snake in the hole, instead of coming after them.

"Grab Rex's collar," he told Hattie, brandishing the snake pole. "When I say, 'Go!' pull him back." To Alex, he said, "Get the gunnysack ready."

"Uh... Ryan?"

"What?"

"When I open the sack to put other one in, what's to keep the first one from getting out?"

Ryan's heart was going like crazy. He wasn't scared, although he should have been. Shoot, they all should have been sacred witless. But he noticed that—like him—Alex and Hattie were boiling over with excitement.

"Get the other sack," Ryan said. "We'll figure it out after we get this one squared away."

The other snake was trying to turn in the small space so it could get at Rex. Ryan pushed the pole forward, the noose dangling wide open.

At what he judged to be just the right moment, he shouted, "Go!"

Hattie pulled Rex back. Ryan dropped the noose over the snake's head and pulled it tight.

"Got him!" he shouted.

Now the truly bone-chilling business began of getting the snake into the sack. Doubly frightening, because Ryan hadn't seen the first operation. He'd been on his back the whole time.

Alex held the sack wide as he could, while Ryan struggled to lift the heavy snake. Alex slid the sack over its tail then started working the sack upward very carefully.

Finally, only the head with its dripping, poisonous fangs remained. The snake was tremendously strong and each time it tried to get at Alex, he staggered back, fingers within inches of those deadly fangs.

"Hattie?" he called out. "Can you get one end of this sack?"

"Coming," Hattie said.

She gave Rex firm orders to stay put, then hurried to Alex's side. Gingerly, she took over one side of the sack's mouth.

"Ready?" Alex asked Ryan.

"Ready!"

He opened the noose and the snake fell the rest of the way into the gunnysack and Alex closed it tight, securing it with a piece of cord.

Alex placed the sack next to the first one. Both snakes were lashing back and forth, rattling like crazy.

"Thought you said they could barely move during a cold snap."

Alex shrugged. "Maybe they got warmed up coming after us," he said.

"Never mind," Hattie said. "That one had to be at least seven feet long as well. We just made fourteen dollars in, like, five minutes."

"A really scary five minutes," Ryan said. "Seemed more like a year when I was on my back with the snake hanging over me."

"Okay, so now we know what to expect," Alex said, getting all business like. "I vote we keep going. We catch seven or eight more of these suckers and we'll be hundred dollar-aires."

"Uh, one problem," Hattie said.

"What's that?"

"We only brought three gunnysacks," She pointed out. "So, after the next rattler, we're gonna have to put in a whole lot more than just one snake. We'll have to hold the bag open, with others tryin' like the devil to get out, while we stick the other one in."

"I don't like the sound of that," Ryan said.

"Well, let's get us the third snake first," Alex said. "Then we can figure things out from there."

The third snake was smaller and so lethargic that Ryan thought he could have just grabbed it behind the head and stuck it in.

Alex said, "The cold probably hit him harder than the others because he was smaller. One of the Professor's dinosaur books had this whole thing about cold blooded and hot blooded critters. And how maybe an ice age killed all the cold blooded ones, like the dinosaurs."

"We're gonna have to start callin' you Professor Alex," Hattie said. "Here we are up to our necks in rattlesnakes and you're goin' on about dinosaurs."

"It was just a point of interest," Alex said. "An observation." But they could tell he was pleased at being called Professor Alex.

"Well, let's go observe ourselves up another gopher hole," Ryan said. "Get back to work on that hundred-aire business."

The next hole was truly a dry hole. And the next. And the next.

Then—bingo! A rattle went off.

Loud!

"We got a big one!" Hattie shouted.

"Eight, ten bucks easy," Alex said.

"I'll get the gasoline and hose," Ryan said.

"Wait, wait, wait," Hattie admonished them. "Not so fast. Wouldn't it be smarter if we figured out how to put him in the sack *before* we caught him?"

A long silence.

"Uh, Good point," Alex finally said.

Ryan went over to one of the sacks. Picked it up, setting off a fierce round of rattling. Inside the bag, the snake threw itself from one side, to the other. He could see from the wriggling outline of its body that the head was near the top.

He grabbed the sack with both hands—holding it well away from his body—and shook it up and down, driving the furious snake to the bottom. Then, moving quickly, he laid the bag on the ground, and slammed his foot down, trapping the snake in the bottom of the bag.

"Tie it off right here," he said, pointing to the area below his shoe.

"Gotcha," Alex said, cutting off a piece of cord and gingerly slipping it around the sack and tying it off.

Ryan held the sack up again. Now, no matter how hard the snake wriggled, it was trapped firmly in the bottom of the gunnysack.

"All we have to do now," he said, "is get the other snake in. Untie the cord and shake the bag until the new guy makes friends with the old guy at the bottom. Tie it off again. And so and so forth…"

"Bet we can get five in each sack," Hattie said.

"Let's get to it," Alex said.

A couple of hours later they had two sacks containing five snakes each and were working on putting the fourth rattler in sack number three.

It was the biggest one of all. Maybe eight feet long and thick as a man's leg. Ryan struggled mightily to lift its weight off the ground and maneuver the hissing reptile over the gunnysack Alex and Hattie were holding open. The other snakes bulked huge at the bottom and their combined weight—on top of the thrashing about—made the sack difficult to control.

Ryan felt like he was operating the nightmare version of one of those Coney Island arcade machines where you maneuvered a claw around, trying to grab a watch, or some other shiny prize.

Rex was as alert as ever. Racing around them, darting in and out whenever a snake tried to escape, but never getting in the way.

"That's one snake-huntin' dog," Alex exclaimed. And then just as Ryan was about to drop the snake into the gunnysack, the bamboo rod snapped with an audible crack!

Instead of falling into the sack, the snake fell across it. The sudden added weight ripped the sack out of Hattie and Alex's hands. Meanwhile, the sudden lack of weight sent Ryan reeling backwards, almost falling over Rex.

"Look out!" Alex shouted.

They scrambled away as the freed rattler coiled itself up, looking for an opportunity to strike.

Then, disaster piling on disaster, the cord keeping the other snakes at the bottom of the sack came loose and suddenly the whole meadow was filled with the sound of angry rattlers.

Warmed up by activity and being packed in close together, the snakes shook off any effects of the cold snap and were slithering about, looking to revenge themselves on their captors.

There was only one thing they could do:

Run!

But the snakes were between them and their boats.

"This way," Alex shouted and he took off for the treeline, the others close behind him and Rex bounding ahead.

Panic overtook them and they kept on running, bursting through the bushes, thorns ripping at their clothes.

Then they tumbled out into a little clearing and stopped, looking wildly about.

"I think we're okay, now," Ryan said. "Maybe we can circle back and—"

"Oh, no," Alex said.

"What's wrong?" Ryan said.

And then he spotted a strange object sitting in the clearing. It was a big tank-like device, with grungy hoses and copper coils leading off into barrels. There was a banked-coal fire under the device and an acrid odor of smoke and chemicals in the air.

"Moonshiners," Hattie said.

Ryan remembered Verne's warnings about moonshiners and their stills.

"Let's get out of here," Alex said.

Rex barked. They looked up, not knowing what to expect.

A deep, harsh voice spoke from the other side of the still. "What the hell you doin' here?"

And then Ryan saw a tall, red-faced man on the other side of the still. He was unshaven and dirty and wore raggedy overalls with the strap of one shoulder ripped away. He had a deep curving scar that ran from his crown to his chin, reminding Ryan mightily of Verne's eye-gouging nemsis.

"Who're them kids, Smoky?" someone called out.

Just beyond the man called Smoky were two other men, and behind them was someone else—someone much younger and cleaner. Ryan couldn't make the guy out, but then saw the flash of a vehicle parked in the brush. It was a pickup truck, with a flame paint job.

But then Ryan saw Smoky bend over and come up with a shotgun and he shouted:

"Run!"

They bolted.

Smashing through the brush just as the shotgun went off, pellets ripping past Ryan's head. He tore branches aside, as he and Hattie and Alex plunged into the woods.

Then he heard angry barking. It was Rex, who stayed back to confront the moonshiners. He heard the men shouting and cursing, then somebody gave a cry of pain and there was another shotgun blast. Followed by a yelp from Rex.

The barking stopped.

They kept running, but then Hattie gave a wild cry and she fell face-first into the bushes.

Ryan and Alex stopped to help her up. But just as Ryan stretched out his hand he saw something that stopped his heart.

It was a woman's body.

A small figure, with a trickle of blood drying on deeply tanned skin. Hooked nose. A battered captain's cap lay next to her. He leaned closer and saw the glitter of a silver St. Christopher's medal around her neck.

"It's Sally!" Alex said in a shocked voice.

"I think she's dead," Hattie said.

TWENTY-SEVEN
Murder on the Seminole

Ryan and the others sat on the riverbank, watching numbly as two litter-bearing deputies carried Sally's body to one of the sheriff's boats.

A loud rattlesnake's buzz made the men jump, nearly dumping the litter on the ground.

"Mind how you go," he heard Hattie say. "There's a whole passel of them around here."

She pointed to the three empty gunnysacks on the ground. "Don't know how they got loose. Must've been fourteen, or fifteen of them."

The deputies looked nervously around, then gingerly continued on to the boat.

Hattie's father, trim and handsome in his Coast Guard uniform, stood over her, a protective hand on her shoulder. Mr. Peters whispered something and her head came up sharply. Her eyes were fierce and her hissed reply made him jolt like one of those spooked deputies.

Ryan had no idea what she said, but he and Alex had learned that when she fixed you with one of "Hattie's looks," it was best to shut up. Obviously, her father had learned the same lesson.

Rex whimpered and Ryan gently patted him. The Dalmatian's head was on his lap. His shoulder was bandaged and his short, black and white fur was blood-stained where several shotgun pellets had caught him.

Luckily one of the deputies was studying to be a vet, and carried an emergency kit for injured animals he spotted on patrol. After extracting the pellets and dressing the wound, he gave Rex an antibiotic shot and something for pain.

"Don't worry, Ryan, he'll be okay," Verne assured him, reaching out to stroke Rex, who nuzzled his hand and got the expected treat hiding there.

"Rex saved our lives," Ryan said. "That man was going to shoot us."

"Good old Rex," Verne said, moisture glittering in his one eye. Then, lower: "Good old Rex."

Verne was crouched to his left. On his right were Hattie, Alex, and Sammy, whose face was pinched with worry for his son.

"Damned moonshiners," he said.

Deputy Tindall came up, flipping through his notebook. Ryan could tell he was very aware of the presence of Verne, the Coast Guard officer, and Sammy. His voice took on a condescending tone.

"Kids," he said. "I want y'all to run all this through for me one more time. Just a quick rundown, okay? I don't want to keep y'all from your homes any longer than I have to."

Ryan, Hattie and Alex complied, although Alex bristled at being called a "kid." But he and his friends had calmed down enough to quickly and clearly repeat all they had seen and heard.

Tindall tapped his notebook with his pencil. He said, "From your description—the knife scar and all—we're lookin' for Smoky Anderson, wickedest moonshiner this side of Miami. We'll pick him up, by and by."

"Wern't just him," Alex said darkly. "There were others."

Tindall looked annoyed at the interruption, especially coming from a colored kid. But there were other people present—parent type people— and his manner quickly shifted back into a friendlier mode.

"Yeah, he's got a whole gang," Tindall said. "We know all about 'em. They're mostly his kin. His brother runs a roadhouse up a ways."

"It was more'n just his gang," Alex said. He turned to Ryan. "Tell him, Ryan. Tell him who else you saw there."

Tindall looked down at Ryan, frowning. "Go on, son," he said.

Another rattler sounded a few feet away, and one of the deputies cursed. Tindall looked back over his shoulder.

"Mind yer mouth, Hank," he said. "We got kids present."

Hank mumbled an apology and Tindall turned back to Ryan. "Go on," he said again.

"Well, I can't be totally sure," Ryan said. "But I think I saw Joe Collins there."

Tindall's head snapped back. "Watch what yer sayin', son," he admonished Ryan. "I know you kids and Joe don't get along. But we're talkin' murder, here."

"He saw him—bigger'n life," Alex insisted. "Tell him about the truck, Ryan."

Ryan gulped, then said, "There was this pickup. Ford, I think. Kind of red, with maybe yellow flames on it. Just like Joe's truck."

"That's a pretty serious charge, son," Tindall said. "His pa ain't gonna be too happy to hear you say somethin' like that."

Verne's grip tightened on Ryan's shoulder. "The boy saw what he saw, Tindall," he said.

"But he also said he weren't all that sure," Tindall said. "Ain't that so, son?"

Reluctantly, Ryan nodded. "Yessir," he said. "There were trees and bushes and a big old still in the way. And I was pretty scared. But, it looked like Joe. And the truck looked like Joe's truck."

"I don't like where this is goin'," Tindall said.

Hattie scrambled to her feet, her father hastily stepping back. One hand went to a defiantly outthrust hip.

"Everybody knows that Joe Collins had it in for Sally," she said. "He was always on her. Even broke up her pullcart and tried to hide it in the weeds."

"There weren't no evidence that Joe done it," Tindall protested.

"There weren't no evidence," Hattie said in a mocking voice.

"Here, now, Hattie," her father said. "Have some respect."

Hattie rounded on him. "Respect? For him?" She pointed a shaking finger at Tindall. "He knew what was goin' on. He wouldn't of done anything about it, either, except Mr. Sullivan leaned on him."

Ryan saw a smile twitch one of edge of Verne's lips and his single eye gleamed in admiration of Hattie's spunk.

And Hattie wasn't done, yet, either. "Deputy Tindall even warned Joe and his folks to leave Sally be," she said. "But nobody put their foot down, leastwise his mom and dad. So Joe kept bein' Joe. Hanging out with crackers. Shoot, he could've even paid Mr. Smoky Anderson to shut poor Sally up. He's got his daddy's money, don't he? Thinks he can do whatever he wants."

There was a popping sound, as Verne rose from his uncomfortable crouch and his joints made their protests known. Ryan could tell that he thought it was time to bring things to an end.

At least for now.

"I'm sure Deputy Tindall is gonna look into all that, isn't that so Deputy?" he said.

Tindall nodded fiercely. "Yessir. I don't play no favorites. Everybody knows that. Besides, the sheriff's sending down his forensic boys. They'll get to the bottom of this in no time."

"We're all relieved to hear that, Deputy," Verne said. He turned to Sammy and Mr. Peters. "I know you gentlemen want to get your kids home. A good hot dinner and a nice sleep in tomorrow and then we can all look on things with fresh eyes."

Mr. Peters and Sammy murmured agreement. Hattie started to protest, but Ryan gave her a sign—later. Her eyes flashed. Her temper was on edge.

Then she took a deep breath and nodded agreement. Later.

A dry rattle sounded.

Then gunfire.

"Got one," Ryan heard a deputy say.

"You oughta bag him," another deputy said. "I hear they're goin' for a dollar a foot."

Despite the terrible scene all about them, Ryan almost burst out laughing. He buried his face in Rex's fur to keep the others from seeing.

"Good dog," he said, stroking Rex. "Good dog."

Rex thumped his tail.

TWENTY-EIGHT
The Crime Scene

It took another wasted hour to "secure the scene," as Deputy Tindall put it. With his deputies swearing and sweating and occasionally shooting when a rattler went off with its spine-tingling buzz.

Ryan thought it was a sound he could never become accustomed to. It went right to some primeval spot, like in one of those Amazing Magazine time travel stories.

Eventually, two miserable deputies were left behind to "assist forensics," as Tindall put it rather self importantly. Another pair set out with the poleboats tied behind their boat—cruising up the river to fetch the kids' bikes and deliver them—and the poleboats—to their homes.

"That's what I call true community service," Verne told a beaming Tindall, who departed thinking he was on firm political ground.

Ryan noticed that Verne had a way of leaving people feeling better about things than when they arrived. And it came to him now that Verne sometimes used it as a tool to get his way. This big, bluff mountain of a man had many hidden talents that Ryan was just starting to appreciate.

Ryan, Alex and Hattie sat in the back of the boat carrying Sally's body, while Verne and the two fathers sat in front with Tindall and the other deputies.

The small bundle that was once the wildly eccentric Gig Light Sally, who had risen up out of a well of misery few could endure, had been placed in the middle of the boat. A ghostly reminder.

Ryan shivered. "It's like she's here with us," he whispered. "Watching and waiting to see what we're going to do."

"Oh, no, no, no," Hattie said. "Sally isn't watching and waiting. That's not her style."

Hattie jabbed a finger at the small bundle. "She's over there swearing a mile a minute wanting to know what we're gonna do about this."

Alex snorted. "Hattie's right. Sally'd want us to hang Joe Collins by his heels like a pig at hog-killin' time."

"I know. I know," Ryan said. "But I can't be all that certain. Like swear on the Bible in a courtroom, certain."

Hattie made a rude noise. "When did you start swearing on bibles, Ryan Karr. Shoot, you don't even believe in it."

"You know what I mean," Ryan said, refusing to get shoved off point, which Hattie was very good at. "I'm not all that sure it really was Joe," he said. "Now things are more calmed down..." He sighed. "I'm just not sure," he insisted.

"That's not what you said before," Alex put in. He was as angry as Hattie. "When it was just the three of us and Tindall wasn't here you said Joe done it! And that's as plain as the Yankee nose on your face," he said.

"I know that's what I said at the time," Ryan protested. "Think about it. We don't want to put somebody in prison for something they didn't do. Or worse, get him executed."

Hattie and Alex looked thoughtful. After a pause, Alex said, "Okay. I hate Joe Collins's guts. But not so much I want him killed."

"Also, there's something not quite right about the whole thing," Ryan said. "I can't put my finger on it. But everything seems... I don't know... screwy."

He shook his head. Frustrated.

Hattie moved closer. "I heard Tindall tell one of the others that she was hit with somethin' heavy, and sharp like." She touched the back of her neck. "Said it nearly took her head off."

Ryan shuddered. He was glad he hadn't seen that.

Hattie added, "And they said there wasn't all that much blood."

"What does that mean?" Alex asked.

Hattie shrugged. "I don't know," she said. "But Tindall seemed to think it was important."

The engine noise cut back and the boat slowed as they neared the landing.

"My guess is they're not going to let us get together tomorrow," Ryan said.

Alex grimaced. "Sunday is not gonna be fun," he said. "After my pa's through with me, my mom's gonna lay into me. Shoot. I'd almost rather she took a belt to me. That look on her face! All hurtin' and everythin'! Oh, man. When she's done with me I'll feel so small I'll be slitherin' under the door on the way out."

Hattie snorted. "My dad better not try that on me," she said. "He'll be the one doin' the slithering."

Ryan didn't know everything that was going on between Sally and her father and mother. But she clearly held her father responsible for her mother's problems. And she was probably right. Her dad got to go home at night after a day of fighting the war. Ryan's father was in the middle of that war, with a whole ocean between him and home.

Then he thought, *But what about before the war, huh Dad? Hmm? What about then?*

He pushed it aside. It was useless to even think about. Especially right now.

Ryan said, "We won't get to talk until Monday after school. So let's keep our mouths shut until we can figure things out for ourselves."

"Deal," Alex said.

Hattie nodded. "Deal," she said.

The boat bumped against the shore. The engines cut. And in that one brief moment between the sudden silence and the returning world Ryan felt like he and Sally had come to the landing at the River Styx.

For Sally the journey was over. For Ryan it was about to begin.

TWENTY-NINE

S. O. S.

Verne said, "I think we'd best plan this in advance. When your grandmother hears this sorry tale, she is not going to be a happy woman."

They were sitting at Verne's favorite spot on the dock overlooking the lake. He'd stopped there after ferrying the others home in the caddy. Then, in the comfort of his big wooden chair and the "jug of kindness" perched on his lap, he had Ryan tell him the tale of the day's events one more time.

Verne listened intently. Single eye closed. Taking little nips from the jug now and again.

When Ryan was done, Verne smacked the cork back into place and set the jug aside.

"I don't suppose I have to lecture you on what a foolish idea it was to hunt rattlesnakes," he said.

Ryan remembered the poisonous fangs inches away as he lowered the snakes into the gunnysack. Yes, it was dumb. But at the time he felt like a genius.

"Nossir," he said. "It was stupid. We won't do it again."

"Next time you need money, ask me," Verne said. "If it's important—even if it's only important to you—I'll help anyway I can."

Ryan bowed his head. "Yessir," he said.

Verne fell silent for a few minutes. Face darkening as his thoughts turned inward. Every once in awhile he'd reach up and adjust his eyepatch. Ryan didn't know what he was thinking, but he felt horrible. The silence was like a knife in his gut.

A look of pain crossed Verne's face. He picked up the jug again. Pulled the cork. Raised the jug to his lips. Hesitated. Then he sighed. Smacked the cork back into place and set the jug back down on the deck.

He said, "You know your grandmother is not a well woman."

That brought Ryan up short. "Nossir. I didn't."

"She had what they said was a mild stroke about a year or so ago," Verne said. "It affected her right side. Gradually, thanks to the doctors, special exercises and Myrtle's perseverance, things returned to normal. But she still tires easily. And her temper isn't all that steady."

Verne chuckled, adding, "Not that it ever was. Myrtle has her views of what's proper and what's not. Firm views, in case you haven't noticed. And she'll go after anyone who disagrees like Patton going after Rommel."

Ryan smiled. "I've noticed, sir," he said.

Moisture glittered in Verne's single eye. "I love that woman, Ryan. Temper and all. We didn't get together until late in life, but I am a better man for knowing her."

He took in a deep breath. "When I say I don't know what I'd do without her, it's not an exaggeration."

There was nothing Ryan could say to that. So he kept his mouth shut. Instinctively, his right hand went to his knee and he started tapping on it: S.O.S. S.O.S. S.O.S.

Verne's voice startled him."What's that you're doing?" he asked.

He stumbled, trying to answer. "Uh… I'm just uh…"

"Spit it out, boy," Verne said. "I'm not a rattler. I won't bite you."

Ryan laughed nervously. "It's just a stupid thing I've been doing lately," he said. "It's Morse Code. Three dots. Three dashes. And three dots again."

Verne nodded understanding. "It's the S.O.S. emergency call signal," he said. "Depending on who you're talking to it means, Save Our Souls. Or, Save Our Ship. That kind of thing."

"Yessir," Ryan said.

But then, to Verne's obvious frustration, he said nothing more.

"Well, come on," Verne prodded. "You told me *what* you were saying. But you didn't tell me *why* you were saying it."

"I'm not sure why I do it," Ryan said. "But lately, whenever I get upset…when I think I can't take it anymore… I tap out S.O.S. on my knee. Or the chair. Someplace no one can see."

He trailed off. This was embarrassing.

"Come on," Verne said. "Give me the rest."

Ryan forced a smile, but his lips were quivering when he said, "Sometimes I get my Morse Code set out and I hold it like a kid with his teddy bear and I tap out S.O.S. over and over again. Like a prayer, you know? Won't somebody… somebody please… rescue me."

Tears threatened and he turned to hide his face. He sensed that Verne was reaching out to lay a comforting hand on him. And he prayed he wouldn't, because then Ryan would totally lose it and start bawling like a baby.

To his relief he heard the chair creak as Verne shifted his bulk. Then a pop! of the jug's cork. And then the sigh of satisfaction after a long drink. Then the sound of Verne clearing his throat.

"I'm okay now," Ryan said, straightening his shoulders and turning back.

"Good man," Verne said, with a smile so warm it melted many of Ryan's fears. If only momentarily.

Verne said, "When we get home I want you to sit down and tell your grandmother the whole story. Go easy on the gory stuff. We don't want to add any more gray to her hair, okay?"

"Yessir."

"Then I want you to apologize like you've never apologized to anyone before," Verne said. "If you have to, get down on your knees and beg her forgiveness and swear to her that you'll never do something so foolish again."

"Yessir," Ryan said.

Verne fixed him with a sharp look. "And you'll mean it, right?" Verne pressed. "Every precious word—you'll mean it."

"Yessir," Ryan said. "I'll mean it.

"Good," Verne said, starting the car. "Now let's go face the music."

"Yessir," Ryan said.

* * * *

The session with his grandmother wasn't as bad as he feared. She didn't cry—that would have torn him apart. She didn't even yell. She listened closely to everything he said. And she took his apology with good grace.

"Very well, young man," she said when he was through. "Thank you for being so forthcoming. And I will take your promises and your apology to heart."

"Thank you, ma'am."

"One thing, though."

"Yes, ma'am?"

"Do you really think it was Joe Collins that you saw?"

"I'm not sure, ma'am," Ryan said.

"Well, whatever it was that you saw, you stick up for yourself. Weak-kneed mealy mouths are not welcome in this family, you hear?"

"Yes, ma'am. I hear."

* * * *

Later, in the privacy of his room, he sat at his desk, flipping through the science fiction magazines Hattie's dad had given them. The wild covers filled with bug-eyed monsters, evil geniuses with bulging brain cases, and whole planets under attack by fleets of alien spaceships.

From the covers one would think that all these adventures featured scantily clad women being heroically rescued by male saviors with bulging muscles.

In reality, most of the tales were thoughtful stories penned by writers with serious issues on their minds who had mastered the art of sweetening high ideas and ideals with just the right mixture of high adventure—and, yes, those scantily clad women—to find a home on the magazine stands.

He grinned, wondering how writers like Isaac Asimov, Ray Bradbury, and Alfred Bester would handle the events of the day Ryan had just experienced. More to the point, what would the illustrators make of them? They'd be hard put to feed the scantily clad women publishing machine with the likes of Gig Light Sally and 12-year-old Hattie Peterson.

And evil geniuses? Surely, not pimple-faced Joe Collins. Or the low-browed moonshiner, Smoky Anderson.

But the next moment the grin melted away before the mental image of the empty eyes and bloody face of his friend. Old Gig Light Sally. A community eccentric. A figure of fun. A woman who made her living in the mosquito-ridden swamps of the Seminole River. Hit so viciously the blow had nearly decapitated her.

He thought back to that moment in the clearing when he first saw her body. Ran it over and over in his mind.

There was either something missing or something that didn't belong in that scene.

Who killed Sally?

Was it Joe Collins?

The moonshiners?

A conspiracy of the two?

Suddenly exhausted he threw himself on his bed. The whirlpool of the day's events making him dizzy.

Eventually, he fell asleep. But it was only for a short time. He woke up, aching all over and his mouth was as dry as sand. He got up for a drink of water, changed into his pajamas, and returned to bed.

But now sleep was impossible. The night air was still, without a hint of breeze from the ocean. The atmosphere was heavy and humid. Sheets sticking. Pillow lumping. He pushed it away, trying to find a more comfortable position.

And... what was that?

Music?

Very faint as if from far away.

No. Not music. Well... yes... maybe there was music. But the faint sound came with little pops! and squeaks! and electronic blips.

And then there it was!

Morse Code!

But then he lost the signal over the sound of his own beating heart. Or maybe it was just his imagination again.

But wait, wait, wait, Ryan. Had it ever really your imagination?

Or was it something else?

Something real.

Forcing calmness and holding his breath he strained to hear the slightest disturbance in the atmosphere.

And there it was!

Not loud.

But certainly plain.

The dots and dashes clearly defined.

A beat of silence.

Then more dots and dashes.

Another beat.

But, wait!

What's that?

Again, he strained to hear.

He couldn't hold his breath any longer and he let go in a long whoosh! And when he breathed in again, he'd lost the signal.

Or was it just one signal.

Was it...?

He bolted upright.

There were two of them!

He was sure of it: two different, but very experienced hands keying Code, listening for the reply, then answering again.

Ryan pressed his ear against the mattress again. Pulled in his breath.

Held it.

And listened!

Listened...

Listened...

But he heard nothing. He tried it again. Still nothing. Then, he started to doubt himself.

Was it real?

Or imaginary?

Had he gone crazy like his mother? Wasn't insanity hereditary?

Confusion and doubt reigned the rest of the night. And when the dawn finally came, his thoughts were a jumble of nonsense lost in a Seminole swamp.

Who were these people?

What were they saying?

Were they close?

Or far away?

And what, if anything, did they have to do with Sally's murder?

Nonsense, Ryan! How could you even bring those two thoughts together? You stupid, stupid, kid!

He pulled the pillow over his head. No one would ever believe him. Nor should they. He was just a crazy kid, with a crazy mom and a father who didn't seem to care.But he couldn't block out the sound in his head:

S.O.S.

S.O.S.

S.O.S.

THIRTY

Beacon to Nowhere

Until Monday rolled around, Ryan and Hattie never knew they had so many close friends at school.

News of Sally's murder had spread like a summer swamp grass fire and all the kids swarmed the two trying to get insider information on the ghoulish event.

Even Mrs. Carlin got into the act. "Oh, you poor darlings," she said, pulling them aside as the other students hurried home after the last class of the day.

"It breaks my heart to think what terrible things you must've seen," she went on, tears welling in her eyes. "To have to witness such a horrible thing at your age. Why, you're only babies!"

She tried to hug them, but both managed to duck her embrace.

"We're fine, Mrs. Carlin," Hattie said. "Really we are."

"And then you poor dears had to be questioned by the police," Mrs. Carlin went on, as if Hattie hadn't said a word. "Murder! The most awful crime of them all."

"Yes, ma'am," Ryan said. "It was awful. Thank you for thinking of us."

The ghoulish glow brightened in her eyes and Ryan feared he may have awakened a notion to "console" them so she could gather more insider details for her friends.

He grabbed Hattie's arm, saying, "I'm sorry to be in such a hurry, Mrs. Carlin, but Deputy Tindall is expecting us."

"That's right," Hattie said, embellishing Ryan's lie. "He said it was really important to go over our witness statements."

Ryan glanced up at the clock. "We'd better hurry," he said. "We're the only eyewitnesses, after all."

"Yes, yes. Y'all had best hurry," Mrs. Carlin agreed. "And please feel free to come back later to see me. My door is always open to y'all."

She dabbed at her eyes with a hankie. "I've had the misfortune of experiencing tragedy in my life," she said. "But I've always managed to hold my head high. And I'd be pleased to share my little story with y'all. It might be comfortin' to know you are not alone."

Ryan and Hattie thanked her and nearly tripped over each other getting out the door.

When they were clear of the building, Ryan said, "Could you believe her? I've known a lot of phony teachers, but hands down, she is the absolute worst."

"At least Mr. Jackson left us alone," Hattie said.

Ryan laughed. "He's too busy helping Roosevelt and Eisenhower fight the war to pay any attention to a little thing like murder," he said.

A little later, when they met up with Alex at their favorite spot atop Hobe Hill, they learned he'd had the same kind of day.

"Never knew I had so many friends," Alex said. "Guys were slappin' me on the butt like I was a fellow jock. Girls were sneakin' me treats. I'd have enjoyed it some, if they all weren't so mealy-mouthed phony about it."

"Did anybody bring up Joe Collins?" Ryan asked.

Alex shook his head. "Not a word."

"Same with us," Hattie said.

"I'm surprised the sheriff's been able to keep a lid on it," Ryan said. "Bet it won't last long, though. No matter how much his folks holler and squawk."

"Well, you've had a couple of days to think on it," Hattie said. "Still of the same mind? Or, not mind, as the case may be. I mean, you can't seem to make up yours."

Alex broke in. "Like did you, or did you not see Joe Collins?"

Ryan sighed. "I'm pretty sure it was him," he admitted.

"Just pretty sure?" Hattie pressed.

Ryan grimaced. "If they put me on a witness stand," he said, "I couldn't say more than that."

"Logic says it can't be anybody else but Joe or the moonshiners who killed Sally," Alex said.

"I think they caught her out by their still," Hattie said, "and one thing led to another and they started to rough her up. And she fought back."

"Sally might've been tiny, but she was somethin' fierce," Alex said. "Might not even have meant to kill her. Maybe they just kinda hit her a little too hard."

"Little?" Hattie said. "Almost took her head off, was what Tindall said."

"Glad I didn't see that," Ryan said.

"Wish I could've seen anythin' at all," Alex said. He took his glasses off. Looked through them. Shook his head, then put them back on. "With these things, I might as well be blind," he said.

Knowing how frustrated his friend was, Ryan tried to ease the mood.

"The sheriff's forensic people will figure all that out," he said. "My Uncle Tom has worked a lot of murders. And he says when they get a body into an autopsy room all kinds of things come out. Like was the victim in a fight before she was killed? There's what he calls defensive wounds, and other stuff that shows up. Bruises and cuts and sometimes even skin under the victim's nails."

Alex said, "Don't go and fool yourself. This ain't Yankeeland with crime labs and test tubes like they have on *Gangbusters*. What Deputy Tindall and the sheriff know about crime bustin' technology you could put in the small end of nothin' and it'd still rattle around."

Hattie looked over at Ryan, who seemed to have drifted off while Alex was talking. She gave him a nudge.

"What's on your mind, Ryan?" she asked. "I don't think you heard a word Alex said."

"I'm sorry," he said. "I just keep thinking back on what we saw. And I don't mean the blood and stuff. It's something else. Something that's either missing, or doesn't belong there."

"Like what?" Alex said. "She looked just like the same old Sally to me. Other than bein' dead."

Suddenly it came to Ryan. "The necklace!" he said, excited.

"What about the necklace?" Hattie asked.

"The St. Christopher medal she showed us," Ryan said.

"Yeah, okay. So what about it?" Alex pressed.

"She said she never wore it during the day," Ryan said. "Said it almost killed her once when it got all tangled up in the bushes."

Ryan was getting excited now. He clearly remembered seeing Sally's body. The blood. The beaked nose. The captain's cap. And there—shiny as could be—was that necklace hanging around her neck.

"She said someone special gave it to her," he said. "Didn't you guys see it? Plain as day. Around her neck."

A long silence followed. Then, in a small voice, Hattie said, "Oh."

A second later, Alex said, "Yeah, it was there all right."

The two of them looked at Ryan. He could see a confusion of emotion running across their faces. Alex's magnified eyes were bigger than he'd ever seen them before.

"So she wasn't killed where we found her," he said.

"That's right," Hattie said. "She must've been killed on the *Celestial Queen*. And then they dumped her body."

Another long silence.

Then Ryan said, "That doesn't make sense. Why would the moonshiners put her body anyplace near their still?"

A long silence as the three thought it over. Then:

"Wow!" Alex said. "We've got a whole new ball game, don't we?"

"We do," Ryan agreed.

"We'd better tell somebody," Hattie said.

Ryan hesitated. Then: "Think they'll believe us?"

"Only one way to find out," Hattie said, scrambling to her feet.

The three of them raced down the hill then biked like fury to town. As they rolled up to Deputy Tindall's office, they saw him and another deputy pulling a familiar-looking man out of the cab. He was handcuffed.

Tindall gave him a shove. "Get along!" he said.

The man stumbled, turning to get his balance and that's when he spotted Ryan and his friends. He fixed them with a murderous glare.

It was Smoky Anderson. Knife scarred face and all.

Tindall spotted them. Gave them a big smile. "Got our man, kids," he said. "This is the fella you're gonna help the good citizens of this here state put in the electric chair."

Laughing, he gave Anderson a swat that staggered him. "Then we'll watch you fry, like. Get'cha nice'n smoky, won't we Smoky?"

The other deputy burst into laughter. "That's a good'un, boss," he said. "Wait'll I tell the boys."

Tindall leaned into the back of the pickup and pulled out an object partially wrapped in brown paper. It was an entrenching tool of some kind, with the shovel part snapped out into the fixed the position. There was blood and dirt on the blade.

"And talk about stupid luck," Tindall continued. "The fool left the murder weapon over by his still. Shoot, even without your testimony, kids, this'll fry him nice and crispy."

Smoky looked at the three of them like they were insects. "You ain't gonna be testifyin' to nobody," he said.

Tindall snorted. "Big man," he said. "Scarin' a bunch of kids." And he and the other deputy hustled Anderson into the sheriff's office.

A minute later, behind the closed door, they heard the sound of a loud blow and a curse.

The three looked at each other. Bewildered. "I don't think anybody is gonna to want to hear about St. Christopher," Alex said.

* * * *

Back on Hobe Hill, they sat in stunned silence, staring out at the lighthouse as if it might hold an answer.

Finally, Ryan said, "What'll we do? Just give up?"

"I think we should go visit the scene of the crime," Hattie said.

Ryan's eyebrows rose. "What?"

"I mean the real scene of the crime," Hattie said. "Sally's home. The *Celestial Queen*."

Surprisingly, Alex was hesitant. He was usually the first to choose a rebellious course. "I don't know," he said. "I made promises to my mom and dad."

"Hang a bunch of promises," Hattie said. "You made them to people who don't know what they're talking about. Sally's death is much more important than a few promises. Or are you just chicken?"

Alex looked hurt. He ducked his head. Took off his glasses. Polished them. Put them back on again.

"I'm no chicken," he mumbled.

"Well, you're sure acting like one," Hattie said.

"Come on, now, Hattie," Ryan said. "That's not fair. Alex has a different situation than either of us do."

Hattie's hands went to her hips. "What about you, Ryan Karr?" she said. "Are you too chicken to go and see?"

Ryan sighed. After talking to Verne and his grandmother he wasn't keen to upset things.

"I have another problem," he said.

"And what problem would that be?" Hattie demanded, her dander clearly sticking up.

Ryan took a deep breath, steeled himself, then told his friends about the mysterious signals. Hattie was especially unimpressed.

"Well, there you go with the imaginary Morse Code signals in your bedsprings again," Hattie said.

"They're not imaginary," Ryan said. He hesitated. Then, "At least I don't think they are."

"Well, you're just full of information, aren't you?" Hattie said. "Let's see, here. First you see Joe and his truck. Then you're not sure it really was Joe, much less his truck. Then you hear these Morse Code signals. In your bedsprings, no less. And then you're not so sure you really did hear them.

"I swear, Ryan Karr. I've heard about all the mealy mouthed Yankee bee-ess that I can handle. You never take a stand one way or the other. And you're almost as bad, Alex. Puttin' kiddie promises over the murder of a friend."

She got up off the ground, dusted herself off and picked up her bicycle.

"Well, when you two decide you've got your nerve back, come on by and see me," she said, mounting her bike. "But you'd best hurry. 'Cause I'm not waiting around forever. By God, I'm gonna do something about it!"

And she took off down the hill. Practically flying by the time she reached the bottom.

Dismayed at possibly losing a friend and afraid of losing another, Ryan looked over at Alex.

"You don't think she's right, do you?" he asked. "That I'm afraid to take a stand?"

Alex avoided his eyes. "I don't know, Ryan," he finally said. "You do seem to have trouble makin' up your mind."

Hurt, Ryan picked up a stick and jammed it into the dirt.

"I'm just not sure," he said.

Alex sighed. "Okay, well, if that's the way it is, I suppose you can't help it," he said.

Then, like Hattie, he got up, brushed himself off and mounted his bike.

"I'd better get home," he said. "My mom said we're gonna have an early supper."

And then he too was flying down the hill.

Ryan turned away, staring out at the red lighthouse.

A beacon to nowhere.

THIRTY-ONE
Stealing Time

At the bottom of the hill, Ryan was turning for Sullivan Island when he saw Verne's big Cadillac tooling down the county road.

He waved and Verne pulled over. "You heading home, son?"

"Yessir."

Verne's good eye took on a mischievous glint. "Got lots of homework, do you?"

Wondering what was up, Ryan shook his head. "No. I pretty much did it all during study period."

Verne stroked his big chin. "Well, if a certain fella I know was thinking of using Captain Frank's engine overhauling problems to play a little hooky, you wouldn't think badly of him, would you?"

Laughing, Ryan said, "Nossir." Then, grinning he kicked the dirt with the toe of his shoe. "Think you and Capt. Frank might need some help on that job?"

"Oh, we do, we do," Verne said. Then he slapped the back seat. "Put your bike back there and let's go. Don't worry about your grandmother, I told her I'd look you up on the way to town."

He waved a beckoning hand. "So, come on, old son," he said. "Come help me steal a little time."

Ryan hopped into the car, sprits soaring. Worries about Sally, mysterious signals, his two friends, the war—everything, were swept away when Verne said, "Let's get a little traveling music, Maestro," and he reached over and flipped the radio on, and turned the volume as high as it would go.

The song blasting out on the magnificent car speakers had been on the top of the charts for weeks now. Verne beat time with one hand, while driving with the other as Kay Kaiser and the other singers belted out the lyrics:

> *Praise the Lord and pass the ammunition!*
> *Praise the Lord and pass the ammunition!*

Verne broke in, bellowing in his big voice:

> *Praise the Lord and pass the ammunition!*

Praise the Lord and pass the ammunition,
And we'll all stay free!

Now Ryan joined in, singing with Verne and pounding on the door to keep time.

Shouting Praise the Lord,
We're on a mighty mission!
Praise the Lord and pass the ammunition,
And we'll all stay free!

And off they drove, heading for a little job of stealing time, while singing:

Praise the Lord and pass the ammunition!
Praise the Lord and pass the ammunition!
Praise the Lord and pass the ammunition,
And we'll all stay free

* * * *

"Dadburn it, Verne!" Mr. Donaldson whined. "I hope you ain't comin' round here to put the dadburned arm on me for dadburned posse duty. I already did dadburned Tom Hopkins dadburned shift here at the station the other dadburned night. And I'm dadburned tuckered."

Verne slapped Donaldson on the back, nearly bowling him over. "Not this time, George," he said. "We're here for the fishin' not the posse'n."

And they continued on toward the *Myrtle*, where a smiling Capt. Frank waited to greet them.

Ryan was moving past the familiar sounds of the telegraph office when he heard Mrs. Wilkinson call, "Ryan!"

He turned and she came rushing up to him. "Just got a minute," she said, glancing back at the office. "I've got a trainee in there. I hope she doesn't go ga-bluey on me!"

"Yes ma'am," Ryan said. "What can I do for you?"

Mrs. Wiklkinson put a hand on his arm. "I felt so bad after I talked to you the other day. I was so adamant in my opinions."

"That's okay, Mrs. Wilkinson," Ryan said. "That was your professional opinion. I couldn't ask for better than that."

"Well, it wasn't good enough," she said. "I talked to a friend. She's an electronics whiz workin' over at the new base."

Ryan nodded. It was common knowledge that a top secret base was being built outside town.

"Anyway, when I told her about you thinking you heard music, and even telegraphy, through your mattress springs she told me that it was quite possible. What with the war and all we've got all kinds of communication devices around us that aren't shielded properly. And that signals could leak through.

"Not only that, but she said dentists report that sometimes radio signals have can be picked up through dental fillings."

Ryan was stunned. He wished he could teleport Hattie and Alex to his side and say, "See? I told you. I wasn't imagining things after all."

"Are you okay, Ryan?" Mrs. Wilkinson said. His face obviously showed his confusion.

"Oh, sure, sure," Ryan said. Then he got himself together and smiled. "Thank you so much, Mrs. Wilkinson. I really appreciate you going to all that trouble."

"It's the least I could do," she said, glancing nervously at the telegraph office. "Science is always better than an uninformed opinion, don't you think?" Then, "I'd best get back to the trainee," she said, hurrying away. Over her shoulder she called back, "I'm sorry, Ryan. I truly am."

At the boat Verne looked quizzically at Ryan. "What's she sorry about?"

"Oh, it was nothing, sir," Ryan said. "I asked her a technical question the other day and she steered me wrong. She was just correcting it."

Verne nodded absently, then turned back to Frank and the two other crew members who were getting the *Myrtle* ready. Ryan wasn't sure why he hadn't told Verne about the signals. Probably because it seemed silly—even childish—on the face of it.

Ryan hesitated to tell him now because he wanted proof of his claims. To accomplish that, he had an idea for a little experiment he wanted to try tonight, or over the weekend.

They cruised off the inlet for a couple of lazy hours, talking and fishing. Actually, the others did all the talking and fishing. Ryan was lost in his own thoughts, but feigned enough interest so no one noticed his mind was elsewhere.

He was fixed on two things: One: Sally's murder. Two: The Morse Code signals. But no matter how he turned them around—individually, or apart—he couldn't make sense of them. Ryan desperately missed his friends' mental powers. When the three of them were together it seemed they could solve almost anything.

Okay, there was the fiasco with the rattlesnakes. But when he thought on it, the scheme had actually worked. They really had caught all those snakes—just like Alex had predicted. It was only a little accident that spoiled things. He'd file that under "Could've Worked," instead of "Didn't Work."

He grinned, thinking Hattie and Alex would appreciate that joke. And then he started working on how he was going to get them all together again.

It was growing dark and Verne was telling a tale of a youthful adventure off the Cuban coast, when Capt. Frank decided it was time to turn back.

Ryan waited until Verne was by himself broached another subject that had been nagging him.

"Sir?" he said.

"Yes, my boy?" Verne said, face jolly, single eye alight with pleasure.

Ryan said, "You know that discussion we had the other day? You know, after the whole snake business?"

Verne chuckled. "How could I forget?" Shook his head in amusement. "Get a laugh every time I think of those deputies jumping like Mexican beans every time a snake let loose." Then, to Ryan, he said, "What do you need, son? Spit it out."

Ryan took a deep breath, then spilled it. "Alex is the smartest kid I've ever known," he said. "But he's got a problem reading. He can get by with just the stuff they teach at his school. The colored school. But they're way behind even us."

Verne nodded. Ryan had told him about the failing of the Jove Beach school and he'd encouraged the boy to study on his own with the books his Aunt Cassie sent.

"But he's got a chance for a lot more," Ryan said. "The Professor's bringing him books and study guides. But it takes so darned long for Alex to get through them—almost word by word, his glasses are so bad—that sometimes he gets such bad headaches he's ready to give up."

Verne frowned. "I heard Alex was up for scholarships," he said.

"Well, with those glasses," Ryan said, voice trembling with passion, "it's gonna be pretty hard for Alex to go up against all those big city kids. The glasses he's wearing now used to belong to his grandfather. And he had cataracts, or something. Nothing to do with Alex's problems. They're just big magnifiers he can hang on his nose."

"I didn't realize that," Verne said. "Sammy never said a word." He snorted. "Of course, he wouldn't would he? He's a proud man."

"Yessir," Ryan said. "Anyway, when you said the other day that if I needed money for something important, that you'd try to help me."

"Yes, I did," Verne said.

"Well, I really have a need for some money," Ryan said. "I need it so Alex can buy proper glasses and get into a good school and all."

Verne thought a minute, then said, "I'm in. He'll get the money."

Ryan was so excited he hugged him. "Thank you, Verne," he said. "Thank you."

"But we have to be careful how we go about it," Verne cautioned. "Sammy is a proud man. He won't take charity."

"Alex is the same way," Ryan said. "Always insists on paying his share. And even standing treat when he can."

"Good. It's settled, then," Verne said. "I'll put my thinking cap on and figure this out." He offered a hand. "Deal?" he said.

Ryan grinned, sticking his hand into a paw so big that his own practically vanished in it.

"Deal!" he said, with enthusiasm.

At that moment there was a distant CRUMP!

Ryan started in surprise.

Then they all turned to see smoke and fire boiling into the fast-closing night skies.

"U-boat!" Frank declared. "They got a freighter!"

Then there were two more explosions. CRUMP! CRUMP!

And the whole sky shattered into sheets of flame and fiery debris.

THIRTY-TWO
Fiery Seas

Blazing objects shot up—looking almost as if they were in slow motion—flying, up and up and up. Then arcing off, trailing fire and smoke until they disappeared into the sea.

"Let's go!" Verne bellowed. "There'll be men in the water."

Capt. Frank turned the *Myrtle* about and churned away, broadcasting distress signals and locations to the Coast Guard and any other boats or ships within range.

Verne helped the two crewmen break out the emergency gear and supplies. Art and Carl were older men—past even volunteer age—but what they lacked in youthful muscle they more than made up with in seamanship.

As they headed toward the smoke, Ryan found a perch where he could fit comfortably with his lifejacket, and peered ahead at the fiery spot on the horizon.

Ryan had noted before that any motion takes a long time on water. But this trip was sheer agony. With night falling, and vision retreating, it seemed to take several eternities before they came within sight of flaming wreck.

It was a ghastly scene. The freighter bulked black and huge with its stern fully ablaze and men were leaping over the rails to escape the flames.

Ryan saw two huge holes in the side, with flaming oil gushing out onto the heaving seas. Somewhere on the ship alarms were blaring, furiously shouting the ship's distress far and wide.

Ryan felt as if he had stumbled into another world. A world of flame and smoke and oily spume. He saw the dark figures of men leaping from the ship and disappearing into the boiling waves.

He tried to see if they emerged again, but the deck pitched under his feet, hurling him to one side.

Verne caught him, steadied him. Then shouted something in his ear. Ryan shook his head. He couldn't make out what he was saying. Giving up, Verne simply held him with one hand, while he cinched a line just below Ryan's vest.

Then he patted Ryan's shoulder. Pointed at the deck and mouthed, "You. Stay. Here." Ryan nodded. Verne glared. He wanted more than nods. He mouthed the word: "Promise!" Ryan crossed his heart.

Satisfied, Verne headed back to the bridge, where Capt. Frank was directing Art and Cal to get ready for action. Emergency gear was neatly secured around the deck, with lines and flotation devices, as well as first aid supplies.

Ryan craned to see, white-knuckling the rail as the *Myrtle* pitched and heaved under him. He heard Verne shout, looked to see him point to the port side—Ryan's side—and then Capt. Frank was spinning the wheel and the *Myrtle* gave a sickening lurch, then recovered in time to gracefully take a large wave.

He glanced to the side and saw what looked to be like part of the bridge sweep by. If Verne's one good eye hadn't spotted the danger, the *Myrtle* very likely would have been hulled. And then they would be in that oily water, along with the sailors.

Now they were slowing and Cal and Art ran to the rails carrying lines. Ryan craned over the side to see a panicked man roiling about in the water.

His mouth was a wide "O" as he screamed for help. And then he over-weighted his lifejacket and went under, only to emerge strangling and lashing about.

Cal tossed him a line, but the hysterical man just smacked it away, as if it were a threat.

Then Ryan saw canny old Art snatch up a pee-vee pole from its clasp. He jabbed at the man. Turning him with each jab. Then, when then man's back was to him, Art snagged his life jacket fastenings and heaved.

Cal jumped in to grab hold. Slowly, surely, they dragged him to the rail, kicking and clawing as if he were being threatened by monsters of the deep, instead of being rescued.

He almost kicked free, but then Verne's immense form moved into view. With one long arm he reached out, grabbed the man by his collar and lifted him bodily up and over the rail. And then he dumped him into the hold.

Verne pointed at Ryan, then at the man. "Help him." He mouthed. Then he turned back as they came on other struggling forms.

Quickly, Ryan loosened his line and slid down to where the man was. He tore open a bundle, found some rags and a blanket. And shoved them into the man's hands. It was almost like turning on a switch. Suddenly the man came to his senses and wordlessly started wiping the oil from his body.

Ryan shimmied up to his previous perch, cinched the line, and settled in to watch the *Myrtle* closing on the freighter. But slowly. Carefully. Big twin engines throbbing powerfully under Ryan's feet.

And then Capt. Frank was shouting, "All aback," and he was reversing the engines and pulling away from the ship.

Verne looked like he was going to protest, but Frank shouted, "She's gonna blow!"

A second later there was an explosion and the whole sea was blanketed with fire.

The smoke was so thick Ryan could hardly breathe. He balled up his t-shirt and held it to his nose to try to filter the air.

But then Capt. Frank was coming about, and the wind shifted and Ryan could breathe again. Until then he didn't realize that the force of the explosion had hurled him to his knees.

He crept along the deck and used the rail to haul himself up to peer out. And what he saw was a hole opened straight into Hell by the Devil Himself.

It was blackness, shot with flame and oily smoke and he could hear men screaming in agony. Then he saw dark figures bobbing in the water.

"Over there," he shouted. "There's more men over there!"

Capt. Frank guided the ship toward the figures and Verne had Art and Cal organized with nets and hooks and ropes. And they started laboriously pulling men in, one by one.

And they came tumbling on the deck in front of Ryan, a ghastly catch for any but the most hardened seamen.

It was all Ryan could do to keep from vomiting from the smell and the violent motion of the ship. But he managed to help claw out the emergency supplies, wipe oil from men's faces and help them cough up torrents of oily water.

Vaguely he became aware of other vessels about. A quick glance showed him that rescue parties were starting to arrive from shore. Everything from expensive yachts to beat up row boats. It seemed like the whole town turned out and all of Jove Beach was involved.

Finally, Capt. Frank said they'd taken in more than they could safely hold and it was time to get these men to shore for proper treatment.

Verne gave the okay and Capt. Frank whipped the *Myrtle* about and charged back to the docks at top speed.

When they came to the dock they found that the whole town had, indeed, turned out to help. Mr. and Mrs. Donaldson, Mrs. Wilkinson, Tindall and the other deputies, even Mr. Jordan and Mrs. Carlin from school were there, including countless other people whose names he hadn't learned yet, but whose faces were familiar.

They were lifting the men off the boats, giving them emergency treatment, and then speeding them to the hospital at West Palm.

And then it was over.

Ryan stood on the deck, dazedly looking around at the oily mess left behind. There were rags and bits of paper and ripped open boxes and discarded life vests covered in blood.

He heard someone shout his name.

Looking up, he saw Hattie. She was smiling and waving to him. Then he saw Alex next to her, waving and hollering like a crazy man.

Verne's heavy hand fell on his shoulder. Ryan looked up and saw a grin on his face.

"You did well, son," Verne said. "I'm proud of you."

Then: "Go on. Your friends are waiting for you."

THIRTY-THREE

Decisions

"You should've seen it," Alex said. "It was like the whole sky was on fire!"

"He did see it, silly," Hattie broke in. "He was there, remember?"

Alex was too excited to pay attention to little things like facts. His hugely magnified eyes were alight.

"Sure, sure," he said. "But, you should've seen it anyway," he said. "The dirty Germans got three freighters. Sank two of them. Killed I don't know many."

It was the next day, school had been cancelled and the three friends were sprawled across the warm grass atop Hobe Hill.

Ryan was feeling disoriented—almost out of body. He still hadn't quite taken in the previous night's events.

"It was pretty awful," he said. "I've never been so scared. Scared for all those people, I mean. It was… It was…"

His voice trailed off. Forced a laugh. "Sorry," he said.

"That's okay, that's okay," Hattie said. Sliding in next to him.

"You'll be fine." This from Alex, closing in from the other side.

The three friends stayed there, very still, for awhile. Almost in an embrace. And then the moment passed.

"Okay, enough of that," Hattie said, sitting up and brushing leaves from her hair. "We've got other things to talk about. Important things. Starting with Sally. And then Ryan's problem with the signals in the box springs."

Ryan slapped his head. "I almost forgot," he said.

And then he filled them in on what Mrs. Wilkinson had told him. That it was entirely possible for bedsprings to pick up stray radio signals and even telegraphy.

When he mentioned that dentists reported that fillings sometimes picked up signals, Alex nodded. "That makes sense," he said. "Goes straight to your auditory nerves."

"But I think the source—or sources—would have to be close," Ryan said. "I can rule out anything local, like the telegraph office and the military communications. Because Mrs. Wilkinson told me they're all heavily shielded."

"What could it be, then?" Alex asked.

"I don't know," Ryan said. "But I'm going to try a little experiment. Tonight. And if nothing happens tonight, then the next night."

He shrugged. "Until I get something," he said, "there's nothing more to be done that I can think of. So let's concentrate on Sally." He turned to Hattie. "Where do we start?"

Hattie laughed. "Where I always said. The scene of the crime."

"The *Celestial Queen*?" Alex asked.

"That's my guess," Hattie said. "If she was wearing that St. Christopher's medal when they killed her she must've been either in bed, or headed to bed for the night. That's when they came for her."

"But what about the booby traps," Ryan said. "She had them all over the place."

Alex shivered. "Ooh, yeah!" he said. "She was a crazy old hide. I loved her, but..." He grinned at his friends. "You have admit she was a little loony tunes. Just a bitty bit."

They all laughed.

"Just a bitty bit," Hattie agreed.

"A weeny," Ryan said.

He turned serious. "Back to the booby traps," he said. "If she had them set they might have gone off and hurt somebody. In which case, it might be kind of messy."

Hattie shrugged. "So it's messy?"

Alex said, "When do we start?"

"School's cancelled the rest of the week," Hattie said. "That wreck has the town turned upside down. Taking people in. Charity drives."

Alex nodded. "Same here," he said. "We're shut tight."

"Then we'll start in the morning," Ryan said.

THIRTY-FOUR

Letter From Philadelphia

They didn't go anywhere the next day. The sun barely made an appearance and the sky remained so dark that the chickens confused day for night and never left their roosts.

The radio warned of a torrential downpour that would dump eight inches or more before the storm cleared the area.

Ryan had heard nothing from his mystery broadcasters the night before and although he returned to his room after breakfast and spent over two hours with his ear pressed to the mattress springs, it was no good.

Verne used the morning calling friends about Alex's glasses. He stuck his head in Ryan's room an hour or so before lunch and gave him a thumbs up.

"I talked to a guy in the Lion's Club in West Palm," he told Ryan. "They have a program for the blind and people with sight problems, with a special emphasis on kids. He said he thinks they can help."

A little later Sammy swung by with the mail from town and to report that the bridge looked in good shape to handle the storm, if and when it hit. Although it was still so dark out Ryan doubted there was any "if" about it.

Verne took Sammy into his office. Ryan tried to linger nearby to big ear what was being said, but his grandmother had Eve bustling about with the vacuum cleaner and so he soon retreated to his room.

A little later there was a tap at his door. It was Verne, sporting a big smile of victory. "Success!" he chortled. "Alex has an appointment next week to get his eyes examined for new glasses."

Ryan was thrilled. "But, how did you get around the charity thing?" he asked.

"I stretched the point a bit," Verne said. "It's a regular Lions Club program for gifted students. Alex is gifted. And a student. Ergo—whatever that means—he gets the glasses."

Ryan laughed. "We'll have to ask Alex what 'ergo' means when he can look up the word with his new specs," he said. "He'll drive us crazy looking things up. He's always complaining that the dictionary print is so small it's almost useless to him now."

Then, before Ryan could say more, Verne turned serious. Reaching into his pocket, he produced an envelope.

"It's from your Aunt Cassie," he said, handing it over. "Your grandmother got one too."

Ryan's heart sped up as he took the letter. He stared at it, afraid to open it and find out what his aunt had to say.

"I'll leave you to it," he heard Verne say—voice sounding as if he were far away.

Then the door closed and he was left alone with the letter.

He put it on the bed. Paced back and forth, staring at it with increasing dread.

Ryan went to his desk, got out his Morse Code kit and sat on the bed, hugging it to his breast. He thought of his father and wondered what he was doing now. Was he thinking of Ryan? Or of his sick wife? He wished mightily that he could speak to him. Plead for words of comfort.

But his father had never been an affectionate man. He was disdainful of weakness. Believed mightily in mind over matter. Before she fell ill, he was always telling his wife to "grin and bear it." An admonition she increasingly resented.

Ryan knew his mother hated military life. She was uncomfortable with the other women, who were mostly born and raised in the Navy. They all had their little ceremonies and teas and PX shopping runs.

"They're all just so phony baloney," she said. "Like they are better than me because I was raised as a civilian."

As time wore on, his mother became convinced they were talking about her behind her back. And that they were laughing at her ignorance of Navy ways and traditions. Over time, it grew worse and she became more resentful and moody.

And then, not long before Pearl Harbor, she'd gone completely to pieces. Fortunately, they'd been visiting her sister, Cassie, when it happened. If they had still been back on the base, Ryan didn't know what he would have done.

It happened at breakfast. Ryan and his cousin, Sandy, had almost finished and his mother still hadn't come down.

"She wasn't feeling well when we went to bed last night," his Aunt Cassie said. "Go see how she is, Ryan, dear. Tell Theresa I'll fix her a tray. And she can have a good lie in if she wants."

His mother didn't answer when he tapped on her door. Finally, he opened it. To his surprise, he found her sitting at her dressing table brushing her long dark hair. She was wearing a flowing blue dressing gown and as he gazed at his mother's face in the mirror he thought he'd never seen anyone so beautiful.

"Mom?" he said.

She didn't answer. Only kept brushing. And she seemed to be humming a little tune to herself.

He went closer. "Mom?" he said again.

Still nothing.

He touched her shoulder.

Crying out in fear, she gave a mighty flinch, and whirled about, striking out at him.

The blow only brushed him but Ryan was so surprised he fell back, grabbing at the dresser as he fell. Several bottles crashed to the floor.

Aunt Cassie and Sandy came running up the stairs and found Ryan there, sitting in a pool of broken perfume bottles.

"I'm okay," he said, getting up. "But there's something wrong with Mom."

She was sitting there, staring straight ahead. Cassie went to her, murmuring, "Theresa? Theresa, darling?"

But she just sat there, brushing her hair, humming a tune.

Cassie reached a hand to touch her.

His mother shrieked, striking out, screaming, "I won't go! I won't go! They can't make me!"

And it was like that all day. Humming softly to herself one moment, then raging outbursts the next.

When Uncle Tom arrived home from work he called a doctor friend who came over to examine her.

She wouldn't let him near her. Striking out at anyone who came close, screaming, "I won't go. They can't make me!"

Days passed. More doctors were called. Sedatives were given. Strings were pulled with the War Department to contact his father. Eventually, she was committed to the asylum. And there she remained.

Staring at the unopened letter, his heart beating like crazy, Ryan put the Morse set in his lap and started tapping the key: S.O.S. S.O.S. S.O.S.

Finally, he calmed down. His heart and breathing slowed. He carefully put the key set aside. Picked up the letter. Drew in a deep breath.

And opened it and started to read:

My Dearest Ryan:

I'm writing to tell you of good news at long last. The doctors say our Theresa is making good progress. True, she isn't very talkative as yet, but she does know who I am on most days.

When our visits end she always begs me to tell her Ryan she loves him. Those are very words, Ryan dearest. 'Tell my Ryan I love him.' Isn't that just marvelous?

Your Aunt Rita was in town for a visit and we had a lovely novena said at the church for your mother.

Now, here is the grandest news of all: The doctors say your dear mother might be well enough to start coming home for weekend visits. And if those visits go well enough, why she might even be allowed to stay longer as time goes by and she heals her poor sick mind.

So, now you know our novenas and prayers are being heard, my darling nephew. From our lips straight to the ears of our sainted Mother Mary.

Love from your Uncle Tom and Sandy…

Your loving aunt—

Cassie

Ryan didn't know whether to laugh or cry. Yes, it *was* good news. His mother was improving. The doctors said so, didn't they? But it sounded like she was far from normal. He wondered if she would ever really get better. And then how long would that last? She'd just be going back to the same life she had before. One that she found so miserable that she had abandoned her son and husband to retreat into insanity.

After dinner, he tarried outside the dining room for a few minutes, listening to his grandmother talking to Verne.

"It's all very well for Cassie to talk about the power of prayer," he heard her say. "But that's nonsense. Prayer never did anybody any good. It's fortitude that is needed. And fortitude is something the poor woman lacks."

Ryan started to get angry. How dare she speak of his mother that way? But then he thought, she's only speaking the truth. Never mind fortitude. His mother just didn't seem to have the strength to bear up under the life she had married into.

His heart gave a jump when he thought maybe she should get a divorce. Just like his grandmother had. But, then, what about his father? And Ryan? Where would that leave them?

He shook it off. Ashamed that he'd started worrying about his own lot when his mother was languishing in a Philadelphia asylum.

And as for prayer—his grandmother was right. Not once in his life had Ryan had a prayer answered. Wishes and prayers were nothing but empty words tossed into empty skies, with less substance than a feather.

At that moment, Ryan became more determined than ever to stay the course. With the help of his new friends, he would crack these mysteries one by one.

He washed his face. Got a cold drink of water, then got out a little note-book and a pencil and carefully positioned himself on the bed, pressing his ear against the mattress.

Nothing happened for a long time. And then it came—a burst of te-legraphy. Ryan strained to hear, desperate to make sense of what he was hearing.

The signal stopped. Quickly, he wrote down what he thought he'd heard.

A moment later and the signals began again. But like the last time he was certain the Code being sent came from a different hand. Another person entirely.

When it stopped he scribbled what he thought were the letters being formed.

The session lasted for about fifteen minutes, then stopped.

He waited patiently for them to resume. An hour of silence passed.

Ryan studied his notes. There were letters grouped into what he thought were words. But even for Code the words were nonsensical.

When the promised storm came, bringing lightning and thunder and torrential rain driven by fierce winds, it found Ryan thoroughly frustrated. But still determined.

By morning the storm was gone and the day dawned bright and clear.

THIRTY-FIVE

Rex

Ryan and Alex struck out after breakfast to meet Hattie. Even on their bikes—and without the pole boats in tow—it was slow going. There was storm debris everywhere. Branches, torn up bushes, even toppled trees littered the island's paths.

To their relief, the newly repaired bridge connecting Sullivan Island with the world had held up. Although it trembled under them when they crossed from the force of the storm-swollen current.

Brown water full of debris churned between the banks. Logs, brush, dead animals—even an entire uprooted banyan tree—hurtled by, slamming into the bridge.

To Ryan's surprise, he saw a dead shark. It was big—eight to ten feet.

"Thought this was fresh water," he said.

"Sharks don't care," his know-it-all friend informed him. "They have super efficient kidneys and livers and can live in both salt water and fresh water, although they prefer the ocean."

"Well, I hope they keep it that way," Ryan said. "Gators are enough for me."

Hattie would be waiting for them at a landing near the Coast Guard base. With only a little wheedling she'd gotten her father to loan them his skiff, which had a nice little outboard engine.

She and Ryan were using the excuse of helping Alex with a science project he was putting together for the Professor to tout his abilities to the scholarship committee. The project was real, a survey of Seminole River wildlife.

Of course, Alex had no intention of working on the project today. It was just their excuse to shake free of adult interference so they could investigate the paddle wheeler with Hattie.

"I felt lousy lyin' to them," Alex said. "They're all so het up about me gettin' new glasses and maybe scholarship money that they didn't question a word I said."

"Yeah, I know what you mean," Ryan said. "I'm going to owe Verne and my grandmother a whole lot of sorries when this is over. But I couldn't think of another way."

"Me neither," Alex said. "If they really knew what we were up to they'd ground us for the rest of our lives."

"And Sally's real killer would literally get away with murder," Ryan said. He sighed. "Even so, I'm with you about feeling lousy."

He patted the pack slung across the handlebars. "But not so lousy," he added with a smile, "that I didn't let my grandmother load us up with sandwiches and stuff."

Indicating the gunnysack Alex was carrying, he laughed and said, "I see it didn't bother you all that much either."

Alex grinned. "Guilty as charged, you smooth talkin' Yankee devil," he said.

They were nearing the county road when Rex suddenly burst out of the underbrush. He barked at them happily and raced alongside the bikes.

Ryan braked to a halt. "Oh, no," he said. "What're you doing here, Rex?"

For an answer, Rex leaped up to brace himself on the crossbars and gave Ryan's face a big lick.

"Aw, yuck!" Ryan said. "That breath!" To Alex, he added, "He's been eating something that was really, really dead."

He noticed that the bandage on Rex's neck had come loose. "Come here, you," he said, dropping the bike on the ground.

After he fixed the bandage he pointed back the way they'd come. "Go home, Rex," he commanded.

The dog didn't budge. Just looked at him with those huge begging eyes.

"Home, I said!"

Rex lowered his head and whined.

"He's breaking my heart," Ryan said.

"He'll just get in the way," Alex said. "Better make him go."

It took a few more "Go home" commands, but eventually, Rex obediently turned and trotted away. Stopping every now and then to stare back at them, making Ryan repeat his commands until there was absolutely no question what he meant, or that he really, really meant it.

When Rex was gone they mounted their bikes and pedaled onward.

They were coming up on the Pennock milk bar when a familiar pickup came screeching around the bend on the wrong side of the road.

Ryan got out of the way in time, but the truck nearly pegged Alex, who veered into a clump of bushes.

There was an angry scream of brakes and Ryan looked back and saw Joe Collins's truck making a U-turn, then come smoking back in their direction. Ryan got off the road in a hurry.

The truck braked violently in front of them. Joe was at the wheel, and two of his sneering buddies were with him.

"Well, lookee who we got here," Joe chortled.

He popped the door and climbed out, his two pals following him.

Ryan and Alex stood together, hanging onto their bikes in case they saw a chance for a quick getaway.

"What do you want, Joe?" Ryan said. "Hope it's not trouble, because Deputy Tindall has warned you off more than once."

Joe looked ostentatiously around. At this hour of the morning the milk bar was closed and the road was likely to remain empty for quite some time.

"I don't see no Deputy Dingleberry around here now, do you boys?" he said.

His friends made loud agreement. "Nope. Don't see nobody," said one. "Coast looks clear to me, Joe."

Collins rubbed the knuckles of his right hand into the open palm of the left. "Guess we're gonna get some scores settled, ain't we, boys?"

More loud agreement.

"What's your problem, Joe?" Alex said. "Your little sister been beatin' up on you again."

"You sure have a big mouth for a colored boy," Joe said. He took a step forward. "Tellin' folks that I was there where that bitch was kilt."

"Don't blame Alex, Joe. That was me." Ryan said. "I'm the one who spotted you. And I'm the one who told Tindall. And I'd do it again."

"Oh, ya would, would ya?" Joe said menacingly.

Ryan looked Joe up and down. They were about the same height, but Joe not only had two years on him, but twenty five pounds or more. Oddly, he wasn't scared. There was no question that Joe would kick his behind. But he'd go home knowing he'd been in a fight.

"Maybe I ought to fix that tongue of your'n," Collins said, reaching for his belt. When his hand came up he was holding a long fishing knife. The early morning sunlight glittered on the serrated gutting blade.

Now Ryan was scared. He reached down for the bicycle pump. It wasn't much, but his grandfather had taught him a thing or two about street fighting.

"Never use an open hand," he'd advised Ryan. "Anything you can wrap your fist around will give you just a little bit more of an edge."

Joe saw the pump and laughed. "What're you gonna do with that, you little Yankee turd?" he said.

"Come closer and you'll see," Ryan said. It was a stupid comeback, but he couldn't think of anything else.

"Happy to oblige you," Joe said and took another step forward, raising the knife.

And then there came a bearlike roar and Rex charged out of the bushes. He leaped straight for Joe, getting him by the sleeve and spinning him around.

Collins screamed as his knife went flying into a ditch. Rex spun around and went for him again. Joe tried to escape into the back of the truck, but Rex got him by the cuff of his jeans, ripping them to shreds.

Still screaming, Joe jerked free and fell over the other side, smashing into the roadway. Momentarily blocked from his target, Rex turned on Joe's buddies, but they leaped into the truck and slammed the door.

A minute later Joe joined them. Rex was on his side now and was going for the open window. Joe got the engine started and peeled away, going just as fast as four wheels and a big damned engine could carry him.

Rex chased the truck for a few yards, then turned around to greet Ryan and Alex with a big doggie grin.

"Good boy!" Ryan shouted.

And Alex joined in with the "good boys" as Rex came trotting up. He sat down in front of the bike and looked up at Ryan. Entreating.

Ryan dropped down beside him and rubbed him all over.

"Okay, okay," he said. "I give! You can go." He looked up at Alex. "He just saved our hides," he said.

"No kidding," Alex laughed.

He mounted his bike. "Come on," he said. "Hattie's waitin' on us."

When they got there, Hattie already had her dad's skiff out of the little boathouse.

"What kept y'all?" she asked. "I've been waitin' for half an hour."

She laughed her head off when they told her the reason for the tardiness.

"Wished I'd have been there to see it," she said, kneeling down to reward Rex with more pats and belly rubs. "Bet Joe messed his britches."

"You could smell him a mile away," Ryan laughed.

THIRTY-SIX
Return to the Celestial Queen

They stashed their bikes in the boathouse with Hattie's. Then, after some tinkering with the throttle, she got the outboard started. They loaded up their supplies, along with an extra can of gasoline, and after Rex hopped aboard, Alex pushed off.

Hattie fed juice into the little engine and away they went. Soon the rushing storm water caught them and they picked up speed.

It was a little scary at first, until Hattie got the hang of it—feathering the throttle to steady the boat against the swift-moving current. Then they were off, flying along the river at a breakneck pace. Rex balanced in the center, nose held high to catch all the delicious odors.

They were moving with the current so after a time Hattie switched off the outboard and they took turns using the pole to keep them centered.

Eventually they came to a quiet place where the rushing water slowed and they were moving along a shady aisle formed by huge red magnolias. Scarlet blossoms spilled down on the gray-green Spanish moss, which fell in heavy drapes, brushing the surface of the water.

As they moved deeper into the shadows the tops of the trees leaned in closer until it was almost like twilight, instead of mid-morning. The canopies were so thick they were like forests themselves.

The sun filtered through the leaves, becoming narrow beams that shone through in a play of multi-colored light. With the cathedral-like atmosphere Ryan half expected to see a priest marching along with a clanking censer, wafting incense blessings into the breeze.

But here the scent was rich and thick and full of life in transition. The perfume of the brilliant magnolia blossoms mingled with the dank smell of rotting vegetation, thick mud and moss covered logs.

Birds flitted among the branches, and fish browsed the shallows, hunting for their breakfast. Giant dragonflies buzzed along, hunting midges and mosquitoes, while dodging the birds and fish who hunted them.

Little animals scurried through the brush and now and then the young adventurers spotted sleepy gators crawling out of their holes to find warm places in the sun.

Just like their previous journey with Sally, a trick of the atmosphere seemed to smother all but the slightest sounds. Ryan heard drops of water fall from over saturated trees to land with a "plunk!" into the river.

Even Rex seemed to be affected. He moved to Ryan's side, gave a long doggy sigh, then rested his head on Ryan's lap. Expecting, and getting, a rub behind the ears.

Hattie was on pole duty now, and he could hear her steady breathing as she set the pole, then pushed, then slowly pulled it out. Reset the pole. Pushed again.

It was a slow, dreamy rhythm—almost a lullaby with the dappling sound of the river caressing the sides of the skiff.

Peering into the shallows, he could see crabs marching along with loot scavenged from the storm—claws waving so they looked like an advancing alien army in one of Ryan's science fiction stories.

Then the current picked up and the skiff became more difficult to manage. Hattie plopped down in her seat and started the outboard. She fed juice into the little engine and the boat settled out and became more controllable.

Nearing a bend, the loud sound of rushing water swept all peaceful feelings aside. Rex popped to his feet and gave a bark. Ryan shushed him, leaning forward to see better. He was on edge, now. His nerves taut.

And then they were coming around the bend and there was the *Celestial Queen* looming before them in all her ruined splendor.

The paddle wheeler was as spooky as the first time Ryan had seen it. The brickwork that had once held the ship's boiler in place looked like broken teeth lining a giant rusted maw.

The gap between the ship and shore was much wider and a piece of the stern had been partly ripped away. It was dangling half in and half out of the rushing water. Bobbing violently up and down.

"Better stop a minute," Hattie said. "Get our bearings."

She disengaged the engine and tossed a canvas anchor over the side. When it filled with water, the boat slowed enough for Alex and Ryan to grab poles and dig in, holding the skiff against the current. Rex obediently stayed where Ryan put him, looking anxiously about.

The three friends sat quietly for a long time, checking around for signs of danger.

Woodsmoke tickled Ryan's nose and he turned his head, trying to see which direction it came from. But then it was gone.

"I think we're okay," Alex whispered. "Let's go."

But then a scaly snout lifted out of the water.

"Stop," Hattie hissed. "Geraldine, remember?"

Ryan remembered very well the toothy maw that had snatched up the offal Sally had dumped over the side when she was cleaning fish for her cats.

"Wait a minute," Hattie said. "I've got something for her."

For a mad moment Ryan wondered if she'd brought along a wind-up clock, like the Peter Pan joke "tick-tock" joke they'd made.

Hattie lifted up a bait bucket. "Fish guts," she said. "Fetched some along just in case." Ryan smiled. Only Hattie would remember important little details like that.

The she hurled the bucket as far away as she could. It splashed into the water and Geraldine slipped out of sight. There was a ripple as she moved toward the place where the bucket had fallen. Then the water churned as Geraldine found her breakfast and gulped it down.

Hot and humid as the morning was, Alex shivered. "Hope she gets indigestion," he said.

Giggling nervously, Hattie said. "Can you imagine the giant Bromo Seltzer?"

They all laughed as she spread her hands to demonstrate just how big that tablet would have to be.

"Okay, let's calm down," Ryan said in normal tones. "We've got booby traps to deal with, remember?"

The others nodded and Hattie engaged the engine and cautiously edged the skiff forward until they touched the side of the ship. Alex found the bolt Sally had used before and tied the boat up.

Rex jumped up, ready to go with them.

"Remember the cats," Hattie warned.

"Oh, yeah," Ryan said, remembering the caterwauling fiends who were Sally's sole companions.

"Stay, Rex," he said.

The dog whined. Not liking this one bit.

"I said, stay!" Ryan repeated, in the deepest, most commanding voice he could manage. It obviously worked because Rex obediently sat back on his haunches and then watched anxiously, as the three friends went up the side.

Ryan was the last in line and he hung by a bolt for minute, waiting for the others to clear the railing.

A few yards away the river was thundering through the gap and he swore he could feel the *Queen* shift. He waited, but the sensation passed, and he continued onward.

Just before she reached the rails, Hattie stopped. "Careful of the cats," she said.

Cautiously, she pulled herself up until she reached the rail. Then stopped. Waiting. Expectant.

But nothing happened.

Puzzled, she continued onward, the others following.

Not a single yowl greeted them when they reached the deck. They looked around and there was not a cat to be found.

"I don't like this," Hattie said.

Neither did anyone else but after a moment they continued onward.

Sally's hand-painted warning greeted them when they reached the main deck.

DANGER!
NO TRESPASSING!

From then on they moved with greater caution. And one by one, they found the booby traps—all of which had been disarmed.

"She must've been asleep when they came," Hattie said. "She said she always disarmed the traps so she didn't trip them accidentally in the middle of the night."

"Yeah, but she had one that she said she always left on," Ryan said.

"Right!" Alex said. "The guillotine contraption. Her Froggie machine with the big old machete blade."

They found it a few minutes later. And when they did, all of Deputy Tindall's murder theories went over the side.

Broken wood and metal and a black pool of dried blood marked where Sally's guillotine had once stood.

Hattie grimaced. "I think she got somebody," she said.

"And she got him good from the looks of all that blood," Alex said.

"Let's check her cabin," Ryan said.

They moved onward in growing dread. The blood splatter had spooked them, even though Sally had assured them that there were no traps set past the guillotine.

They smelled the awful odor of death before they reached Sally's cabin. They covered their noses with their shirt tails and moved onward.

The door was partway open. Ryan reached out to push it wider then jumped as something darted past him. Alex and Hattie made little noises of surprise.

"A rat!" Hattie said. "I hate rats!"

"Ain't too fond of 'em, myself," Alex said.

The three looked at each other. Nobody wanted to go in that cabin.

Finally, Ryan steeled himself, pushed the door the rest of the way and stepped in.

Instantly, he jumped back, startled by the loud buzzing of tens of thousands of flies lifting from the floor.

"Let me by," Hattie said, stepping past Ryan.

She had piece of board that she used to shoo clouds of flies out the door. Ryan didn't know how she could stand it.

The cabin was like something out of a pre-Hayes Code horror movie. Everything had been ripped apart. The sleeping bag had been torn to pieces. The Spanish moss mattress ticking scattered everywhere. The library shelves had been pulled down and books and charts dumped on the deck.

The whole cabin was covered with a thick layer of black blood. The walls and deck turned into a charnel house.

More horrible still were the dead cats. There were three of them and they looked like they had been hacked in half.

Flies continued to buzz everywhere and the stench was awful.

"Oh, Jesus, Lord," Alex said, rushing from the cabin. Ryan and Hattie close behind him.

They stood in the passageway, chests heaving with sobs. Choking and gagging. Tears running down their faces.

"Oh, poor, poor Sally," Hattie said.

Ryan started to say something, then turned aside and doubled over to heave.

Outside they head a crash of thunder.

"Ah, geeze," Alex said. "We're gonna get hit with another storm."

"Maybe we'd better go," Ryan said.

"Not until we're finished," Hattie insisted.

The three retreated topside, only to be greeted by a stiffening wind and a few drops of rain.

The sky was dark now. There were flashes of lightning followed by rolling thunder.

Ryan ran to the side and looked down. Rex saw him and barked. He wanted badly to come aboard. But Ryan didn't dare chance it.

Ryan pointed at him. "Stay," he croaked. Voice rough from sickness. "Stay!"

And it was if the gods were listening in, because the rain lessened. After a moment the three moved inside to discuss their findings.

"Moonshiners didn't do that," Alex.

"Neither did Joe Collins," Ryan said.

"Well who, then?" Hattie said.

"Anybody who got hit with that guillotine," Ryan said, "is either dead, or in the hospital."

"Or, hiding out," Alex said.

The two looked at him. Alex shrugged. "He'd need somebody to take care of him," he said. "But it's possible."

Alex leaned out to look at the skies. They were a little lighter. The rain had all but stopped.

"Looks okay," he said. "For awhile, anyway."

"Good. Let's look around some more," Ryan said.

Steeling themselves against the very real possibility of new horror, they investigated further.

In the kitchen, they found a heap of bloody rags and gauze.

"I'll bet they tried to treat somebody here," Ryan said.

Hattie was at the stove. "That's not all," she said, displaying a dirty frying pan. "They did some cooking, too."

She sniffed the pan. Poked around a little heap of greasy stuff. Shook her head.

"Don't know what this is," she said.

Ryan took the pan, frowning as he tried the smell test.

"Sausage," he decreed. "But not country style sausage. More like you get in a delicatessen."

Alex frowned. "Never tried any delicatessen food," he said. "Bet none of those moonshiners have either."

Ryan said, "Yeah, but Collins might have. His old man's rich enough."

"Maybe so," Hattie said. "But he'd still have to go all the way to Miami to find anything that looked like—or even smelled like delicatessen food."

"What's this?" Ryan said, reaching into a trash bin and coming out with a hunk of what looked like hard roll.

He broke it in half. Scraped it with a finger. Sniffed it. "Sesame seeds," he said. "This is definitely not local bread," he said.

"Let's take a look in the wheelhouse," Alex said.

They climbed up to the wheelhouse, which had only been partially fixed up by Hattie. There was a tall barstool pushed up against the place where a window used to be.

The rain had started up again and was splashing inside. The three were too overcome by what they were finding to pay it any mind.

"Bet Sally used to sit up here like a ship's captain," Ryan said, indicating the barstool. "Smoking her pipe and studying the river."

"What's this?" Hattie said, going to a wide shelf beneath the empty window pane.

She displayed what looked like a nautical chart of the Seminole River. There were pencil scrawls, but the recent storms had all but obliterated what had been written there.

However, Ryan could see the indentation marks of a pencil following a route along the river. Looking closer he could make out other routes that had been traced.

Unrolling the chart more he spotted the blurred remains of a large "x" marking a specific spot.

"This is us," he said, indicating the mark. "*The Celestial Queen*. And all the lines go out from there."

He traced the lines with a finger. "This one goes up behind the Coast Guard base," he said. "And this one goes to Hobe Hill. And then this one that goes to... Hmm... I can't make it out."

"Blowing Rocks," Alex said. "That's where it goes. Blowing Rocks."

"Why'd anyone want to go there?" Hattie said.

"Especially if they had some poor sap who was hurt," Alex added.

"I'd like to hurt him some," Hattie said, "after what they did to Sally. And the cats."

"Yeah, but why would anyone do something like that?" Ryan wondered. "If we had a hurt friend we'd want to get him to a doctor, or a hospital. Not hang around and cook dinner and then go sneaking off into the bushes."

Alex shrugged. "Bunch of revenge happy crazies," he said. "First Sally, for the booby trap. Then the cats, for maybe scratching one of them. Least, that's how it looks to me."

"We have to tell somebody," Ryan said.

"Yeah, but who's gonna believe us?" Hattie said. "You have to admit it's all pretty far-fetched."

"Then, we'll bring them out here and show them," Ryan said, rolling up the map. "These are facts. They can't deny facts that are staring them right in the face."

Alex gave a nasty chuckle. He said, "You ain't been around Jove Beach too long, have you?"

Then, as if acting on some contrary celestial cue, lighting crashed and thunder boomed and the rain began to fall in earnest.

Underneath them, the *Queen* suddenly shifted. This time, so hard, it hurled them to the deck.

"We'd better get out of here," Alex shouted over the thunder and the torrential rain.

Ryan stuffed the chart in his shirt then followed his friends out onto the deck. They ran for the rail, slipping and sliding on the wet surface. Rex was barking his head off now, warning them.

Not that they needed a warning. The ship was creaking and cracking and shifting violently about. Meanwhile, above them, lighting flashed, thunder sounded and rain came crashing down in blinding sheets.

As they clambered over the side, the *Celestial Queen* gave a great groan and a shriek and lurched forward, nearly throwing them into the water.

They dropped into the boat, pushing an anxious Rex aside.

Alex cast off the line. Hattie got the outboard going. And Ryan grabbed his pole and pushed off just as the paddle wheeler's stern started to come slowly around.

Then with an enormous CRACK! it split away from the ship and came rushing down on them.

Hattie goosed the engine and they roared away just in time—the stern going past like an express train.

The heavy current caught them, spinning them around. Hattie fought for control. But it was a losing battle.

"Let's just get to shore," Alex shouted.

The rain was so heavy that Ryan could barely see. But then he made out a little finger of shoreline about ten yards away.

Pointing, he shouted, "Over there," and Hattie turned in that direction.

Pieces of the wreck banged into the boat, but Hattie managed to maintain control.

Then, agonizingly, she got turned toward the shoreline. Minutes later they slammed against it.

Rex went over the side. But Ryan caught his collar and hung on until he got his feet under him. The water was waist deep, but moving fast, pulling against them.

Finally, he got Rex ashore, then turned back to help Hattie and Alex beach the boat, then pull it up higher on the bank so the rising river wouldn't carry it away.

They got the outboard off the boat, tipped the skiff on its side, then crawled under it. Ryan pulled Rex in with him.

The dog whimpered and shivered as forks of lightning split the sky and thunder boomed like artillery fire.

Ryan hugged him close, soothing him, while his fingers tapped out S.O.S. against his fur.

Knowing all the while there was no one to save them.

THIRTY-SEVEN
The Professor

When the three weary friends reached the boathouse a few hours later it was a bright, shining Florida afternoon.

They were tired and bedraggled and more than a little dazed from their experience. Huddled under the skiff, watching the *Celestial Queen* slowly break apart while the storm raged around them. Meanwhile, reliving the horror they'd seen. And feeling more and more helpless and isolated.

The paddle wheeler had been jammed into the channel for many decades, constantly pummeled by the Seminole River. Later, Alex surmised that more than likely the pressure of the river had pinned the wreck against the embankment until it was almost part of it. Eventually Florida's violent weather won out. Now she was slowly coming to pieces before their eyes.

Ryan watched the wheelhouse come off and crash into the water. And then it was bobbing downstream, hitting the banks. Sticking. Then bumping onward, carrying debris with it.

The boiler was next. The last of the brickwork gave way—a river of old brick cascading down the side. Then the boiler groaned free and fell, taking more of the ship with it as it smashed against the side then plummeted into the river.

And then—as if some cosmic engineer had turned a shut off valve—the torrent became a drizzle, the skies calmed. And the storm ended.

Numbed by their experience, they crawled out from under the boat. Without speaking they wrestled it up and into the water. Attached the outboard. Found their places. Hattie gave the little engine one pull. Then another. On the third try it coughed into life, then caught and off Hattie went, dodging the debris that was piling up on the far side of the bend, then shooting out into mid-channel.

Gradually they made their way through downed trees, broken limbs and dead animals. The gators were out in force feeding on the storm's bounty.

And now their journey was over. The skiff had been cleaned and returned to its place in the boathouse.

They looked at each other. Gradually coming back to awareness.

And Ryan said, "The hard part's next."

After a long moment, Alex sighed. "You're right," he said.

"I don't know about you two," Hattie said, but I need a minute to think. To get my mind in order."

Ryan said, "The milk bar's just down the road. My treat."

* * * *

Several of their classmates were in the milk bar when they entered, including Marla and her boyfriend, Tom.

She reacted in surprise when she saw Ryan. "What are you doing here, Ryan?" she said. "I thought you were stuck on Sullivan's Island."

Ryan's eyebrows rose. "Why would I be stuck?"

"Because the bridge is out again, silly," she said.

"Must'a been fixed," Tom, a skinny kid with a huge Adam's apple, said. "Or, he wouldn't be here."

Ryan turned to his friends. "I'd better call Verne," he said.

He went up to the counter, where another of his classmates worked part time.

Handing her a dollar, he said, "Can I get a chocolate malt, Patty?" Then, indicating Hattie and Alex: "And get them whatever they want."

Patty sniffed at Hattie and gave Alex a suspicious look. She clearly did not like colored people. But like most people of her ilk in Jove Beach—where it was considered impolite to express hard core racial views and where there were too few people to turn away business—she kept her feelings to herself.

"But first," Ryan said, "may I use your phone to call home?" He pointed at the phone mounted on the wall. "My grandmother is going to be worried about me."

"I suppose so," she said, reluctantly. Yankees were also not among Patty's favorite people.

While Patty got Alex and Hattie's order and started assembling them, Ryan went to the phone, gave the handle a few twists, and the operator answered.

"Mrs. Richards," he said. "This is Ryan. Ryan Karr. Myrtle Sullivan's grandson?"

"I know who you are, hon," Mrs. Richards said. "Your grandfather's gonna be pleased as all get out to hear from you. He's been callin' all over town askin' about you and Alex and Hattie." A pause, then, "Is everybody okay, hon?"

"Oh, we're fine, Mrs. Richards," Ryan assured her. "We're at the milk bar getting some malts."

"Well, that's a relief," Mrs. Richards said. "The town's already in an uproar over Jim Collins's kid."

Ryan was rocked back. "Joe? What happened to him?"

"Oh, didn't you hear?" Mrs. Richards said. "He's been arrested on a murder charge. Gig Light Sally's murder."

Ryan gulped, then said, "Thanks, Mrs. Robinson. Now, could you put me through, please?"

A moment later Verne was the line. "Ryan!" he exclaimed. "Are you okay? We've been worried sick."

"I'm sorry, Verne," Ryan said. "We were stuck until the storm was over. We didn't mean to worry anybody. But everybody is safe and sound. I just stopped by the milk bar to give you a call before we came home."

Verne sighed. "Well, that's going to be a problem, Ryan. The bridge is out again."

"I heard," Ryan said. "What about the ford where we crossed before?"

"It's impassible," Verne said. "I was just down there and a big piece of the embankment came away. It won't be safe to cross until the water level drops."

Before Verne could continue, Ryan broke in: "I just heard about Joe Collins. I really need to talk to you about that."

"Sure, sure," Verne said. "But first let's get our own problems settled. I already talked to Hattie's father and he said he could put you and Alex up until we can get across the river tomorrow."

Before Ryan could reply, Verne said, "Another thing. And this is important. Sammy got a call from the Professor. He'll be coming into the station aboard the *Florida Special* this afternoon. The train gets in at 3:30. He has some sample tests for Alex. And he wants him to get to work on them right away. The scholarship committee will be meeting pretty soon."

"That's wonderful news, Verne," Ryan said. "But I have to talk to you about Joe Collins. He—"

Just then crackling noises overwhelmed the phone. He could hear Verne saying, "Ryan? Ryan?" But it sounded like it came from a distant planet, instead of a few miles away.

Desperate, Ryan gripped the phone harder. "Listen, Verne. Please. People are making a big mistake. Joe didn't have anything to do—"

But before he could say more, the line went dead. A split second later Mrs. Richards was back.

"I'm sorry, Ryan," she said. "The line is down. We won't be able to get a crew out that way until tomorrow."

Stunned, all Ryan could say was, "Oh."

"But don't you worry, young man," she said. "If you and Alex have nowhere else to go, y'all can stay with us."

Ryan sighed. "Thanks, Mrs. Richards," he said. "That's very nice of you. But Verne said Hattie Peters' folks were going to put us up until he and Sammy can get across the river."

"Oh, that's nice, hon. Now you take care, you hear?" And she was gone.

He turned to find Hattie and Alex staring at him, wondering what was going on. He put a finger to his lips, signaling silence.

Patty walked over to him, hand extended with his change.

"Thanks, Patty," he said, taking the money. "Say, is it okay if we take our malts outside? Rex is out there and he's still pretty upset about that storm."

Apparently Patty' prejudice didn't extend to dogs. She was immediately sympathetic. "Poor thing," she said. "My little Mitzy is terrified of storms. I have to hold her the whole time."

She reached into the fridge and came out with a hot dog. "Here's a little treat for him," she said. "Bring the glasses back when you're done."

He thanked her, got his chocolate malt and followed Alex and Hattie out the door. Rex was waiting patiently outside. He didn't look the least bit upset, but enjoyed the hot dog immensely just the same.

"What's going on?" Hattie asked.

"First off," Ryan said, "Alex and I are stuck on this side of the river until tomorrow."

"Ah, geeze," Alex said. "Closest people I got are my cousin down in Del Rey."

"Don't worry about it, Alex," Ryan said. To Hattie he said, "Verne already talked to your dad and he said we could stay at your place."

Hattie paled. For some reason this bothered her. Then, after getting her bearings, she said, "There really isn't any room at my house. Dad must mean the bungalow next door. It's empty until the next Coast Guard family moves in. But it's furnished. And we've got plenty of sheets and blankets and stuff."

Ryan shrugged. Compared to what he had to say next, it seemed unimportant.

"Mrs. Richards said Joe Collins was arrested for Sally's murder."

Alex nodded. "We already got that bit of news from Patty," he said. "Guess they picked him up not long after he hassled us."

"Patty was happier than a pig in a wallow," Hattie said. "So were Tom and Marla."

"Guess Joe doesn't have a whole lot of friends," Alex said with a grin.

"Yeah, but he didn't do it," Ryan said.

"I know that. And you and Alex know that," Hattie said. "But the question is the same as before. What do we do about it?"

"I was going to suggest we start with Verne," Ryan said. "Get him on our side first. He'll know what to do."

"Maybe," Alex said. "Except now we don't have any evidence. The *Celestial Queen* is a goner, remember?"

Ryan sighed and tapped his shirt, where he had the rolled up chart. "Just some illegible marks on an old chart," he said.

"That's not much better than nothing," Hattie said.

Ryan didn't like it, but he had to admit she was right.

He said, "In any case, I guess we'll have to wait until tomorrow when Verne can get off the island." He looked at Hattie. "Unless you think your father can help?"

She shook her head. "He hates to get involved with the locals," she said. "He's always been like that." She looked down at the ground. "Makes it even harder on my mom. She doesn't get along with the other Coast Guard wives. For them, it's Coast Guard, Coast Guard twenty four hours a day."

Ryan knew the problem very well, but he didn't think Hattie was into a big discussion about it just now. She was still too storm battered.

Then he remembered Verne's other message. "Alex," he said. "Your dad talked to the Professor. He wants you to meet him at the train station this afternoon. He's got some sample test papers. Something about the scholarship committee meeting soon."

Alex perked up. "I've got the *Florida Special's* schedule memorized," he said. "It gets in at 3:30."

Ryan peered through the milk bar window at the clock on the wall. It was 3:15.

"We'd better hurry," he said.

Hastily, they returned their milkshake glasses, hopped on their bikes and pedaled like crazy for the train station.

* * * *

The last passengers were scurrying aboard the train when they reached the station. When they spotted the Professor, he was pacing anxiously back and forth, a large parcel under one arm.

When he saw them, his face split into a relieved grin.

"Alex!" he cried. "Am I happy to see you. We are about ready to depart."

As if on cue, the engineer gave a blast of his whistle.

The Professor shoved the parcel into Alex's arms. "Study these like you've never studied before, young man," he said. "If you do well—and I expect you will—I can reliably predict that your whole life will be impacted favorably."

"Thank you, Professor," Alex said. "And I'm getting new glasses any day now. So that will be a big help."

The Professor clapped him on the back. "Your father told me all about it."

He turned to Ryan. "I understand that your grandfather had a lot to do with it," he said.

Once again, Ryan decided not to correct him about his relationship to Verne. Besides, he had something more important to ask.

"Professor," he said. "I know you don't have time for me to tell you the whole story, but I've been receiving these odd telegraphic messages. The biggest problem is, I can't make head or tails of the words. I'm either writing them down wrong, or the words are way outside of my vocabulary."

The Professor frowned. "I seriously doubt that, Ryan," he said. "You are much too bright. You might be stumped by a single word. But not several."

To Ryan's dismay, the train whistle blasted through the station.

The Professor took a step toward the passenger car's open door. "Sorry, I really have to go. Can you give me just one quick example?"

Ryan nodded. "Sure. And it's a short one, too. It's spelled N-E-I-N. I don't even know how it's pronounced."

"It's pronounced 'nein,'" the Professor said.

Ryan frowned. That didn't make sense. "You mean, like the number nine? And they just misspelled it? A typo? If so, they made the same mistake four or five times."

The Professor shook his head. "No, no. Not the number nine. But 'nein,' as in the German word for no. I don't speak German. But I do know a few basics. 'Nein' for no. 'Ja' for yes."

Ryan was rocked back on his heels. "German, you say? Are you sure?"

The Professor nodded. "Yes, I'm sure. It's German, alright. Next time I'll bring a little English to German dictionary with me. Make things easier for you."

Before Ryan could say another word a third and final blast sounded and the train started to move and another conductor shouted "All aboard!"

The Professor grabbed a rail and stepped up on the platform. "See you next time through," he said.

He stood in the open doorway and waved as the train slowly picked up speed, then disappeared around the bend.

Ryan turned to his friends. Dumbfounded he asked, "Did you hear that? The Professor said it was German. I've been picking up German signals."

Hattie got it immediately. "It has to be a U-Boat," she said. "Morse Code signals from a U-boat! Talking to somebody onshore."

"Yeah, but, who are they talking to?" Alex said.

"The people who killed Sally," Ryan said.

THIRTY-EIGHT
The Base

The lighthouse towered over them as they walked their bikes along the pathway leading to the family bungalows on the edge of the Coast Guard base.

"Wow, now that is somethin' else!" Alex exclaimed. "Never seen anythin' that high. Even in West Palm Beach."

"Haven't you ever been here before?" Ryan asked.

Alex snorted. "You must be kiddin'," he said. "They barely let me in the milk bar. Surprised the stuffin' outta me that the sentry let me on the base with you two."

Ryan had noticed the nasty look of appraisal the young sentry had given Alex. He'd been oh, so friendly with Hattie and polite to Ryan. But even with orders from Mr. Peters to let all three of them on the base, he was clearly reluctant. Almost to the point of rudeness.

"I'm really sorry about that, Alex," Hattie said, embarrassed. Then, fiercely, she added, "If he had said something I would have given him a piece of my mind."

"But he didn't," Alex said, soothingly. "So why fight when you don't have to? Besides, it's not your fault."

Anxious to change the subject, he pointed up at the lighthouse. "See how they've got all but a skinny horizontal window blacked out? Can't let out that much light."

"Dad told me all about it," Hattie said. "These U-boat attacks have them caught between a rock and a hard place. Too much light makes the freighters easier for the U-boats to see. Too little, and the freighters might miss the channel and run aground, or hit a reef."

Ryan stopped to look out at sea. After the storm, the Atlantic was at peace. It looked like paradise. Blue skies. Bright sun. Low rolling swells. Soaring sea birds and leaping fish. Spread out along a stretch of dazzling white beaches, lined with palm trees and coconuts. And tropical foliage ablaze with color.

But somewhere out there a U-boat lurked—waiting for its next target.

"Come on," Hattie said, shaking him out of his reverie. "It's getting late."

Hattie's house—a cheery little bungalow with a well-trimmed yard—was on the far edge of the neighborhood. The bungalows were all new, or newly refurbished, and all but a dozen or more seemed to be occupied. Kids were playing in the yards, housewives were at the clotheslines, taking in the wash, and men were unloading moving vans, transferring the contents into newly occupied homes.

"The base is growing like crazy," Hattie said, as they neared the house. "When we first got here from Georgia most of the places were empty. It looked like a ghost town."

"It's said that the lighthouse was built on Indian burial grounds," Alex said. "So maybe it really was a ghost town."

Ryan leaned down to pat Rex. "Hear that, Rex?" he said. "That's your job. Keeping your eyes peeled for ghosts."

Rex woofed. Alex laughed, but Hattie—strangely—seemed preoccupied, and edgy.

"You won't think it's so funny," Alex said, "when some haunt in a feather headdress comes after you tonight with a tomahawk."

"I'll just sic Rex on him," Ryan said. But then he noticed Hattie's nervousness. "What's wrong, Hattie?" he said.

She shook her head. "Nothin'," she said. Then, "You guys wait here while I check in with my dad." She pointed to another, identical bungalow, next to hers. "That's where you'll be stayin' tonight."

"Thanks," Ryan said. "It looks nice."

"Another thing," Hattie said. "My dad has a little pocket German dictionary the Coast Guard gives out. I'll grab it for you."

"That's great," Ryan said. "Next time I'll be ready for them."

Hattie just nodded, then licked dry lips. Clearly on edge. Like a tightrope walker ready to take her first step. She approached the house as if in dread. The reason for the dread became apparent the next moment when they heard the crash of broken crockery.

And then a woman was shouting, "Where'd you hide it, Steven? I'm not in your damned Coast Guard. You're not my commanding officer."

There were more sounds of broken glass. Then they heard a man pleading: "Now, Bridget. You know how you get when you drink. I'm only doing it for you, honey. Remember what the doctor said. It's gonna kill you, baby. Kill you!"

Hattie turned back to look at them. She started to speak. But she just shook her head and then ducked into the house.

A minute later they heard Mr. Peters say, "Look who's here, sweetheart! It's Hattie. Hattie's home." His voice was overly loud, the tone of one speaking to a child, or an addled adult.

And then Mrs. Peters was saying, "Hattie, honey. Where have you been? I've missed you so."

They heard Hattie's voice, but she was speaking so softly they couldn't make out what she was saying, although her tone was soothing and gentle.

"Oh, Hattie," Mrs. Peters exclaimed. Then she burst into tears.

Alex nudged Ryan. "Maybe we ought to make ourselves scarce." He indicated the adjoining bungalow. "Let's go see what our digs look like."

Inside the bungalow, they switched on the lights and found a comfortably furnished living room, with cane-backed chairs, a long couch and a glass-topped coffee table. They sat on the couch, Rex between them.

"That's terrible," Alex said. "I knew Hattie had it rough, but not that rough."

Ryan sighed. "You don't know how lucky you are, Alex," he said. "You have a great mom and dad. And sisters who love you, even if they do drive you crazy."

Alex gave him a penetrating look. Perhaps seeing things in Ryan that he hadn't been aware of before.

"It's that bad, is it?" he said.

Ryan's throat thickened. His eyes were suddenly wet. Instead of answering, he gently stroked Rex's head.

After he composed himself, he said, "It's hard to explain to an outsider what's it like when your father's in the military." He drew in a deep breath, then let it out. "Some people can't seem to ever get used it."

In a low voice, Alex asked, "That what happened to your mom?"

A whole raft of conflicting emotions and confused thoughts welled up in Ryan. He wanted so badly to spill his guts to Alex. Tell him about all the things that had happened. He opened his mouth several times to speak, Alex leaning closer to hear. But then it all collapsed.

He shrugged. "I guess," he said.

For a moment he thought Alex was going to push the issue. Try to draw him out. He almost wished he would. But then he felt ridiculous. Here was Alex, a colored, half-blind boy with a father who only had one hand, living in world that sometimes treated him like a festering thorn that it desperately wanted to pull out and dispose of. Compared to all that, Ryan's problems were baby stuff.

Just then, there came a great CRUMP! The whole bungalow shook and windows rattled in their frames so hard Ryan thought they'd explode.

Rex leaped to his feet, barking. And then there came another CRUMP! and Ryan and Alex were running outside to see what had happened.

Looking out to sea they spotted twin columns of smoke rising on the far horizon. Then sirens were wailing and people were shouting and Hattie's dad came bursting out of the house, pulling on his uniform jacket.

He shouted at them, "Stay here!"

Which was quite unnecessary. Where would they go? Then he was sprinting down the road to the Coast Guard headquarters.

Then, to Ryan's surprise, he found Hattie moving in between him and Alex.

"Another U-boat attack," Hattie said. The second this week." She looked at Ryan. "Probably your Germans," she said.

"Yeah," Ryan said bitterly. "My Germans."

THIRTY-NINE
The Boy Who Cried U-Boat

Verne put a big arm over Ryan's shoulder. "Are you ready for them?" he asked.

Ryan gulped. "Yessir, I'm ready," he said.

Verne looked at his two friends. "How about you two?" he asked.

In the light beaming through his office window, they looked drawn and weary.

Alex started to reply, then licked dry lips and merely nodded.

Sammy patted his son's arm. "You sure, son?"

Alex drew himself up. "I'm sure, Pop," he replied. Firm.

Attention turned to Hattie, who pulled in a deep breath, then expelled it. "I'm ready," she said. "I just wish my father had shown up. But he wouldn't listen. Said it was all a bunch of hooey and went off to work."

"If you can convince the three men waiting out there your father will come around," Verne assured her.

Hattie blurted, "Momma always said he had problems listening." Immediately after she looked mortified. "I'm sorry," she said. "I shouldn't be talking about family business."

"No sorries needed," Verne said. "You're under a lot of pressure. But when you're out there—" he pointed to the door that led to the living room… "- it'd be wise to watch your tongue."

"Yessir," Hattie said, chastened.

"Now, let me warn you," Verne said. "I twisted arms into pretzels to get everybody out here to Sullivan's Island because it's neutral territory. But they're going to be pretty hostile. They've got their suspects—Smoky Anderson and Joe Collins. And they've got all the evidence they think they'll need to convict them."

Verne shook his head. "And now you three come along with a whole other theory. And a pretty far-fetched one at that. German saboteurs. Sounds like the plot of a Saturday morning movie serial."

Ryan was suddenly alarmed. "But you believe us, don't you, sir?"

Verne sighed. "Let's put it this way," he said. "I think you sincerely believe you saw what you claim you saw. And that you are equally sincere in your conclusions."

"But you think it could be our imaginations, right?" Ryan pressed.

"I honestly don't know," Verne said. "You are three of the most level-headed kids I've ever had to pleasure to meet."

"But we're still just kids," Hattie said, an edge of bitterness in her voice.

"And one of us is the wrong color," Alex added, his jaw set to its most stubborn mode.

Sammy came in. "You'll be facin' that your whole blessed life, son," he said. "Least this time you'll be facin' it with friends at your side."

Alex frowned, then the frown suddenly turned to a grin. "We've already done rattlesnakes and moonshiners," he said to his friends. "Guess we can handle a couple of cops and a Coast Guard officer, huh, guys?"

Ryan and Hattie laughed. "Sure we can," Ryan said.

"Piece of cake," Hattie said. She giggled. "Of the pineapple upside down variety."

Verne smiled. "That's the spirit," he said. With that he rose from his overstuffed chair, then he and Sammy escorted them into the living room.

Their newly found high spirits turned leaden the moment they walked into the room. There were three very serious men waiting for them: Deputy Tindall, his boss, Sheriff Plant and Lt. Matheson, head of security at the Coast Guard base.

Plant was a portly, middle-aged man with a uniform tailored to hide his expansive gut, and two heavy gold rings on his right hand. Ryan had heard whispers that he used those rings with some effect when questioning suspects.

Matheson was in his late 30's, trim in his uniform and his eyes had the steely, far away gaze of a man who spent a lifetime at sea.

Tindall was nervous in their company, his bald dome glistening with sweat.

They were seated in a semi-circle around a long couch. A tray of ice cold sweet tea and cookies had been set on a low table between their seats and the couch.

Ryan noticed that his grandmother had taken up position in a far corner of the room. She had her sewing basket out and was busying herself repairing one of Verne's work shirts.

The three friends sat in the couch, while Verne and Sammy pulled up more chairs and sat next to the inquisitors.

Verne said, "I want to thank you gentlemen for taking time out of your busy schedules. But I wouldn't have asked you here if it wasn't a matter of utmost importance. Justice, as they say, must be served."

Tindall snorted. "Justice for a moonshiner," he said. "Don't that beat all!"

Sheriff Plant frowned. "Now, deputy," he said, "we're also talkin' about the son of one of our most prominent citizens."

Chastened, Tindall ducked his head. "Yessir," he said. "Sorry sir."

The sheriff turned back to Verne. "Havin' said that, I've heard a little bit of what this is about from Lieutenant Matheson. And what I heard sounds pretty far-fetched to me."

"After listening to Hattie's father," Matheson said, "I almost declined to come." Then he chuckled "But Mr. Sullivan here can be most persuasive."

In the corner, Ryan's grandmother spoke up. "I expect you're all enjoying those pool tables he donated to the officers' club a couple of months back."

Laughter all around at that, although Ryan saw that his grandmother hadn't cracked a smile. She was dead serious. For the first time he realized she was actually on his side. It emboldened him.

"May I speak?" he said.

"Go ahead, son," Verne said. "That's why we're all here."

"There's no denying that what we have to say sounds far-fetched," Ryan said. "But it is all true. And based on hard facts."

"Let's hear those facts, then, young man," Sheriff Plant said.

Ryan said, "It all started with Morse Code signals that I started picking up a month or so ago."

"I understand from Mrs. Wilkinson down at Western Union that you're an amateur telegrapher," the sheriff said.

"Yessir," Ryan said. "My dad's a submariner. The chief telegraph operator aboard the boat. He gave me a Morse Code set and I've been practicing pretty regular."

The sheriff nodded. "So you started hearin' these signals on your receiver," he said. "And it made you suspicious." He looked the other men. "That's understandable."

"Nossir," Ryan said. "I didn't pick them on a receiver. I don't have one."

The sheriff frowned. "Then how did you hear them."

Ryan glanced at his friends, who looked at him with great sympathy. Feeling like he was about to high dive from a cliff, he took a deep breath.

"Through the mattress springs in my bed, sir," he said.

There was an explosive, "Nonsense!" as Lt. Matheson jumped to his feet. "That's the stupidest thing I have ever heard," he said.

He turned to Plant and Tindall. "I don't know about you two, but I'm not wasting anymore of my time."

"Just a minute, lieutenant," Verne said, heaving himself to his feet. Peering down at Matheson from his great height, he added, "I don't appreciate you calling my grandson stupid," he said. "Now, instead of name-calling and making hasty assumptions, why don't you sit down and hear the boy out?"

Matheson gulped. "Sorry about that," he said. "There's no excuse for rudeness. But I'd be lying if I didn't tell you that in my mind the boy has an overactive imagination. Hattie's father said young Ryan is a science fiction fan. But come on—Morse Code in mattress springs. That's beyond science fiction."

"Just the same," Verne said, "I would take it as a personal favor if you sat back down and heard the boy out. And try to keep an open mind."

Matheson sighed. "Very well," he said, returning to his seat. "Go ahead, son," he said.

"Yessir," Ryan said. "But about the mattress springs. I talked to Mrs. Wilkinson about it and she agreed with you. She said it was impossible."

Lt. Matheson nodded. "Naturally," he said. "It's a simple matter of science."

Ryan raised a finger. "But that's not how it turned out," he said. "Later, she spoke to a friend who is an expert on telegraphy. She works over at the new base they're building."

"She?" Lt. Matheson said, scornful. "Mrs. Wilkinson's expert is a woman?"

"Yessir," Ryan said, not sure why gender had anything to do with it. Especially since a moment ago Matheson was supporting Mrs. Wilkinson's mistaken opinion.

Verne must have thought the same thing, because he loudly cleared his throat. Matheson glanced at him, caught his stern look and folded.

He waved for Ryan to continue. "Go on," he said. "Sorry to interrupt."

"Yessir. Anyway, Mrs. Wilkinson's friend said it was definitely a possibility. It had to do with atmospherics, antennae arrangements, shielding. And a lot of other stuff I haven't started reading up on yet."

Ryan took a deep breath. He'd hardly started and he was suddenly feeling tired. And his throat was sandpaper dry.

"Want some sweet tea, Ryan?" Hattie broke in, leaning forward to pour him a glass from the frosty pitcher on the table.

Gratefully, Ryan drank long and deep. Hattie poured him some more, but this time she picked up the narrative.

"At first, we all thought Ryan was crazy too," she said. "Isn't that so, Alex?"

Alex nodded vigorously. "Ryan's got a wild imagination," he said. "We were both funnin' him for awhile. But after hearin' from Mrs. Wilkinson,

I went down to the library in Jove Beach. They got a whole new section on electronics, there. 'Cause of the war and the new base, I suspect."

Ryan looked at him. Alex had never mentioned this. His friend grinned at him. "Well, you didn't think I was just gonna take a couple of people's word on it, did you?"

Ryan shook his head—No.

"Anyway, I looked it up," Alex continued, "and although electronics aren't part of my regular studies, I could make enough sense of what I was reading to see that Mrs. Wilkinson's friend was right. I also got confirmation that dentists have reported that some of their patients pick up radio signals in their fillings."

He looked over at Lt. Matheson. "I can give you the names of those books later on, if you'd like."

Matheson looked offended that a colored boy was offering to share his knowledge with him. Glancing at Plant and Tindall, he could see that they were of the same low opinion about the worth of such information.

"That won't be necessary," Matheson said. "We have a more than adequate technical library at the base."

"Boy, would I love to see that," Alex said. "Maybe someday I could get a peek."

"Sorry, Coast Guard personnel only," Matheson said—just a little too hastily.

"Yessir," Alex said, sounding genuinely disappointed. Then to Ryan, he said, "Go on. Tell them about your two telegraphers theory."

"Two telegraphers?" Matheson said, frowning.

"Yessir," Ryan said. "I learned from my dad—and from listening on my own—that every telegrapher has a distinct hand. A manner in which they tap out the Morse Code. And there's a distinct difference between one guy and another."

"That's true," Matheson said, with undisguised reluctance. "But everyone knows that."

"Yessir," Ryan said, not knowing what the heck that had to do with anything. "Anyway, I started to realize that two people were talking to each other. Also, that the signals were coming from two different places. One near. And one a little distance away."

"And how could you tell that?" Matheson wanted to know.

Ryan shrugged. "Volume levels. Interference. It was easy."

"Go on," Matheson said.

"Well, then I started trying to write down what was being said. But nothing made any sense until I talked to the Professor."

Matheson frowned. "The Professor?"

"Yessir," Ryan said. "He's a genius. If you talked to him out of uniform you'd never know he was a conductor on a train."

Matheson looked horrified. "A common train conductor?" he exclaimed.

Ryan shook his head violently. "There's nothing common about him," he said. "Ask anybody. He's a genius, alright. Shoot, he's read the entire Encyclopedia Britannica!" He leaned forward in his excitement to press this point. "Practically memorized the whole blamed thing. From A to Z!"

Matheson was unimpressed. "I suppose he's colored too," he said. "Being a conductor and all."

"Indeed he is, sir," Verne said. "Which makes him no less a genius. You may take the word of Verne Sullivan on that!"

Sammy broke in. "The Professor has tutoring been my son," he said, eyes full of pride. "Alex is up for a full college scholarship, you know."

Matheson rolled his eyes. "Isn't that just grand," he said.

The look and tone made Sammy seethe. He appeared ready to punch the man out. Although he was small in stature and missing one hand, Sammy was immensely strong and Ryan didn't give the lieutenant much of a chance.

Ryan jumped back in before Sammy's temper got the best of him. "That's when it all came together," he said. "When I showed the Professor the code words I picked up he informed me right off that they were German."

Matheson gave him a blank look. "So?"

That was enough for Hattie. "So?" she said. "That's all you have to say—'So?' Shoot, how'd you ever make lieutenant?"

"Hattie!" Verne said, warning. "Don't be disrespectful. Your father wouldn't like it."

Chastened, Hattie ducked her head. "Sorry, sir," she said.

Ryan picked up the thread. "It means that the Morse Code signals are coming from Germans. The only Germans around here, as far as we know, are the ones on the U-boats attacking the freighters."

Sheriff Plant broke in. "That's all very interestin'," he said. "But not to me. I'm here investigating a murder. Not a U-boat full of Germans, imaginary or not."

Hattie broke in. "Don't you get it?" she said. "Remember the second Morse Code hand Ryan mentioned? The one transmitting close in? It has to be more Germans, but they're probably hiding out somewhere around here. Probably up river, in the swamps."

Plant frowned. He said, "What are y'all talking about? Saboteurs? Isn't that pretty far- fetched?"

"It's not far-fetched at all," Ryan said, getting desperate. "They're always warning us on the radio to look out for German saboteurs. Shoot, you even have posses patrolling the beaches at night."

"Don't you get it?" Alex said. "That's who killed Sally. Dirty rotten German saboteurs. Not Joe Collins, or some cracker moonshiner."

Plant snorted. He said, "If that's so—and I don't believe for a minute that it is, then they'd be long gone. Doing their nasty work up north in the factories and shipyards. They wouldn't be hanging around here."

"And that's what they would have done," Ryan said. "But when they ran into Sally, one or another of them also ran into one of her nasty booby traps. And got hurt. Really hurt. They're probably stuck right now with a guy who's dying. Can you imagine the infections he must've been hit with, hiding out in our swamps?"

Alex said, "The swamps are practically one giant Petri dish full of germs and diseases."

"That's a pretty interestin' theory," the sheriff said. "But where's your proof?"

"We found all kinds of proof yesterday," Hattie said. "It was at Sally's place. Aboard this big old paddle wheeler."

"What, now we've got paddle wheelers too?" Matheson broke in. "First U-boats. Now old paddle wheelers. What next? Pirate ships?"

"Please, sir. Just hold on a minute," Ryan said. "Let us tell you the whole thing from start to finish."

In next ten minutes or so, the three friends told them all about their first encounter with Sally. Their tour of the *Celestial Queen*—the wrecked paddle wheeler deliberately blocking one of the Seminole's tributaries. And the amazing home Sally had turned it into, complete with all the deadly booby traps she'd set for security.

"You should've seen the one that got the German," Alex said. "She called it her Froggie machine. Kind of a guillotine with a big old machete blade set into a weighted beam. Shoot, when it came down it'd practically cut you in half!"

He demonstrated, bringing the edge of his hand down hard into an open palm, adding, "There was blood all over the place."

And then Ryan told them the most crucial fact of all. Sally's treasured St. Christopher's medal that she faithfully left aboard the ship when she went about her daily business. But when she was found dead there it was hanging about her neck. Which means she had to have gone to bed when the saboteurs went after her.

When they were done they looked expectantly at the sheriff, then Tindall, then the lieutenant. To their dismay, none of them seemed particularly impressed.

Finally, Sheriff Plant said. "Tell you what. I'll assign Deputy Tindall here to take a crew up the river and look for this so called *Celestial Queen*. And if he finds it, he'll gather up any clues and bring them to me. Then we'll look them over and decide."

The sheriff looked up at Verne. "Sound fair to you, Mr. Sullivan?"

Verne sighed. He motioned to Ryan. "Tell him the rest," he said.

And so Ryan told them about the storm and paddle wheeler breaking up and being washed away downstream.

"In other words," Matheson said, "all you've got is a big fat zero."

"Not exactly, sir," Ryan said. "We found this."

He dug out the battered chart and spread it across the coffee table. "It's one of Sally's charts. I think the Germans were using it to figure out some kind of game plan. You can see where they marked it up."

Everybody bent close to see. But the marks were so faint they were barely visible. Most of the ink had been washed away during their very wet ordeal huddled under the skiff.

Lt. Matheson snorted derisively and rose to his feet. "Gentlemen, I for one am sick of having my time wasted," he said. To Verne, he said, "Thank you for your hospitality." Turning to Ryan's grandmother he added, "The cookies and sweet tea were delicious, ma'am."

Myrtle didn't even look up from her sewing, when she said, "You are making a big mistake, young man. One that you will live to regret."

Matheson started to reply—and from the look on his face it was going to be a sarcastic reply—but then he glanced over at the glowering giant who was her husband and he wisely kept his counsel.

Instead, he turned to Hattie. "I'll be speaking to your father about this," he said, menacingly.

Hattie didn't answer, but Ryan could see she really wanted to give the man a piece of her mind. She kept glancing over at Verne and it was only her great respect for him that kept her from ripping into the Coast Guard officer.

Plant and Tindall also climbed to their feet. "We'll all be going, now," Matheson said.

"That's it?" Ryan said, aghast. "You're just going to leave? What about Joe?"

Sheriff Plant broke in. "Well young man," he said, "at this point in time Joe is the court's problem, not mine."

"What led you to finally believe that Ryan was telling the truth when he said he spotted Joe at the still?" Verne asked. "Couple of days ago you were adamant that it was all due to an over active imagination. Just like you are doing now?"

"At first," the sheriff said, "Joe denied even being there. But Smoky Anderson contradicted him, confirming Ryan's sighting. He said Joe was one of his middle men for hooch sales. He's been hustling booze to the young soldiers at the base. He was at the still to pick up another load.

"But then when it looked like we were going to pin the murder on Smoky he finally spilled the beans. He said Joe was there trying to get Smoky's help disposing the body. Offered him a hundred bucks. Kicked it up to a hundred and fifty when Smoky refused."

"What did Joe say to that?" Verne said.

"He denied it, of course," Plant said. "Although he finally admitted that he was at the still after all, but insisted he was buying another supply of moonshine to sell at the base."

"Let me guess," Verne said. "Smoky is turning state's evidence in exchange for having all charges against him dropped."

"That's the deal his attorney worked out with the DA," Plant said. "Adding to Joe's problems is that he had a hundred and fifty dollars on him. The exact amount of the alleged payment to hide Sally's body. And Smoky and his boys didn't have more than thirty, forty bucks among them."

"So Smoky didn't do anything illegal?"

Plant sighed. "No sir, he didn't"

Verne grimaced, "I suppose you're going to have to let him go."

With great ostentation, Plant checked the time on his fancy vest pocket watch. "His buddies are probably waiting for Smoky in the parking lot right about now."

Alex burst in. "Wait on up," he said. "Are you sayin' that Joe's gonna take the whole blame?"

"That's how I see it," Plant said. "The DA might take a different view. But we usually see eye to eye."

"Tain't fair," Alex said with deep emotion.

Ryan was stunned, as were the other people in the room. Joe and Alex had a notorious hate on for each other. Some feared that it might end badly someday—probably for Alex. Why in the world would Alex speak up for him so passionately now?

"Careful, son," his father warned. "Show respect to these gentlemen."

Alex started to defy his father. His temper was dangerously on the rise. With great visible effort he forced it down.

Hanging his head, he said, "Yessir." Then, in a low voice: "But Joe ain't guilty. He just ain't."

Just then there was the sound of a car roaring down the driveway and screeching to a halt. A shower of seashells peppered the sides of the verandah.

A moment later, someone was knocking on the front door and shouting, "Hello! Plant? Tindall? Are you two in there?"

It was Joe's father, Jim Collins.

The man Ryan saw waiting on the verandah was a far cry from the arrogant, sneering figure he'd met on the beach.

Collins's eyes were hollowed and bloodshot from lack of sleep. His skin had an unhealthy pallor, despite the deep Florida tan. And he had an edgy, palsied look about him.

When he saw Plant he said, "Sheriff, I just heard that the Sullivan kid has changed his eyewitness statement. He's no longer sayin' that my boy was at the murder scene."

Plant frowned. "Now, hang on there just a minute, Jim," he said. "I don't know where you got that information."

"Word's out all over town," Collins said, "that Verne called a big pow wow and y'all were comin' out here to Sullivan island. What other reason could there be?"

Plant gave Tindall a disgusted look. If there was a leak, the sheriff knew who to suspect. Tindall turned deep red, confirming his suspicions.

The sheriff turned back to Collins. "Jim, I don't know exactly what you heard," he said. "But if you're talkin' about young Ryan here recanting his testimony, well, that's just not true, sir."

"Then what are you doin' here?" Collins demanded. "Don't look like a social call to me." Indicating Lt. Matheson, he added, "You even have the Coast Guard out here."

Matheson snorted. "Don't you try pull the Coast Guard into this mess," he said. "We've got nothing to do with it, sir."

And with that, he stalked over to his Jeep, climbed in and drove away.

Collins looked at Ryan. His face was flushed with anger. "So, you're still tellin' lies about my boy, Joe?"

Verne stepped forward. "Careful, Jim," he said. "You don't want to be saying things you'll come to regret."

Myrtle, who had come up behind the group, spoke up. "Don't you be calling my grandson a liar, Jim Collins. I won't stand for it, you hear?"

Before it could go any further, Ryan jumped in. "Excuse me, Mr. Collins," he said. "I feel just awful about Joe." He indicated his two friends. "We all do." Hattie and Alex nodded vigorously. "We know for a fact that he's innocent. And that he had nothing at all to do with poor Sally's murder. No matter what Smoky Anderson said."

"You see!" Collins said to Plant, practically shouting. "Straight from the horse's mouth! It's a case of mistaken identity. He just thought he saw my son."

Then, forcing a calmer voice, he said, "I know how it must've been, Ryan. It was all pretty scary with those moonshiners and stuff. So, you were scared half to death and only thought you saw my boy."

Ryan shook his head. "Nossir," he said firmly. "I saw Joe. And I saw his truck. He was definitely there!"

Collins looked stricken. One moment he'd had the gift of his son's innocence. A second later it was being snatched away. Innocence once again in doubt.

"What's happening here?" he said, almost wailing. "Why has everyone turned against me?"

"Nobody's turned against you, Jim," the sheriff said. "If your boy is innocent, then you can rest easy. My best advice is to get the best lawyer money can buy and let the justice system take its course."

Stricken, Collins stood there, frozen. Not knowing what to say or do.

To Verne, Plant said, "We'll be gettin' out of your hair, now, Verne. And if we get any more information, I'll let you know."

Then, to Tindall: "Come on, deputy. We've taken enough of these people's valuable time."

And they piled into the sheriff's spanking new Chevy sedan and drove away.

Ryan looked at Collins, who was practically in tears. "Honest, Mr. Collins," he said, "we know Joe's innocent. And I swear we will do everything we can to prove it."

Grasping at straws, Collins said, "If you need anything at all, just call. Any time. Day or night. Money is no object."

Then, nodding at Verne and Myrtle, he said, "Sorry to barge in on you. I'll be going now."

"You be sure to give our best to Sarah," Myrtle said. "Your wife has always made me feel welcome since I first came to Jove Beach."

Collins nodded. He was in such a daze, Ryan wasn't sure he heard.

"Thanks, Myrtle," he said.

He got into his car and drove slowly away, so out of sorts that he almost bumped into Myrtle's favorite cherry tree. She winced, then sighed with relief as he straightened the car out just in time.

Meanwhile, Ryan moved closer to his friends. "Stay near the phone tonight," he said in a low voice.

"Easy. My dad's on duty tonight," Hattie said.

"The lamp next to the phone is the best in the house," Alex said. "And I'll be studyin' the scholarship stuff way past my folk's bedtime."

Then Sammy was calling out. "Come on, Hattie. Alex and I will give you a lift."

Ryan leaned closer. "Same signal as last time," he whispered. "Cold snap."

Alex grinned. "Except this time, no rattlesnakes," he whispered.

"Yeah, no snakes," Hattie said. "But still with an "s" word."

And she hissed: "Sssssaboteurs!"

FORTY

A Tale of Three Marriages

"That was just one hell of a thing," Verne said, pacing back and forth like an angry bear. "One hell of a thing. I thought Matheson was a sensible man, and then he practically calls Ryan a liar."

Myrtle was sitting straight as a board in her caned back chair, a glass of sherry in her hand.

"I almost turned them all out of our house," she said. "I am furious. Simply furious."

Verne stopped in his tracks. "I'll call that sugar cane big shot in Tallahassee," he said. "Get somebody down here to look at things."

"That could take forever," Ryan said. "Meanwhile, Joe's in jail. And we have German saboteurs hiding out up the river."

"We don't know they're saboteurs," Verne said. "It's more than likely just some landing party. Reconnoitering targets. Shoot, by morning they'll probably be back on their boat with their Heil Hitler buddies."

Ryan didn't agree one bit, but he could see it was hopeless arguing. He'd been surprised at the firm support Verne and his grandmother had given him. Actually, Verne didn't surprise him so much as his grandmother. He was beginning to realize how much he'd misjudged her. Still, there was not a chance she would support what he had in mind.

Verne resumed pacing. He said, "And there's that federal guy. The one on the Orange Juice Board." Shook his head. "Always on my case to expand my orchards and increase production."

Verne slapped his chest, making a sound like a bass drum. "That's the ticket," he chortled. "I'll ask his advice about expanding and then hit him with the mess going on down here."

He started for his office, saying, "Don't worry, Ryan. I'll rattle the hell out of their cages and get some action."

When he was gone, his grandmother reached over to the decanter and poured herself a rare second glass of sherry.

"Come sit by me, Ryan," she said. "I've been wanting to talk to you." She peered over her glasses, took a deep breath, then added: "It's about your mother."

Ryan felt a chill go through him. "What… What about her?"

His grandmother patted the chair next to her. "Come sit. Please."

Reluctantly he lowered himself in the chair, sitting right on the edge as if he was about to bolt.

"I received a letter yesterday from your Aunt Cassie," she said. "The doctors were trying a new medication and apparently your mother had a relapse."

"Oh," Ryan said. Flat. He rolled it around in his mind, felt his fingers go automatically to his knee to tap out Coded relief. Then he stopped and pulled himself together.

"What does that mean?" he asked.

"I'm not exactly sure," his grandmother said. "Cass wasn't all that specific. But from what I gathered they're thinking about resuming electric shock treatments."

"Oh," Ryan said, emotions roiling. "She… she hated it before. Said all she wanted to do was to… to die."

Myrtle sighed. "I'm sorry, Ryan," she said. "I truly am. I know you don't think that I have a very high opinion of your mother."

Ryan felt a surge of resentment. He said, "You… you acted like you thought she was weak. That it was all her fault."

"Oh, Ryan," she said, voice tight, "don't you see, that's just my way." She laid a fist against her breast. Pressing down—hard. "Sometimes I feel… so helpless. Frozen. When I saw your mother last I wanted to shake it out of her. To tell her to stand up and fight."

Ryan dropped his head. "She's not very strong," he admitted. "She's like Hattie's mom. All that Navy wife stuff piled up on her until she says she can't breathe."

He gave an angry swipe at his eyes. Damn it! He would not cry!

"At least she didn't start drinking like Hattie's mom," he said.

"Yes, that's a blessing," Myrtle said. A wry smile. "Why do we say that? A blessing. As if we were granted some great gift from a bearded man in the sky. Like Santa Claus. I don't believe in blessings, Ryan, dear. You have to make your own blessings. And even then, it's safest to expect the worst. To expect betrayal."

Ryan stared at her. He was finally getting a glimmer of who his grandmother really was. "Is that what happened to you?" he asked, emboldened. "Did someone betray you?"

Myrtle stared at her sherry glass as if looking for an answer in the rosy depths. Then she sighed, and took a sip.

"I suppose I blame my own mother," she said. A long pause. A wry smile. Then, "She had the temerity to die on me when I was thirteen."

Ryan was rocked by this. Motherless at thirteen. Just a year older than he was now. And he thought—*she knows what it's like!*

"We were a poor family," his grandmother continued. "Twelve children, including my father, who, like Hattie's poor mother took to drink. I was the oldest so it was up to me and I became a house maid to help support us."

Ryan goggled at her. "You?" he said, amazed. "A maid?"

Myrtle smiled. "I was very good one, too," she said. "Although you'd never know it from my employer. She was an unkind creature. An unforgiving woman. Quick with her hands and sometimes a switch. I bore up under it for a long time. Then, several years later, I met the man who would become your grandfather."

Ryan nodded. Aloysius Karr. A man his own father never mentioned. The grandfather he'd never met.

"He was thirty eight," Myrtle said, "And I was seventeen. The perfect age difference for an older man to control a young woman. I lived for a once-in-a-blue-moon smile he might deign to gift me with. And cried for hours for his daily cruelties. They weren't physical, you understand. He used words, rather than a switch. And once, the back of his hand."

She paused, lifted her sherry glass, then put it down again without taking a sip.

"We were married for fifteen miserable years," she said. "And then one day he came home from work, after stopping at a bar to gather courage, and informed me that he wanted a divorce."

Ryan was shocked, blurting "But why?"

She sighed. "Who knows the why of another person's heart?" she said. "He had his reasons, which he spelled out in cruel detail. He said he'd outgrown me. That I was ignorant. "

Myrtle shook her head. "It was true. I had no education. I never finished high school. But I did my best to make up for it. I became an avid reader. A regular visitor of the library. Hardly an education to boast about. But I did my best. I truly did."

Ryan nodded. His grandmother always had a book nearby. Mostly fiction, mixed with biographies.

"The real reason, as it turned out," she continued, "was another woman." A rueful smile. "Or, should I say, another seventeen-year-old girl. Someone else to control and mold to his liking. Apparently, I'd questioned his pronouncements one time too many. Even contradicted him. The fault of the library, I suppose."

A bitter laugh. "In fact, he once said that he should never have allowed me obtain a library card. That it gave me notions above my station and intelligence."

She raised a finger. "That was marriage number one," she said. "He not only divorced me, but he still had so much power over me that I allowed him to talk me into using his lawyer for the divorce. It was to save money, he said.

"The result was a disaster. I was awarded very little alimony and child support. For several years times were difficult. I became a housemaid again—it was all I knew—or thought I knew. We were so poor I had to send your father to live with my relatives because I didn't make enough money to feed and clothe the two of us.

"Things were so bad I swallowed my pride and went to see your grandfather to beg him for help. But he said it was impossible. That he didn't make enough. And besides, he had another mouth to feed. Another son."

Ryan was astounded. "You mean I have another uncle?"

Myrtle nodded. "You do," she said.

"Dad never mentioned it," Ryan protested.

Myrtle frowned. "I know," she said. "I urged him to. But your grandfather made it plain that your father was not welcome. He said if he turned up at his door he would send him away and if he refused, he would call the police."

"He'd set the police on his own son?" Ryan said, aghast.

"Oh, very much so," his grandmother said. "Aloysius was always a man of his word." Reflecting, she took a sip of sherry. Then added: "As long as it didn't include marriage vows."

Ryan didn't know what to say. It was just too horrible to contemplate.

"So your father continued bouncing from one relative to another. They were all so very poor they could only keep him for a month or so. Then it was back with me and moldy bread and spoiled meat until I could beg another cousin to take him in."

She leaned closer to Ryan. "One thing I've learned about being poor and being around poor people," she said, "is that they are more generous than the moneyed class. I suppose it's because we know in our bones how desperate life can be."

Ryan nodded. He'd seen that for himself these past few years. Witness his Aunt Cassie and Uncle Tom. They weren't poor, but they had a large family of their own to feed and yet they generously took Ryan in and treated him like their own.

"Finally," Myrtle continued, "your father was old enough to take matters into his own hands. He'd worked hard in school and got his high school diploma at seventeen. Then, after getting my permission, he joined the Navy the summer after he graduated."

Deeper understanding was starting to dawn on Ryan. He'd never heard the reasons why his father had joined up so young. Now he knew. It had been a matter of survival.

"Meanwhile," his grandmother said, "I met another man. This time, the age difference was on his side. I was several years his senior."

She laid a hand against her breast. "He was very handsome, although not in a dashing sort of way. He was sickly. Consumptive. And yet he had the soul of a poet. He sold insurance, but he spent more days in his sick bed than out selling. Despite his infirmities, he was the most kind and supportive man I had ever met.

"He cozened me into taking business courses at night and I learned to type and file and keep books. Eventually he talked a business acquaintance into taking me on as a secretary.

"And for the first time in my life I felt important. Worthwhile. My employer counted on me. Respected my opinion. Trusted my intelligence and judgment."

She hugged herself. "I can't explain what a marvelous feeling that was," she said. "To be someone people knew they could rely on."

Ryan smiled. Having been on his own most of his young life he knew the feeling very well.

"We were married for three years," his grandmother said. "And then he died."

Ryan was shocked. His mother had only said—in a decidedly disapproving way—that his grandmother had been married a scandalous three times. She'd held up three fingers when she'd said that. Shaking them for emphasis—Three times! And then she'd talk about how terrible it had made her father feel. How ashamed he was of his own mother. Of course, his father had never complained.

But Ryan's father was a man who never showed emotion. Ryan got the rare pat on the back. Although, he could see now that the gift of the expensive Morse Code set was meant to take the place of all those years of neglect.

Before he shipped out this last time he'd listened to Ryan practice and said he'd done pretty good. "That's a pretty good hand, Ryan," he'd said. "Keep it up." Ryan had lived on that "pretty good" for months.

"Time went by," his grandmother continued. "And then you were born. I was so happy. Not just for me. But for your father. He'd always wanted a son. Said he'd make up for how his own father had treated him."

Myrtle saw the pained look on Ryan's face and hastily added. "I know he's not demonstrative, Ryan," she said. "Lord knows I'm not. But I've had to steel myself my whole life. And so has he."

"Okay," Ryan said. Everything else was too confused—too much in a turmoil—to say more.

"But back to my own small tale," Myrtle said. "I continued working at the insurance office. And then one day another man came into my life. A man unlike any I had ever met before. He was so big it was frightening at first. And that poor eye of his—the missing one. It was horrifying. I used to make excuses to absent myself when he came.

"He persisted. Inventing his own excuses, I realize now, to return to our insurance offices to buy one annuity after another. Always insisting that he see me so he could personally thank me for the work I'd done for him. Gradually, I began to see his true self. The real Verne Sullivan. A man so large because his heart required a body that size to contain it."

Ryan grinned. He felt himself swell with pride for just knowing, and having won favor and affection, from someone like Verne Sullivan.

"He's made me happy ever since," she said. "Although, I have to admit that I live in fear that he will be snatched away from me. That I'll be abandoned once again.

"At least he's too old to be caught up in this damned war," she said. "Unlike your father."

She lifted the sherry glass, peered at the contents a moment, then finished it.

"But you know very well how I feel about that," she said. "You have been forced to live with it yourself."

Ryan nodded. More than a few families in Jove Beach had been visited by uniformed men these past days and weeks with news that a father, or husband, or brother was dead, or missing in action. He wasn't sure which was worse. Knowing, or being left in the agonizing limbo of waiting to learn their fate.

"Now, to return to your mother," Myrtle said. "You have heard my life story. In its ups and downs it isn't that much different than other people's lives and in so many ways my troubles are nothing compared to what other people have suffered, or are suffering this very minute because of the war. Or, just because life handed them the filthy end of the stick.

"Some people are more capable than others at handling life's dirty tricks. Unfortunately, your mother is not one of those people."

Ryan sighed. "No, she isn't," he admitted. "I've thought about it a lot. And I don't think she ever will be."

Myrtle patted his knee. "I'm afraid you are right, Ryan," she said. "It isn't that she doesn't want to. Or that she doesn't love you. But life has put her in a spin and to be brutally honest with you, she may never recover."

Ryan felt wetness come to his eyes. He wiped them away. "I know," he said.

"Well, you are strong, my dear Ryan," she said. "Where this strength came from, I don't know. My family certainly doesn't possess it. Nor did your grandfather's. But you've proven to me these past few months just how strong you really are.

"And so when the time comes, I hope you use that strength to help your mother. To shore her up. And to do all those things she should have done for you. And my mother might have done for me—if only she had lived."

Ryan felt a spark of what he would later understand was self knowledge. Of sureness. Of promise.

"I will," he said.

"I know you will, Ryan," his grandmother said.

Suddenly she stretched out her two arms. "Now, come give me a hug, please," she said. "And then go finish planning whatever it is you have on your mind."

Ryan was jolted. She knew. *She knew.*

He got up and embraced her. Arms around his neck, she pulled him close with a surprising strength for one so small.

"I love you, Ryan, dearest one," she whispered. "So very, very much."

FORTY-ONE
Signals in the Night

He went to bed early that night, anxious not to miss a transmission from the U-boat. He stretched out full length on the bed, ear firmly pressed flat against the mattress. Clutching paper and pencil.

He waited for what seemed like hours, pushing away all the night sounds of crickets and frogs and the occasional bellow of a lustful bull gator.

Finally it came. First the faint sound of music. Then static. Then a series of dots and dashes. He concentrated as hard as he could, trying to make out full words of any kind.

Then it ended. But, thankfully he thought he had something. Three short, but complete words.

Hastily he jotted them down.

. .-. / .. ... - / - --- -

Then he translated the dots and dashes to words: Er ist Tot.

Fingers trembling, he got out the little pocket German dictionary Hattie had borrowed from her father. Flipped pages back and forth until he came up with the translation.

"He is dead."

Ryan was electrified. He jumped to his feet and started pacing, running it over and over in his mind. *"He is dead. He is dead. He is dead."*

But who was dead? That part of the message had seemed to come from the hand Ryan thought of as the shore party. The saboteurs.

If so, they were most likely referring to the man who had been injured by Sally's booby trap.

And if that was true, it seemed to Ryan that there was no reason for them to continue hiding out in the swamp. Which would mean that they'd soon be on their way to accomplish whatever missions had been assigned to them.

But wait! There were two other strings he'd made out. Two words. The second word was the same both in English and German, and he'd easily translated the dots and dashes in his mind.

That word was "radio." Expressed in Morse as: .-. .- -.. .. ---

He jotted down the dots and dashes for the first word: -. . ..- ...

That came out as "neus."

It was so similar to English he almost didn't have to look it up. In German, neus meant new.

New radio. New radio. What did that mean?

Then it came to him that they were being told they were getting a new radio. Why? Maybe the one they were using had been damaged in the swamp, or the storm. Neither of which was a happy home for electronic devices.

If so, how would they get it? Of course! It could only mean that a second party would be coming ashore from the U-boat with the new radio and anything else they might need. Maybe even a guy to take over the assignment of the dead saboteur.

He got out the battered chart and went over the marks that had been made by Sally's killers. There were three possible routes, all of which eventually led to places where a boat could be easily landed with no danger of being discovered. Not too difficult a task on Florida's wild coast.

He drew an "X" to mark each of the three spots.

Ryan looked at his bedside clock. It was 9:30. Not too late.

He crept into the living room—Verne and Myrtle had adopted early to bed country habits, so there was no one around.

Quietly, he asked the night operator for the Davy residence. Someone picked up immediately.

"Yes?" came the voice, almost a whisper. Thankfully, it was Alex.

"Cold snap," was all Ryan said.

He hung up. Then asked for the Peters' residence. Once again his luck held and it was his friend who answered and not a parent.

"Hello?" Hattie said.

"Cold snap," Ryan said.

"Gotcha!" Hattie said.

Ryan went back to his room and gathered the things he'd need for tomorrow, starting with his Morse Code key set. Then the little spark transmitter. He carefully wrapped them both in oilcloth against the wet.

Then he wrote four notes. The first was to Verne and his grandmother:

> Please forgive me for what I am about to do. I know it's wrong, but I don't see that we have any choice. No one else is going to do anything about finding Sally's murderers, so I guess it's up to me and Alex and Hattie to track them down.
>
> I'm pretty sure I know how to find them and when we do we are going to need everybody's help to catch them before they hurt anyone else.

I'm taking my Morse Code set and the spark transmitter I made that caused all that trouble with the radio station and Western Union. When we find the Germans, I'll send an S.O.S. and the location. The transmission will blast out the radio station and the telegraph office. Please leave all the radios on tuned to the local station and the minute you here the static noise, call Mrs. Wilkinson at Western Union. She'll be able to translate the Morse Code for you and you can come running with all the people you can get. We figure they'll land at one of three places. Charlie's Point. Ibis Landing. Or, Blowing Rocks.

Just so you know, we're also leaving notes with Sammy, Mrs. Wilkinson and Mr. Peters. I'm not leaving one with Deputy Tindall because he'll just mess things up. I know what we're doing is going to make you mad and that you'll be worried. I am very, very sorry about that, but I don't know what else to do.

I love you both very much.

Ryan

When he was done he wrote the other notes, heart racing, hands trembling, but still firm in his resolve.

* * * *

Ryan and his friends huddled over the chart, the golden rays of the rising sun illuminating the places he'd marked. A pelican settled on the roof of Mr. Peters' boat house. Rex lifted his head to bark, but Ryan quickly shushed him.

Squinting at the chart through his bottle-neck glasses, Alex said, "I think the best bet is Blowing Rocks. It's a lousy place for surf fishing and nobody goes there except maybe tourists."

"Not a lot of those, lately," Ryan said, "what with the war and all."

Alex nodded, "Plus the guys bringing the new radio can land on this little beach right here." He stabbed a finger at his chosen guesstimate.

"I don't know," Hattie said. "The other places Ryan marked look pretty good to me." She shrugged. "But you've lived here your whole life, Alex, so you'd know way better than me."

"Yeah, but if Alex guesses wrong we're sunk," Ryan said. "And we're going to be in a whole lot of trouble from the ruckus we've raised."

He'd spent a good part of the night tossing and turning with visions of enormous people surrounding his bed, glaring at him and they all had the faces of Verne and his grandmother, Sammy and Ada, along with Mrs. Wilkinson and Mr. Peters. Even Mr. Donaldson got in the act, wagging an admonitory finger and muttering "Dadburn boy and his dadburn friends."

Hattie shrugged. "Rather be in a little trouble," she said, "then let those murdering Nazi swine get away with killing Sally."

"Not gonna let that happen if I can do anything about it," Alex said. "Besides, if they get loose, no telling what they'll sabotage."

Ryan said. "I get nightmares about that all the time. Like, what if my dad's sub was attacked and all they had was dud torpedoes and stuff to fight the enemy off. If these guys get loose and something happens to him I'll feel like it was my fault."

"Well, sitting around talkin' about it isn't gonna get it done," Hattie said. "Let's pick a spot and go."

Alex snorted. "We need a better plan than that," he said. "What'll we do, flip a danged coin?"

"Last time we were on the *Celestial Queen* I smelled wood smoke," Ryan said. "And maybe somebody cooking. Like campers, or something."

"Lousy place to camp," Alex said. "Mostly muddy ground and swamp. And the skeeters would drive you crazy."

"Maybe we ought to start there," Ryan said, "then track them to see which way they're going. He patted Rex. "Old Rex will sniff them out, won't'cha, boy?"

The dog thumped his tail appreciatively.

"Sounds good to me," Hattie said. "We ought to have enough time before everybody finds those notes we left."

In the past hour they had left notes for their families to find. Plus, they'd dropped off notes at the closed Western Union office and the Collins residence.

Now, the boat was gassed up and loaded with the few supplies they'd need. As an extra precaution they'd brought along their palmetto spear guns.

When he'd put them in the skiff Alex joked, "I almost feel sorry for those Nazi pigs. Rubber band guns versus Schmeisser mitzer machine-guns."

He raised one of the spear guns, which looked more like toys than anything else. "Take that, mein herr," he said in a fake German accent.

Laughing, Ryan said, "They don't stand a chance against the Jove Beach Musketeers."

"That's not all we have," Hattie said and to their surprise she pulled a .45 automatic from her knapsack.

"Wow! Where'd you get that?" Alex said.

Hattie snorted. "My dad, where else?" she said. "Keeps it in a drawer in the living room. He won't miss it until later." She displayed several clips loaded with bullets. "Brought some extra ammo just in case," she said.

Ryan was nervous about the gun. "I don't know," he said. "You know how to use that thing?"

Hattie and Alex scoffed at him. "'Course she does," Alex said. "She's not a Yankee scaredy cat like you. Her daddy probably taught her when she was eight or nine years old."

"Seven," Hattie said. "He taught me to shoot when I was seven. But it was a .22." She hefted the big automatic. "This thing would've knocked me on my behind."

"Just don't shoot me by mistake," Ryan said.

Laughing, Hattie said, "If I shot you it wouldn't be a mistake."

She shoved the .45 back into her knapsack and hopped to her feet. "Let's go," she said.

A minute later they were in the skiff and she was goosing the engine upriver on the hunt for Sally's killers.

FORTY-TWO

On the Stalk

The only thing left of the *Celestial Queen* was the ruined bow jutting up from the green waters of the Seminole River like an accusatory finger.

A breeze carried the terrible smell of rotting carcasses as they drew closer to the bank. Rex growled, frightening a half-a-dozen or more turtles that plopped off the remains of an alligator.

"Yuck!" Ryan said. "I didn't know turtles were scavengers."

"Waste not, want not," Hattie said. Then she grimaced. "Guess that'll put me off turtle soup for a hundred years or so."

"Look over yonder," Alex said, pointing to an area just to the right of the gator's remains. "Mud's all tracked up. Like somebody was scramblin' ashore."

Hattie nosed the skiff against a place where the embankment had caved in. There were deep bootprints in the mud and the distinctive outline of a small boat.

"Good a place to start as any," Ryan said, gingerly hopping ashore, Rex following.

Alex tossed him a line then stepped out of the skiff. They pulled the boat in close and tied it to the giant roots of a banyan tree. A minute later Hattie joined them.

Rex sniffed at the bootprints and wuffed.

"Think he smells Nazi stink?" Alex said.

"Maybe," Ryan said.

They followed the bootprints to a higher point where a large area had been tramped down.

"Looks like they rested here for a bit," Alex said.

Ryan scratched his head. "You'd think the storm would have washed all these prints away," he said.

"Maybe this was done after," Hattie said. She glanced around. "When you smelled the smoke, which direction was it coming from?"

"Oh!" Ryan said. "I didn't think…"

"You never do, yadda, yadda," Alex teased.

Then Ryan remembered. "It came from that direction," he said, pointing to the far bank. "So, maybe when we were here last time they were holed up on that side of the river."

Hattie grimaced. "Maybe they were watching us the whole time," she said. Then, shivering, she added, "Gives me the willies just thinking about it."

"Okay, so now maybe we're startin' to get a picture," Alex said. "They killed Sally, but one of them gets hurt real bad by her booby trap."

Hattie broke in: "So, they take him over to that side and do what they can to fix him up. They hide out there for awhile, doing whatever Nazi creeps do after a hard day of putting thumbscrews on people."

"They were probably scared half to death," Ryan said. "They had their orders, but then one of them gets stupidly hurt. If they'd left Sally and the *Celestial Queen* alone and just gone about their sneaky business they'd probably be in New York or Chicago by now."

"Instead they were stuck in the swamp," Alex said, "sending messages like crazy to their U-boat captain."

"Driving you nuts listening to their messages in your bedsprings," Hattie said.

"Then, surprise, surprise, we show up at the *Celestial Queen*," Ryan said. "Can you imagine them sitting over there, putting out the campfire quick as they could, while we poked about the Queen?"

"I'll bet that at one point," Alex said "they thought about comin' over and shuttin' us up. Just like they did Sally."

"But then we got hit by a big darned storm," Hattie said. Her eyes widened in sudden realization. "That storm probably saved our lives," she said.

Ryan's heart trip hammered when she said that.

"Oof!" Alex said, doubtless thinking along the same lines.

"Let's nose around and see what we can see," Ryan said.

The area they were in turned out to be nothing more than a wide hummock. There were deep drag marks—probably made when they hauled their boat from one side to the other. There they found a small, muddy beach where there were more bootprints and the now familiar outline of the saboteur's boat being pushed into the water.

Confirming their guesses, Rex trotted back and forth, sniffing at the ground, clearly following the trail left by the Nazis.

On the far side he picked his way along what appeared to be a narrow deer path. He kept turning back and woofing at them.

"I think he's sayin' 'They went thataway, pardner,'" Alex said.

"Let's get the boat," Hattie said.

Thankfully, the skiff was lightweight so they quickly got her to the other channel, remounted the outboard and shoved off.

It was hard going at first. The channel was clogged with storm debris and Alex and Ryan had to continually hop off in the knee-deep water to clear the way, while Hattie throttled the skiff through.

"Watch it," Alex said at one point. "Looks like a place where a gator might dig a hole."

Ryan had no idea what he was supposed to watch, so he just steeled himself and moved on.

After about a hour they came to a little beach that seemed to find favor with Rex. On closer inspection, they discovered bootprints and a mud wallow where the Germans had apparently decided to come ashore.

After tying up they followed the bootprints for a few yards, but then Rex "woofed" at the same time Ryan smelled wood smoke. Immediately, he grabbed Rex's collar and raised a hand to stop the others.

He motioned ahead. "Smoke," he whispered.

Waving them back, he crept forward, Rex at his side. Then he spotted the ring of stones surrounding a cold firepit and relaxed.

He got to his feet, saying, "They're long gone."

Alex went to the firepit and squatted next to it.

"Let me try out one of my gen-u-ine Seminole Indian tricks," he said and put his hand on one of the rocks.

Immediately, he snatched it back. "Ouch!" he said.

Ryan and Hattie laughed. "I guess 'ouch' is Seminole for 'not that long, kemosabe'," Ryan said.

"Funny guy," Alex said.

Now that they seemed to be getting close, excitement rippled through the group. Even Rex was infected. He woofed and trotted about the camp area sniffing the ground and pawing at places where the earth had been disturbed.

Ryan dug down in one spot and found a trove of empty ration cans and packages with German writing on it.

He sniffed at one the cans. Looked at the writing on the side: *Eiserne Portionen*. Then he dug out the pocket dictionary and flipped the pages until he came to the translation.

Nodding, he held the can up for the others to see. "If we ever needed proof that Germans were around," he said, "This would do it. It means 'Iron Portions.'"

"Man, when you are right, you are right!" Alex said, holding up what was obviously an empty first aid kit, with German writing on the side."

"And look at this," Hattie said, using a stick to lift some nasty-looking rags out of a hole. "Bandages. Covered with what looks like blood."

Ryan thought a minute, then said, "We could go back right now and show everybody what we found. They wanted proof. And we've got it here."

Hattie and Alex gave him pitying looks. "You really think this'll do it?" Alex said. "That they're gonna look at this stuff and say, 'Oh, wow! What fools we have been. How could we have ever doubted those three genius kids."

Hattie snorted. "Sure they will! One's a castoff Yankee. The other's a dirty little girl with a dipso mother. And the other..." She looked at Alex and shrugged, leaving the rest unsaid.

Which Alex did not. "And the other's a creepy little colored kid with weirdo glasses."

"Then we go on?" Ryan asked.

"I vote, hell yes!" Hattie said.

Alex raised his hand. "Double hell, yes," he said.

Ryan raised his own. "That's three, 'hell yeses," he said.

He scratched Rex's belly, who gave an appreciative woof. "Four out of four," Ryan said. "A clear majority."

They got out Sally's battered chart and spread it on the skiff's bench.

Alex stabbed a finger at the map, just off the channel they'd recently left. "We're about here," he said. "We figured there were three ways to go. Here: Charlie's Point. And here: Ibis Landing. Or, here: Blowing Rock..."

"From where we're at now," Hattie said, "Charlie's Point looks out of their way. And rough. More channels and weavy lines on the chart to cross."

"Okay, try this," Ryan said. "We forget Charlie's Point. We stay with this channel until we hit the fork." He tapped the point on the chart. "And we can decide the rest of the way from there. How's that sound?"

No vote was needed. They all nodded, took a minute to munch on cookies Alex had lifted from his mom's pantry and then continued on their way.

The next stage was easy. The channel clear. It was a beautiful Florida morning. A refreshing breeze blew off the Atlantic, carrying the scent of far horizons. Water oaks and sweet gums and red maples stippled the banks, in between banyans and magnolias and the rare bald pine.

Swamp hens were doing their aquatic dance, skimming across the water on delicate feet. A tall, stately gray heron stood guard over a rock eddy where small fish liked to hide. A white ibis sailed overhead, snowy wings, tipped charcoal black, spread wide and free.

The scene was so peaceful that Ryan was nearly fooled into relaxing back into his inner self and letting his mind soar away, following that graceful white ibis into cotton candy skies, ruled over by a benevolent sun.

And then Rex gave a woof and his hackles rose.

Ryan hissed, "Hattie. Cut the engine."

Without a moment's hesitation, the ever alert Hattie chopped the engine. And Alex, who also needed no urging, picked up his pole and silently pushed them toward the towering roots of a banyan tree.

When they got close, Hattie and Ryan grabbed thick roots and pulled the skiff through a curtain of Spanish moss that spilled over the entrance of a vault beneath the roots.

Moments later they heard voices. Rex's throat rumbled, but Ryan shushed him. Rex settled down, but his hackles prickled under Ryan's soothing hand.

They heard an outboard engine approaching and they peered through a gap in the mossy curtain in time to see a boat with three rough looking men move slowly past them.

One of the men turned his way and for a minute Ryan thought the man was staring right at him. To his astonishment, it was the moonshiner, Smoky Anderson, knife scar and all.

Ryan jerked his head back in reaction, but to his relief he was not seen.

"It's Smoky Anderson," he whispered. "What's he doing out here?"

"Beats me," Alex whispered back. "But thank God he's goin' the other way."

The minute he said it Smoky cut the engine and a frightening silence settled over the river.

Hattie glared at Alex, as if to say, *You and your big mouth.* Alex winced and mouthed: *Sorry!*

Then Smoky spoke up, his voice so loud they nearly jumped out of their skins.

"I still think we oughta go back there and skin those old boys out," he said. "Smelled like easy money to me. Buncha strangers, too. Nobody'd know they was missin'."

"They might'a had money, Smoky," a short, fat moonshiner said, "but it didn't smell like easy money to me."

"I think one of them had a Tommy gun," the third man said.

"I didn't catch that," the fat guy said, "but I did spot a big old sawed-off on one of those guys. Betcha dollars to doughnuts they're bank robbers, or somethin'. Hidin' out until the coast is clear."

Anderson snorted derision. "They ain't bank robbers," he said. "But even if they are, just gives us even more reason to go on back there. They didn't see us when they took that turnoff to Blowing Rocks."

Ryan and his friends exchanged meaningful looks. The answer to their most important question had just fallen into their laps. But then they turned back in awful anticipation of what Smoky Anderson was planning.

"All we gotta do," Anderson told his friends, "is wait until night. Then we slip in there when they're sawin' logs, cut their throats, slit their bellies, stuff 'em full'a rocks and stick 'em in some big ole gator hole."

"Smoky," the fat man said, "you just got your cracker ass outta jail on a murder charge. The kid's takin' the whole blame. Our mouthpiece has got the sheriff believin' you're squeaky clean and that the kid is tellin' a pack of lies."

Smoky laughed, sounding like a rusted boiler. "I was just in the wrong place at the wrong time, boys," he said. "And like the man said, I fell into bad company."

The third man snickered. "Bad company. And it's Jim Collins's kid, too. What a joke."

"I'm gonna miss the kid," Smoky said. "He was bringin' us in a pretty penny from all those enlisted men. MPs won't let us near the base."

"Better that than an accessory to murder charge," Fattie said.

Then he reached past Anderson and gave the engine cord a tug. It went, "chachufa!"

"Come on, Smoky," he said. "Let's get on back to honest work. Makin' shine. To hell with a buncha kid killers and bank robbers."

Anderson gave a long sigh, then grabbed the cord from his buddy. Gave it a hard yank and bang! the engine fired up with a shot so loud Ryan nearly fell out of the skiff. Then Anderson's boat was roaring away.

Ryan was outraged. "Can you believe that?" he said. "They're taking the word of that throat-cutting moonshiner over ours! Joe Collins is guilty, no matter what we say, or how much evidence we pile up. That really, really ticks me off!"

Alex shrugged. "Welcome to my world," he said. "But in case you didn't notice, Kemosabe old buddy, they just saved us a whole lot of trouble. Now we know where the real killers went. The Nazis, remember? Hello?"

"Yeah, but that's not the point," Ryan said. "The point is—" And he stopped.

Feeling a little stupid he looked at Hattie. The whole time they were talking, she'd been fiddling with one of the outboard's valves. Clearing the line with a twig.

"That'll do her," Hattie said. "Thought she was gonna have a coughing fit back there. She looked at her friends. "Now, are you two through groaning and complaining about stuff we can't do anything about?" she asked.

A little embarrassed, Ryan and Alex nodded.

"Good," she said, and gave the outboard cord a mighty tug.

"Next stop, Blowing Rocks," she said.

FORTY-THREE

Shootout at Blowing Rocks

They took the right hand fork to Blowing Rocks, where they found the channel so jammed with debris that it was difficult to move at more than a snail's pace.

In some places they had to remove the outboard, haul the skiff over the next obstacle, then rematch the skiff and engine on the other side.

Their nerves were stretched to the breaking point, making them clumsy and a little careless. Ryan cut himself from being too much in a hurry. Fortunately it was only a minor cut to his forearm. Using the Coast Guard first aid kit Hattie had scrounged, they stopped the bleeding by sprinkling a packet of sulfa on the wound and bandaging it.

"We'd better slow down," Hattie said, "or somebody could get hurt a lot worse."

"We can't go any slower," a frustrated Ryan said. "If we don't speed things up they'll get away."

Hattie looked like she was about to argue, but then glanced over at Alex who nodded.

"He's right," Alex said.

"Okay, but let's not be so much in a hurry that we suddenly find ourselves in the middle of them," she said.

They moved onward, but heeding Hattie's warnings they were more careful, their brush-clearing movements more deliberate.

Oddly, their pace seemed to quicken and in a short time they could hear the boom of waves and smell the salt air as they neared the ocean.

Then Rex woofed and Hattie immediately cut the engine.

They sat very still, pushing all their senses forward.

Nothing.

Only the crash and hiss of the waves coming onshore.

Ryan nodded and Alex stood up to pole the skiff forward.

Another woof. And Ryan could feel the big Dalmatian's hackles rise under his hand. He signaled Alex, who stopped poling and crouched low.

The embankment was high, so their vision was limited. On the other hand, that meant they couldn't be spotted either.

"Why don't I take a looksee?" Ryan whispered.

The others agreed. After ordering Rex to stay put, he got out of the boat and crept up the side of the embankment.

He smelled cigarette smoke. Then, very faintly, he heard men's voices drifting through the sound of the crashing waves.

Ryan peered over the rim and felt an electric thrill shoot through him when he saw the Germans for the first time.

There were five of them, huddled around a rubber boat they'd pulled ashore where the channel spilled into the ocean. Beyond them he could see the distant tower of the lighthouse.

The men were dressed in nondescript clothes—dungarees and work shirts—and looked entirely American. One of the men paced back and forth in the sand, binoculars in hand. The others sat on the edges of the rubber boat, or relaxed in the sand. One of the men was spooning food out of a can, while two others cleaned what looked like the Tommy guns and the sawed off shotgun the moonshiners had mentioned.

The fifth man crouched over a transmitter in the boat, ear phones clamped to his head, fingers of one hand busy tapping out a message.

With a thrill, Ryan realized the man was actually communicating with the U-boat, which must be hiding somewhere close.

And then he nearly jumped out of his skin as a wave crashed against the boulders with a mighty KABOOM! Followed by a thunderous roar as the seawater geysered up and up, then came crashing down, with another KABOOM! Followed by the long hissssss of the retreating waves.

Suddenly, Ryan was overwhelmed with emotion and his hands started shaking. After all these days and weeks of listening to the mysterious signals in his bed, wondering if he were crazy, or stupid, afflicted with an overheated imagination, or all of the above.

Now, here he was, looking at the Germans he'd said were there all along.

Sally's killers.

And would-be saboteurs.

The man working the radio stopped to listen to the U-boat's reply, pressing the earphones against his head to hear better.

Suddenly the German looked up and snapped his fingers at the man with the binoculars, trying to get his attention. The man turned, words were exchanged, and the radioman went back to transmitting while the other continued his pacing, pausing now and then to sweep the horizon with his binoculars.

Then there was another thunderous KABOOM! as the waves exploded through the passage ways Nature had carved through the rocks over many thousands of years.

Ryan flipped over on his back and slid back down the embankment to his friends.

"It's them," he whispered.

Hattie and Alex goggled at him, as if in disbelief.

Ryan snorted disgust. "See for yourself," he whispered.

To his surprise, they did. Scrambling up the embankment, then peering over edge.

A KABOOM! and a CRASH! and Alex jerked back, startled. Hattie seemed unaffected. She turned around, a big grin on her face, and gave Ryan a thumb's up.

As they slid back down to the skiff Ryan got busy, unwrapping the oil-cloth protecting his Morse key set and the little spark transmitter.

"Help me, Hattie," he whispered. "Gotta get to the battery."

She nodded, and—brandishing a screwdriver—she popped a cover off to expose the small battery. Then she carefully unscrewed the nuts from the battery posts and pulled the wires free.

Ryan grabbed the leads running off the transmitter, then attached them to the battery posts, which Hattie tightened back down.

Rex whined and Ryan patted him, whispering a few soothing words. Then looked up at his friends.

They were staring at him. Trembling with anticipation, excitement and—he had to admit—a little fear.

"You ready?" Hattie whispered.

Feeling a little sick, Ryan drew in a deep breath. Let it out, forcing calm.

Then: "Better go back up and keep watch," he whispered.

Hattie nodded, then dug out the .45 from her knapsack, shoved it into her belt, and went back up the embankment. Alex, meanwhile, was arming himself with a palmetto spear and tucking a few extra bolts into his belt.

He fixed one spear to the rubber strip and tested the bow, pulling it back further and further and then he almost let loose as another wave smashed against the Blowing Rocks formation, with a loud KABOOM!

Alex grimaced at Ryan, mouthing "Sorry," and relaxed the bow.

"Okay," Ryan whispered, bending over the key. "Here goes nothing."

He took a deep breath. Let it out and started tapping away.

S.O.S.:

...---...

A pause, then—

Blowing Rocks:

-... .-.. --- .-- .. -. --. / .-. --- -.-. -.- ...

Another slight pause, then—

Saboteurs:

... .⁻ ⁻... ⁻⁻⁻ ⁻ ...⁻ .⁻. ...

And again:

S.O.S.

Blowing Rocks.

Saboteurs.

And once again:

S.O.S.

Blowing Rocks.

Saboteurs.

Sweat dripped from his forehead, falling on the keys as he tapped out the words with extreme care. Emotion roiled within, pushing him to get it done as fast as he could so they could get the hell out of there before the Germans discovered them.

Carelessness could cost them their lives and let Sally's killers get away. So he bent low, concentrating, tapping out his message. Imagining static electricity blasting through speakers all over Jove Beach. Especially the one in a certain living room on Sullivan's Island. The others at Alex's and Hattie's homes. The Western Union office. And Mr. Collins's place.

And in the background there was the KABOOM! and the CRASH! of the waves.

Suddenly, as he tapped out the message, he heard a loud static BUZZ! And then another: BUZZ! And another: BUZZ! Then, the longer: BUZZ, BUZZ, BUZZ and to his terror he realized the static exactly matched his actions as he tapped out the Code for S.O.S.

Hattie hissed down at him. "It's coming from their radio!"

But how could that be? Surely their equipment had wartime shielding like the Coast Guard.

Experimentally, he tried again. And he jumped as once again he heard the BUZZ, BUZZ, BUZZ, of static coming from the Germans' radio. The only thing he could think of is that Germans must've accidentally disconnected their earphones, freeing the radio's speaker.

And then Hattie was sliding down the embankment.

"They're looking this way," she said. "We'd better get out of here!"

Clumsily, Ryan started unhooking his key set so Hattie could reattach the battery cables. But then Alex was next to them.

"No time," he said. "Two of them are coming this way."

Ryan grabbed Rex's collar before he could bark, ripped the Morse Code set free, tucking it into his shirt, and then they were all were splashing through the water as fast as they could.

Someone shouted something in a foreign language. Had they been discovered?

And then a Tommygun let loose, bullets stitching the water next to Ryan, but leaving him miraculously unscathed.

They got around a bend and Alex was pointing at an immense banyan tree up ahead.

"That way," he said, and started sloshing toward the tree.

Ryan followed, half dragging Rex who wanted to go back and fight.

Then he realized Hattie wasn't there and he turned to see her step out into the shallows, giving her a clear view of their pursuers.

And them a clear view of Hattie!

She raised the .45 and fired. BOOM!

The force of the recoil slammed her onto her back. But somehow she kept control of the gun.

She came up to a sitting position and fired again. This time the pistol flew from her hands.

There were shouts of fear from the Germans. Hattie scrabbled for the gun.

"Leave it," Ryan cried.

And she left it, rushing to join him and Rex. They made their way to the Banyan tree and got to the other side.

There a tree-lined creek emptied into the channel.

"This way," Alex said. "It doubles back."

And he ran for the treeline. Ryan and Hattie followed, but Rex broke away.

"No!" Ryan shouted.

But Rex was gone, racing off to meet the enemy.

Ryan started to go after him, but Hattie grabbed his sleeve.

"Come on!" she cried. "Or they'll get us all."

Reluctantly, he followed her into the cover of the trees.

Behind them they heard Rex roar in fury and the ratatattat of a Tommygun.

And then an awful silence.

"Oh, God," Ryan said. "God. God. God."

"Never mind God," Alex said, "we need to get under cover."

And so they ran for cover, racing through the trees, crashing through the underbrush, dodging around and through heavy tree limbs.

Amazingly, there were no sounds of pursuit.

Alex found a clump of trees that overlooked the beach and the back side of Blowing Rocks.

To their surprise, they saw all five of the Germans gathered there.

Hattie pointed out to sea. "Look," she said. "Another boat."

Ryan's head jolted up and he felt a thrill when he saw another German lifeboat riding clumsily through the waves. Ryan couldn't tell how many men there were on board. As if it mattered. No one was chasing them now.

He turned to look out toward the red lighthouse. When help came, it should come from that direction.

His stomach clenched as he thought, *"If help came."*

Ryan was beginning to despair as the supply party's boat moved closer to shore.

"Hope to heck they heard it in town," Hattie said.

"They must've," Alex said. "The Germans sure did."

"Sorry," Ryan said. "I wasn't counting on that." His voice trembled. "I got Rex killed."

"It wasn't your fault," Hattie said.

"It was the Germans," Alex said. "Just like Sally."

Ryan looked out at the approaching boat. More and more it looked like they had been too late.

Then Hattie was clenching his arm. "Look!" she said.

He turned to see small dark shapes in the distance. And then they were getting larger and began to take form.

It was the posse! Led by Verne, who was astride the magnificent Big Red. Thundering along the beach, getting closer by the second.

He heard shouts. The Germans had also spotted them. The supply boat had just cleared the breakers and was only a few yards from shore.

Now the saboteurs spotted the posse and were waving their shipmates away. Two of the saboteurs turned, as if to run for cover, but the radioman—the obvious leader—shouted and waved for them to come back.

He and the other three were pushing their boat out to sea. They'd try to escape to the U-Boat.

Gunfire! *Boom! Boom! Boom!*

And the saboteurs were turning back to face the posse.

There was the ratatattat of machinegun fire. Bullets stitching the sand, but not finding their marks and Verne and the others shooting back. Boom! Boom! Boom!

Alex shook him. "Look! Look!" he was shouting.

Behind the posse a half-a-dozen vehicles appeared and leading them all was Sammy in his Model T. And he was pointing a rifle out the driver's window, bracing his crippled arm as he opened fire on the saboteurs.

A cry of pain and the three friends turned to see the German with binoculars fall, clutching his chest.

The others ran for the trees, but now Verne was almost on them.

The radioman whirled about to shoot, but Verne knocked his gun away. Wheeled Big Red about in one magnificent sweep, then he reached out with a long arm and grabbed the German by his hair, lifting him bodily off the ground, kicking and screaming.

Now the other rescuers were on the Germans and there was more gunfire, but it was all one-sided.

And in a few minutes it was over.

As if to mark the moment, Blowing Rocks made its most spectacular display of the day. KABOOM! And then up and up and then crashing down, KAPUSH! and the white spume shattered into rainbows, all aglitter like broken cathedral glass.

Then Ryan heard a "woof" and his heart jumped as he whirled to see Rex trotting out of the trees, alive and well and as bouncy and full of life as if he'd just come from a nice doggy afternoon of rabbit chasing.

Ryan jumped to his feet and heard cries of joy from his friends when they saw the big Dalmatian. Rex jumped up, planting his forefeet against Ryan's shoulders to happily lick his face.

The boy dropped to his knees, hugging the dog and scratching him and whispering nonsense in his ears.

Then Hattie and Alex joined him in the embrace and soon they were all laughing and blubbering, while Rex had an orgy of face licking.

Ryan heard a noise and he looked up into the big beaming face of Verne.

His single eye a dazzle of blue.

He said, "I got your message, son."

* * * *

Ryan opened the screen door and stepped out of the hot Florida sun into the dark cool of the house.

His grandmother stood across the room. Bathed in backlight he couldn't make out her expression.

He just heard her say, "Oh, Ryan," in a warm, soft, welcoming tone he'd never heard from her before.

And then Verne pushed him forward and he found himself in his grandmother's amazingly strong embrace.

She pulled his down to her level and whispered in his ear:

"I want you to know, Ryan, dearest one, that I never doubted you.

"Not for one second."

FORTY-THREE
The Last S. O. S.

The Professor cried, "All aboard!" and Ryan stepped up on the platform, turning to wave a last goodbye.

There was Alex, sporting a stylish pair of glasses—looking almost handsome in a goofy sort of way. And there was Hattie, smiling and wearing, wonder of all wonders, the first dress Ryan had ever seen her in.

And then there was Sammy and Ada and the twins, Esther and Phebe, and the rest of the Sullivan Island gang, here to see him off.

Finally, there was his grandmother and—yes—his by god grandfather, not step grandfather—Verne.

Both astride horses. Verne on Big Red. His grandmother, comfortably astride Sheba, looking almost youthful in her riding outfit, topped with a broad-brimmed Spanish style hat.

Verne had made a ceremony about Ryan leaving the same way he'd arrived. Sammy drove his grandmother ahead in the Cadillac, accompanied by Alex, Ada and the twins while Ryan and Verne took the longer Hobe's Creek route riding Big Red and Sheba.

It was a leisurely ride. They stopped to let Ryan give Bertha one last belly scratching with the rake in exchange for a piggy kiss.

And for one final time Ryan breathed in the marvelous Florida countryside air, full of orange blossoms and tropical flowers and the rich scent of the Spanish moss that fell in curtains from the banyans, palmettos and showy magnolias.

Splashing across the creek, he saw baitfish dart out of the way, and imagined the lovely mullet and catfish just waiting for a boy with a bucket of baitfish and a lazy day to kill.

Then Orville swooped down with his showy wings for one last graceful farewell.

Down the way he saw a gator, startled by a barking Rex, plunge off the bank into the water. Rex woofed and then turned to race ahead, tail held high in doggy victory.

Then they were in town, with all the familiar places: the milk bar, the movie-lot/sundries store, the school, closed for the summer, Western Auto where, thanks to Alex and Verne, he took possession of the marvelous bike. And so many other places he and his friends had haunted during his stay in Jove Beach.

Everybody met them at the train station, and Mrs. Wilkinson wept a little, and Mr. Donaldson dadburned a lot, and Deputy Tindall harrumphed and kicked the dirt. Jim and Joe Collins might have been there, but Ryan wasn't sure and certainly didn't care, no matter how many apologies he and Alex and Hattie had received.

His grandmother and the whole Sullivan Island gang was waiting in the station. To his surprise, his grandmother took possession of Sheba, Sammy boosting her into the saddle.

And now she sat there, flushed and smiling, looking proud beside her husband.

Ryan made his farewells to everyone then pulled aside the two most important people, Hattie and Alex.

To Alex Ryan said, "Looks like you're all set. New glasses, scholarship, the whole—ahem—dadburned thing."

"Yeah, that's me, dadburnit—Set!" Alex said, grinning and, like Ryan, holding back tears.

Ryan turned to Hattie, but before he could say a word, she stopped him with a finger pressed against his lips.

"Don't ask," she said, "or I'll embarrass us—me most of all—by turning into a water fountain."

"No water fountains," Ryan said. "Remember. We're the Jove Beach Musketeers."

Alex raised a hand and shook his head. "Nope. No water fountains here, d'Artagnan old buddy."

"You've got my address in South Carolina, right?" Hattie said.

Ryan patted his shirt pocket. "Here," he said. "So I won't lose it. Don't want you to miss the next thrilling episode of Ryan Karr, boy radio wonder."

His friends laughed.

"They sure made a fuss over us," Alex said. He grimaced. "Didn't like it much."

"War's moved on now," Hattie said, "So's the fussin'."

In reality, the war hadn't exactly moved on. Locally, the Coast Guard had increased its presence four-fold. They'd hunted down and sunk the U-boat that had been hiding under a reef just off the coast. Then set up patrols so others couldn't take its place. And the base was going full force now, vastly improving the coastal defenses.

"You goin' straight through to Connecticut?" Alex asked.

Ryan shook his head. "Stopping in Philadelphia first to pick up my mom. My dad's meeting us in Connecticut. He's got desk job, so maybe things will go better."

Hattie gave him the knowing, fellow military brat look. But all she asked was, "How's your mom?"

Ryan sighed. Held out a hand and rocked it back and forth in a so-so motion.

Hattie grabbed it. Squeezed. Meaning, *just like mine.*

And then they all jumped as the train whistle blew. Echoing from one end of the station to the other.

The Florida Special was about to depart.

"Oh, so fast!" Hattie said, brushing away a stray tear.

"Remember, no water fount-," Alex started to say, then his voice broke.

Ryan pulled his two friends close.

"We'll write," he said.

"Absolutely," Alex said.

"Without fail," Hattie said.

Another whistle blast and Ryan was running to his grandfather and grandmother for a last round of hugs and kisses and then the Professor was shouting "All Aboard" and Ryan was sprinting for the train as it creaked and jolted, chains rattling, and just in time he jumped on the platform, heard a "woof" and turned to see Rex trying to clamber aboard after him and he sobbed and pushed his friend away, and Alex and Hattie were grabbing Rex and holding onto him as the train gathered momentum.

Ryan ran to a window and looked out at the receding scene and the last thing he saw was his grandmother, sitting ramrod straight in the saddle.

And then Verne, that magnificent man of all men: big as a mountain, strong as John Henry and Paul Bunyan wrapped into one, and even then his magnificent body was not large enough to accommodate his heart.

As he watched, Verne leaned forward and tapped Big Red's left leg and that marvelous animal dipped down in a bow, while his grandfather swept off his Panama Hat for a final farewell, Verne Sullivan style.

His heart ached at the sight and deep inside he somehow knew it would be the last image that he would ever have of the man.

Ryan waved, but he didn't think they saw him. The Professor and gave his shoulder a warm, all-encompassing squeeze that made Ryan feel stronger.

"You'll be back," the Professor said.

"Sure, I will, Professor," Ryan said, sinking into his seat, then swiveling to stare out the window.

He saw the red lighthouse getting smaller and smaller, until the lighthouse, Sullivan's Island, Hobe Hill and then the entire town of Jove Beach vanished in one long blast of the engineer's whistle.

He desperately wished he could climb into a time machine and make a grand jump into the Future to see if Tomorrow would bring all that back.

His hand went to his knee and his fingers began tapping that old familiar melody:

He did it once:

…---…

Each formed letter shouting in his head: S.O.S.

Then another: …---… S.O.S.

And then one final plea that would echo through his mind from now until very end of time: …---…

S.O.S.